Death of a Stray Cat
An Affair of the Heart
Two Novels by
Jean Potts

Introduction by Curtis Evans

Stark House Press • Eureka California

DEATH OF A STRAY CAT / AN AFFAIR OF THE HEART

Published by Stark House Press
1315 H Street
Eureka, CA 95501, USA
griffinskye3@sbcglobal.net
www.starkhousepress.com

DEATH OF A STRAY CAT
Originally published by Charles Scribner's Sons, New York, and copyright © 1955 by Jean Potts. Reprinted in paperback by Berkley Books, New York, 1961; Penguin Books, Harmondsworth, 1961.

AN AFFAIR OF THE HEART
Originally published by Charles Scribner's Sons, New York, and copyright © 1970 by Jean Potts.

Reprinted by permission of the Jean Potts estate. All rights reserved under International and Pan-American Copyright Conventions.

"Jean Potts and Classic Crime" copyright © 2023 by Curtis Evans.

ISBN: 979-8-88601-005-3

Book design by Mark Shepard, shepgraphics.com
Proofreading by Bill Kelly
Cover Art by James Heimer

PUBLISHER'S NOTE:
This is a work of fiction. Names, characters, places and incidents are either the products of the author's imagination or used fictionally, and any resemblance to actual persons, living or dead, events or locales, is entirely coincidental.
Without limiting the rights under copyright reserved above, no part of this publication may be reproduced, stored, or introduced into a retrieval system or transmitted in any form or by any means (electronic, mechanical, photocopying, recording or otherwise) without the prior written permission of both the copyright owner and the above publisher of the book.

First Stark House Press Edition: May 2023

DEATH OF A STRAY CAT

Marcella is a born victim. She brings out the worst in men. But someone has taken it too far and murdered the poor girl. Alex knew her from the previous summer, during a brief affair when his wife was away. So when her body is discovered in their beach house, he feels as guilty as if he had murdered her himself. But Walt, who had been carrying on with her too, is the one who doesn't have an instant alibi. So he's the one they arrest. But no one really thinks Walt would have strangled her. Everyone knew Marcella—anyone could have killed her. His friends Brad and Dwight certainly knew who she was. And Jimmy, her conniving husband, was supposed to have a meeting with her that day. Horace Pankey must have seen her as well—he was working on Alex's patio that afternoon. But who hated this stray cat enough to choke the life out of her? And why?

AN AFFAIR OF THE HEART

Kirk Banning and his wife Hilda run an advertising agency, but ever since Kirk's heart attack, Hilda has been trying to get him to slow down. His mistress, Lorraine Walsh, also wants him to slow down. But all Kirk wants to do is leave Hilda and marry her. Which seemed like a good idea to Lorraine a year ago, but now…. So when Kirk is found dead of an apparent heart attack in Lorraine's apartment, there is a scramble to cover up the situation to protect Hilda. But the bigger question is, what happened to his heart pills that he always kept with him, the pills that could have saved his life? Is it possible that someone didn't want Kirk to survive a second heart attack, and took measures to prevent it?

"You'll find subtlety, sensitivity and a gentle, late-summer sadness….a well-shaped plot, an attractive young hero and the quiet authority of a first-rate craftsman."—Anthony Boucher, *New York Times*

"The terror that can invest the ordinary and the way people under stress can talk themselves into a corner are the author's special forte."—*Kirkus Reviews*

"Potts has a turn of phrase that cuts like a knife."
—Paul Burke, *NB*

7
Jean Potts and Classic Crime
By Curtis Evans

11
Death of a Stray Cat
By Jean Potts

151
An Affair of the Heart
By Jean Potts

234
Jean Potts Bibliography

Jean Potts and Classic Crime
By Curtis Evans

After publishing her final crime novel in 1975, Jean Potts, like so many other mistresses of mid-twentieth-century crime and suspense fiction, sadly saw her books largely fall out-of-print and remain so until they were finally reprinted, over the last several years, by Stark House. Although Jean Potts continued to place the odd short story in the redoubtable *Ellery Queen's Mystery Magazine*, publishers for decades gave her crime novels frostily cold shoulders, with only one exception of which I am aware: British publisher Chivers Press, who produced at least four Potts titles under its Black Dagger Crime imprint, which was largely aimed at libraries. This quartet of titles, which Black Dagger reprinted during the years between 1988 and 1998, were *Go, Lovely Rose*, *Home Is the Prisoner*, *The Only Good Secretary* and one of the two novels included in this volume, *Death of a Stray Cat*, which is in my view Potts' finest essay in what has been termed "classical detection."

In his foreword to Black Dagger's 1996 edition of *Death of a Stray Cat*, the late Robert Barnard (1936-2013), one of the leading figures in what I have termed the Silver Age of the detective novel (around 1950 to 2000), lauded Jean Potts as a shamefully underappreciated American exponent of the classic whodunit which at that time was viewed almost as the exclusive property of British detective writers, particularly the so-called British Crime Queens (Christie, Sayers, Allingham, Marsh and sometimes Tey). American mystery writers of the Golden Age, Barnard noted, were associated almost completely (and erroneously) with "the private eye novel, with all that term implies, in terms of tone, setting and style." Barnard himself knew better, having been old enough to have read Jean Potts in his late twenties/early thirties, when she was reprinted in Penguin paperback editions during the 1960s. "I bought *Home Is the Prisoner* the day before flying from Australia to Britain in the mid-sixties, and I bought it on the strength of having enjoyed *Go, Lovely Rose*," he recalled. "An hour or two before the flight left I dipped into it. Fatal. It was a simple, even clichéd, plot line, but the telling made it impossible to put down. [Having finished the novel before takeoff] I had an even more boring than usual thirty hours on the flight."

Robert Barnard recognized *Death of a Stray Cat* as an estimable American version of the classic Golden Age English detective novel, though he argued that what demarcated Jean Potts' characters "from the English classic whodunit's cast list" was their "ordinariness." "The characters of Christie and Marsh may be essentially ordinary," he allowed, "but they are ordinary gentry. They seldom, for example, do what the average person would call work for a living." To me this seems too sweeping a generalization, but I agree that *Death of a Stray Cat*—even the title has a classical ring to it—is in essence an English Golden Age crime novel skillfully updated to the mores and attitudes of the bustling American mid-century.

At about 65,000 words *Death of a Stray Cat*, which was Jean Potts' second mystery novel and originally published in 1955, is significantly shorter than its more maundering English model, taking place over a spare two days on a Labor Day weekend on Long Island and leaving no room for inquests and lengthy disquisition on material clues, be they tobacco ash, loose hairs, muddy footprints or bloodstains. Swiftly the novel moves, like a sleek 1955 Ford Thunderbird, from the short opening prologue, where Marcella Ewing pathetically meets her maker at the beach home of bookseller Alex Blair and his beautiful wife Gen, to the encountering of her strangled body by the vacationing Alex and Gen and their flighty, bohemian, not-entirely-comic-relief employees Mr. Theobald and Vonda, to the spread of the dark stain of suspicion, from Marcella's bluff former "keeper" Walt Bowman, to her handsome if thuggish "piano man" husband Jimmy, to Alex himself and his and Gen's vacationing bachelor friends, handsome player Brad Stone and retiring scholar Dwight Abbott.

No brilliant and eccentric aristocrat amateur sleuth is in the offing, and though there is a somewhat plodding police chief, Ed Fuller, the murder of Marcella is solved by several ordinary individuals, with Gen Blair ultimately playing the most decisive part in its elucidation. The setting is classical in essence as well, an enclosed location with what is effectively a village setting—"on one side of the road W. Gertz, Meats and Groceries, and across from it the filling station and Rudy's Bar & Grill"—and assorted locals like monkey-faced Rudy and his wife and daughter, clamming and tippling odd jobs man Horace Pankey and his mother, lovelorn gas-station attendant Floyd and brassy, hash-slinging, Ava Gardener wannabe Lil and her mother. Then there is Dwight's beach front property, inherited from his father, "a full-fledged estate, with a house twice as big as Dwight needed—plus a cottage, originally intended for a caretaker"; it essentially is the country mansion of detective novels of yore.

It is in the breadth and depth of the characterization that *Death of a Stray Cat* most distinguishes itself from the Golden Age English detective novel. The "villagers," as it were, are not stock butts-of-the-joke figures, as they so often are in Golden Age mystery, but rather genuinely interesting individuals, sympathetically presented, while several other characters are remarkably well conveyed for a so-called "middlebrow" popular novel. Most notably, Marcella Ewing, the figurative "stray cat" of the title, is slain in the novel's first few pages, yet her presence grows throughout the story rather than diminishes, like some revivifying specter taking on material form, and you surely will not forget her after you finish reading.

As one character puts it of poor, maddening Marcella: "She struck me as a congenital victim type ... Or a stray cat ... Some people *are* like stray cats, you know. They follow you home, so to speak. You don't want them, yet there they are, making you feel guilty for not taking them in...." The phenomenon of a natural murderee, a "feeb" so relentlessly pathetic that she unconsciously transmutes human sympathy into the violent rage to kill, is a fascinating one, ably developed by the author.

Contemporary reviewers welcomed *Death of a Stray Cat* with open arms, with many of them pronouncing the novel superior to the author's fine first effort at mystery, *Go, Lovely Rose*, which earlier that year had won the Edgar Award for the best first crime novel of 1954. "Formally this is an unusually well-constructed detective story," pronounced American's revered dean of mystery criticism, Anthony Boucher, adding: "But its virtues are even more novelistic than deductive...." I agree entirely with Boucher. With *Death of a Stray Cat*, Jean Potts managed to infuse a formal novel of detection with the thematic and emotional resonance of a so-called mainstream novel, making it to my mind one of the undoubted classics of mid-century mystery.

■ ■ ■

The punningly titled *An Affair of the Heart* (read it to see the title's double meaning), one of Jean Potts' final novels, was published fifteen years after *Death of Stray Cat* and is written in the author's later, much pared-down style. At about 40,000 words, the novel (or novella, arguably) might be termed, borrowing from novelist and essayist Willa Cather, a mystery *demeuble*, or "unfurnished mystery." Like *Stray Cat*, *Heart* is set in New York, but the setting is sparsely set, leaving the focus firmly on the interplay of the pieces in the puzzle of businessman Kirk Banning's death: his second wife, his mistress, his two young adult children (an alienated boy and an intensely devoted girl) from his first marriage, and the mistress' sister and "GBF" (i.e., gay best friend).

Looking at the novel today, from the vantage point of over a half century later, perhaps the most striking thing about it is the author's inclusion of a GBF character, Teddy. The homosexuality of Teddy is taken for granted by his friends Lorraine (Kirk's mistress) and Lorraine's sister Mary, who matter-of-factly reference his latest squabble with his boyfriend Ernest. Doubtlessly Potts' depiction of Teddy as a fairly flighty "queen" type is dated (like that of the queen character in the film *The Boys in the Band*, which premiered the same year), yet ultimately the author's portrayal of him and his fate achieves a certain poignancy.

As for the rest, Allen Hubin, who briefly succeeded Anthony Boucher as the crime fiction reviewer at the *New York Times Book Review* after Boucher's death in 1968, aptly summarizes the book's virtues: "A slender yarn, simply told, of the eternally fruitful—for mystery fiction at least—wife-husband-mistress triangle ... the husband dies ... and all, including his moody adult offspring, begin concocting stories to keep each other from the truth." In this succinct duel of wits between author and reader, who will emerge victorious?

—February 2023
Germantown, TN

Curtis Evans received a PhD in American history in 1998. He is the author of Masters of the "Humdrum" Mystery: Cecil John Charles Street, Freeman Wills Crofts, Alfred Walter Stewart and British Detective Fiction, 1920-1961 (2012) and most recently the editor of the Edgar nominated Murder in the Closet: Essays on Queer Clues in Crime Fiction Before Stonewall (2017) and, with Douglas G. Greene, the Richard Webb and Hugh Wheeler short crime fiction collection, The Cases of Lieutenant Timothy Trant (2019). He blogs on vintage crime fiction at The Passing Tramp.

Death of a Stray Cat
Jean Potts

To the Brownies

ONE

It was deserted, this stretch of beach, except for the girl and an occasional, busy little troop of sandpipers who scurried along the ocean's edge, just not getting their feet wet. The girl sat, as she had sat all afternoon, watching them. What funny little things they were, twinkling along on their twig-like legs, intent on nipping sand fleas out of immensity! Just as she was nipping a crumb of comfort from their minute presence. Because everything else was so vast—the boundless sea-surge, the infinity of sand, the empty summer sky above, deepening now as the afternoon ended. She shivered. End of the day. End of summer, too, or very nearly. Labor Day weekend.

Like the man in the grocery store had said. "You'll have it all to yourself this afternoon," he had told her. "Tomorrow, tonight even, they'll all be coming out, but this afternoon there'll hardly be a soul. You're ahead of most folks, getting Thursday off too. You're lucky," he had said.

Lucky.

Such a nice, friendly man. She hadn't felt at all timid about asking him where Alex's house was. He told her exactly how to find it. "It's quite a considerable walk," he warned her. "A good two miles, I'd say. And I don't hardly think you'll find anybody there. They generally stop in and load up the car with groceries on their way out."

"I know," she said. "He's not coming out till tonight. But I—I got off early, so I decided not to wait. I can spend the afternoon on the beach."

"You can't miss the house. White roof. Set a ways back from the road, and two great big willow trees in the yard. Go right down the highway here, turn left when you get to the Motel, and keep going. You can't miss it. The beach is on a ways, behind it. Can't miss that either, I guess."

They had both smiled at this mild joke, and for a moment she felt half-inclined to linger in the neat safety of the grocery store. But then some other customers came in. "Will that be all, Miss?" said the nice, friendly man, dismissing her, and she picked up her candy bar and bottle of coke and set off down the highway. It was all just the way he had told her. She turned left at the Motel onto a winding, narrow road, and after a while, sure enough, there was a house with a white roof and two big willow trees. No one was there yet. But it was Alex's house. His name was on the mailbox: Alex Blair. The name itself had a solid, kindly ring, and the house had the same quality. There it was, and there it intended to stay, a sturdy shelter against all the world. The girl eyed it wistfully.

But she did not linger there, either. This haven was not for her, any more than the grocery store had been. Still, she had caught a glimpse of security; she could come back later. Perhaps. Of course she could come back later. She let herself be drawn on (it was like some overpowering magnet pulling her) down the path, to the great sweep of beach. She sank down on the sand, unresisting and nerveless as a pebble, or as one of the shells strewn there by the tide. She had gathered a handful of the most delicately colored ones, and now as she looked at them a childish, dreamy smile stole over her face. Perfect, pretty little things, some fluted, some still hinged, like lockets, to show how neatly they had encased whatever soft, helpless creatures had once lived inside them. It would be nice, she thought, to have a shell like that to live in. How snug and safe you would feel, curled up inside your little fortress, and when at last you died, as of course some day you would die …

Again the girl shivered. I shouldn't have come here, she thought. I must go back. But the magnet still held her. It was stronger even than the terrifying sense of her own nakedness (though her flowered cotton skirt was still there, her off-the-shoulder blouse, her sandals, and her scarf). I haven't any shell, she thought. Not even the fragile, brittle protection of a seashell. I've never had any shell at all.

"Marcella!" called the voice, softly, quite close. "Marcella!" And all the little sandpipers started up in fright and sped off. The girl, too, started up, her heart fluttering like the birds' wings, her long, limber fingers still clutching the handful of shells.

She was frightened. But she was not surprised. It seemed almost as if this was what she had been waiting for, all through the long, trance-like afternoon. She had never really believed that she would carry out her secret plan. (Secret! He must have guessed it from the beginning.) She had known he would find her first. That was somehow why she was here.

"Why did you have to come?" he asked. "I told you—"

Yes, he had told her. And yet, as she turned, she did feel one more foolish spurt of hope. Because the voice sounded so gentle, quite harmless; because its owner had been—like the others—so good to her, at first. But then she saw his face, and her legs, which knew nothing about hope but all about danger, sprang instantly into flight. They found again the path by which they had brought her here. Up the slope of beach they carried her, through the tangle of bayberry and coarse grass, and now the ground under her flying feet was rockier, there was the dark shelter of trees above her, and on ahead—or was hope playing another cruel trick?—on ahead a remembered haven.

Panic sharpened all her senses to an agony of alertness. Her eyes, straining ahead, caught the glint of failing sunlight on glossy leaves, the lazy sway of branches in the breeze, the twitch of a squirrel's tail as it scampered out of her way. The ache in her laboring chest swelled beyond imagination; she was acutely aware of sweat stinging along the backs of her legs, and of the bruising pebbles inside her sandals. Above all, her ears recorded with terrible clarity the tearing, gulping sound that was her own breathing, and the thud of footsteps. Not just hers. Those behind her, too; ominous as thunder, heavier than her own, sure of their goal.

A goal. Had she ever had one? Only a vague memory now, of a place that had been a comfort, because she could come back later ...

It was there, it was there, shimmering in front of her like a mirage. White roof. Two big willow trees. You can't miss it. Alex's house. She stumbled, half-fell. Behind her the footsteps were closer, surer than ever, almost tangible against her frantic heels. She fled on across the grass and the clam shell driveway (no car, no one here yet, no one to open the door to her) and up the porch steps.

Miraculously, the door opened under her hand. She plunged into the cool dimness, and even as she felt the first, painful surge of relief, knew that it was too late, she was lost. The door gave against her trembling shoulder. The merciless fingers closed over her wrist.

She started a hoarse scream, turned it into a whimper as the fingers twisted and dug into her arm. There was no one to hear, anyway. From over by the fireplace came the sprightly chirp of a cricket. No other sound, except their panting, hers and his.

"No. Please. No," she whispered.

"Why did you have to come?" he asked again. "I can't stand it. Don't you see? I have to." The fingers moved up her two arms, encircled, almost tenderly, her long, pulsing throat.

TWO

"I really don't know what's gotten into me," said Gen. She rolled the car window up half an inch, searching for the point at which it rattled the least, and looked out at the stream of cars, headed, like theirs, for the shore and the long weekend. "I feel gay as a lark. It worries me."

"I don't blame you," said Alex gravely. "There's nothing worse. This awful, uncontrollable feeling of gaiety. I get it too, every once in a while. Times like now, for instance, when I'm starting on a vacation with my favorite wife. Why, I have to wrestle with myself to keep from feeling downright happy."

"Aren't you funny." But she couldn't help laughing. She slid over closer to him and tucked her arm under his. He was such a darling, with his amiable moon-face and his receding hairline and his leisurely jokes.

"Beats last year's vacation," he said. "Doesn't it?" And anybody but Gen would have thought it was as casual as it sounded.

"Yes," she whispered, admitting for the first time, even to herself, that last year's separate vacations hadn't been such a rip-roaring success. It had been Gen's idea; she couldn't bear, she said, to think of their turning into one of those stodgy married couples who wouldn't dream of doing anything separately. Deliver her, she said, from such people. No individuality. Might as well be half of Siamese twins. She still felt that way. The principle remained sound, even though circumstances had contrived last summer to produce the dismalest month of Gen's life.

"Personally," said Alex, "I had a gruesome time last year, and I don't mind admitting it."

"A likely story. You probably had a high old time chasing blondes and carrying on behind my back." In a way, thought Gen, she was teasing herself as much as Alex. It was like the delicious shudders she used to get, when she was a child, listening to ghost stories that she knew weren't true. The plot had changed, that was all. No more rattling chains or spectral groans. In their place the idea—equally horrendous, equally bogus—of Alex's ever wanting anybody else instead of her.

"Gruesome," repeated Alex. "And I intend to make up for it, beginning right now. What's wrong with feeling gay as a lark?"

"Not a thing. All I meant was—"

All she meant was that it didn't seem normal, for her to keep right on feeling gay today, in view of all the circumstances.

The back seat, for instance, was full of Mr. Theobald and Vonda and books. Ordinarily that alone would have been enough to put Gen on edge. Not that she disapproved of the books exactly (though it would be nice, just once, to go someplace without hauling along a load of second-hand books) but Mr. Theobald and Vonda— Well, they were a preposterous pair. Not a brain cell between the two of them.

Alex admitted it. "They mean well, though," he always added mildly. "Best-hearted, most obliging creatures in the world. They'd do anything I wanted them to."

"Why shouldn't they?" Gen would ask. "They wouldn't have a penny if it weren't for you. Nobody else would give them a job. Nobody else would put up with them for two minutes."

It never did any good. The truth was that Alex had a weakness for the human oddities of the world, the strays, the misfits. The incompetence of Mr. Theobald and Vonda didn't exasperate him at all. It amused him.

The original arrangement had been for them to mind his little Fourth Avenue bookshop while he was away on scouting trips; somehow they had turned into more or less permanent fixtures. Almost any day you would find them there, busily misfiling correspondence, mixing up orders, misinforming customers, and garbling telephone messages. They lived next door to the shop, in an incredibly cluttered loft (and in sin; and in a happy, hazy, make-believe world of their own) so, even on the days when they weren't "working," Vonda was likely to show up with a thermos of coffee or tea for Alex. "Time for a little collation. Mustn't wear ourselves out, you know," she would carol. Her voice was an extraordinarily pleasant one; what she said seldom made much sense, but it was nice to listen to. She was much younger than Mr. Theobald—a small, very dark woman with a great deal of wildly curly hair, which she handled in a variety of ways, all of them interesting. Today it was pulled back and bundled into what appeared to be a small gilt gunnysack. She also wore, for her jaunt to the country, a navy crepe dress with bead pockets, and a pair of thong sandals. (Gen, who wrote fashion advertising, was always frankly fascinated by Vonda's costumes.)

She glanced back now at the two of them crammed in among the books. They were blissfully holding hands. They hadn't been out of town in years; this Labor Day outing was a real treat for them. It had taken quite a bit of doing on Alex's part. They couldn't afford to rent a place, of course, and Gen (and possibly even Alex himself) would have balked at installing them in the spare bedroom of the Blair house for a whole weekend. But then Alex thought of Dwight Abbott. The beach property Dwight had inherited from his father was close by, and it was a full-fledged estate, with a house twice as big as Dwight needed—plus a cottage, originally intended for a caretaker, vacant now for many years. Dwight, who loved doing favors for people, had been delighted with the whole idea. He would have been more than glad to give Vonda and Mr. Theobald a ride out, in addition to the use of the cottage, except that he wasn't sure he could get away until tomorrow. So Alex was providing transportation.

Mr. Theobald caught Gen's eye and waved his free hand at her in a gesture at once courtly and exuberant. He looked a little like a seedy version of Liszt. His longish white hair streamed in the breeze; even in the twilight Gen could see how his eyes were shining.

"The ozone! The delightful, intoxicating ozone!" said Mr. Theobald, drawing in a rapturous breath of the motor exhaust-laden air.

They had planned on getting an early start. But Mr. Theobald and Vonda had no sense of time. So here they were, crawling along in the thick of the weekend traffic—and it made no difference, Gen simply felt gay instead of irritated.

Very mysterious. There was also the question of whether or not they were going to have Brad Stone for a weekend guest. Not that Brad posed any problem—or if he did, it was a pleasantly piquant one. But a hostess liked to *know*, thought Gen.

"I don't suppose Brad committed himself?" she asked.

"Naturally not," said Alex. "You know Brad. If he doesn't get stuck in the office. And if the redhead stays mad at him."

"You mean he's still buying lilies for the redhead?" They were not ordinary lilies, the chaste white flowers that were Brad's trademark; the one unvarying element in the long list of his romances. He himself always referred to them, respectfully, by their correct name of *Eucharis*. It was his friends who reduced them to plebeian lilies, and to whom the expression "buying lilies" had become synonymous with courtship.

"For the redhead," said Alex, "but not exclusively for the redhead, I gather. That's why she's mad. Seems the silly girl has notions about monopoly."

"With Brad?" Gen laughed. Though actually, she thought, it was sad that Brad had never yet found a girl who understood him. He shouldn't be expected to be faithful. He should just be appreciated for his gaiety and charm ... There she went, making excuses for Brad, the way people so often did. No doubt about it, he was too engaging for his own good.

She moved a little closer to Alex. "Don't tell anybody," she whispered, "but I hope he doesn't come."

Alex's smile was pure, grateful joy. In spite of his own liking for Brad, in spite of all his efforts to be sensible and civilized about these things, Gen suspected that Alex was a little bit bothered by the half-playful, half-serious passes Brad made at her. He must know that they meant nothing. But he must also know that Gen enjoyed them. There might even be black moments when Brad—with his fine advertising job, his ambition (Alex had very little), and his surface charm—seemed to him like real competition.

"I guess it's okay either way," he said now, magnanimously. He negotiated the turnoff with quite a flourish. "It won't be long now. We can stop at the corner and pick up some groceries."

"Let's stop at Rudy's, too," said Gen. "Have a drink, for old times' sake."

Alex all but blushed with pleasure. Because Rudy's evoked, for both of them, their honeymoon, and you could say what you wanted to about the rest of it, there had been nothing wrong with their honeymoon. It floated in Gen's memory, a flawless, enchanted island of time. Three summers ago. Sometimes it seemed much farther away than that, impossibly far away. But today she felt—well, in love again, as if she and Alex were sailing back to their magic island across a golden sea, instead of rattling along in a car that had seen better days, headed for Rudy's very ordinary Bar & Grill.

No use trying to analyze this happy state of affairs, thought Gen. Just be thankful for it, relax and enjoy it while it lasted. Except, why couldn't it last forever? Why— There she went again. Fussing. Focusing on the imperfections, missing the roses on account of the thorns.

I'll reform, she promised herself dreamily. I won't ever be bitchy again. So Alex hasn't much ambition, he's too easygoing with other people ever to get very far in this high-pressure world. So what's the difference? He's such a darling ...

Her head settled against Alex's shoulder, and she drifted into a delicious little doze. When she woke, it was no longer twilight but genuine dark. Swarms of stars in the sky, and in the air the tang that Mr. Theobald had been imagining (and enjoying) ever since they left Fourth Avenue. They were slowing down for the turn, and in front of them gleamed the familiar lights—on one side of the road W. Gertz, Meats and Groceries, and across from it the filling station and Rudy's Bar & Grill.

"Groceries first," planned Alex happily. "Then drinks and dinner at Rudy's."

But he had overlooked Mr. Theobald and Vonda. They never drank, and they had just embarked on a miraculous new diet of yoghurt, blackstrap molasses, and dates—three items not ordinarily available at Rudy's Bar & Grill. They had foreseen that this would be the case, and had come prepared.

"So all right," said Alex. "Groceries first, then we drive you out to Dwight's cottage, stop at our place and dump the groceries in the icebox, and then come back."

There was a storm of protest from the back seat. Neither Vonda nor Mr. Theobald would *think* of putting Alex to all that trouble. Mr. Theobald said he would like nothing better than a nocturnal stroll through the ozone, and why didn't they walk? Alex said nonsense, it was all of four miles from here to Dwight's cottage, and what about their luggage?

"I have it!" cried Vonda, bouncing with such inspiration that her hair all but slipped its gilt gunnysack moorings. "If you'll let us take your car, Alex, there is no problem whatsoever. We can even stop at your place first, if you'll tell us how to get there, and leave your groceries for you, and you and Mrs. Blair can just relax and enjoy your dinner without a worry in the—"

"Wait a minute," Alex broke in. He turned around to peer at her. "Can you drive?"

Certainly, Vonda assured him blithely. Since the age of twelve. She had a license and everything. (She just might have, thought Gen. Every once in a while, Vonda came up with some puzzling possession out of the past—a genuine mink muff, a sketchy knowledge of shorthand, a clarinet. Why not a driver's license?)

"I could draw you a map," said Alex, half to himself, "so you won't get lost. You can't miss either our house or Dwight's, anyway. There's a key under our doormat. I left it there for Horace Pankey. He was supposed to fix the patio this week. And we can always bum a ride home with somebody at Rudy's."

So it was settled. They all trooped into the grocery store, where Mr. Gertz greeted them, genial and talkative as ever. Alex and Gen were favorites of his. "Better keep an eye on that husband of yours," he told Gen, winking at her to indicate that this was a joke. "Wouldn't trust him if I was you. He's got the girls chasing him now, instead of the other way round."

"My irresistible charm," Alex explained modestly. "What girls? Who's chasing me now?"

"Didn't tell me her name. Just asked me how to get to your house. Not a bad-looking girl, on the skinny side. She stopped in along in the afternoon, early. I told her I didn't think you was out here yet, and she said she knew it, but she'd got off early and was going to spend the afternoon on the beach. No kidding. I thought she was somebody you'd invited out."

Gen and Alex raised their eyebrows at each other. "We didn't invite anybody but Brad, did we?"

"Of course not," said Alex. "It must have been somebody who just happened to be driving through and—"

"She wasn't in a car," reported Mr. Gertz. "Afoot. Came out on the train, I guess. She didn't exactly say you was expecting her, come to think of it. I just took it for granted, when she wanted to know where your house was."

"How weird." Gen poked absentmindedly at a head of lettuce. "Tomatoes, Alex. Let's get lots of tomatoes. Who do you suppose it could have been?"

"It beats me," said Alex cheerfully. "A spy, maybe. A rival bookseller in disguise. One of Brad's string. Whoever it was, I guess she'll keep a while longer. Got everything? Hurry up."

They loaded the groceries into the car and watched as Vonda and Mr. Theobald, armed with Alex's map and detailed instructions, set off in a cloud of dust.

"They'll probably wreck the car," said Gen.

"I doubt it." Alex grinned as he raised his hand in a final wave. "God's got a special full-time angel looking after them."

Gen was suddenly so happy that she reached up and kissed him, shamelessly, right there in the lurid neon lights of Rudy's doorway.

Rudy's was lively tonight. Summer people, unmistakable in their carefully nurtured tans, their sunback dresses and splashily printed shirts, milled around the little bar and overflowed into the dining room in the rear, where the juke box pulsed with many-colored lights and soulful sound, and Rudy's wife and young daughter scurried back and forth with loaded trays. But Rudy's was also popular with the natives; they hunched on the bar stools in their overalls, stubbornly refusing to be displaced by these outsiders.

"Look," whispered Gen. "Our table's still vacant. Waiting for us."

It was indeed. The one in the corner, beside the phone booth. Waiting for them, thought Gen; the fitting backdrop for their honeymoon homecoming. Rudy himself brought their ceremonial martinis.

"Blair Special," he told them, as he always did. His ugly little monkey face beamed in welcome. "I waved the vermouth bottle once over lightly. You just out for the weekend, or you going to spend some time with us?"

"Vacation," said Gen. "Three great big beautiful weeks."

"Good for you. I'll see you later, if this mob ever thins out. They're running me ragged tonight." He streaked back to the bar, where someone was bellowing for him, and Alex and Gen raised their glasses to each other and lapsed into the lingo of their honeymoon.

"Viva la Geneviva," said Alex.

"Alex darling," said Gen. "We're going to have a fine time."

"I know it. I've known it all day. We always do when you feel gay. That's all it ever takes for me to have a fine time. You witch."

"Poor Alex. Think how much simpler life would be if you'd married a nice pliable clinging vine instead of me."

"Quiet, please. It's none of your business who I marry. Besides, who wants a simple life?"

"Oops. Sorry. Beg your par—" The solid, beefy-faced man who had barged into their table on his way to the bar broke off in the middle of his apology. He looked very warm and definitely tight. He wore city clothes, except that his tie was missing and his collar undone; and he was staring at Alex fixedly, his mental machinery obviously grappling with some vague memory. "Hey, haven't I met you some place? Sure I have. Alex. Sure. Good old Alex. Howsaboy?"

"Fine," said Alex. He too was mentally grappling, and he too emerged victorious. "It's Walt, isn't it? That's right, Walt."

They continued to stare at each other, and Gen became aware of an acute embarrassment between them. They can't think of each other's last name, she thought in secret amusement.

"Never forget a face," said Walt rather feebly. Then he seemed to get hold of himself. "Howsaboy, Alex? How's the book business?"

"Can't complain. What are you doing out in these parts?"

"I been waylaid," explained Walt pompously. "That's what I been. Waylaid. I'm on my way out to the end of the Island. The missus and kids are out there, been there all summer, and I'm sneaking out a day early to spend the weekend with them and bring them back to town. I had to stop for gas, and here was this bar right next door, and Jesus, look at the time. The missus is going to give me hell."

"You ought to be like me. Never set foot inside a bar unless my wife is along. Gen, this is Walt. My wife, Walt."

Walt's eyes, china-blue in his flushed face, travelled over Gen appreciatively, and he extended a moist, freckled paw. Again, embarrassment descended, thick as a fog. "Uh. Well, I got to shove off. Nice to run into you again, Alex boy. Be seeing you around."

"Who's he?" asked Gen, when Walt had lurched on his way. "A customer?" He didn't look like the literary type, but then you never knew.

"Lord no," said Alex. He swished the olive around in his drink. "He sells something, I forget just what. Electric light fixtures, something like that." He looked up, smiling once more, and touched his glass against hers. "Well, well. Small world, isn't it?—as Walt would be the first to say, if he'd only thought of it. Drink up, Mrs. Blair, you're way behind."

The phone in the booth next to them pealed, and Rudy's daughter, sailing past with her tray, ducked in to answer it. She was little and wiry, like her father, with stringy hair and an anxious expression. Always going somewhere at a dead run. Gen could hear her shrilling into the phone: "Rudy's. Who? Yes, he's here ... What? Who do you want? Hey, wait a minute—"

She stuck her head out the door of the booth, looking more than anxious, downright alarmed, and her piercing voice cut through the juke box music and all the other racket. "Pop! Police! Mr. Blair!"

"Me?" said Alex. "Somebody wants me?"

At the bar big Ed Fuller, chief of police, set down his glass of beer, heaved himself off his stool, and steered his majestic stomach in their direction. For a minute it was unnaturally quiet.

"I don't know who they want," gulped Rudy's daughter. She pushed her straggly hair back of her ears. "First it was a man asked for Mr. Blair, and then it was a woman kind of screeching 'Police! Help! Police!' And then they hung up on me."

"Vonda. Mr. Theobald," said Gen. She and Alex were both on their feet. "They've wrecked the car or set the house on fire or—"

"Well, let's go see," said Ed Fuller reasonably. "Where did they call from? Mr. Blair's house?"

Rudy's daughter didn't know. But it seemed likely. They set out in Ed's car, and Ed might amble when he was navigating under his own power, but not when he had a motor to haul him. They shot out of Rudy's driveway, down the highway and on to the tree-lined dirt road, quiet and dark under the summer stars.

"Don't worry," said Alex, tightening his arm around Gen's shoulder. "You know how excitable Vonda is. Maybe all they did was run over a rabbit."

"Maybe it wasn't even them. It might be somebody's idea of a joke. In which case, ha ha."

There were no signs of disaster along the way. And when they got to the house, it looked its normal, substantial self. The lights were on in the living room, and the car, undamaged, was parked in the driveway. But as soon as they opened the door the comforting sense of normalcy evaporated. Even before she took in the physical signs of trouble—the overturned chair, the rug all askew, Vonda and Mr. Theobald, huddled together, sobbing, on the window seat—Gen felt the shock, the terror in that pleasant living room. It was like a potent odor, permeating the whole place.

Then she saw the girl. She lay on the couch, a rather tall, slender girl in a flowered cotton skirt and an eyelet-trimmed blouse, one slim hand trailing the floor. Her brown, slightly curling hair was shoulder-length, but it did not hide the terrible thing that had happened to her throat and her face. And her feet seemed to Gen somehow most pathetic of all, set neatly side by side, with the chipped red polish on their toenails showing through the cheap, ill-fitting sandals.

"We found her," Vonda blurted out. "I—I stumbled over her, opening the door, and oh, the poor girl, the poor, poor girl—" A fresh fit of sobbing swallowed up the rest.

"Then you moved her," wheezed Ed. His shrewd little eyes switched thoughtfully from Vonda back to the girl on the couch. "You should have left things the way they were. Looks to me like somebody strangled her."

Mr. Theobald wiped his eyes on his shirt sleeve and offered a tremulous explanation. "She looked so uncomfortable on the floor. We couldn't bear to leave her there, all twisted up. And then we didn't know for sure, we thought perhaps we might be able to revive her."

Such a possibility, thought Gen, wouldn't occur to anybody in the world except Mr. Theobald and Vonda, poor blundering innocents.

"No use crying over spilt milk," said Ed philosophically. "Pull yourselves together and show me just where she was laying, if you can remember, when you found her. Who is she?"

The question startled Gen. For no good reason: of course the girl was more than just a pitiful, wrecked body cast up on their living room couch. She had been, not so long ago, a living person, someone with likes and dislikes, with friends, relatives, perhaps a job. Certainly with an enemy. A living person. Someone with a name and address and telephone number.

She took a step nearer and looked down, in awe and compassion, at the discolored face which must, once, have been rather pretty.

"It's nobody we know," said Gen. "Nobody we ever laid eyes on before."

No one else spoke, and as she turned again, she caught the extraordinary expression on Vonda's and Mr. Theobald's faces. They looked, both of them, as if they were holding their breath, and their eyes were fastened on Alex.

"Alex—" she began. Her own breath caught. She had a panicky impression that the earth's foundations were shifting under her feet. Alex's face, usually so round and wholesome, had gone quite white, quite drawn-looking. He had not said a word, she remembered now, since they had walked in the door.

"I know her," he said at last. "That is, I did know her for a while last summer. Marcella. It's Marcella, of course."

THREE

"Oh," said Ed Fuller. "So she's a friend of yours?"

"Not exactly a friend." Alex swallowed, but it didn't help. He felt hollow, and somehow all out of commission. Especially his brain. It seemed to be in violent—and completely ineffectual—motion. Like one of those nightmares where you run like crazy and never move an inch from where you started.

Not exactly a friend. Then what had Marcella been? An acquaintance? That sounded altogether too casual. It hadn't been casual at all. He remembered, when it was over, his curious feeling of having made a hairbreadth escape. Though it was hard to imagine anybody in the world less dangerous than Marcella. Utterly defenseless, in fact. As pitiable in life as in death.

Why then, had he said *It's Marcella, of course*, as if her murder were no surprise to him?

"Not exactly a friend," prompted Ed, and waited.

Gen was waiting too. She had her head pulled up high, proud as a race horse, and there was a yellowish gleam in her eyes. The hollow feeling got worse. How could he ever explain Marcella to Gen?

He swallowed again. "I didn't really know her very well. I haven't seen or heard from her in months."

Vonda let out a kind of bleat. "Oh, my! I just remembered—" She clapped her hand over her mouth.

"Go on," said Ed. "Nobody's going to bite you."

"I just remembered that she called. Marcella called you at the shop, Alex. Now let me think when it was. This morning? No, you were in all this morning, so it must have been yesterday. That's it. That's exactly it. Late yesterday afternoon, Mr. Abbott had dropped in, and I was doing the filing, so I must have put the message in the folder with the W's. Just said to tell you she called. I recognized her voice right away."

"Such a soft little voice," Mr. Theobald recalled. "Like a child's."

"So you knew her too," said Ed. "You all knew her. All except Mrs. Blair."

"What of it?" Gen pulled her head up even higher. "Alex and I know lots of people separately. Any number of people."

"Well, sure, Mrs. Blair. I'm just trying to get it all straight. What was she doing out here?"

"I can't imagine," said Alex, and knew at once that it was false, he could imagine. "I don't think she even knew I had a place out here."

"Oh, I told her," Vonda explained. "We had quite a little chat. I told her we were all driving out tonight, and she was so sweet about it, wished us all a happy vacation—" Overcome, she buried her face once more on Mr. Theobald's shoulder.

"She must have been the girl Gertz was telling us about." At last Alex's brain caught hold of something concrete. "You remember, Gen, he said some girl had been there, asking how to get to our place. It must have been Marcella."

"Evidently," said Gen crisply. She did not look at him.

"We'll have to get Gertz up here." Ed's stomach heaved in a sigh. "And the coroner. And God knows who all. What's her last name? Where did she live?"

"Marcella Ewing." He saw the name, crudely printed, above the doorbell that was almost always out of order; the dingy, narrow hallway; the carpet on the stairs, so threadbare that only the ground-in dirt held it together. He heard the gentle, mourning dove voice; he had had to lean forward to catch it. "Marcella Ewing. I don't know if that's her married name or her maiden name. She'd been married, I think she told me, but she wasn't living with her husband when I knew her. She had a little apartment. Leroy Street, I think it was. I don't remember the number. I hired her to do some work for me, typing and so on. She needed a job, and I felt sorry for her."

"When was this?" asked Ed. "How long ago?"

"Last summer. In August." August. The month of vacations, separate and otherwise. Gen, Gen, you must stop thinking what you're thinking, you must give me a chance to explain, you must give yourself a chance to understand. His eyes fastened on her face—that charming, willful, heart-shaped face, with its amber-colored eyes and its bang of dark brown hair. Every inch the queen; Gen never looked haughtier than when she was on the verge of tears. Gen, he thought hopelessly, Gen, and turned back to Ed. "She worked for me a week or so."

"Then what? Did you fire her?"

"Not exactly. It was just a temporary typing job. When she finished it, I didn't really have anything for her to do, and I couldn't pay her much, so I told her she'd better look for something else."

"How about you?" Ed switched his gaze back to Vonda and Mr. Theobald. "What did you know about her?"

"She had a little cat," Vonda offered timidly. "That was why she liked to work at home. The cat got lonesome and misbehaved when she left it alone. You know, on the rug. So she did the typing at her place, on Alex's portable."

There was a short silence. "And you haven't seen her since?" Ed asked finally. "That's all you know about her?"

"That's all." The words came out mechanically, falsely. Of course it was not all. At Vonda's mention of the cat the whole remembered scene sprang into focus before his mind's eye: that miserable derelict animal, and Marcella's imploring eyes, and the meaty red face ... *It's Walt, isn't it? That's right. Walt.* Alex himself had come up with the name, back at Rudy's, half an hour or so ago. Why couldn't he repeat it now, to Ed? Surely it was twisting the arm of coincidence too far, for Walt and Marcella both to turn up in this neighborhood on the same afternoon. And yet Alex's tongue remained locked between his teeth, refusing to do its plain duty. Once more the old bond of shame-faced sympathy, shared guilt, whatever it was between them, held fast. Me and Walt, me and Walt. He had thought that it was buried for good, like all the rest of the oddly disturbing episode.

Well, he had been wrong. Here it was, right in front of him, and what he had to do was get away from everybody (even Gen? Yes, even Gen) and face, undistracted, what he had chosen not to face last summer. Pin it down. Dissect it. He had to, he had to.

Ed didn't show any signs of leaving any of them to themselves. He was pinching his lower lip in a worried way, studying Marcella as if he still expected some sort of explanation from her. "She must have had some folks," he insisted, "or something. A pocketbook. Women always got pocketbooks. Where's her pocketbook?"

Rather to Alex's surprise, it turned out that Marcella had one. They found it jammed back of the door. A shabby straw affair, decorated with a bunch of cloth violets that had this much in common with real ones: the ability to wilt. It hurt Alex to see this flimsy little safe of Marcella's broken open, its poor treasures exposed to Ed's probing eyes and hands. There wasn't much: thirty-nine cents in the coin purse, a plastic compact, two keys on a paper clip, lipstick and comb, a few stray bobby pins, a broken-backed cigarette. The imitation leather billfold was empty except for a pasteboard identification card, dim behind its sheet of cellophane. Marcella Ewing. The address on Leroy Street. Age: 25 yrs. Ht. 5'6". Wt.: 114 lbs. Social Security Number. That was all, except for two small sheets of lined paper that looked as if they had been torn out of an address book. On one was written Alex's name and the address and telephone number of the Fourth Avenue bookshop; on the second another name—Walter Bowman; Ed read it off laboriously—with a lower Broadway address and phone number.

"Walt," said Alex involuntarily, and Ed looked up sharply. "You know the guy? This Walter Bowman?"

"I—" Once again Alex's non-conformist tongue might have locked in silence (quite pointless, of course; nothing could keep Walt out of it now) but Gen pounced on the name before he had a chance to find out.

"Walt? That man down at Rudy's, the drunk one that stopped and spoke to you. His name was Walt. Is he the one?"

No help for it. "He knows her," Alex admitted. "At least he did last summer. I don't know about now. He was at her apartment once when I stopped in to see her about the job. That's the only time I ever met him before tonight. She told me later that he'd—broken off with her."

"You mean he was this Marcella's boyfriend?" Already Ed looked less worried.

"Something like that, I gathered."

"He's married," said Gen. "He mentioned his wife and family." Her glance fell, cutting as a winter wind, on Alex. "Not of course that that would deter him."

"And he was at Rudy's? And drunk?" Ed hitched up his belt and headed ponderously for the telephone. "Looks like we're getting some place. What's this guy look like?"

Alex let Gen describe him. She did it tersely. "Typical visiting fireman. Hail fellow well met, and pretty tight. Red face, blondish, not exactly fat, but solid." She paused, and added in a small, awe-struck voice, "He didn't act at all like a—a murderer."

"None of 'em do," Ed told her, and picked up the receiver.

First he called the police station and ordered somebody to pick up the coroner and get out here on the double-quick and somebody else to get over to Rudy's on the same. Then he called Rudy himself and relayed Gen's description of Walt, together with instructions to "keep the guy there if it takes everybody in the place to do it. There's a young lady been murdered out here at Blair's."

"We'll wait till Whitey gets here with the coroner," he announced to the room at large, when he had finished his calls. "Then I'll shoot back to Rudy's and pick this Walt guy up. Rudy says he don't see him at the bar, but even if he's already left it won't take us long to nab him. Wouldn't surprise me if we got the whole thing cleaned up tonight." He gave them all, including Marcella, a reassuring nod. "Long as we're here, I'll take a look around, just see … Say, wonder how they got in? You kept the house locked up, didn't you, Alex?"

"But that was the funny thing!" exclaimed Vonda. "It wasn't locked. When we couldn't find the key, we tried the door, and it wasn't locked at all."

"Horace Pankey," said Alex. He wrenched his mind away from its secret preoccupation and focused it on the key, the unlocked door. "I left a key under the doormat for Horace Pankey. He promised to fix the patio this week, so I told him to come in and help himself to beer whenever he felt like it." He smiled wanly. "You know Horace. You've got to prime the pump if you want to get any work out of him."

Ed knew Horace, all right. "And then like as not you'll overdo the priming, and he'll decide to go clamming instead. Where is this patio?"

Alex flipped the light switch, and they peered out through the big side windows at the square of freshly laid cement. It was really a sort of unenclosed extension of the porch; "patio" was Gen's name for it. Her idea, too. "We can sit in the sun and drink whiskey sours and meditate," she had said.

Well, there it was. Finished. All it lacked was the sun and the whiskey sours and the two happy meditators. The pile of empty beer cans beside it testified to the amount of priming that Horace had found necessary.

Gen turned away abruptly. "There's the key," she said, pointing to the top of the desk. "He left it inside. Maybe he saw—whoever it was."

"You got something there, Mrs. Blair." Ed plucked an envelope from the desk cubbyhole, whisked the key into it, and consigned it to his shirt pocket. "We'll round up Horace and find out what he saw, provided he ain't too drunk by this time to remember. There's Whitey," he added, as a car pulled up in the driveway. He cleared his throat in an embarrassed way. "Got to ask you folks to go back with me. Because it was your friends here found her, and you knew her, Alex, and Mrs. Blair—"

"Me?" said Gen. "I'm just along for the ride. Don't worry, we'll go quietly." She gave Ed a kind of smile, and her head was as high as ever. But her hands, as she gathered up her purse, fumbled; for a split second Alex had the crazy notion that she was going to wring them.

FOUR

The frightening thing, thought Gen, was that she couldn't identify her own feelings. Anger she would certainly have recognized; she had lost her temper before—oh, many times—with Alex. Or jealousy, though she had to cast her mind back to high school days to remember what it felt like to be jealous. A thrust and twist in your chest, a hot haze that distorted your vision, monstrously magnifying your rival's charms, monstrously minimizing your own. Inconceivable, to feel like that toward a poor wispy dead girl. All that Marcella had inspired in Gen was a sorrowful aversion, a half-ashamed desire to get away from her. That was Marcella dead, of course. Marcella alive might have been something quite different. A nice, pliable little clinging vine, perhaps, the kind of wife that would make life simple for Alex? Yes, but even so …

Not exactly jealousy. Not exactly anger. Deeper than either, some nameless feeling: a crumbling under her feet, a boiling in her chest.

Alex drove their car back to Rudy's, and all the way (they bucketed along; the lights of Ed's car behind them seemed to shove them on relentlessly) Gen sat with her hands clamped in her lap, waiting for Alex to say something.

Not a word. Not a mumbling word. Once or twice she felt his eyes on her, as if he might be hoping for a sign from her to break the deadlock. Well, let him hope. Her neck stayed stiff, her own eyes remained stubbornly averted. It was only once or twice, anyway. Most of the time he stared straight ahead, shutting her out, withdrawn in some queer absorption of his own. The way he had been out there at the house.

In the back seat Vonda wept voluptuously, and Mr. Theobald murmured, "There, dearest, there." The lucky, uncomplicated innocents.

They had known Marcella, too. Everybody. Everybody except you, Mrs. Blair. And it's all very well to say you and Alex know lots of people separately. Name one, name just one that you know and Alex doesn't.

Even the most casual acquaintances, the people at the office, the strays left over from your unmarried days—Alex knows them by hearsay, if not by sight. You've told him about them all. You've held nothing back.

It had never crossed Gen's mind that Alex—her guileless, open-faced, devoted Alex—would shut her out of any part of his life, however trivial. That was the thing. She was shut out; and Marcella, whatever else she might have been, was not trivial. "Not exactly a friend," Alex had said. And, "I didn't really know her very well. I haven't seen or heard from her in months." False; so patently a lie that she wouldn't have blamed Ed Fuller for laughing in his face. Then, too, there was his silence about Walt. Unaccountable; he must have thought of Walt in the instant of recognizing Marcella. Yet he had left it to Gen to make the obvious connection, had seemed in a way to be trying to shield Walt. The little encounter at Rudy's began, in Gen's mind, to take on a sinister tinge. How embarrassed they had been, both Walt and Alex! She had smiled to herself over it, had chalked it up to their not being able to remember each other's last names. It seemed no longer amusing, nor anywhere near as simple as that. It was tangled up with Marcella, and again Gen had been shut out.

Alex cleared his throat. But all he said was, "Here we are."

The first person they saw when they got out of the car was Brad Stone. He galloped up to them, and the sight of him—that stylishly homely face of Brad's, and the Brooks Brothers suit, and the crew cut—brought a lump to Gen's throat. It was just that he looked so exactly as usual, flesh-and-blood evidence of the safe, familiar world which in the last half hour had dissolved before her very eyes.

"What the hell goes on?" he burst out. He pressed Alex's arm briefly, deposited a hasty kiss on Gen's left ear. "Thank God you two are all right. I just got here, and there's been so much sound and fury I haven't got anything sorted out. All this nonsense about murder ..." He gave Gen and Alex each a searching glance, and abruptly stopped talking.

Ed Fuller cleared his throat, and Alex came out of his fog enough to explain who Brad was. Ed nodded at him affably. "You know this girl that got killed, Mr. Stone? This Marcella Ewing?"

"Marcella Ewing?" repeated Brad. His tone was blank, but Gen didn't miss the split-second flick of his eyes toward Alex. (So everybody knew her. All except you, Mrs. Blair.) "I don't think I do. Should I?"

"You might have heard me mention her," said Alex. "She worked down at the shop for a while last summer. Maybe you remember seeing her name on a check. You may even have met her."

All very reasonable, thought Gen. Brad had a small investment in the bookshop—no more than a token, really, of his recurrent dream of escaping from the advertising rat race into a pleasanter, more leisurely life. Alex had made the break; it was unlikely that Brad ever would. He liked money too much, the kind of money people made in advertising. If the truth were told, he probably liked the pressure, too, the rush and push that he complained of so bitterly. But the wistful dream persisted. Some day he would get wise to himself, like Alex (only would Alex have found it so easy, if he had been as successful as Brad?), some day he would kiss the big money goodbye and relax with Alex in the easy-going, not-very-lucrative bookshop world. Some day. If he didn't drop dead first.

"Could be," he said now. "You know me. It's sometimes all I can do to remember my own name. Look, kids," he added, as Ed Fuller made a small, restive gesture toward the crowd—quite a little crowd, Gen noticed, all clustered in Rudy's driveway, around a car with a New York license plate. "Look, leave us not obstruct justice or whatever's going on here. I'll stick around, in case you need moral support. Stiff upper lip, you know, and all that." He gave them both a warm grin. "Nothing like a nice quiet weekend in the country, is there?"

The crowd made way, respectfully, for Ed and his little procession. One of Ed's henchmen seemed to be in charge. "I waited for you," he reported. "Don't look like he's going to give us any trouble. Rudy spotted him out here in his car before I got here."

In the front seat, his head lolling half out of the open window, sprawled Walt. He couldn't have looked less like a murderer of defenseless girls, thought Gen. Defenseless, in fact, was the word that seemed to fit Walt himself at the moment. All unaware of his audience, his light hair plastered against his forehead in sweat-dampened curls, his lower lip puffing in and out with each clearly audible breath, he slept as peacefully as a baby in its crib.

He roused up when Ed jerked the car door open. "Hey," he mumbled, "what the—?" Blinked, startled but not alarmed, at the faces peering at him. Scratched his chest. Yawned. Grinned sheepishly. "Must've dropped off, I guess," he remarked.

"All right, let's have it," said Ed, very gruff and official. "What do you know about Marcella Ewing?"

"Marcella Ewing?" There could be no doubt that the name was a familiar one to him. Wariness flickered in his china-blue eyes; he pulled himself up straight. "What's it to you, what I know about Marcella Ewing? Who wants to know?"

"Police, that's who. Don't try any funny stuff. We know you're mixed up with her."

"Police? Marcella?" For the first time Walt seemed to sense danger, possible hostility in the group of people watching him. He blustered a little. "Say, what the hell is this, anyway?"

"Murder," said Ed. "She's been murdered out at Mr. Blair's house. Now you going to talk?"

"Murdered!" Walt's jaw dropped. He forgot to be wary. He simply goggled at Ed. It looked real, but Gen remembered what Ed had said: None of 'em act like murderers.

There was a little bustle in the group back of them. Rudy was pushing forward the weedy young fellow who tended the gas station for him. "Go on. Tell Ed, the way you told me. Is that him?"

The kid, all scared eyes and protruding ears and bobbing Adam's apple, peered in at Walt. "That's him, all right. Stopped for gas and asked me the way to Alex Blair's place. This afternoon, long about three, three thirty." He ducked back out of sight, apparently overcome by the sensation he had created.

Something like a sigh—whether of satisfaction, sympathy for Walt, or plain excitement Gen could not tell—shook the cluster of people. She had no doubt about Ed's reaction. Straightforward satisfaction. All he needed to clinch the case. For a moment Gen saw it as clearly, as flatly black-and-white as it must seem to Ed. "Boyfriend" of the victim. Or ex-boyfriend. Married man playing around behind his wife's back, having his fun on the side. Fun at first. After a while, for one reason or another, a nuisance. The man gets tired; or the girl gets tired, gets too demanding … Anyway, a nuisance. So the man gets rid of her.

A fairly common little story, Gen supposed. And, if Walt had been trying to find Alex, why hadn't he mentioned it when they ran into each other at Rudy's? That was odd, come to think of it. Very odd.

"That right?" Ed was shooting questions at Walt. "You found out from the filling station how to get to Alex's place? You knew the girl was going to be there? So maybe you got a good story about what happened after you got out there? It better be good, brother, it better be good."

"Wait a minute!" Walt stumbled out of the car and onto his feet. "Lemme get this straight. You think I—" Swaying slightly, rumpled with drink and sleep, he looked around him incredulously. What they thought hit him at last. It drained blotches of color out of his face. "All right. So I knew her. That was last summer. All washed up. We been all washed up since last summer." (Alex had said that too. Haven't seen or heard from her in months.) "So we went out there. That was Jimmy. His idea. He got me to drive him out. But she wasn't there. Nobody was there but a guy drinking beer and mixing cement. Ask him. Ask Jimmy. He was there, he'll tell you." He took a deep breath and got his voice back under control. "All you got to do is ask Jimmy. He'll tell you. Where is he?"

"Yeah," said Ed. "Where is he? And who is he?" He turned back to the filling station kid. "Anybody with this guy when he stopped for gas? Did you see this Jimmy?"

"There was a fella with him, all right," the kid stammered. "Young fella. Hitchhiking out to Montauk."

"I know the one you mean," Rudy broke in excitedly. "I heard him talking at the bar about a job in Montauk. Sharp-looking young guy. Flashy dresser. He was talking to—Hey, Lillian! C'mere, Lil, tell Ed about the guy that was buying you the Tom Collinses. You know the one I mean."

"Who, me?" Considering the limitations of her stage, Lillian contrived to make quite an entrance. At some point in her short life, it was obvious, somebody had told her she looked like Ava Gardner, and she had worked hard at it ever since. Her gait was an extraordinary combination of prance and slither, her haircut Italian, the outer corners of her eyes equipped with the standard provocative tilt. Gen remembered having seen her around before; like a good many other local girls, she had a summer job as a waitress in one of the restaurants in town.

"Oh, you mean Jimmy," drawled Lillian. (Sultry heroine tangling with meathead cop.) "So he bought me a coupla Tom Collinses. You want to make something out of it?"

"Not a thing," said Ed patiently. "I just want to find out who he is. Last name. Where he was from, where he was going, where he is now. Like that."

"How should I know? I go to the little girls' room and when I come back—no Jimmy. I should beat my brains out looking for him? Not me. There's plenty more where he came from." The carefully tousled haircut tossed, the hoop earrings bounced, to indicate how Jimmy rated with Lillian. "Jimmy. That's all the name he told me. He had this job waiting for him out in Montauk, playing the piano with some band. His own car broke down, back in New York, so that's why he was hitching a ride—"

"His own car! Job in Montauk!" Walt's voice all but broke with the weight of desperation. "He was handing this kid a line, that's all. I'll tell you who he is, you'll find it out anyway, he's Marcella's husband!"

Once more everybody seemed to sigh in unison. Ed blinked a couple of times.

"Her husband, eh? What are you trying to sell me? That you and him were pals? First time I ever heard of a girl's boyfriend and her husband …"

"Ex-boyfriend! Ex-husband!" Walt's whole face quivered with the force of his point. "They split up years ago. And Jimmy is sure as hell no pal of mine."

"Oh, so that's the pitch. Kind of lucky, ain't it, for you to have Jimmy, whoever he is, around to put the blame on? Yep. It sure would be handy for you, wouldn't it?"

"I'm not putting the blame on him! We went out there together! He'll tell you, he's got no more to hide than I have. Ask him, just ask him. Where the hell is he? Jimmy!"

But Jimmy was nowhere to be found. Neither was Horace Pankey, who, having drunk his beer and laid his cement, was no doubt fishing or clamming in his customary blissful fuddle. He would turn up in the morning; he always did. Whether he would remember anything about this afternoon (aside from the fact that Alex owed him some money) was another matter.

Walt made one last frantic appeal before Ed took him off to the police station for further questioning. "But *why* would I do it? Answer me that. A person's got to have a motive. *Why* would I kill her?"

"Maybe she got a new boyfriend and you didn't like being out in the cold," Ed told him amiably. (Beside her Gen felt Alex give a convulsive start.) "Or maybe she had her hooks in you, threatened to tell your wife if you didn't come across, something like that. It's happened before."

"Oh my God." Walt turned his face up to the starry sky, as though he realized he was beyond all earthly aid and were consigning himself, without much hope, to some higher power.

But it was an earthly voice, after all—Alex's—that spoke in his defense. "She never would have, she never would have." Somehow Gen got the impression that the words were being yanked out of him, and a curious glance, half-guilty, half-comradely, passed between him and Walt. "It's got to be something else. You're making a mistake, Ed. There's still Jimmy—"

"Don't worry, we'll find him." Ed paused to give Alex's arm a friendly pat. "Look at it this way, Alex. Supposing you're a hitchhiker, on your way to a job some place, and supposing the guy that picks you up gets mixed up in bad trouble. What would you do? Wouldn't you lose your head and scram?"

"I might." Alex looked him in the eye. "I know damn well I'd scram if the bad trouble happened to be my ex-wife getting herself murdered."

"We'll find him," Ed repeated, a shade more thoughtfully. "You're going to be around, aren't you, Alex?" He couldn't quite keep his eyes from sliding in Gen's direction. "Might have another question or two, later on."

When your wife isn't around to be embarrassed. He might as well have said it in words. No sense hurting the little woman's feelings; I know how wives are, always making a mountain out of a molehill. I understand. No need to stir up any more trouble. What she doesn't know won't hurt her.

The boiling feeling in Gen's chest got worse.

Ed roared off for the police station with his captive; his henchmen disappeared, presumably in search of Jimmy; people began to drift back into Rudy's for another drink and the endless rehashing that would be their conversational meat for weeks to come.

Brad was nowhere in sight; he had no doubt adjourned to the bar. Typical of him, thought Gen. Not that Brad or anyone else could have done much about the way she felt. She tried to smile at Vonda and Mr. Theobald. Poor souls, with their ecstatic vacation plans. Something would have to be done about Vonda and Mr. Theobald ...

"Mr. Abbott! " trilled Vonda. "How nice to see you here!"

It was Dwight, all right, and Gen felt a surge of relief at the sight of his round-shouldered figure in the shapeless seersucker suit. He could at least take charge of Vonda and Mr. Theobald, get them out to the cottage on his place that was to be theirs for the long weekend.

"Good Lord, what a mess!" he said, and shook hands solemnly, all around. Like a funeral. "I just got here, finished up in town earlier than I expected and decided to come on out tonight instead of tomorrow. Look, Alex, if there's anything I can do—" He paused, peering wistfully at Alex and Gen. Behind their glasses Dwight's eyes always looked red and strained, as if he had been up all night reading footnotes. Which more often than not was the case; ever since he finished college he had been immersed in the task of writing the definitive life of somebody, Gen couldn't think who at the moment.

His dull, anxious-to-please face brightened. "Well, of course there is something I can do. You're not going to want to stay at your place, so come on home with me. Loads of room—you know how I rattle around out there all by myself. I'll be more than glad to have you. The cottage is all ready for you," he added, turning to Vonda and Mr. Theobald. "At least I hope it is. I told Mrs. Pankey to air it out and fix it for you. I can drive you out right now if you want me to."

"Thanks a lot, Dwight." Alex was making an obvious effort to pull himself out of the trance that had its grip on him. "Why don't you do that? You'll be back here for dinner, won't you? Maybe we'll take you up on the invitation. Right now I could use a ..."

"Drink, of course," supplied Brad, materializing out of the gravel. Or so it seemed to Gen. "I thought as much. That's why I've been keeping a couple of martinis in the warming oven for you. No trouble at all, I'd do it for anybody." He held up his hand, as if to ward off a shower of thanks, and showed all his nice white teeth in a smile, aimed principally at Gen. "Hi, Dwight. How's tricks?"

"Very well, thank you." Dwight's expression grew faintly stony, as if he were bracing himself against flippancies, possibly indignities. Past experiences with Brad had made him wary. But no one was going to accuse Dwight of not meeting his fellow man halfway. "I was just telling Alex, he and Gen are welcome to stay at my place, in view of the circumstances. And of course you are, too. I've got plenty of room, you know. Glad to have you."

"Delighted," said Brad promptly. "I can't thank you enough, in view of the circumstances. We can all get drunk together. Don't look down your nose at me, Mrs. Blair, I was never more sober in my life." He kissed her lightly on the neck. "Think nothing of it, pet. It's sex, just sex."

Dwight did his best not to look disapproving, and turned with relief to the business of loading his weekend tenants into his car and driving off with them.

"Good old Dwight," said Brad sententiously. "Always the friend in need." Then he turned back to Gen and Alex with one of his shrewd, perceptive glances. The light touch was still there, but subtly changed. "I shall now exit. Only as far as the bar, you understand. I'm not deserting you. It's just that I have this uncanny instinct about domestic crises. Remember, the martinis and I await within." He nodded brightly and crunched his way across the gravel to Rudy's door. The juke box was going again in there, and a hubbub of voices.

Talk, talk, talk. That was what she and Alex must do. Talk.

Only Alex had shut her out. She had a desolate feeling that she couldn't make him hear, that she couldn't reach him at all—though he was right here next to her, his sleeve actually brushing her arm. Should she try? Should she touch his hand, his face that had such an unfamiliar, preoccupied look? It was that withdrawn expression of Alex's that stopped her. She might have swallowed the bitter pill of her pride, but fear—of another rebuff, another door shutting in her face—froze her.

So it was Alex who spoke first, and of all the wrong things he might have said (could anything have been right?) he chanced on the one that seemed most abysmally wrong to Gen.

"Gen," he said, "you've got to let me explain."

Instantly they were reduced to the hackneyed stock characters of every play since the world began: aggrieved wife, erring husband, classic compromising situation.

It was her cue to say, "Go ahead. Explain." So she said it. That was the appalling part. She said it.

And it was his cue to stammer. So he stammered: "Marcella and I—"

Stop it, stop it, she was crying inside. This is cheap, this is what Walt and his wife are going to say to each other, this isn't us. But her voice went on, apparently of its own accord, shrill, wifely, bitter: "You said you hardly knew her. Hadn't seen her in months. What was she doing at our house, then? Why did she go there?"

"I don't know. That is, I'm not sure. Honest to God, Gen, it isn't what you think."

"How do you know what I think?" She clenched her hands up against her boiling chest, but there was no help for it, the seething rose ungovernably. "You don't know anything about it! You never have, because you're a fraud! A great big stupid lug of a fraud! You're a—a *Walt!* That's what you are, and I can't stand it. You're a Walt!"

He must have put out his hand (too late; everything was too late now) because she wrenched away and tore across to the car.

"Gen! Where are you going? Gen, you can't do this!"

"Oh, can't I! " She grappled with the car door, flung it open and herself into the seat. "I'm going back to town. To gay Paree. To darkest Africa. To Podunk. Who cares?"

At the corner she looked back, and he was still standing there in the sickly neon lights of Rudy's driveway. She couldn't see him very well, though. Tears were streaming down her face.

FIVE

He didn't blame Gen. That wasn't unusual; Alex had a weakness for Gen, he hardly ever blamed her, even when she was utterly unreasonable. Which she could be, all right, if she put her mind to it.

But nobody could have said tonight was her fault. Gen, for all her touchiness and quick temper, wasn't mean or small-minded. She took a lot of understanding, but she could give it, too. A surprising lot of it. You had to know how to handle her, that was all. And Alex, who knew and loved her, who was aware of all the thorny spots in her nature—Alex had treated her tonight as if she were just any suspicious, sharp-tongued wife. No wonder she had yelled at him and left him standing here in front of Rudy's to face whatever had to be faced alone.

He had behaved like a—well, all right—like a Walt; and the reason was somehow Marcella. Marcella, unaccountably creeping back into his life and dying there. Marcella, raising in his mind all the haunting uneasiness of last August, so comfortably forgotten until now. Pin it down. Dissect it. He must, if he was ever to be himself again. That was the real urgency. That was the secret preoccupation that had numbed him to Gen's feelings—so thoroughly that he had wound up by driving her away from him.

Alone at last, he thought wryly. No more questions to be answered, for the moment, no more nagging little details to explain. He had been inwardly screaming for solitude all evening. Well, now he had it. What was he going to do with it?

(Gen. Like the tolling of a bell. Gen. Gen.)

This sort of thing would get him nowhere. He must get back to Marcella. Begin at the beginning. Dredge it all up and examine it. The first time he ever saw Marcella, that steamy August day in the park. On his way back to the shop, he had dropped down on a bench out of inertia, had sat there trying to wring an illusion of coolness out of the listless trees. A few pigeons pecked half-heartedly at some peanut shells, a dog barked, a fretful baby wailed. He wouldn't have noticed the girl, except that, as she passed his bench, she stumbled and the heel came off her shoe ...

"Where's Gen?" It was Dwight, back again, still earnestly bent on good deeds. There was no escape. Even if Alex had had the heart to snub Dwight and his neighborliness, he couldn't afford to, stranded as he was. Just like the old days, when they were kids, spending their summers out here. Alex and the rest of the gang had let Dwight tag along for financial reasons—you could always count on him for hot dogs and cokes if you were halfway decent to him. What noble creatures we are, thought Alex, all of us.

"She decided to go back to town." Let Dwight make what he wanted to out of it; it was just something else for Alex to endure, like the hour or two that lay ahead. Drinks, dinner, conversation. You bet. Lots of conversation. Brad would be on hand, too, and you never knew for sure whether Brad was going to be in the mood to ease the strain, or add to it. But, at the end, solitude. Eventually Dwight and Brad must fold up and leave Alex to his long, long thoughts. "No reason for her to stick around here. Ed told me to stay, or I'd have gone back with her."

Dwight's head bobbed up and down in hearty understanding. "Naturally, naturally. What a shock for all of you. Come on, let's have a drink. You look done in."

Brad detached himself from the mob at the bar and sauntered over to their table as soon as they found one. And Alex had to hand it to him, he didn't ask where Gen was. Well, he ought to be an expert on domestic crises; he'd had a world of first-hand experience. For the moment, Alex noted gratefully, Brad was in one of his quiet phases—still bright-eyed and alert, but not making much noise. Not even baiting Dwight. The way he sat there with his head tilted a little (it was a characteristic pose of Brad's) made him look like an intelligent, observant dog. A terrier,

Alex decided, a sleek, dark-haired, sensitive terrier. And old Dwight—they were about the same age, but Dwight had always seemed at least ten years older than anybody else—Dwight was like a wire-haired dachshund. Well-meaning and clumsy and scraggly.

He began to feel quite philosophical about his companions. Rudy's was full of specimens that would have been harder to put up with than Dwight and Brad. Rudy himself, for instance, nervous and inquisitive as a monkey; or Frank Gertz, who wallowed, goggle-eyed, in the memory of his brief encounter with Marcella: "I never gave it a second thought. Nice looking girl, you know, and I told her, I said, 'It's quite a considerable walk,' when she asked about Alex's place, 'a good two miles,' I said, and then she said ..."

It was obvious that Dwight was doing his conscientious best to curb his curiosity. He didn't permit himself a single question until they had their drinks in front of them and their cigarettes lighted.

"I gather from what Vonda said that she was somebody you knew, this girl that was killed?" He put it out tentatively, like a feeler, ready to withdraw at the tiniest discouraging sign from Alex.

"I knew her, yes. Slightly." With an inward sigh, Alex resigned himself to the inevitable. Dwight would plod along, as he always did; deliberately, methodically digesting each fact before tackling the next. "She did a little work for me last summer, on that lot of books I got from London. You know, the Dreiser items." Dwight had moused his way through the lot, Alex remembered, on the off-chance that there would be some reference to his boy, Vachel Lindsay. Lindsay's life, if Dwight ever got it finished, was certainly going to be the most tediously detailed slide ever subjected to the literary microscope.

"I remember." Dwight put down his glass abruptly; it wasn't like him to make such swift, unexpected gestures, and Alex saw with surprise that he had turned quite pale. "Good Lord, is *that* the girl! Why, I met her, she came into the shop one day when I was there, going through the Dreiser stuff. She'd been working on the descriptions—I remember because it was one of the most slipshod jobs of typing I ever encountered."

"She wasn't any ball of fire when it came to efficiency," Alex agreed.

"Why, good Lord," said Dwight again. Shock made his face seem bigger and plainer than ever; he blinked helplessly at Alex, and ran his hands through his already rumpled, lifeless-looking hair. "I didn't realize that was the one. Tall, undernourished looking girl. No self-assurance. Why would anybody want to kill a harmless creature like her?"

"Why not?" Brad asked the question suddenly, with the mixture of suavity and irritation he so often showed toward Dwight. His quiet phase, inevitably, had passed. Too good to last. "She struck me as the congenital victim type. That's right, I met her once, too. Down at the shop, where everybody seems to meet everybody. At least, I met a girl that fits the description. I never clutter up my mind with people's names. Sure, she was harmless. So are rabbits harmless creatures. That's their undoing. You might say they're lethally harmless. Absolutely irresistible to hawks. Like I said, a congenital victim. Natural-born prey."

Dwight blinked at him. "Rabbits? Hawks?"

But Alex knew that Brad—maybe just by chance—had hit on something basic about Marcella. He didn't remember that Brad had ever met her. Of course it might have slipped his mind. Or Alex might have been out of the shop at the time. Anyway, Brad had come through with a deft and penetrating thumbnail sketch of Marcella.

He evidently felt the same way. Carried away with his own eloquence, he was soaring on: "Or a stray cat. (Gad, what an artist I am with words! Sometimes it almost frightens me.) Some people *are* like stray cats, you know. They follow you home, so to speak. You don't want them, and yet there they are, making you feel guilty for not taking them in ..." He shot one of his mischievous glances at Dwight. "Didn't somebody write a poem on just that theme? I'm sure of it. James Whitcomb Riley, Eugene Field, Lindsay, Edgar A. Guest. One of those boys."

Here we go, thought Alex wearily: Brad up to his favorite tricks, and Dwight rising, as always, to the bait. "I can't vouch for what the others may have written," he was saying, in his stuffiest tone, "and may I remark in passing that your classification of Lindsay impresses me as irresponsible, to say the least—but I can assure you that Lindsay never ..." (The bell tolled inside Alex's head again. Gen. Gen.)

There was nothing to do but draw the mental curtain and wait for solitude. They must have eaten, because they were drinking coffee when Ed Fuller, with his impressive stomach leading the way, steamed back to their table and settled down, wheezing, across from Alex and Dwight.

"Your wife go back to town? I don't blame her. Hell of a way to start a vacation." His eyes, shrewdly inquisitive, met Alex's. "How about it? You figured out any reason why this Marcella should turn up at your place?"

"I don't think she had many friends," said Alex. "She struck me as kind of a rootless person. She might have needed work and turned to me just because I gave her a job last summer. That's the only thing I can think of."

"You don't think she had any ideas like—" Ed cleared his throat delicately. "—like stirring up a little trouble between you and your wife?"

"It would never in the world occur to her. Never."

"Well, supposing there was somebody else putting her up to it? That's the story this Walt Bowman's been giving me. Claims her husband, Jimmy—the fellow everybody else says was just a plain hitchhiker—has been putting the screws on him for the past year, ever since he quit paying Marcella's rent. On a small scale, you understand. Ten bucks here, twenty-five there. According to Walt, it griped the hell out of him, but he figured it was less trouble to pay than to have his wife find out he'd been two-timing her. So he paid. And today, he says, when Jimmy cadged a ride out here with him, Walt thought he was trying the same little game on you. How does it sound to you?"

"I'm not sure," said Alex truthfully. It was going to take him a minute to get used to the idea of himself as a likely candidate for blackmail. "She might, if somebody else put her up to it. She was—pliable."

"Yeah. That's what Walt says. Pliable. All you had to do was give her a kind word, and she was all yours." Ed paused. "Did you ever have any dealings with Jimmy?"

Alex shook his head regretfully. He would like to have been able to back up Walt's story. He believed it, but he didn't think Ed did. Still, there must be other people who could identify Jimmy, not as a casual hitchhiker, but as Marcella's husband. Meanwhile, all Alex could do was tell the truth. "I knew she'd been married, but I got the impression the husband had deserted her. A first-class heel, I gathered, the kind that might very well go in for a spot of blackmail."

His flimsy little efforts in Walt's behalf were not lost on Ed. "So Walt's a pal of yours? How long have you known him?"

"I don't really know him. I told you, I met him once at Marcella's place last summer. I just don't think he murdered her, that's all."

"Well," said Ed comfortably, "everybody's got a right to their own opinion. When we get our hands on Jimmy we'll be considerable farther ahead."

"You mean you haven't found him yet?" Alex couldn't resist rubbing it in. "I should think it would be a cinch to nab a jobless hitchhiker, especially one that had lost his head and scrammed. And how about Horace Pankey?"

"If you find Horace, let me know," put in Dwight drily. "I've been trying to get him to fix my roof for the last three weeks. He keeps promising he'll be right over, and his mother keeps promising she'll send him right over, and that's all that ever happens."

"Oh, Horace'll turn up," Ed assured them. "He always does, sooner or later. The boys haven't found him yet, but that doesn't mean anything.

He's probably trying out another new clamming spot. I doubt if we get much sense out of him, anyway. Not after all that beer." He made a motion to rise, and Alex, struck by a sudden thought, put out his hand.

"Wait a minute. I just thought of something, Ed. What if Marcella came out here because she knew Jimmy was going to try to blackmail me and wanted to warn me? I think she might do that. I honest to God can't see her as a blackmailer herself. What if she objected to Jimmy's little game, and they got in a quarrel, and—"

"Quite a mess of if's there," Ed said, and resumed the process of hoisting himself out of his chair. "If Jimmy really is her husband. And if he's really been putting the bite on Walt. And if Marcella knew he was going to try it with you. Why didn't she warn Walt too, if she was such a Girl Scout?"

"Maybe she didn't even know it was going on. Jimmy could have been doing it all on his own."

"He could have. But she had yours and Walt's address and telephone number written down, in her purse. Seems funny she'd hang on to those all this time, for no particular reason."

"It doesn't," said Alex hopelessly, "not if you knew Marcella."

They didn't linger long after Ed left. Brad, who had applied himself diligently and on the whole silently, to a procession of Scotch and sodas (though he had been listening, Alex was sure of it; not missing a word) staggered a little as they made their way out. Not that it worried Alex. Brad was less a problem drunk than sober. He usually went to sleep.

Alex took a deep breath of the quiet, moonlit night when they got outside. It was a welcome contrast to the buzz of voices and overcharged atmosphere of Rudy's.

"'How sweet the moonlight sleeps,'" intoned Brad, "to quote the immortal lines of Lindsay—or was it that second-rate hack Shakespeare?"

But for once Dwight ignored the bait. He was busy with other thoughts. "Ed's a reliable character, you know," he offered, as they got into the car. "He lacks formal education, of course, but he's sensible. Thorough, too. He'll check Walt's story, you can depend on it."

Alex, however, was wondering whether Gen would remember to buy some gas (she probably wouldn't; it always came as a complete surprise to her when she ran out) and didn't bother to answer. And Brad, apparently under the impression that they were riding in a rowboat, was trailing his hand out the open window and remarking on the coolth of the water this evening. After that he lapsed into a vibrato rendition of Little Redwing.

The estate that Dwight's father had built (he had been *the* Dwight

Abbott; it was fifteen years since his death, but the royalties from his sharp, witty plays still amounted to a nice piece of change) no longer seemed grand to Alex, as it had in his childhood. It just looked pompous now, and a little depressing, with its formally laid out grounds, its veranda where no one ever sat, its museum-like façade with all the steps. The cottage, where the caretaker used to live and where tonight Vonda and Mr. Theobald were no doubt feasting tearfully on blackstrap molasses and yoghurt, provided the only inviting touch.

"I hope they're going to be comfortable there," Dwight said as he drove on past the cottage to the big house. "It hasn't been used in years. Mrs. Pankey's got her hands full, just keeping the part of the house that I use livable. But at least they'll be near the beach."

"Don't worry about them," Brad put in, unexpectedly. "Happiest people in the world. You know why? They got no brains. That's what wrecks the human race. Brains. Intellect. Gray matter. Heap bad medicine." He returned to Little Redwing.

"It doesn't always work that way," said Alex. "Marcella didn't have any brains to speak of, either."

And she hadn't been happy. Crying the first time he ever saw her; sitting there on the park bench with her head bent, while she tried to fit the heel back on her shoe and the tears fell hopelessly down on her long, limp hands. "Look," he had said, after he whacked the heel on for her, "you're not crying about your shoe, are you? What's wrong?" She lifted her face, with its drowned, imploring eyes. Oh Lord, he had thought—aware, even then, of something obscurely dangerous in her, or in himself—Oh Lord, what am I letting myself in for? "He was so good to me, at first," she said, in a remote, strangled voice ...

"We'll go in the side door." Dwight's eager, bustling air as he led the way up the steps made Alex feel conscience-stricken. How little company he must have, to be so pleased over these two guests—Brad, who took such malicious delight in ridiculing him, and Alex, who was merely using him to suit his own convenience. "The front of the house is all shut off. The upstairs, too. The only rooms I use are the study and kitchen and a couple of the downstairs bedrooms." He switched on the lights in the study, that somber, dark-paneled room where his father had presumably written all his clever lines. Massive furniture; rich dark red drapes; marble mantelpiece; two walls book-lined, and the third covered with photographs of the stage celebrities of two decades ago.

Brad, after a moment of swaying in the doorway, made a beeline for the couch, where, after removing his shoes and testing the springs, he stretched out. "Accommodations seem to be satisfactory," he announced briskly. "That will be all for now, boy. Ask the desk clerk to ring me at nine, if you please."

"But there's no necessity for you to sleep here!" protested Dwight. "You'll be much more comfortable in the bedroom."

"He couldn't be any more comfortable. He's asleep already," Alex pointed out.

It was true. Sleep had come to Brad as to a child, with touching suddenness. All the sharpness was smoothed out of his face; he looked innocent and candid. Dwight went over and turned out the light beside the couch. He and Alex exchanged an indulgent, rather parental smile.

"Now make yourself at home, Alex," urged Dwight. "If you want to turn in right now, all you have to do is say so. Or, if you'd like to join me in a nightcap—" He paused, his eyes fixed anxiously on Alex's face. Hoping; and yet, from long experience, prepared for disappointment, resigned to yet another brush-off.

Oh well, what the hell. "A nightcap sounds good to me," said Alex, and Dwight hurried happily off to the kitchen for glasses and ice.

There was a telephone on the big desk, and Alex eyed it speculatively. But Gen would hardly have had time to reach the apartment yet—if she went there at all. It wouldn't be a cheery place to come home to. All the windows shut, the refrigerator empty and turned off for vacation, the slip covers at the cleaner's. She might go to her sister's place instead, or even a hotel. In which case, how would he ever find her? He swallowed nervously, and at once a couple of other horrid possibilities sprang to his mind. Even at her calmest, Gen was an erratic driver. Car trouble, an accident ...

He made himself pick up a magazine from the table beside him. He made himself thumb through it. It was one of the glossier periodicals, not, one would think, Dwight's dish. But then Alex remembered what was so overwhelmingly easy to forget—Dwight's poems. Of course. Here it was, in the middle of the book, a flip little number called "Vacation Vacuum." This sprightly streak in Dwight, this knack for light popular verse, never failed to give Alex a jolt. You would as soon expect a maiden aunt to break out in a bump-and-grind routine.

"I see you're in print again," he remarked as Dwight came in with his loaded tray.

"Oh, that." It was impossible to tell whether Dwight was pleased or annoyed. He habitually took—or pretended to take—a disparaging attitude toward his poems, treating them as a frivolous sideline. And yet they constituted his sole claim to distinction. The slick magazines snapped them up; an eminent publisher had brought out two slim volumes of them; critics called them "delightful," "deliciously amusing," "fresh as paint."

"More of that nonsense," said Dwight. "I thought maybe you meant this one." And, steadying the tray against the table, he pulled out one of the gray, obscure quarterlies that he was so devoted to. Sure enough, it opened of itself to what Alex recognized at once as another chunk of Dwight's scholarly prose on the subject of his boy Lindsay.

"I've had a letter on it already," he told Alex proudly. "From an elderly lady out in Keokuk, Iowa, a distant cousin of one of Lindsay's teachers. She remembers Vachel as a boy, and writes that she has some of her cousin's records, lesson plans and the like. Of course you never know what's going to come of these things. It may be of no significance, and then on the other hand ... But here, let me fix you a drink. I'm boring you."

"Not at all," said Alex feebly. You sucker, he told himself. He had been on these Lindsay excursions many times before; nobody who knew Dwight escaped them. What a pity, that not a drop of the sprightly streak ever seeped out of its airtight compartment into Dwight's conversation. Witchcraft, Gen had said once, or spiritualism; Dwight's poems probably got themselves written automatically, like the messages on slates.

Gen. Alex's eyes strayed back to the telephone. In case of an accident he would of course be notified. Maybe not right away; but eventually.

He took a sip of his brandy (it was excellent; Dwight's father had been quite a connoisseur) and shifted a little in his chair, so as to get the breeze that was swelling the curtains. The smell of the ocean, and occasionally its sound, the endless slap of waves, crept in. The sound that Marcella must have listened to this afternoon—there had been sand in her shoes, Alex remembered; sand and a few crushed shells on the living room floor. With unearthly clarity he saw her on the beach under the bright afternoon sky, leaning back on her elbows, watching the waves rush in, smiling that dreamy, mindless smile of hers. She was like a child in her capacity for watching, indefinitely, anything that moved. The bus rides she used to take; rides with no destination, merely for the sake of the wind blowing against her face, and the city streets, the buildings and people and cars sliding past beyond the window. So she must have spent this final afternoon, and whether or not she had foreknowledge of its dark destination would have made no difference, she would still have let herself drift, half-hypnotized by the infinite ocean swing.

Foreknowledge ... Alex's mind seemed to give a little jerk at the impact of this fresh idea. Had Marcella known? Was that why she had been trying to seek him out—to appeal, in desperation, to him because he, like the others, had once been good to her?

"Can I refresh yours?" Dwight had apparently abandoned the elderly lady out in Keokuk, Iowa, for the moment, and was bending over him with the brandy bottle in his hand. "No?" He filled his own glass, took an absentminded sip, and with a sigh of contentment resumed his monologue. "As I say, it's these trivialities that breathe life into a man. We're too prone, we biographers, to see our subject in terms of genius, literary trends and achievement, rather than as a human being. We lose sight of the fact that ..."

The telephone gave a shrill, demented peal. Alex felt his heart lurch.

"Yes, he's here," said Dwight, and Alex took the phone from him and produced a smothered-sounding "Hello."

But it wasn't Gen, or any word of her. He recognized Vonda's voice, in spite of the fact that she seemed to be whispering. "A prowler. No, dearest—" This disconcerted Alex, until he realized that it was directed not at him, but at Mr. Theobald. "Not an animal. Positively not. Human. A human beast prowling around outside, sniffing, and that poor girl he murdered ..."

Inevitable, thought Alex. Vonda would be hearing human beasts prowling around for weeks to come. Then he remembered Jimmy, presumably still at large. It made him feel less like pooh-poohing.

"Stay right where you are," he said. "Just sit tight. We'll either get the police, or investigate ourselves. It's probably just a— Well, anyway, sit tight."

SIX

"A prowler?" There was a pause, while, with his customary maddening deliberation, Dwight examined the problem.

On the couch Brad still slept, undisturbed by the telephone or possible perils. The only sound in the room was the deep rhythm of his breathing.

"It's probably just Vonda's imagination." Alex couldn't quite keep the impatience out of his voice. It was true that impetuosity would get them no place. On the other hand, he felt, there was such a thing as carrying the deliberative process too far. "We can call Ed Fuller. Or we can bust out on our own and take a look. I don't suppose you've got a gun, have you?"

"A gun?" Dwight pinched his upper lip thoughtfully between thumb and forefinger. "Why yes, I have a gun. Look here, Alex, in my opinion it's not necessary to call Ed Fuller. In my opinion our best course is to arm ourselves with the gun, turn on the floodlight—the switch operates from the side porch and it illuminates virtually the entire grounds—and—"

"Okay. Let's go."

By the time Dwight got all his opinions formulated and his decisions made, Alex was convinced, the prowler would be long gone. Assuming that there was a prowler. So he was doubly surprised when the floodlight—he flipped the switch, according to Dwight's plan of synchronization, while Dwight stood by with the gun—revealed an unmistakably human figure scuttling around the corner of the cottage.

"Halt!" Dwight cried out in his thin, pompous voice. His next words betrayed the intense excitement which he had kept so well hidden until now. "Shoot or I'll halt!"

For a minute nothing happened. Then their quarry responded with a cackle of laughter. "Go ahead and shoot, Mr. Abbott. Or halt, if you've a mind to. Either way I bet you don't hit me."

"I'll be damned," said Alex. "It's Mrs. Pankey."

Horace's mother—Alex's identification had been accurate—emerged from behind the cottage and proceeded up the driveway toward them. She was a large, lumbering woman in sensible oxfords, a cotton housedress, and a sweater buttoned uncompromisingly over her prominent front. "Turn off them lights," she called. "Enough to blind a person."

Dwight obeyed. "I beg your pardon, Mrs. Pankey," he said when she had toiled up the steps to the veranda. He shifted the gun uneasily from one hand to the other and finally put it in his pocket. "We were under the impression ..."

"What the hell are you up to, Mrs. Pankey?" asked Alex good-humoredly as they shook hands. "A young thing like you, sashaying around the country this hour of the night. It's not safe."

Mrs. Pankey bridled and flashed her dentures at him. But there was a worried look in her eye. "I'm looking for Horace, that's what I'm doing. That boy's going to be the death of me yet." (Horace was forty if he was a day.) "Waiting supper for him till all hours, and the police calling up, wanting to know where he is, and that girl getting herself murdered. Just you wait till I get my hands on him."

"It's my guess he's gone clamming. He usually does when he—"

Mrs. Pankey broke in firmly. "He'd have come home first." Never in her life had she admitted that her son drank. He was feeling poorly. Or his nerves were bothering him again. Or he had eaten something that didn't agree with him. "He'd have come home first to get his clam rake. He took it out of the truck last night and left it home."

"Where is his truck, by the way? Ed Fuller ought to be able to track that down."

"Vic Anderson's got it. Asked for the loan of it—his broke down and he had to go to Mineola. So he dropped Horace off at your place, with his tools and the cement for your porch, and Horace was figuring to walk home or get a lift with somebody, one or the other. Only he never showed up."

"Now don't worry. Like as not he borrowed my clam rake. It's right there under the back porch, and he knows he's welcome to it."

"That's so." Mrs. Pankey brightened a little. "Sometimes, when his nerves are bothering him, he comes over here and lays down on that bench back of the cottage. So I just thought I'd take a look. I'll be getting along home now. I didn't aim to upset anybody."

"Wait," said Dwight. "Let me give you a ride home, Mrs. Pankey."

"Why, it's no walk at all." Mrs. Pankey's work-roughened hands fidgeted with the buttons of her sweater. "I don't like the idea of Horace being out. I know Ed claims he's got the fellow that killed that girl up at your place, Alex, but I just don't like the idea of Horace being out."

Horace would turn up, both Dwight and Alex assured her. But she still looked worried, as she lumbered down the steps and into the car with Dwight. Like a mother hen, thought Alex, with one chick instead of the dozen she should have had. And that one none too bright. Oh, Horace was a whiz at fixing things, all right. He seemed to know by instinct what to do about electricity or plumbing, just as he knew how to build in shelves or staircases or closets, how to paint woodwork, paper walls, and finish floors. But these talents, in Horace, seemed freakish, like the uncanny ability of an idiot child to work arithmetic problems in his head. He was not a fool, and yet he had the air of one—or of an addleheaded, amiable, hulking child. It was hard to get him started on a job, and there was never any guarantee against his getting tired and quitting in the middle. Grinning bashfully, ducking his head, he would listen to the scoldings and coaxings of his employers—then do exactly as he pleased. There was no harm in Horace, even when he was drunk; all he asked was time to go clamming, plenty of beer, and payment in cash. Checks didn't seem like real money to him.

No wonder his mother worried about him. She mustered up a half-hearted goodbye smile for Alex. Then he went back to the study, where Brad had apparently not stirred. The telephone was still there too, right there on the desk.

But there wasn't any answer.

He hung up after quite a while and just sat there at the big desk staring at the ivory letter opener which, like practically everything else in the room, had belonged to Dwight's father. There was hardly an imprint of Dwight's own personality, except for the papers and magazines. Oh yes, and the photograph of Dwight's wife Clarice. It was a pathetic touch, thought Alex, that memento of what must have been a fumbling, painfully self-conscious little romance. Pathetic, for one reason, because Clarice was dead, killed in the crash of the plane that had been bringing her across the Atlantic to join her brand-new husband. She was an English girl; they had met and married in London, during the war. Pathetic also because of Clarice's face—that long bony peninsula of a face with its undershot jaw, weak eyes, and distressingly coy hairdo. Had she been beautiful, to Dwight? Had he, to Clarice, been the dashing hero of her girlish dreams?

It wasn't easy to imagine Dwight in love.

She had inscribed the photograph, in a surprisingly bold, distinctive hand: "From your devoted, your one and only wife Clarice."

The bell in Alex's head tolled again. Gen. Your one and only wife. Gen.

He got up abruptly and went down to the cottage to set Vonda's mind at rest about the human beast. By the time that was accomplished Dwight was back.

"I'm bushed," said Alex, determined not to be trapped again. "Where do I sleep?"

Dwight was all hostly contrition. "I should have told you before. Right in here, and the bathroom's here." He fussed around interminably, producing pajamas, slippers, towels, an extra blanket. At last he said goodnight, and Alex was alone.

He stretched out on the window seat where he could see the mysterious moonlit world and feel the fresh breeze. Now that the long strain of the evening was over, he felt at loose ends. His brain seemed to shift like a kaleidoscope, producing one disjointed pattern after another. Marcella and Gen, Marcella and Walt, Marcella and Jimmy, Marcella and himself. Death and Marcella.

That must be the focus. Violent death—murder—and Marcella. He looked at the idea squarely; it did not shock him. It had not shocked him, even in the first moment of recognition. *It's Marcella, of course.* Had he expected this, all along?

Not consciously. Certainly he had never said to himself, in so many words, someday someone will murder Marcella. But he must have felt it, in the subterranean, labyrinth part of him where the daylight of words never penetrated. There was no other way to account for that curious absence of shock. Or for his feeling of having made a hairbreadth escape on the day last summer when he put an end to the affair with her.

If you could call it an affair. It had lasted only a week. But you had to call it an affair, because he had gone to bed with her. Right away quick. The minute Gen's back was turned. The minute Walt cleared out.

Which he did, the day after the episode in the park, when Alex had progressed from repairing Marcella's shoe to hiring her for the typing job. (Out of pity. Alex honestly hadn't noticed, at first, that she was a rather pretty girl. Very slim, long-necked and limber looking, like the sketches of girls in the Sunday advertisements. Nice, delicate coloring. He just felt sorry for her. Any reasonably decent human being would have been touched by her drab little tale about the husband who had deserted her, and the baby who died, and now Walt, who had been so good to her at first but he was changing, Marcella could see it, and she didn't know what to do.)

The job—or more likely Alex himself as a potential successor—must have seemed to Walt like a heaven-sent opportunity for escape. After his own week with Marcella Alex could see that; he could even sympathize with Walt, in a secret, shamefaced way. But not at first. At first he had thought of Walt as a brute, a coarse, meaty-faced animal with no sensibilities or heart. They had met only once, that one sticky evening in the Leroy Street apartment, when Alex toiled up the stairs, through the layers of stale cooking smells, with his typewriter and the first batch of work for Marcella. Third floor rear. Just the sort of slightly seedy apartment Walt would pick for his clandestine love nest. The place had a transient, hotel room atmosphere, which Marcella's little attempts at home-making—the artificial bouquet, the skimpy drapes, the dime store knick-knacks—did nothing to dispel.

The next evening Alex went back. Or rather, he was drawn back almost against his will, certainly against his better judgment. But Marcella had not turned up at the shop with the finished work, as she had promised, and he couldn't find her number in the phone book because it was unlisted, and he got to thinking about Walt and that cat ...

Even now, Alex found, his mind stalled when it came to the cat. Simply shied away and refused to go on.

Anyway, he went back, and found Marcella collapsed and drenched in tears. Walt had decamped, leaving a note which Alex remembered word for word: "Sorry but I can't stand it any longer. I'm getting out. There's money in the desk, right-hand drawer."

He took her out to dinner—anybody would have tried to cheer her up—and when he brought her home, he kissed her lightly because she looked as if she might be going to cry again. That is, he meant it to be a light kiss; he couldn't possibly have foreseen how she would cling.

"Don't leave me," she whispered frantically. "Please, please. Don't leave me."

A year ago. Alex sat up on the window seat and hugged his knees, looking back contemptuously at himself, a year ago, with Marcella in his arms. The Woman's Home Companion, he thought; that's me. A great little ever-present aid and comfort. Not one whit less of an animal than Walt.

For, in spite of Marcella's air of delicacy, it had been a strictly animal affair. Not that Marcella was by nature voluptuous, or even especially passionate. But somewhere along the line she had picked up a good many little lovemaking tricks which made her seem so, that first night. He suspected, later, that she trotted them out automatically and dutifully, in the forlorn hope that they would buy security for her.

It took him only a week to catch on to what Marcella was doing to him. And what was that, exactly? She ... Well, all right, the phrase was ridiculous, but it was the only one that seemed to fit. She brought out the beast in him. She couldn't help it; there was just something about Marcella that aroused in other people the bully, the streak of cruelty that is always there, no matter how deeply buried. She insisted on being victimized.

So that what had begun as a kindhearted gesture on Alex's part flowered into a nightmare of guilt and the constant, almost irresistible desire to hurt her. Even while it was happening, it seemed incredible to him. Often as he watched her (the way she used to sit, with her feet drawn back under her chair in a self-effacing way; all concave lines, even a little dish-faced) there would flash into his mind's eye a picture of Gen with her verve, her high-headed, fiery pride. I don't belong here, he would think; what am I doing here, anyhow?

A week for him; a year for Walt. So he got a gold star for speed. Otherwise there was no difference between them.

Marcella knew, when he said goodnight to her that last time, after the cat ... (Again Alex's mind balked.) Just as she had known that Walt was going to leave her. Her eyes held an expression of frightened, hopeless awareness. She knew already. Without his telling her—which he hadn't the courage to do, face to face. Without the letter—which he wrote as soon as he got home. He made it sound quite smooth and plausible. "Called away. Business. Enclosed find check."

The muffled clang of the mail box shutting. The heady feeling of escape. Not merely from a cheap, shameful entanglement that he had drifted into unintentionally—though that was all he permitted himself to think at the time. He knew better now. The real escape was from something far more deadly than a trivial extramarital fling.

The real escape was from murder. Murder committed by himself.

Alex sat quite still on the window seat. His hands were suddenly clammy with sweat. Me a murderer? But I'm a good guy, he thought, everybody says I'm a good guy, a sucker, a pushover for any hard-luck story. I don't even like to swat flies.

Nevertheless. Nevertheless. If for some fantastic reason he had *had* to keep on with Marcella ...

The little cruelties would no longer have sufficed. (He remembered them all; they had given him an agonizing pleasure. The times he had kept her waiting, the dates broken at the last minute, the withering words: "Why don't you go out and buy yourself a decent dress for a change?" "Do you *have* to hang on to my arm like that? Isn't it hot enough, without you twining yourself around me like a damn trailing arbutus?") But it was like dope; he would have had to keep increasing the dose. And Marcella would have gone on, abjectly accepting whatever was done to her, turning on him that mutely imploring gaze, seeping all through him until he couldn't have stood himself another minute.

He was shivering from nerves and the chilly night wind. He had escaped. But someone else had not; because Marcella had been murdered. Victim, murderer. Not to be confused with one another. Remember that. He stared out the window. Remember that the victim and the murderer are two separate and distinct—

Was that the figure of a man, sliding along in the shadow of the wall, beyond the stretch of lawn? He couldn't be sure. Moonlight was tricky, and his eyes were too tired to be dependable. There it was again. The barest flicker of motion.

He felt more irritated than alarmed. Whatever it was, it ought to be investigated, he supposed. He shuffled over to the door, stepped quietly out into the hall, and bumped smack into Brad, who was holding one of his shoes in each hand, as if he were prepared to clap them together, like cymbals. "Traffic seems to be moderately heavy," he said. "What's on your mind?"

"I thought I saw somebody out there by the wall. I might have imagined it ..."

"I might have, too. In which case we're soul mates. So what do we do now?"

"It could be the police, of course, looking for Jimmy. On the other hand, it could also be Jimmy. Or Horace." (I sound just like Dwight, thought Alex. Standing here deliberating.) "Dwight's got a gun, if we want to get him in on the act."

"God forbid. Whoever it is, they're not going to hang around while Dwight makes up his mind whether to take the first step with his right foot or his left one."

"Okay. How about turning on the floodlight?"

But if they did that, they would have everybody—not only Dwight, but

Vonda and Mr. Theobald as well—in on the act. Their best bet, they decided, was to duck out to the wall and give it a fast going-over.

The grass was chilly with dew. Alex's scuffs kept slipping off; he finally gave up and carried them in his hand. Moonlight spilled across the tranquil lawn. A windless, beautiful night. They scurried from one patch of shadow to another, until they reached the wall which encircled the grounds. There was no one to be seen. No sound anywhere. Which wasn't surprising. The prowler—if he had been there at all—had had plenty of time to get away. Feeling foolish but somehow committed to their fruitless project, they made the rounds.

"Well, anyway," Brad said, "it's a nice night for it."

He looked cheerful and a lot fresher than he had any right to, when you considered all those drinks and the fact that he had been sleeping in his clothes. When they got back to the steps, he sat down on the top one, lit a cigarette, and looked up at Alex with a wry smile.

"Courage, brother," he said. "She'll be back, in case that's what's preying on your mind. Gen's like all the other ladies. They go, but they return."

Alex didn't often lose his temper. He did so now, thoroughly. "Gen's not in the least like anybody else, and you can damn well keep your—" He stopped, amazed and humiliated by what he had been about to say. Not, "You can damn well keep your nose out of our business and your views on women to yourself." But—of all irrelevant, primitive things— "You can damn well keep your hands off her."

This, then, was at the root of all his resentment of Brad—which, in spite of their long, close friendship, he had always known was there. Only he had rationalized it away so convincingly. There was a certain native slickness about Brad (he had told himself) that bothered him. Brad was glib, he was superficial; success came to him with what seemed to Alex irritating ease. True, all true. And all beside the point. Brad could be as rich and slick as he chose, and Alex would never really turn a hair. But those half-playful passes at Gen, those casual caresses that didn't mean a thing—Alex resented them right down to the marrow of his primeval bones. The revelation shook him; it was like looking in the mirror and seeing an ape.

Thank God he hadn't given himself away entirely. He hadn't finished the sentence out loud. What unholy delight it would have produced in Brad! Even richer fun than he got out of heckling Dwight. Maybe that was the way Brad saw him—as another Dwight, to be goaded into making a fool of himself. The possibility (of course it was possible; why should he be immune, any more than Dwight?) crept over him like a blight.

But when he looked down into Brad's mobile face, he saw neither malice nor amusement there, but a queer, sorrowful hunger, as if there were something Brad wanted and knew that he was never going to get.

"Look, Alex, you pointy-headed genius—"

But this sentence, like that famous one of Alex's, never got finished. The door behind them opened, and there stood Dwight, blinking at them like some absurd, puzzled bird in his skimpy cotton robe. In one hand he held a flashlight, in the other his gun.

"Oh," he said. "It's you." Finally, with an embarrassed air, he slipped the gun into the pocket of his robe.

"We don't deny it. It's us. We, I mean. Don't I? It's we." Brad stood up. The mischievous gleam was back in his eye.

Alex came to the rescue with a quick explanation of why they were here. It seemed to him that he could see the ponderous machinery of Dwight's mind getting into gear, deliberately going to work on this new bit of intelligence. There would be the question-and-answer period, he thought resignedly, and after that the discussion period; Dwight had never been known to leave a subject unexhausted.

But for once Dwight surprised him. For a minute he said nothing at all; when he did speak it was not in his usual well-rounded measures. "Strange," he murmured. "It seems so strange. Life. Death. Do you ever have the feeling—" He made a clumsy gesture toward the moon-drenched lawn.

"What feeling?" Alex prompted.

"I don't know. Unreal. That it's all—unreal. You know what I mean?"

It struck Alex as not exactly a sensational disclosure, after all that build-up. Brad's eyes flickered toward his: half a smile, half a wink, and Alex felt himself drawn back into the old charmed circle of companionship. How could he stay angry at Brad? And how could he have believed, even for a moment, that he was only another Dwight to Brad?

"Sure," said Brad. "Who doesn't?" There was a gentle, not unkindly amusement in his voice. He flipped away his cigarette and put his hand, briefly, on Dwight's arm. "Come on, let's go back to bed."

SEVEN

Lillian, stealing another glance at herself in the mirror back of Rudy's bar, tilted her head and tried out an Ava Gardner pout. Not bad. Should she use it, or the slow, subtle smile, by way of greeting when Jimmy came back? The pout would show that she wasn't accustomed to this vanishing act treatment. But the smile was more sophisticated.

He'd be back. She was sure of it. Jimmy wasn't like the run-of-the-mill summer characters.

Oh, Lillian knew them, all right. She ought to; she'd been around enough by now to know just what to expect from summer characters. She'd learned plenty since four years ago, when she was fifteen and got her first job waiting tables at The Seashell in town. What a dope she'd been, running her legs off for the summer theater crowd (they weren't even good tippers), hanging on their every word, living for the moment when one of them, noticing her at last, would say, "You're lovely, my deah. Have you ever done any acting?" What a dope! A couple of them had noticed her, all right; but the kind of acting they had in mind wasn't anything you did on the stage. And for free, too. You were lucky if you got a couple of beers out of the deal.

There wasn't any percentage, either, in the college types that spent their vacations out here at their family places. They might give you a whirl, for practice, but just let one of those college type *girls* show up, and you'd find out quick enough how you rated. You might be twice as good-looking; you still didn't have a prayer. Lillian knew. It had happened to her.

But this Jimmy, the one who had bought her the Tom Collinses before he vanished without a trace—Jimmy was different. She had known he was different, the minute she laid eyes on him. Just the way he strolled in, took his time about looking the place over, and then slid on to the bar stool next to hers. All over again, Lillian felt the anticipatory shiver of that moment when Jimmy's bold blue eyes had travelled over her and he had said, "Hiya, Babe. What you drinking?"

She let him have the sultry, sideways glance and the lifted eyebrow. "Well, well. Look what comes in when they leave the doors open."

She knew right then, and so did he; she could tell from the way he laughed. They understood each other. This was it.

He would come back, she insisted to herself. No matter where he had gone, he would come back. She had felt serene about it, at first; had expected every footstep beside her, every slap of the screen door at Rudy's, to bring him back. Now, way past midnight, the serenity was beginning to wear thin. Not that she doubted. Just that the waiting got her down.

She wasn't the only one who was waiting for Jimmy. She knew that, all right. She knew why Ed Fuller kept hanging around, always on the side of the bar that faced the door. Ed Fuller and his questions. Well, he hadn't gotten anything out of her, thought Lillian with satisfaction. (For the moment she was half-persuaded that, if she had wanted to, she could have told Ed Fuller plenty.) She had done her part, and Jimmy was going to make Ed Fuller look even sillier when the time came. Jimmy of course would have all the answers. It would be like in the movies, when the hero's name is mud in capital letters to everybody except this one gorgeous girl, whose faith in him is never for an instant shaken ...

So what if Jimmy was married to the girl who had been murdered out at Blair's house? Lillian doubted it; that fellow named Walt was just trying to get Jimmy into trouble out of spite. (Calling her a kid, insinuating that Jimmy had been feeding her a line!) But even if that part of his story was true, so what? Jimmy wouldn't be the first guy to marry the wrong girl. Like as not he was out right now, solving the whole thing, while dopey old Ed Fuller hung around, waiting to ask another load of questions.

Lillian stopped dead, in the middle of lighting another cigarette. It came over her that quick, like a flash of lightning. How dumb could you get? She was just as much of a meathead as Ed Fuller! Sitting here waiting for Jimmy, here of all places, with not a brain cell working! Naturally Jimmy was bright enough to figure out what Ed Fuller's move would be. Naturally he wasn't going to walk into any such a trap as this. Why, Rudy's was the last place in the world to wait for him.

Where, then? Automatically her glance returned to her own reflection in the mirror; automatically she adjusted one of her coquettishly disheveled curls. Well, why not tomorrow at The Seashell in town? She had told him she worked there, had just happened to mention that her hours tomorrow would be noon till after dinner. So why wasn't that the logical place? Her mind seized upon the idea gratefully. All she had to do was go home and wait for tomorrow and the moment when Jimmy would stroll into The Seashell, back into her life. She saw him as he had looked this afternoon at Rudy's—wearing his plaid sports jacket with careless grace, his dark hair combed slightly upwards on the sides and breaking into a deep wave on top, his boldly roving eyes narrowed against the smoke from his cigarette. Saw herself too, as she would look tomorrow in her pale green uniform, pausing to give him the slow, sultry stare. "Well, well," she would say, "look what comes in when they leave the doors open."

Smiling enigmatically, she finished her beer. "Goodnight, kiddies," she told her neighbors at the bar. (All local talent; nobody worth bothering with, though Floyd of course would insist on walking her home.) Sure enough, he was on his feet before she had slid off her stool. A drip, if she ever saw one; Floyd would be working at Rudy's filling station for the rest of his natural life and never know the difference. Oh well, she'd give him a break, he wasn't hard to get rid of, and if she left by herself Ed

Fuller might get some screwy idea that she was going to meet Jimmy some place. Not that Ed seemed to be paying any attention to her, but it was smarter to play it safe.

She gave a little wriggle to straighten out her skirt, tossed her earrings, and let Floyd follow her out the door.

He got his usual death grip on her elbow, as if she were a bicycle that he was wheeling uphill, and cleared his throat in preparation for social conversation. "Funny about that young fella," he ventured. "The one Ed was asking you about, the one that was hitchhiking—"

"Jimmy," she said impatiently. "What's funny about him?"

"Funny they haven't found him. Wonder where he's at?"

"I haven't the foggiest. Couldn't care less, either. He's nothing to me."

"Well, me neither." Floyd laughed nervously. "Gee, Lil, I didn't mean he was anything to you. Why get sore at me?"

"Why not?" she snapped. "You're as bad as Ed Fuller, snooping around in other people's business. For crying out loud. Just because some joe buys me a drink I'm supposed to know the history of his life, and where he is, and why!"

"I didn't mean—"

"Well, if you didn't mean it, what did you say it for?"

She felt better, after that. And it shut Floyd up; he loped along in unhappy silence the rest of the way home. It was only a short way down the highway. For a while, after Lillian's father died, Mom had tried to make a living out of her garden and chickens. But the summers, no matter how backbreaking and busy, hadn't made up for the long, dead winters with nothing coming in. So finally Mom's brother offered her a job working nights as a short order cook at his diner, and she took it. She worried about leaving Lillian alone, but then worry was Mom's prevailing state of mind, and had been for so long that she would have been lost without her troubles. She and Lillian both did their best to keep the house looking nice; it was all they owned, and they were proud of it. It needed a coat of paint, but Lillian kept the lawn mowed, and Mom's rock garden with the wooden flamingoes circling it did a lot to spruce the place up. Mom had wanted the family of ducklings marching across the lawn, instead of the flamingoes, but Lillian talked her out of it. There was more class to flamingoes.

When they got to the screened-in side porch Lillian stopped and turned to face Floyd, as a signal that this was the end of the line for him. Sometimes she invited him in, but tonight she was in no mood for Floyd's fumbling conversation and his even more fumbling advances. The contrast with Jimmy's smooth self-assurance was too sharp.

Floyd put his arms around her awkwardly and planted an inexpert kiss on her jawbone. Even if she closed her eyes, she couldn't pretend it was Jimmy.

"Goodnight," she said firmly.

"Wait a minute, Lil." She could feel his heart thumping away. "How about tomorrow night? Rudy'll let me have the Ford, and we can go to the Pavilion, or anywhere you want. How about it, Lil?"

"Some other night, Floyd. I'm busy tomorrow." She crossed her fingers and prayed, silently and fervently, that it would come true.

Floyd swallowed a couple of times in disappointment. The poor dope. You'd think he'd get tired of asking. She paused on the porch step a minute or two, watching his gangling, dejected figure as he went down the sidewalk. He couldn't help his Adam's apple and his big ears, she supposed; when it came to that, he probably couldn't help being a creep. Some people were just born that way.

Others were born like Jimmy. The moonlight poured down, like silver dripping through the trees. It seemed to Lillian that it was pouring through her, too, drenching her in magic light. She took a deep, ecstatic breath. Thank God, she thought, others were born like Jimmy.

She stepped inside the porch, hooked the screen door behind her, and was fumbling in her purse for the door key when she heard a scuffling sound over in the corner, back of the wicker chair. It didn't frighten her; every once in a while the neighbor's dog nosed his way into the porch, if they hadn't been careful about shutting the screen door tight.

"Here, Spot," she began. But the next sound told her it wasn't Spot. She stood very still.

"Shhh," came the whisper again. "Keep quiet. Don't be scared. It's me, Jimmy."

"Jimmy?" Her heart leaped up. "What are you—"

"Shhh" He crawled part way out of the corner, still keeping his head below the part of the porch where the wooden siding ended and the screening began. His face was ghostly white in the moonlight. "For God's sake don't wake up everybody in the house!"

"There's nobody inside," she whispered back.

"You sure?" It made her uncomfortable, the way he stayed down there, crouched on all fours, peering up at her anxiously. "Listen, Lillian. Listen, Babe, you going to help me out? I'm in a jam."

Was she going to help him out? How could he ask? "Come on inside," she said shortly. "Get up off of the floor."

He sidled in behind her, flattened himself against the living room wall while she flicked on the lights and pulled the shades. For a minute more he stayed there, his eyes darting around the room, his head cocked, listening for any suspicious sounds. He looked nothing at all like the smoothie who had strolled into Rudy's this afternoon with the world on a string. His fawn-colored gabardine slacks and plaid jacket were torn and dirty; there was a scratch on his cheek; and the once triumphant crest of his hair straggled forlornly across his forehead. She could see little beads of sweat there, too, and he kept licking his lips nervously.

"Did they find the guy?" he asked.

"Sure they found him. They've got him in jail right now."

"In jail?" For the first time his voice rose above a whisper, to a kind of incredulous gasp.

"Well, of course. They found him right out in front of Rudy's, passed out in his car."

"Oh," said Jimmy. "Him. You mean Walt."

"Who else? He told them about you. So they're looking for you too."

"I know it. Christ, do I know it. I been dodging them all night. I been all over the place. Alleys. Woods. Some big estate with a wall around it." He licked his lips again. "Listen, is there a drink in the house? I need one."

"There's beer," she said. Out in the kitchen she paused with a cold beer can in each hand, staring down at the worn linoleum.

She felt so funny. So kind of let down and—not scared. Just funny.

When she came back into the living room Jimmy was inspecting himself in the mirror back of the sofa, hunting in the breast pocket of his jacket for his comb.

"Got a comb? Mine's gone, must have slipped out of my pocket." She dug hers out of her purse for him, and watched him stooping a little so that he could see while he carefully combed up the sides, carefully pinched in the wave on top. It was like a plume; with it in place he regained his air of jaunty confidence. And she lost her funny feeling. Things were all right again.

"That's more like it." He turned and flashed something like his old smile at her. "No wonder I scared the hell out of you. Jumping out at you, looking like a bum."

"I wasn't scared."

"Yeah. You sure had a funny look on your face." He advanced, teasingly, flipped one of her earrings before he took his can of beer. "Brother, this is for me. My tongue's hanging out a foot. I thought you never were going to come home."

"How did you know where I lived?" But even as she asked it, she remembered that she had told him. The house down the road. With the flamingoes. She had just happened to mention it, like her job at The Seashell, and the hours she would be working tomorrow. She had done her share of talking, all right. Jimmy was the one with things to explain. "So you're in a jam. What's it all about?"

"And what a jam." The shifty look came back in his eyes; he darted a glance over his shoulder at the door. "Look, what's the pitch on your folks? They liable to come busting in here?" He watched her intently while she explained about Mom's job and how she wouldn't be home till six thirty in the morning. "If you're lying to me—" he said gently, and it was like something cold trickling down her back. The next minute, though, his smile flashed on again. "I'm kidding. I know you wouldn't lie to me, Baby. I know you're going to help me out. I knew you were for me, the minute I saw you."

The words worked instant magic for her. It took quite an effort to remember the things Jimmy had to explain. "This Marcella," she faltered. "Walt said you were married to her."

"Sure he did. I knew he would. That's why I scrammed when I found out what had happened to her." While he talked he guided her smoothly over to the sofa and sat down beside her with his arm around her. His hand, brushing her shoulder, made a little tingling spot there. "I know the kind of a rat Walt is. He wouldn't pass up a chance like this to get me in it up to my neck. I bet he tried to sell them a nice mess of bilge about me. Didn't he?"

She told him, as nearly as she could remember, what Walt had said. "It didn't keep him out of jail, though. Ed Fuller thinks he did it and was just trying to put the blame on you. I told them about how your car broke down in New York and you were just hitching a ride out to Montauk, and so did Floyd. He works in the filling station, he's the one that told you and Walt how to get out to Blair's."

"Yeah. I remember him. He's the jerk that brought you home tonight, isn't he? Strictly for the birds."

"Oh, I don't know," Lillian drawled, spuriously loyal. "Floyd's not so bad, once you get to know him."

"So who's got time to waste getting to know him?" Again he flipped her earring; his eyes made another of their exciting journeys over all of her, from her rope-soled sandals to the curl on her forehead.

"We're getting off the subject," she said, but it didn't sound as smart and unflurried as she meant it to. "Why did you go out to Blair's? Walt said it was your idea."

"What did I tell you? The rat. For Christ's sake, why would I be looking for Marcella? I got fed to the teeth with her three years ago and haven't changed my mind since. Sure I was married to her. If you want to get technical, I guess I still am. That's no crime. They can't arrest a guy just because his wife gets herself murdered."

"But then why—"

"Look, Lillian, I'll give it to you on the level. I wanted to get out of town this weekend on account of a little deal that's neither here nor there. Nothing to do with this business, so help me. Just a matter of raising some cash, and I figured the job out in Montauk would do it. Well, like I told you, after my car broke down I happened to run into Walt and he offered me a ride part way out. He wasn't just a stranger that picked me up, I'll grant you that. I'd met him up at Marcella's quite some time ago. Seems she latched on to him after I pulled out."

Lillian stared at her beer can. "I thought you and her were all washed up."

"Oh well, you know how it is." He made a large, easy gesture. "She used to call me up once in a while, when she was broke. Not that I owed her anything. But hell, that's the way I am. What's a few bucks more or less? So I knew she and Walt were shacking up. No skin off my nose."

"He claims he hasn't had anything to do with her since last summer."

"That's his story. Can't prove it by me. All I know is that he wanted to go out to this Blair's house because she was supposed to be there."

"He claims she wasn't there."

"Can't prove that by me, either. All I did was sit in the car and wait for him. He went inside the house, I know that. There was a guy out there mixing cement, so the door was unlocked. Walt went inside and after a while he came out and said she wasn't there, and that's all I know about it." He paused, as if in thought. "He was hell-bent on getting drunk afterwards, come to think of it. If I'd had my way, we'd have gone on, but he insisted on stopping at Rudy's."

"I still don't see—" Lillian swallowed painfully "—why you had to scram. Why couldn't you tell the police what you've just told me?"

"Because I know a frame-up when I see one, that's why!" His hand against her shoulder was suddenly a tense fist. "You think they're going to take my word against Walt's? If you do, you're nuts. He's the one that looks like a solid citizen, with his job and his wife and kids and all the rest of it. Me, he can make me sound like a bum. Every damn thing has gone sour on me for the last six months. No regular job—they think all piano players are hopheads anyway—and what they'd do with this deal I told you about, all I need is a little cash to clear it up. But what they'd do with it. Brother, they'd crucify me!"

Yes, she saw it. Lillian herself was just near enough to the wrong side of the tracks to know that he was right. "I haven't got any money," she said finally. "I mean, I can't help you out that way—"

"Oh now look, Baby." He put his hand, tenderly, over her mouth. "I'm no prize package, but that's one thing I don't do, is take money from dames. All I want you to do is help me keep out of sight for a couple of days, till this blows over. That's all. It would be different if I knew anything that would help them. But I don't, so why should I stick my neck out? It wouldn't do anybody any good."

"You mean you want me to hide you?" She felt suddenly out of breath. "Here in the house? But supposing they found you?"

"Why should they?" He gave her a sharp look. "Unless you told them something—"

"Not me. They didn't get anything out of me."

"That's the stuff. I knew you were okay, the minute I saw you. Otherwise I wouldn't have come here. And you can count on me—even if they found me here, I wouldn't let them pin anything on you. So what have you got to lose?"

"There's Mom. She'd blow her top if she found out."

"Then don't let her find out. Look, honey, there must be some place. An attic, or a cellar, or some place."

"The summer kitchen." She sat up straight and gave an excited laugh. "We don't use it anymore, just to store stuff, and Mom won't go in there because she saw a spider once. She's got this thing about spiders."

"We're in business. Lead me to this summer kitchen. You smart little cookie. You doll."

He was jubilant. And so was she; a feeling of delicious danger and high adventure swept through her. But before she let it engulf her entirely she made one last gesture of caution, of thinking twice.

"Jimmy," she whispered. "Just so long as you're telling me the truth. You are, aren't you? You didn't—kill her?"

"Who, me? Why, Baby, you know me better than that." He turned so that he was looking straight into her eyes; his were clear, almost transparent blue, with lashes thick and black as fringe. Ah, that bold, sparkling glance of Jimmy's! "I can think of better things to do with a dame than strangle her," he said. His hand tightened on her shoulder, his mouth came closer, closer, and the silver, the moonlight, whatever it was, poured through Lillian, drenching her in magic.

EIGHT

What made it rougher than ever was the way the old lady started right in, the minute she opened the door and saw who was there. They had roused her out of bed, though she got to the door so quick that Ed Fuller doubted if she'd been asleep. But anyway, she had her hair in a braid down her back and her teeth out, and she was cinching up the cord of her green and pink bathrobe as she peered out at them. And she started right in.

"No, Horace ain't home yet, if that's what you've come for, and don't you think I'm not going to give that boy a piece of my mind, when he does show up! Staying out till all hours, with people getting themselves murdered. And another thing, Ed Fuller, I'd just like to know what you think you're doing, getting me up out of bed, this hour of the night ..." Something must have showed in his face, because her voice—rubbery-sounding, without her teeth—all at once petered out.

"Mrs. Pankey," he said. "Uh." And he couldn't think of a thing to do but shake hands with her. "I'm afraid we've got some bad news for you. That is, uh, there's been an accident ..." They stared at each other, locked in a paralysis of mute, agonized question and answer. She let her hand drop from his; her chin worked in and out.

"A bad accident," he mumbled.

She snatched at it in desperation. "He's hurt? Horace has got himself hurt bad?"

"Dead, Mrs. Pankey." His eyes shifted from her face to her poor old feet, bulging out of a pair of dilapidated felt slippers. "Whitey and the boys found him down at the bay, half ways in the water. Drowned. The way we figure it, he went down there clamming, slipped and fell—got a dizzy spell, maybe—anyway, fell face down in the water and drowned himself."

"Drownded?" said Mrs. Pankey shrilly. "Why, he's never done such a thing in his life! Been clamming for years, knows every inch of the bay, why, Horace wouldn't no more drowned himself than I'd fly!"

"Now, Mrs. Pankey." Motioning Whitey and the others to wait for him outside, he took hold of her arm and steered her into the living room. "Let's sit down a minute till you get yourself together." He planted her in one of the overstuffed chairs—she sat bolt upright, stiff as a poker—and eased himself down into the other. "Doc's going over him now, to find out what happened for sure. But that's the way it looks. Could've been a heart attack, Doc says." (That wasn't exactly a literal translation of Doc's comments, which had been to the effect that Horace like as not had enough beer inside him to drown him and two other guys.) "It wasn't very far from Alex Blair's place where they found him. Looks like he went down there to the bay after he finished work."

"I just can't—" There were two lace doilies, one on each arm of her chair, and Mrs. Pankey kept smoothing them down, smoothing and patting for all she was worth. "He didn't have his clam rake with him. I guess maybe he borrowed Mr. Blair's."

Ed cleared his throat. There hadn't been any clam rake anywhere around. Whitey and Ed had both given the place a good going-over. There had just been Horace, spread out face down, hulking in his faded, wet overalls. When they turned him over, his face, which had a couple of bruised places from the stones, had an expression of innocent astonishment, as if he couldn't believe what had happened to him any more than his mother was believing it now.

"I say," repeated Mrs. Pankey, "I guess maybe he borrowed Mr. Blair's."

"We didn't find it," Ed admitted. Not that it meant anything; get Horace drunk enough and he'd just as soon dig clams with his teeth. "Here's all we found near him. Guess it must have slipped out of his pocket when he fell."

He held it out to her—a cheap blue pocket comb. Like as not she'd want to keep it, the way women did keep every damn last belonging of somebody that was dead. But she was shaking her head slowly, with her eyes riveted on the comb, like somebody in a trance. "It ain't Horace's," she said. "He didn't own any such a comb as that. Never carried one with him, anyway. It ain't Horace's."

"No?" All at once the comb felt supernaturally heavy in Ed's hand; it seemed to grin up at him with all its blue teeth. He slipped it back in his pocket with what he hoped was an easy air. "Oh well. Then it probably belongs to one of the boys. I'll ask Whitey. If you're sure it wasn't Horace's."

"I'm sure." Mrs. Pankey suddenly stopped smoothing the doilies and twisted them instead, crumpled them up in her two fists. "I'm sure of something else, Ed. Sure as I'm sitting here. It wasn't an accident. They murdered Horace, whoever it was killed that woman up at Blair's. They killed Horace too, they murdered my boy ..."

"Now, Mrs. Pankey. Horace was a good boy, everybody liked him. Why would anybody want to kill him?" He got up and patted her shoulder, uncomfortably aware of a very good answer to his own question. Alex Blair's wife had spotted it hours ago, when they first found Marcella's body. Maybe Horace saw whoever it was, she had said. That was why they had been searching for Horace, to find out what he might have seen. But there wasn't any reason why the same possibility mightn't have occurred to the murderer. It might very well have been certainty, not possibility, with him. Horace wouldn't have had the sense to keep his mouth shut. Ed could see him, the big, lumpish, friendly child-man, staring bug-eyed and all unaware of his own peril, at the murderer. (He could have seen the whole thing, thought Ed with rising uneasiness, through that patio window. His truck hadn't been there; nothing to advertise his presence, especially to a man with murder on his mind.) "Why, Mr. So-and-So," Horace might have blurted out, "what were you doing to that girl? You hadn't ought to do that, Mister ..." And then what? A threat from the murderer, some gesture that would alert

Horace at last and throw him into a clumsy, befuddled gallop for safety. Horace was big, but he didn't know a thing in the world about how to fight.

Never hit anybody in his life. Never had to; nobody had ever raised a hand to him, everybody liked Horace ...

Now look here, Ed told himself, you're getting pretty far off the ground with your might-have's and could-be's. Stick to the facts. All you know for sure is that Horace—drunk or sober—got himself drowned, and if somebody hit him first Doc's going to find it out. Likewise with the blue comb. Meanwhile, keep your shirt on.

"You oughtn't to be here alone," he told Mrs. Pankey. "I'll get one of the neighbor ladies to come over and stay with you. You just take it easy now."

She didn't seem to have heard him. "Murdered," she said. She looked up at him fiercely; her mouth worked in and out, and she twisted the doilies in her hands as if she were wringing them out of the washtub.

"I could bawl," quavered Mrs. Pankey. "Oh, I could just *bawl*."

NINE

Alex heard about it from Ed Fuller himself.

He had wakened early, if you could call it waking after the fitful dozes of the night, to find the sun shining jubilantly (this affronted him; how dared the day be fine, with Gen gone?); Dwight and Brad still asleep (he had to admit this was a break); and still no answer when he tried to call the apartment in town. He had tiptoed out to the kitchen, made himself a cup of instant coffee, and then—still without disturbing either his host or his fellow guest—had let himself out the back door and set off in the direction of the beach.

It was not yet eight o'clock, and in spite of himself he found the gayety of the day irresistible. The whole world sparkled—every blade of grass, every grain of sand, every rollicking, dancing wave in the ocean. And he had it all to himself. Not even Vonda and Mr. Theobald were abroad yet to revel in the ozone. Or if they were, they had gone the other way. He walked along the beach, automatically heading for his own house. No purpose in mind; not much of anything in mind. To tell the truth, he was rather proud of the strict mental embargo he was maintaining. Gen was not permitted to emerge above the surface, nor Marcella, nor Walt, nor certain animals such as cats. It took all his energy to keep them underground; he wondered how long he could manage it.

Not very long, as it turned out. Because as soon as he emerged from the thickets and scrubby trees of the path he saw Ed Fuller's car in the driveway, and Ed himself mousing around the newly finished patio.

"Morning," Ed wheezed, and then he told Alex about Horace. "No reason why it couldn't have been an accident, according to Doc," he wound up. "Drunk, of course. He could have hit his head on a rock when he fell and knocked himself out there at the edge of the water. His face was bruised up. We found him along about two this morning, and Doc says he'd been dead for seven, eight hours. Doc says it could have been an accident."

"Accident my eye," said Alex. "If you believe that, you're dumber than you look. First of all, did you ever know Horace to leave his tools scattered around like this?" He pointed to the spade and trowel, still caked with cement, the half-empty bag tilted against the wheelbarrow. "Never. Even when he was boiled to the eyebrows, Horace cleaned up his tools and put everything away. The only time he ever gave me a cross word was when I forgot and left the saw out. It was a mania with him."

"Yeah," said Ed glumly. There were pouches under his shrewd little eyes; his whole fat face, even his majestic stomach, seemed to droop this morning. "Okay, Sherlock Holmes. You notice anything else that strikes you funny?"

Alex's eyes made a slow tour of the pile of empty beer cans. One had been left standing on the upended bucket. He picked it up, and it was more than half full.

"I know." Ed beat him to it. "It ain't like Horace to go off and leave any beer in the can, either." And as Alex bent to peer under the porch, he added, "Your clam rake's right there, if that's what you're looking for. He didn't take it, and he didn't have his own, though that may not mean a damn thing. There was plenty of clams caught, I expect, before anybody ever thought to invent a clam rake."

"It means something when you put it with the other things, though," said Alex. "The tools. And the beer in the can. It means he lit out of here in a hurry, unexpectedly. He was either chasing somebody, or—more likely—somebody was chasing him."

Ed nodded.

"Yeah. Horace hadn't any more fight in him than a month-old baby. He never did anybody any harm, and by God if they did kill him—" Ed's face turned a wrathful red; he cleared his throat, apparently embarrassed by his own show of feeling. "Well, I can't stand here gabbing all day. I got to get into New York and check up on Marcella and her husband. If she had one. The Lord knows where he is by this time. We checked every place in Montauk, and nobody had hired a piano player from New York named Jimmy or anything else."

"Gracious me," said Alex. "You mean your innocent little hitchhiker wasn't telling the truth?"

Ed gave him a dirty look. "I wouldn't bet on every single word your pal Walt says, either, if I was you. You want a lift some place? If you want to go into the city, I'll be leaving in half an hour or so. Got to stop at the office first."

Alex hesitated. What did he want to do with this disgracefully splendid day? It was worthless, without Gen. But to go tearing back to the city with Ed, before he had located her, seemed pretty risky. That left the prospect of a day with Dwight, or Brad, or both of them. Dwight alone was deadly; the two of them together were nerve-wracking at best; and Brad alone ... Last night's spurt of anger had died as quickly as it came. But somehow Alex didn't relish the idea of Brad today, either. Maybe he was just unfit for human consumption.

"I might take you up on that. Drop me off at the drugstore in town and let me make a couple of phone calls," he said. "I'll meet you at your office if I decide I want to go in with you. Is Walt allowed visitors? You don't need to worry, I won't slip him any files. But maybe there's something he'll want me to do for his wife or—"

"His wife." Ed chuckled as he backed his car out of the driveway. "Boy, that wife of Walt's. If you're aiming to get tangled up with her, you're in for something. She hove in last night, and I hope to tell you! Not a bad-looker, but that woman has got a tongue like a buzz-saw. Couldn't make up her mind who to light into the hardest—Walt for two-timing her, or me for arresting him. My good Lord, but she was sore!"

Alex got out at the drugstore. He waited, sweating a little, in the stuffy phone booth, while the telephone dutifully rang its head off in the apartment in town. "Sorry, sir," said the operator at last, "they do not answer."

No, they do not. They do not answer. Are they, perhaps, sitting on the couch with their fingers in their ears and their topaz eyes fixed on the phone, willing it to stop its noise? Or racing up the stairs outside, fumbling for the key, reaching for the phone one heart-breaking minute too late? Or maybe they are miles away from the apartment, already pushing the old car for all it's worth back here where they belong ...

Wherever they are, whatever they are doing, they do not answer.

After a brief mental conflict, he gave up and called Gen's sister, who lived a full, rich life out in Jersey with her husband and three little monsters of children—all of whom, he remembered while he waited for the call to go through, just loved to answer the telephone. If he got one of those piercing childish trebles this time, it would be the last straw.

But God was with him; the voice that answered belonged to Bertha, who came in to do the cleaning.

"Hello, there, Mr. Blair," she greeted him chattily. "They all picked up and took off early this morning for the beach."

"Oh," said Alex. "Is that so? I was just wondering if Gen—uh—"

"She went with them. Came out on the train late last night. Wasn't it nice she could make it? She told me you might call, Mr. Blair. Said if you did to tell you she left the car on 12th Street and she won't be wanting it."

"Oh," said Alex again. "Is that so? I see. Okay, Bertha, thanks ..."

Well, so that was that. Ride into town with Ed and drive the car back. It would be abandoning Brad, in a way, but he couldn't help it. Brad would simply have to shift for himself. He ought to call Dwight, he supposed; though of all the things that didn't appeal to him at the moment, the one that didn't appeal most was a long, detailed, rehashing session with Dwight.

"Why, Alex, I can just as well drive you in, if you want me to. Be more than glad to. I suppose Gen's coming back with you?"

"I doubt it," said Alex. (How understated could you get?) "Thanks a lot, Dwight, but Ed's going anyway ... Sure I'm sure ... Yes, I heard about Horace. You're right, a damn shame ... Look Dwight, Ed's waiting, thanks a lot, see you tonight ..."

Ed was tied up on the phone, he discovered when he walked across the street to the chunky brick building that constituted police headquarters and jail. "Go on back and call on your friend Walt," Ed told him, "and watch out for that wife of his."

Alex saw what he meant, all right, as soon as his eyes lit on Walt's wife. Which was practically immediately. She was standing outside the door of Walt's cell, a woman—it struck Alex at once—that you couldn't possibly miss. If you happened to be blind, you would still have heard her, and for the benefit of those who might be both blind and deaf there was her perfume, plenty of it, the kind the advertisements characterize with words like exotic and subtle. She wore a bright green suit, platform pumps, and a little pill box of a hat with a feather in front that stood right straight up, trembling with indignation. Her face was built a good deal like a Peke's, and it was tricked out with all the cosmetics known to womankind. Her hair, like her voice, was pure brass.

Walt, who looked as if he wasn't sure yet what had hit him, greeted Alex with a mixture of relief and surprise. "Shirley honey, this is Alex. The one I been telling you about. Mr. Blair. Meet the wife, Alex."

Shirley extended a set of fingernails dark as garnets and said she was glad to meet him. But her prominent, bright brown eyes were hostile.

"It was your house, wasn't it? I understand you knew her, too. Walt says that's how he met you, through her."

Alex admitted it. "I just thought I'd stop in and see if there's anything I could—"

"Well then, why aren't they holding you, too?" demanded Shirley.

"Now honey," said Walt feebly.

"Well, why aren't they? Why does everybody right away decide it's Walt instead of you? After all, it was your house. For my money, you're as mixed up in it as Walt, and don't think I haven't told them so. What does *your* wife think about it, by the way?"

"Gen?" stuttered Alex. "Why, she—uh—"

"For Pete's sake," pleaded Walt. He sat down on the bunk and put his head in his hands. "Lay off, for Pete's sake."

"Lay off, he tells me! That's rich. It's all very well for you to tell me to lay off. How do you think I feel about it?" Shirley paused dramatically, her eyes snapping, before she went on to explain, in minute detail, how she felt about it. It was like being shut up in a small living room with a brass band; there wasn't anything to do but wait for the end of the selection. It came at last. "Where'd you be without me, I'd like to know? I'm going out now and camp on that lawyer's trail till he gets you out of here. Or know the reason why. Get up here and—" Her voice broke in a sudden sob, which she high-handedly ignored "—and kiss me goodbye, you lug."

Walt sprang to obey, and after several loud smacks Shirley swept past Alex and the guard, who had taken up his post at a discreet distance, and marched off down the gray hall, the feather on her hat vibrating with purpose. All three men watched her respectfully.

"She's a great kid," murmured Walt as he wiped the lipstick off his chin. "Oh, she's got a temper. But when the chips are down, she's right in there pitching. What I mean is, how many guys got a wife they can count on, in a situation like this? A great kid. You don't want to take it personally, Alex, what she said to you. For Pete's sake, why should they hold you? You weren't even out here when it happened. You got witnesses."

"You'll have one too," Alex reminded him, "when they find Jimmy."

"That louse." Walt heaved a great sigh. "To think I got to depend on him. You ever meet him? No? You're lucky."

"Why did he want to go out to my place? You said it was his idea."

Walt's eyes shifted to the floor. "Hell, I don't know. He said it was to see Marcella, but maybe he figured you'd be there too and he could put the bite on you like he did with me. All I wanted to do was get rid of him. But there wasn't anybody there but the fellow mixing cement—"

Cautiously, he looked back at Alex. "You hear about what happened to him? He could have told them there was nobody there. He wasn't exactly sober, but he could have told them."

"He could have told them plenty," said Alex briefly. It was a curious thing that Horace's murder (if it was murder) should seem to him so much more of an outrage than Marcella's. True enough, Horace—as Ed Fuller had pointed out—never did anybody any harm, hadn't any more fight in him than a month-old baby. But the same could be said of Marcella. "Look, Walt. If Jimmy knew Marcella was going to be out here, that means he must have talked to her or seen her recently. And that means he was still mixed up with her. And that means—"

That he might have murdered her? The idea trembled wordlessly between them. Here was the point that made Horace's death somehow crueler than Marcella's. Horace had been the victim-by-chance, the freakish casualty, the hapless bystander hit by a stray bullet, so to speak. But whoever killed Marcella had known her, had been mixed up with her, so hopelessly that there had been no other way of escape. The difference between the incidental and the inevitable. Inevitable, thought Alex. It was the right word for Marcella's murder, and the odd bond between him and Walt was simply this: they both knew it was the right word.

"Mixed up with her," repeated Walt. He stared down at one of his big, meaty hands, working it open and shut as if to grasp with it the words he was groping for. "I'm not so sure Jimmy was mixed up with her that way. You know what I mean? Yeah. You knew Marcella, too. He saw her once in a while, when he thought he could get a buck or two out of her. He'd steal the pennies out of a blind man's cup. I know she used to give him money sometimes, when I was shacked up with her, but I figured what the hell, they'd had this baby that died, and you know how women are about stuff like that. He walked out on her three, four years ago."

Hail, brother, thought Alex. Me and Walt and Jimmy. A great little fraternity.

"So maybe I was wrong, maybe he was mixed up with her that way." Walt frowned with the effort of cerebration. "How did he do it? I mean, when? Because she wasn't there when we went out together. I was the one that opened the door and looked inside. Nobody there."

"Unless he went back later. Could he have done that without your noticing?"

Walt looked startled. "I guess he— Sure he could have. Why not? I didn't pay any attention to him after we went into Rudy's. I told you, all I wanted to do was get rid of the louse. He'd stuck me for twenty-five bucks on the way out here, damned if I was going to pay for his drinks.

My idea was to have a drink and maybe a bite to eat and shove off, and Jesus, if I'd only kept it down to one drink—" His china-blue eyes clouded wistfully. "Well, you know how it is. I ran into a guy back in the dining room, in the same line as me, electrical fixtures, a hell of a nice guy, and the next thing I knew I was pie-eyed. Sure, Jimmy could have been in and out of there a dozen times, for all of me. He could have taken my car, too, because I left the keys in it. Didn't figure on staying more than half an hour."

"He could have, then," said Alex. "If he was still mixed up with her. And if he wasn't, somebody else was. Somebody must have been keeping her for the past year or so. Otherwise she'd have starved to death."

"Yeah. She was a—a funny girl." Walt's hand opened and closed again, helplessly struggling for words. "That's the part that gets me, is how I ever got into the whole damn mess in the first place. If she'd been the type I go for ... I like 'em with some pep. Like Shirley. You too, I guess. You take somebody like your wife, I could go for that. But Marcella. And for damn near a year! How long was it with you?"

"A week," said Alex curtly. "Just about a week." All at once he couldn't bear Walt or anything about him. Him and his Shirley (bracketing Gen with that one-woman brass band!) and his meaty face and his insufferable way of assuming that he and Alex were soul mates.

But Walt, all unaware of Alex's resentment, was still grappling with his memories. "That cat of hers," he said. "Remember that goddam cat?"

Alex's mind, surprised into facing what it had balked at yesterday, automatically produced for him the picture, as sharp-edged and as shameful as if it were happening all over again. Two pictures, really. The first one was of Walt snatching Marcella's cat (a scrawny, calico animal that looked as if it had been made out of left-over scraps) as it slunk past his chair. Snatching it by the nape of its neck, and letting it dangle like a limp, dusty fur piece, and then stuffing it into that little wicker hassock affair, and holding the lid on, and laughing. Watching Marcella and laughing. That hateful, gloating laugh of Walt's—it still rang in Alex's ears, along with the piteously imploring voices of Marcella and the cat. Intolerable. Alex had wrenched the lid from the basket, had almost thrown the cat toward the kitchen door ...

So much for picture number one. The second was a replica. Scene: the same. Time: a week later. Just one slight change in the cast. This time it was Alex snatching up that abject animal, Alex with its dangling, swinging weight in his hand, Alex— But I didn't do it, he assured himself. Ah, but he had wanted to. His foot had touched the little wicker basket beside his chair, he had felt the ugly, exultant smile crawling over his mouth, and more than anything in the world he had wanted to shove the cat into that basket, and watch Marcella's face, and laugh.

What had saved him? Something trivial—the clock in the neighborhood tower, striking eleven. He had put the cat down. His hands were shaking. He had gone right home and written the farewell letter and mailed it. He had escaped.

So there it was. He could shudder his fastidious little heart out, but the galling fact remained: that goddam cat made him and Walt brothers.

He said his speech about if there was anything he could do, suffered through Walt's long-winded thanks, and beat it.

The trip into the city was silent for the most part. Like Alex, Ed seemed sunk in his own private thoughts. At one point, while they were waiting for a light, he fumbled in his pocket and pulled out a small blue comb. "Before I forget it," he said, "you got any idea who this belongs to? Does it look familiar to you?"

"Well, it's not exactly an exclusive model, but I don't recognize this particular one. I prefer black, myself."

"You wouldn't know if Horace had one like this? Or Walt, maybe?"

Alex shook his head. "For all I know, they neither one of them ever combed their hair. Why?"

"Just wondered." Ed put the comb back in his pocket and lapsed again into silence and his concentrated brand of driving.

The sun, which had sparkled so gaily on Long Island, pressed down, steamy and blurred, on Manhattan and its hurrying Labor Day crowds. Even Ed was slowed down to a crawl; he kept muttering bitterly. As for Alex, he had gotten himself involved (now that the cat episode was taken care of) in another diabolical mental hassle. If he, not Walt, had wound up in jail, would Gen have come through with Shirley's flying colors— a great kid, right in there pitching when the chips were down? He couldn't leave it alone. It was as absorbing, and as excruciating, as a toothache. It kept him busy all the way across town.

"Good luck," he remembered to tell Ed as he got out at 12th Street. "Thanks for the lift. See you later."

He found the car, just as Bertha had said; when he unlocked the door a blast of stored-up heat and smells—cantaloupe, celery, Swiss cheese— hit him in the face. Oh God, last night's groceries, still there in the back seat, along with the load of books he had planned to sort out if there were any rainy vacation days, and his bag. Gen's was gone. But it was the groceries that set off, like a sound track in his mind, Gen's voice, flickering with happiness: "Vacation. Three great big beautiful weeks ... Alex darling, we're going to have a fine time." And Gen's face, the way her mouth curled up at the corners, and the crick in her left eyebrow, and her sturdy, proud little neck. He could have put his head down on the steering wheel and howled like a deserted dog.

And still the spark of feeble-minded hope would not quite expire. He explained to himself that his reason for going back to the apartment was to take a shower and have a bottle of beer and a sandwich in peace; his real reason was to see whether she might not, after all, have stopped there last night and left him a note, some tiny sign.

There was nothing. He opened the windows to get rid of the stale overnight smell; he turned on the refrigerator and even started up the clock, just for company. Then he sat down on the couch, naked without its slip cover, and drank a beer and ate his delicatessen sandwich. There was nothing at all. She must have gone straight out to her sister's in Jersey.

It was nice and quiet up here. That was one thing about a rear apartment, you didn't get the street noise. He nodded wisely at the ailanthus tree, shimmering in the haze and soot outside the window. Nice and quiet. After a while, when he felt that something a little stronger than beer was indicated, he poured himself a shot of gin. To this he thoughtfully added the thin film of ice that had already formed in the trays. That was one thing about a refrigerator in a rear apartment, it made ice fast. And you didn't get the street noise.

She would have to come back here eventually. So the thing to do was to leave her a note. Feeling very shrewd and purposeful, he extracted from the desk drawer a pencil and an old envelope. He took a sip of gin and wrote: "Dear Gen, I am taking the car ..."

The gin diminished, inch by inch; the ailanthus tree continued its shimmering and the refrigerator its busy, conscientious purring; the note did not get itself written.

Once in a while he would read it over again, to see if it had gotten any better while he wasn't looking. Once in a while—between sips of gin; between his long, long, meandering thoughts about death and Marcella, about life and Gen.

"Dear Gen, I am taking the car." Not exactly an inspired outpouring of what was in his heart. He used to think of himself as quite an articulate fellow, but look at the way he had botched up his explanation to Gen last night. Walt himself couldn't have done a more thorough job of it. "You've got to let me explain ... Marcella and I ... It isn't what you think." His own inane phrases came back to set him cringing all over again.

Would it be any different if Gen were here now? Had he found, since last night, the right words? Good questions, one and all. And so what if he didn't know the answers? She wasn't here, she wasn't here.

He stood up, and at once made three discoveries. Number one, he was a little bit drunk. Number two, it was well past four o'clock. And number three, he was waiting for the phone to ring and Gen to say "Darling, I love you."

Which was a fantastic and brainless thing to be doing. He must put a stop to it at once.

The doorbell rang, and he lunged to push the buzzer. Brainless again. Why would Gen be ringing her own doorbell?

It was Ed, very damp and wilted-looking. "Find your car okay? I didn't know but what you might want to ride back with me, after all, and I was right in the neighborhood, so I rang your bell." He sank down in the big chair and mopped his forehead. "I'm beat. You're damn right I could use a beer." He took a deep, grateful draft of the bottle Alex brought him.

"How'd you make out?" asked Alex. "Got the case all sewed up?"

"Oh, sure. She strangled herself with her bare hands. Plain case of suicide." Ed tilted his bottle once more. His face brightened a little. "One thing, I got the dope on Jimmy. He was married to her, all right. Jimmy Ewing. Quite a boy. We're not the only ones that are looking for him. He's a real artist with the check book. Calls himself a piano player, but when things get tough, he makes with the checks. Piddling little stuff. Neighborhood groceries, stationery stores, a couple of his ex-landladies. He moved pretty often. Business reasons, you might say. The last landlady says he skipped out night before last, owing a month's rent. She trusted him because he had such thick eyelashes, just like her nephew that was killed in the war."

"Charming fellow," said Alex.

"Yep. It looks like Walt may have been telling the truth. Or at least part of the truth. Jimmy needed money, all right, and he needed to get out of town for a while, till things simmered down. No wonder he scrammed. He couldn't stand much investigation—whether or not he had anything to do with killing her."

"He can't hide out forever," Alex pointed out. "If he hitched another ride somebody's sure to report it, and he doesn't sound like the type to take to the woods and stick to it for very long."

"I don't know." Ed sighed. "A fellow could live on clams and blueberries for quite a while. I've got the boys beating the bushes for him, but there's a hell of a lot of bushes to beat. Of course it's quite a jump, from phony checks to murder, but just the same, Jimmy's going to have plenty to explain when we catch up with him."

"Had he been seeing Marcella lately? I should think the other tenants at Leroy Street could help you out on that."

"A couple of the women remembered Jimmy—he sure has a way with the ladies—but they couldn't make up their mind how recently they'd seen him. One of them thought two weeks ago, and the other one thought longer ago. They remembered Walt, too. According to them he hasn't been around in a year or so. But I checked his office, and his secretary had a message that Marcella called while he was out, day before yesterday. And somebody called on Marcella night before last. The woman across the hall heard some man arguing with her. Didn't see him. Just heard him. Till all hours."

"Did Marcella have a job?" asked Alex.

"No sign of it, if she did." Ed stared glumly at his beer bottle. "The woman across the hall got in a couple of digs on that subject. Said it looked to her like Marcella worked nights, but it wasn't for her to say what kind of work that might be. All she knew was that Marcella didn't go to business in the daytime, and more often than not she was out all night. Apparently she wasn't particularly friendly with any of her neighbors, except for a young fellow with a harelip that lives beneath her. Didn't get much of anything out of him."

No friends, thought Alex, no job. "Look here, Ed," he said, "somebody must have been keeping her for the past year. Who paid the rent?"

"She did," said Ed. "Cash. Right on the dot, according to the landlord. So it doesn't sound like Jimmy. Sounds like some married man, or anyway somebody anxious to keep well out of sight. I didn't find a single lead in her place. No letters, no address book, no nothing. It's a hell of a note, Alex. Most people got some kind of ties with somebody, but this girl ... She wasn't always such a question mark. Seems like everybody in the neighborhood knew about her and Walt. Several of 'em knew about Jimmy. There was even one that remembered you, and how you gave her a temporary job. But after that, nothing. It don't seem natural."

No, it didn't. Alex remembered how eagerly, at the first friendly word from him, Marcella had poured out the whole story of her life. It was as if the sense of her own rootlessness impelled her to confide in any stranger who would listen, however casually. She wasn't secretive. But Alex's successor—he was the one with a secret. He had not only kept it himself; he had somehow persuaded Marcella—by flattery? by threats?—to keep it too. For a whole year. Alex corrected himself. Forever. Marcella would never again sit on a park bench and pour out her own or anybody else's secrets.

"... going round in circles," Ed was saying. He cast a moody, belligerent eye on Alex. "You got me started on it. You and your 'somebody must have been keeping her.' I got enough on my hands, with Walt and Jimmy. There doesn't have to be anybody else. She could have just been playing the field. She was young and kind of pretty." He hoisted himself up out of his chair. "I've got to get back. What you going to do, stick around here?"

"No," said Alex shortly. Another wave of desolation broke over him. Stick around here—for what? He closed the windows. Turned off the refrigerator. Then—with Ed waiting for him at the door—his eye fell, once more, on the note he had started to Gen. "Dear Gen, I am taking the car." He picked up the pencil and added, "Viva la Geneviva." Broke the point of the pencil doing it.

It didn't matter. There was nothing else to say, anyway.

TEN

"Take it easy, Dreamboat, you got all the time in the world," said the bus driver (it was the young, fresh one tonight) as Lillian hurried on to the bus. He had seen her running down the block from The Seashell and had waited for her. "I wouldn't go off and leave you. Not me. Never. Don't you trust me, Dreamboat?"

Usually Lillian was right there with a snappy comeback, but tonight all she could produce was a dreamy smile. The seat right back of the driver, where she was in the habit of sitting, was taken, and for once Lillian was glad. She felt too—too precious, too out-of-this-world, for kidding with comedian-type bus drivers.

It had been like that all day. She had glided through her hours at The Seashell, carrying in addition to her tray load of shrimp cocktails and broiled lobster and lemon chiffon pie the magically glowing jewel of her secret. It alone was real to her. All the rest—the old ladies who couldn't make up their minds, the drunks, the brats who spilled their milk—slid past her with no more substance than shadows on a wall. The memory of Jimmy surrounded her like a golden haze, and each time she closed her eyes his face was there, thrillingly close.

She kept her eyes closed most of the way home.

Mom hadn't suspected a thing. Which, to Lillian, was a little miracle in itself; how could the rest of the world be so blind? How was it possible for no one to notice that inwardly she was flashing like a neon sign? Never mind; it was possible. Mom had been all wrapped up in the news about Horace Pankey getting himself drowned and the murder up at Blair's house. Poor Mrs. Pankey, said Mom, she's had more than her share, all right. And to think that Lillian had been alone in the house, with a murderer running around loose—well, not loose, of course, they had the fellow in jail. Just the same, Lillian must come right straight home tonight, Mom wouldn't draw an easy breath otherwise, right straight home and lock all the doors, because there was that other fellow, the one that disappeared, it just *got* Mom, to think that Lillian had talked to him, picked up with a stranger like that ...

"Oh, Mom," Lillian had said, with an elaborate yawn, "after all! I've been around a little, I know what the score is. He didn't have anything to do with it, anyway, all he did was hitch a ride with the guy that did it. What? How should I know where he disappeared to? He probably got a ride the rest of the way to Montauk."

(She had dropped her spoon on purpose, so Mom wouldn't see her face. If Mom only knew, if Mom only knew!)

She hadn't dared risk a trip to the summer kitchen before she left for work at noon, not with Mom still up and yakking away. But Mom spent her afternoons sleeping, and she would be leaving not later than ten for her night's work at the diner, and then; and then ...

"Wake up, Dreamboat!" called the bus driver. "Here's where you live. Remember? Unless you want to give yourself a break and ride to the end of the line. I don't mind. I'm used to dames that can't tear themselves away from me."

Rudy's was the regular bus stop, but he always made a special stop for her, right in front of her house. "Thanks," she murmured as she swayed down the aisle and out the door. "It's been too, too divine."

The porch light was on, and Mom was out there in the wicker chair working on her quilt blocks. Sewing rested her, she always said, and besides—Lil could turn up her nose at hope chests all she wanted to— but some day she'd thank her, she'd be glad she had one with something in it.

"Pooped?" she asked sympathetically, as Lillian dropped down on the glider and kicked off her shoes. But she didn't wait for an answer. "I just got back from Mrs. Pankey's, thought I'd run over and see if there was anything I could do. She's taking it hard, poor soul. Well, there was lots worse boys than Horace, I've always said I never saw his equal when it came to carpentering, drunk *or* sober. Not that his mother would ever in this world admit that Horace drank. But what *got* me, Lil, she's made up her mind he was murdered. Yes sir. No accident about it, according to her whoever murdered that girl up at Blair's murdered Horace too ..."

Yak, yak, yak, thought Lillian amiably. Through her private golden haze she halfway listened to Mom's recital of "she saids" and "I saids"; halfway watched Mom's worried-looking face, surprisingly thin on top of her heavy, sagging body. Her gold side tooth gleamed occasionally as she talked, and her frizzy home permanent was stowed away in a hair net, all ready for her night's work. But it was the funniest thing, the way the light hit her face, casting the shadow of her eyelashes against her cheek and making her look—not pretty, but as if she might once have been pretty. The idea was startling to Lillian, and somehow embarrassing. Mom pretty? Mom young and light on her feet and not worried about anything? Mom ... in *love?*

"... said Ed Fuller told her they'd found it alongside Horace's body, just assumed it belonged to him, but Mrs. Pankey says not, Horace never carried a pocket comb, and—"

"A comb? A pocket comb?" Lillian sat up so suddenly that the glider creaked in protest. Her mind seemed to freeze in its tracks, unable to budge beyond the simple registering of those words. *Comb, a pocket comb.*

"Well, for heaven's sake, Lil, snap out of it! That's what I've been telling you! They found this comb alongside Horace, only Mrs. Pankey says—" The honking of a car horn interrupted her; Uncle Stan was here to pick her up and drive her out to the diner. Mom shrieked at him: "Be right out, Stan!" and struggled to her feet. "Now you promise me, Lil. Don't you sit out here alone. You go inside and lock the doors and stay there. I'll try and call you, if I can get a minute before midnight. Night, honey. See you in the morning."

Lillian lifted her face for the routine goodnight kiss. Then, automatically obedient, she went into the living room, locked the door, and switched on the floor lamp. There he had stood, right there in front of the mirror, combing his hair with her comb because his was gone, must have slipped out of his pocket. So what about it? It happened all the time, people losing their combs, all kinds of people, all kinds of combs. Her eyes moved away from the mirror to the sofa beneath it. That was where they had sat last night, with their beers (forgotten, left unfinished) and Jimmy's hand tingling against her shoulder and then pulling her closer, and then his urgent mouth on hers, and his voice, shaky with excitement: "I knew you were for me, Baby, the minute I saw you."

Yes, he had known, had trusted her and no one else, had put himself in her hands without a second thought. (Well, hardly a second thought.) They had both known. This was it, the real, once-in-a-lifetime thing. To fail Jimmy—even to doubt him for a moment—was to deny love itself. She was either the stuff that heroines are made of, destined for romance and high adventure; or she was too earthbound, too petty and cowardly to rise with the tide that, once missed, would never come again.

In plain words, she was either chicken or she wasn't.

Aware of a portentous thumping in her midriff, Lillian searched her face in the mirror. For a long, motionless moment. Then her head lifted in decision; she reached for her lipstick and began, skillfully and steadily, to paint on her Ava Gardner mouth. When it was finished, and her hair coaxed into the properly mussed look, she smiled secretly into her own eyes.

"Who's chicken?" she whispered, and went out to the summer kitchen, where Jimmy and Love and Kismet awaited her.

It was a little bit disappointing, the casual brush of a kiss he gave her. But then, as he pointed out, he had had a rugged day, cooped up in this hot, airless place with nothing to do but count the cracks in the ceiling and worry about who was walking past.

"All clear," whispered Lillian. "Mom's gone to work, and you can come inside."

He scuttled into the kitchen ahead of her and flattened himself against the wall until he was sure all the shades were down. He looked hunted and wild, what with his unshaven face and his uncombed hair. (Comb. A pocket comb, thought Lillian, in spite of all she could do.)

"Let's have a drink," she said gaily. "I'll fix us one while you get cleaned up. Want a shower? I'll get you a towel."

Bustling around seemed to make her feel better. And Jimmy would feel better too, once he got a shower and a shave; no wonder he wasn't in the mood for moonlight and roses, after the day he'd put in. They would sit on the couch with their drinks, and it would be like last night only even more thrilling because she had grown up since last night, she was now a woman of the world, caught up in a tide of real-life romance, risking all for Love and counting the cost as nothing.

She was in the living room, arranging their drinks—Tom Collinses, of course—and the ash trays and cigarettes on the coffee table, when she looked up and, in the mirror, saw him coming toward her. His smile was restored, and the gallant plume of his hair, and the bold sparkle in his eye. She stood quite still, watching the two enchanted mirror-figures, until his hands reached around her, tenderly capturing her breasts, and his head bent to the curve of her neck. Then her eyes closed; her whole self melted, and for a moment there was nothing in the world but the golden haze. This was the way it should be—and would be for always, once Jimmy got out of the jam he was in, the little deal that was neither here nor there but that made it wise for him to get out of town this weekend. This was what Lillian had been waiting for all day, all her life.

Meanwhile, however, there *was* the jam.

"So what gives?" he asked when they were settled on the couch, with his arm around her and the tall, cold glasses in their hands. "Has Walt confessed yet?"

"No, but they're still holding him, and they're checking up on everybody in New York that knew Marcella. On you, too, I guess."

"Oh sure. You might know they couldn't leave me out of it." Jimmy laughed bitterly and took a nervous sip of his drink. "Just because I was married to her ... That's no crime. They can't pin anything on me. What else?"

"Horace Pankey," said Lillian.

There was a little silence. Well, naturally. Jimmy would be waiting for her to go on. "Who?" he asked. "Who's he?"

"He got drowned last night. They found him at two o'clock in the morning. Drowned. At first they thought it was an accident, only—"

Again the silence. Jimmy had taken his arm away from her shoulder; he was holding his glass in both hands, staring down at it. She couldn't see his eyes. "Only what? What is this, a guessing game or something? You trying to be funny?"

"No. Only now they think maybe it wasn't an accident. His mother does, anyway. Because Horace was working up at Blair's house yesterday afternoon."

"Oh. That guy. I saw him, when Walt and I went up there. Drunk as a skunk. The shape he was in, he could drown himself and never know the difference. Wouldn't know the bay from the ocean."

Lillian's throat felt funny; it was hard to swallow. "I didn't say the bay," she said at last, very low.

"Neither did I," said Jimmy quickly. "Was it?"

"Yes. The bay. His mother thinks Horace saw whoever it was that killed Marcella, and so they killed him too."

"Sounds screwy to me. If Walt did it, I mean. The guy was still there when we left Blair's. Unless Walt went back again. Say," Jimmy turned so she could see his eyes; they looked unusually bright. "Say, he could have, at that. I wasn't paying any attention to him, after we got to Rudy's. He could have gone back while you and me were having those drinks at the bar. I wouldn't have noticed."

It hurt Lillian, somehow, to remember those drinks at the bar and how happy she had been. Because—no use ignoring it—she wasn't happy now. Something frightening was happening to her mind; against her will, it kept noticing things, remembering things. It swooped back now, to last night, when she had found Jimmy, cowering on the porch on all fours, and almost the first thing he had said: "Did they find the guy?" She had taken it for granted he meant Walt—only he knew Walt by name, he wouldn't have referred to Walt as "the guy." Would he? Wouldn't he? Her throat went dryer than ever. And when she had said of course, they had him in jail, Jimmy had looked at her as if he couldn't believe his ears. Supposing—helplessly she watched her mind careening down its own twisting, perilous road—supposing he hadn't meant Walt at all, but Horace? Horace, whose body hadn't been found then, whose name Jimmy had never heard. "Did they find the guy?" And then: "Oh. Him. You mean Walt."

"Walt could have gone back," Jimmy was persisting. "With all that mob coming and going at Rudy's, it wouldn't be noticed. He sure as hell could have, for all of me. I wasn't paying any attention to anybody but you. Remember? I spotted you as soon as I walked in the joint."

She nodded dumbly. Jimmy's alibi, all neatly arranged. Maybe a little too neatly. Would an innocent person be quite so careful about reminding her?

"Well, say something!" Jimmy burst out irritably. "What the hell's eating on you, anyway? What are you looking at me like that for?"

"I'm not. I mean—like what?"

"I don't know. Funny. Like you thought I—" He paused, and she had a feeling his mind was racing. Measuring her, calculating, deciding. He turned on his smile. "Lil Baby, I'm sorry. I didn't mean to use that tone of voice with you. I'm just so damn on edge I don't know what I'm doing. It's like everybody in the world was against me except you, Baby—" Confidently he took her face between his hands and leaned forward to kiss her.

"Don't!" She pulled away from him so sharply that she knocked her drink off the coffee table; she heard the miniature crash and felt dampness against her knees, but her eyes remained frozen on Jimmy's face. He wasn't smiling any more. There was a curious pinched look about his nose.

"You're holding out on me. Aren't you? There's something you're not telling me." His hands bit into her shoulders. She felt her head bobbing helplessly back and forth as he shook her. "And you're going to be sorry, sweetheart, I'll find out what it is if I have to beat it out of you. You been blabbing to the police? Answer me! Have you?"

"No, Jimmy, no. Honest and true. You know I wouldn't." Again her mind was off on a panic-ridden path of its own. Had she locked the kitchen door? Had she? Hadn't she? Could she get out there on some pretext, make a break for it? Escape, she must escape from this new, terrible Jimmy, and from the withering chill inside her, like something dying there.

"You're hurting me, Jimmy. Let go of me."

"I'll hurt you worse if you don't come clean. I'm not kidding, Lillian. You're going to be sorry—"

The phone let out a shrill, demanding peal that went through them both like an electric shock. Hope surged up wildly in Lillian. But Jimmy's hands tightened on her arms; his eyes went narrower than ever.

"Oh no, you don't," he whispered, and the phone pealed again. "You don't need to think you can pull a fast one like that. You're not answering any phones tonight, sweetheart."

A good, healthy spurt of anger shot through Lillian. She stopped trying to twist herself free and looked Jimmy straight in the eye. "Okay, wise guy. It's your funeral. Because that's Mom calling, that's who it is, and she's going to think it's awfully funny if I don't answer. Because she gave me strict orders to stay home tonight. So she's going to get scared, and you know what she's going to do then? She's going to send my Uncle Stan or somebody over here to find out what gives. Maybe she'll even call the police. How'd you like that, wise guy?"

It shook him, all right. He licked his lips nervously, and his eyes kept shifting from her to the phone, still ringing its head off. At last he shoved her toward it. "Okay, answer the damn thing. But if you're lying to me, if I hear one word out of you that sounds fishy, so help me, I'll—"

"Hello," said Lillian into the phone. Quite calmly, when you considered that her heart was beating harder, and she was thinking more furiously, than ever before in her life. There had to be a way to get it across to Mom, somehow, without giving herself away to Jimmy. There had to be a way.

Only the voice at the other end of the wire was not Mom's. It was Floyd's. Of all times for him to call! Of all the drips in the world, to be stuck with this one, who never caught on to anything unless you beat him over the head with it!

"Lil?" He sounded the way he always did. Uncertain. Apologetic. Flustered. "Gee, Lil, I'd about decided you wasn't home, took you so long to answer. I guess maybe you're busy?"

Lillian set her teeth and plunged desperately. "Oh hello there, Mom. I've been waiting for you to call, Mom. You said you would, you know, if you got a chance. Everything okay, Mom?"

"Huh? Hey, Lil, this is Floyd—"

"Sure, everything's fine. I'm just sitting here having a coke and—" she could feel Jimmy's eyes boring into her, his ears straining to catch every word "—and listening to the radio."

"Lil. You all right? You out of your head or something? This is Floyd, and Rudy says I can have the Ford, so I thought I'd just call in case you weren't busy, after all—"

"Oh, Mom, there's nothing to worry about." (Oh, you dope. Please,

please catch on. Help me, you poor dumb dope, save me.) "Don't be such a fuddy duddy. They've got the guy in jail, so how could he be prowling around?"

There was a bewildered silence. She could see Floyd, standing there goggle-eyed, with his Adam's apple bouncing up and down, and not a brain cell working. Then he started stammering again. "What's going on? What's wrong, Lil? How come you keep calling me Mom?"

"I told you before, Mom, I'm all right." She couldn't go on. It was no use. Tears of pure frustration flooded her throat. "Okay. I'll see you in the morning. Good night, Mom." She fumbled the phone back into its cradle, made a blind, hopeless little rush toward the kitchen.

He was too quick for her, of course. And too strong. In less than a minute he had her two hands pinned back of her, in one of his. "Going somewhere?" He was smiling coldly. "What's your hurry? Wait a while. We're going to have a little talk, only just for kicks, I'll let you do all the talking. You can start right now. What goes on?"

"I told you. Horace Pankey got drowned, and—" Tears were running down her face, and no hands to brush them away with. It seemed like the final humiliation. She twisted her head against her shoulder, and once more caught a glimpse of the two of them in the mirror over the couch. But how cruelly different from the enchanted mirror-figures of half an hour ago! Her own face was an ugly mask of fear, and above her loomed the terrible new Jimmy-face. Once so tender, now so menacing. She blurted out the rest: "And they found this comb. Somebody dropped a comb beside him."

She caught the tell-tale, involuntary twitch of Jimmy's free hand toward his jacket pocket, the flare of fear in his eyes. "So that's it. I get it now. So you're the bright kid that puts two and two together and gets a hundred and four. They can't pin anything on me. I never saw the guy before. A goddam stinking comb, and—" He drew a breath and got his voice back under control. "What kind of a comb?"

"Just a—a comb. Pocket comb. That's all I know."

"It's not. You're lying. You're still holding out on me, and you're not going to get away with any more of your cute little tricks. Why didn't you just turn me over to the police tonight instead of inviting me in here, falling all over me the way you did?"

"Because I—"

"Shut up. I'll tell you why. Because it's a trick, they put you up to it. Thought you could frame me, didn't you? You double-crossing little bitch—"

She wasted no energy on denials. She was beyond words, or even a shake of the head. What difference did it make what he thought of her, anyway? All that mattered now was survival; the bright, shallow, fear-crazed glare in Jimmy's eyes told her the peril she was in. Her arms were still pinioned behind her back. No use wasting energy there, either. So that left her feet. She shut her eyes tight, and with all her force she stamped and kicked. She remembered her teeth, too, and sank them in his arm until she tasted blood.

Grunts. Curses. Her own harsh-drawn breath. Her ears, sharpened by her extremity, caught the hum of traffic on the highway, cars whipping heedlessly past. The people in them wouldn't believe ... Neither could she. Except that it was happening. The coffee table crashed over; Mom's rug, the best glasses, it couldn't be happening except it was, the cars buzzing past ...

She was imagining it, of course. She had not really heard brakes squealing in front of the house, or a car door slamming, or footsteps coming up the walk. It was all a fabrication of her madly straining ears, the impossible, last-minute rescue that you could always depend on, in the movies. Nowhere else, though. Nothing, nothing, was like in the movies.

But Jimmy had heard something, too. She felt him shudder and stiffen; when the pounding began on the front door she opened her mouth to scream, and was staggered by a blow that caught her along the jaw. She sagged halfway to her knees. Heard, through the explosion of blinding wheels in her head, Jimmy's furious promise: "I'll get you for this, goddam you. They may get me, but I'll get you first." And felt his hands closing mercilessly on her throat.

She thought, no, No, NO. No to the unbearable bracelet tightening, tightening around her neck. No to her own futile thrashings, the failing strength of her clawing and kicking. NO. I won't die, she thought. I will not die. I will not. I will ...

ELEVEN

"You're sure you don't want to come on home with us?" repeated Gen's sister, when they got to the George Washington Bridge. "No, Pammy. I told you before. No more lollipops, and if you wake the baby, I'm going to— You're sure, Gen? It'll be cooler than your apartment, and I have this awful feeling you're going to just sit there by yourself and brood—"

"Stop fussing, Ann. Of course I'm not going to brood. Never been known to brood in my life."

"I don't know. You've got that look in your eye." With the hand that wasn't holding the baby, Ann reached out abstractedly and plucked Junior, who was leaning halfway out the window, back to safety. "Gen darling, if we'd only had a chance to *talk!*"

They hadn't, of course, and Gen should have known better than to hope. The day had been one long hassle of lost sandals and shovels, wails and fights and sudden, ear-splitting fits of giggles, trips for ice cream cones and hot dogs, spilled suntan oil and broken balloons. Not a chance for three consecutive words. Motherhood was like that. The old days of long, satisfying heart-to-hearts with Ann were probably gone forever.

"It's been a dandy day," Gen insisted. "It's done me a world of good." And they looked sadly into each other's eyes, agreeing that it had been not dandy at all. Even the moment of bleak honesty was cut short. The baby woke up howling. "You can let me out here, Bob," Gen said hastily. "I can nip right down in the subway and be home in nothing flat. I'm all right, Ann. Honestly. I'm perfectly fine."

Sticky kisses from the kids. Thanks. Goodbye, goodbye. Call me, Gen, and think twice, don't be too hard on Alex ...

The ride downtown on the subway seemed wonderfully peaceful to Gen. She shouldn't have worried poor Ann, she shouldn't have expected her to make sense. Motherhood was like that; enough to addle anybody's brains. And Ann had always been long-suffering, too tolerant for her own good. "Don't be too hard on Alex." It wasn't Ann's problem, anyway. It was Gen's. Nobody in the world could help her solve it.

It was a lonesome thought. She was up on the street again; not a breath of air stirring; only the jaded, late-afternoon glare, and all the other lonesome people scurrying for home, or the next train, or an air-conditioned bar. All right, so life was a lonesome business. It was what Gen had always maintained, wasn't it? You're on your own, and you might as well face it. You're born alone, you die alone, and you live alone. Even when you love somebody, you live alone, except for rare moments—and maybe they're not real, maybe they're only a kind of wishful thinking. Maybe? No maybe about it. Gen was through with wishful thinking.

So she assured herself. But as she pushed the elevator button and made the stately, shuddering ascent, her assurance suddenly turned tail and fled. Nothing was left but the wishful, yearning thought: If only Alex would be there, waiting for her. If only ...

The apartment smelled of cigarette smoke. Very stuffy. Utterly empty. But someone had been here: the clock was ticking away busily. Ten minutes after six. And the note. "Dear Gen, I am taking the car." That was at the top of the envelope. Farther down, very large and with a headlong look: "Viva la Geneviva."

She turned her face to the wall and wept.

Things had settled down to a steady drizzle when the doorbell rang. She stared around the room wildly, caught a glimpse of her blotched swollen face in the mirror, decided to answer it, not to answer it, to answer it. After all, Alex had seen her in tears before. Not that she expected it to *be* Alex. Not for a minute. It was probably the Fuller Brush man.

"Hello, dear," caroled Vonda, when she opened the door. "How lovely you look. So fresh and cool. I *do* hope I'm not intruding? What a delightful little place you have here. Charming, dear. Simply charming." She looked around ecstatically at the furniture, stripped of its slipcovers, and the rugless floor, already dim with grit and dust.

"Hello," said Gen weakly. "What are you doing back here in town?"

"Dwight—Mr. Abbott, except I already feel as if I've known him for years—had to make a flying trip in. Business." (Vonda always sounded very brisk and knowledgeable when she mentioned business.) "And so I came along. Just for the ride. It's a lovely day, isn't it?"

"It's a miserable day! And the place doesn't look charming, it's a mess! And so am I. 'Lovely. Fresh and cool.' I'm a—a shambles!" Gen broke off, astonished at her own outburst.

Vonda, however, didn't bat an eyelash. "There, dear. Isn't it lucky, I brought along a thermos of iced tea—" and sure enough she had; she held it up gaily "—just the thing, I always say, with plenty of lemon. That's the secret. Don't spare the lemon, when it comes to iced tea. Now you just sit down there, where you'll get the breeze, while I find us some glasses ... Here we are. Just the thing."

There was a soothing, babbling-brook quality about Vonda's voice, and the iced tea wasn't bad, even though, as it turned out, she had forgotten the lemon. Gen began to feel better.

"I'm sorry I blew up," she said. "I was just feeling so—"

"Of course you are," Vonda assured her heartily. "And so is he. Poor dear."

Gen immediately became wary. It was always possible to be mistaken, with a mental free-wheeler like Vonda, but she couldn't help suspecting that the "poor dear" was meant more for Alex than for herself. They were all alike, she thought bitterly. Ann and her don't be too hard on Alex. Vonda and her poor dear. Nobody saw Gen's side of it. Nobody understood how it felt to have doors slammed in your face and the solid earth crumbling under your feet.

Vonda (she was wearing a shrieking orange job today, with a rhinestone belt and earrings like chandeliers) nodded sympathetically.

"Shut out," she said, as if she had somehow heard Gen's thoughts. "That's what I told Dwight. Shut out, I said. Not in the least disloyal."

"Disloyal?" echoed Gen. "But it's not as if Alex were in any trouble over this. Nobody could possibly imagine that he had anything to do with—Vonda! It isn't anything like that, is it?"

"Who? Alex? Why, what a question, dear. But he's very much disturbed. And so are we, Dwight feels just the way I do. We're all very much disturbed. When he was at the cottage last night, after we heard the prowler and all, Mr. Theobald and I both remarked on it. Not like himself at all. So drawn-looking and—what's the word?—abstracted. That's it, the very word. Abstracted, and then, *after* the prowler, the news about that poor man, such a tragedy, and—"

"Vonda," said Gen a little wildly, "you have got to stop this. You have got to make sense. Who's very much disturbed? Who's abstracted? What prowler? What about the poor man?"

"I've confused you?" Vonda looked politely incredulous. "Perhaps I didn't make myself quite clear. It's just that I felt I understood better than Dwight, being a woman, and—"

The doorbell cut her off in mid-flight. It's probably Mr. Theobald, thought Gen as she pushed the buzzer, he probably came along for the ride, too. On account of its being such a lovely day. That's all we need, is Mr. Theobald. She felt on the verge of hysteria. What had she done to deserve this visitation of iced tea and baffling conversation? It couldn't be called disloyal, to walk out on someone who had shut you out and didn't need you, anyway. Didn't want you, either, for all his "Viva la Geneviva" notes. When it came to disloyalty, Alex himself was the original offender. Nobody except Gen seemed to notice that.

She opened the door. There stood a woman in a bright green suit and a hat with a feather that stuck right straight up. "Mrs. Blair? Excuse me for barging in like this, but I'd like to talk to you, if you can spare a few minutes. I'm Mrs. Bowman. Shirley Bowman."

"Mrs. Bowman? Oh, of course. Walt's wife."

"Right." They went through the motions of shaking hands, but neither of them let this interfere with the main business at hand—a swift, thorough survey of each other. Flat-face, thought Gen; not enough nose. Like one of those yappy little dogs. Yappy-dog eyes, too. Prominent, bright brown, belittling everything in sight. Gen became acutely aware of the sand in her hair, the wrinkles in her cotton skirt, her blotched face.

"And you're Alex's wife," Shirley was saying. "Look at it one way, and I guess we've got quite a bit in common."

That was one way of looking at it, all right. "Won't you come in?" said Gen, and introduced Vonda, who twittered socially—though not for very long. There was something a bit intimidating about Shirley's purposeful air.

She sat down, with her big, shiny handbag planted in her lap and her ankles crossed, and waded right in. "I suppose you wonder why I'm here. Well, here's the way I look at it. So okay, Walt's been a damn fool and he's wound up in the soup. Okay. They're not going to hang a murder on him, if I've got anything to say about it. I know what to expect from that bunch of dumb cops. I wouldn't trust them to figure out who ate the canary, not if the cat was sitting right under their nose licking up the tail feathers. All they want is somebody in jail, to make it look good. So it's up to me to do some investigating on my own."

"I see," said Gen. She felt distracted and inadequate; the room still seemed to clang with the brassy echoes of Shirley's voice. "Have you made any headway?"

"I have, and I haven't." Shirley extracted a cigarette from a flashy tortoise-shell case, tapped and lit it. "I dug up that guy that Walt was talking to at Rudy's yesterday afternoon, if that's any help. And it may be. He was there when Walt and Jimmy came in, and he left right after you and Alex showed up. They tied one on, him and Walt, and he's ready to swear Walt didn't leave the place all afternoon. That's in case anybody tries to say Walt went back again, without Jimmy, and choked the dame. Now if that rat Jimmy would just back up Walt's story, or if the guy that was mixing cement hadn't picked last night to get himself drowned—"

"Horace?" cried Gen. "Horace Pankey drowned?"

"I told you, dear," murmured Vonda. "Didn't I? Of course I did."

"You didn't! Nobody's told me anything!" Gen's throat suddenly ached for Horace Pankey—the rose bushes he had set out for her, the kitchen shelves he had built, the clam shells for the driveway, the way he ducked his head and blushed when she scolded him ...

"So I'm telling you now. They found him down at the bay early this morning, drowned. The police are investigating. Quote, unquote." Shirley's voice dripped sarcasm for the bunch of dumb cops. "All I can say is, it's damn convenient for whoever killed Marcella, and it's another piece of tough luck for Walt. Nobody now to prove that she wasn't there when Jimmy got him to drive out to your house. Nobody but Jimmy, and from all I hear, God help anybody that has to depend on that son of a— Do you know him?"

"Me? What are you talking about? Why would I know Jimmy?"

Gen spoke more sharply than she intended; Shirley's head reared up like a war horse's at the sound of the bugle. "I beg your pardon," she said elaborately. "Pardon me for living. Naturally you're above such things. The whole affair. Too, too sordid, don't you know."

"If you want to take it that way," snapped Gen, "it's your privilege."

"Well, let me tell you something, Miss Social Register, whether you like it or not, you're in just exactly the same kettle of fish I'm in, and don't you forget it."

"I am not. Alex—"

"Alex is in it up to his precious neck, for my money. What was she doing out at your house in the first place? And these buddies of his that found her—he's got them wrapped around his little finger. Anybody can see that with half an eye. They'd swear white was black if Alex told them to. No telling what went on out there before they reported it to the police."

"You mean Mr. Theobald and I—" Vonda was beginning, with great dignity.

But Shirley's outraged stare did not shift from Gen. "You walked out on him, didn't you? That proves plenty, for my money. You're not standing by him, so what's all this hands-off-Alex routine? You can't have it both ways, honey chile."

"For your information—" Gen drew a deep, invigorating breath to steady her wobbling voice. "For your information, I did not walk out on Alex, and I have no intention of doing so. I came into town last night to— to do a little investigating on my own, because I haven't much more faith in the police than you have. We have so much in common, haven't we? What was that lovely phrase of yours? We're in the same kettle of fish." She smiled sweetly. "But not, please, in the same apartment. You've come to the wrong place to investigate. Do you mind, honey chile?"

"Mind?" gasped Shirley. "I couldn't be more enchanted!" She scooped up her purse and whizzed out the door, leaving behind an almost tangible current of sultry perfume and unadulterated female fury.

Just one more thing they had in common. The fury, thought Gen, not the perfume. Her knees were knocking against each other like a couple of eggs boiling. She was hopping mad, and it was wonderful.

She turned (poor, gentle Vonda, they had probably scared her out of her wits) and said, laughing shakily, "She's a hell of a poor hand at investigating, for my money."

Vonda was looking as calm as a bowl of cream. Downright smug. "Let's do," she said. "I wonder who she left her cat with."

TWELVE

It was eight thirty when at last the lights of Rudy's Bar and Grill flashed their neon welcome and Alex maneuvered his car into the last parking space available. No lack of customers tonight. Labor Day weekend was in full swing. Alex's head ached with fatigue and tension. Traffic had been brutal all the way out; he had made no attempt to keep up with Ed's impassioned and expert driving. What was the hurry, anyway? He slammed the car door disconsolately behind him and crunched across the gravel. Here, just here at the door, Gen had reached up and kissed him last night, without warning or reason; there beside the phone booth was their special table, which Alex took pains to avoid tonight. He deliberately detached himself from the racket around him (a mental trick, like turning off a hearing aid, which he had cultivated for years), found a booth in the back, and ordered a drink. Not a martini, though that was what he wanted. Already, he found, he had laid down for himself a rigid, superstitious set of laws. No more martinis, saith the law, until such time as he had one with Gen.

"Has Dwight been around?" he asked, drearily aware of his duty.

"Yep," reported Rudy. "He went into the city too. You guys, nothing but a damn bunch of commuters. He said to tell you he'd be back some time tonight, and make yourself at home. Mrs. Theobald went in with him."

"Mrs. Theobald? Oh. Vonda. Wonder what they went in for?"

Rudy shrugged. "Some book, or bunch of papers, God knows what, that he forgot yesterday and he can't live without it. You know Dwight. He don't know how to take a vacation. Work work work. She went along for the ride."

"She would," said Alex. "How about Brad? You know him, he's been out here with us before. Fellow with a crew cut." Rudy knew him, all right. But he hadn't seen hide nor hair of him today.

There was a rather tentative pause; each waiting to see if the other would mention Gen. Neither of them did. So, thought Alex cheerlessly. Rudy's got it all figured out, he's sparing my feelings.

"Nice pot roast tonight," said Rudy, with the air of a nurse trying to tempt an invalid's finicky appetite. "Nice shrimps, too. Or steak. Steak's always good."

Alex summoned up a grin. "All in good time. First things first. I'm not in any hurry."

He dawdled through a couple more drinks and a steak, which lived up to Rudy's recommendation and improved his disposition. Afterwards he had a brandy at the bar, where the conversation centered on Horace Pankey's death (no accident, most of the experts agreed, darkly, zestfully) and the elusive Jimmy (still no sign of him).

What with one thing and another, it was eleven when Alex left. It occurred to him that Gen might be trying to call him at Dwight's; he was all at once in a hurry. For some occult reason it was taboo (that tyrannical set of laws that now ruled him!) to try to call her from Rudy's. One attempt from Dwight's—but only provided neither Dwight nor Brad was back yet—was permitted.

He backed out onto the highway and gave her the gun. He was rolling down the window to get the breeze when he passed the house with the rock garden and the circle of wooden flamingoes, and that was how he happened to notice the Ford pulling away from there like a bat out of hell, and the frantic figure galloping down the walk to the highway.

He slowed down, and caught an earful of hoarse, confused shouts. "Stop him! Go after him! Go get the doctor, quick! Police! Somebody help me! He's killed her, the son of a bitch's killed Lil …"

It was Floyd, wild-eyed and sobbing. He gripped the half-open window and stared in at Alex. His nose was bloody, and he kept making aimless, yet terribly urgent flailing gestures. "Killed Lil, and now he's stole Rudy's Ford! For God's sake, do something!"

The Ford was already out of sight. Not a prayer of catching it with this old jalopy, anyway. "Okay, okay." Alex had to shove Floyd aside to get out of the car. "Come on, we'll call the police and the doctor from the house. Quicker than going after them. Where is she? Inside?"

Floyd's head waggled up and down. They sprinted up the walk and into the front door, which stood wide open. Alex' heart sank when he saw her huddled there on the floor with blood trickling out of the corner of her mouth and her bright, cheap little dress every which way. The poor kid looked dead, sure enough. He did the telephoning—Floyd was practically beyond words, except for "Lil Lil!" The doctor first. Then Ed Fuller, who was still at the police station. "Rudy's Ford. Yep. Stolen. The guy took off east on the highway. That's all I know, but Floyd's here, he can give you the dope. So get over here fast." He had to ask Floyd for Lillian's last name. Schroeder. Lillian Schroeder. He knelt down and lifted her limp wrist, feeling under the three charm bracelets for her pulse.

"She's not dead," he whispered, after a minute. "Out cold, but not dead. Calm down, Floyd, so you can make sense for Ed when he gets here. Who was it?"

With a heroic working up and down of his Adam's apple, a series of desperate shudders and blinks, Floyd got a grip on himself and made sense. "Jimmy," he gulped. "The guy that was with Walt yesterday. Rudy said I could have the Ford, so I called Lil, and I couldn't figure it out, she sounded so funny—"

"Funny?" prompted Alex.

"Like she was out of her head, or something. I don't know. She kept calling me Mom, and when I'd ask her a question she'd answer like it was some other question. You know? I just couldn't figure it out. At first it made me sore, but then I got to thinking there was maybe something wrong ... Look, Mr. Blair, couldn't we lay her on the couch or somewhere?"

"I don't think we ought to move her, in case anything's broken. Doc'll be here any minute. What did he do, choke her?"

Floyd swallowed convulsively, and nodded. "I couldn't get in the front door, and by that time I was damn good and sure there was something wrong, so I went around to the back, and it was unlocked. He had her by the neck—"

Another spasm threatened. Alex looked the other way and waited. Strangled, like Marcella. Only this kid had put up a fight. The coffee table was knocked over, cigarettes strewn over the rug, an ash tray, a smashed glass, another one that looked as if a bite had been taken out of it ... Two glasses? Lillian had been having a drink with someone?

"I took a poke at him," Floyd was going on, "and then he socked me and busted out the door, and time I got out there he—"

"What's going on here?" Dr. Nichols, with Ed Fuller at his heels, bustled in. The doctor, a chubby, bald man in a wild-colored sports shirt and slacks, dropped to his knees beside Lillian and opened his little black bag. "Clear out of here, will you? Let me see what's what. If I need any help I'll holler."

Obediently—though Floyd cast a yearning, worried glance behind—the three of them retreated to the kitchen. Ed had had a hard day, and he looked it. His voice sounded even wheezier than usual. "Okay, son. I put Whitey on the stolen car deal, he's got the license number from Rudy, and he's notifying the highway patrol boys, so the guy isn't going to get very far. What happened?"

He listened, without comment except for an occasional grunt, to Floyd's halting little story. When it was over, he still made no comment. In the silence the faucet in the kitchen sink dripped busily; there was an occasional rustle, or a small, mysterious thud, from the living room where the doctor was at work.

"If she dies," Floyd blurted bleakly, "it'll be my fault, because I didn't get here soon enough. The one time when she needed me—"

"Looks to me like you did all right." Ed padded over to the sink and gave the faucet a good hard twist. "Anything I can't stand it's a leaky faucet. I'd of done just what you did, Floyd. Tell the truth, I don't know as I'd catch on to that phone call as quick as you did."

"He must have been here with her when you called," said Alex. He hesitated, then went on. "I noticed two glasses had been knocked off the coffee table. So she must have been having a drink with somebody. I suppose it could have been with Jimmy."

"Sure," said Floyd, without resentment. He glanced down at his own lanky, knobby frame; his sports jacket didn't quite fit anywhere, and his tie, handkerchief, and socks were all one bright, relentlessly matching blue. "He's a real smoothie. Lil likes a sharp dresser, somebody with a smooth line. You know?"

"So he turns up from wherever he's been since last night," said Ed, laboriously putting the pieces together, "and she lets him in and fixes him a drink. But then something happens and she gets scared, because when the phone rings she makes as good a stab as she can at letting you know that something's wrong. Looks to me like Lil's going to have plenty to tell us, too."

"Okay," called Dr. Nichols, and they trooped back into the living room. (Alex caught himself tiptoeing.) Lillian still lay on the floor, but straightened out now; there was a great bruised lump on her jaw, and dark, sunken places on her throat. "You can help me, Floyd. What we'll do is put her on the glider mattress and get her to the hospital in the station wagon. Can't tell yet whether her jaw's broken or not."

"Is she—?" croaked Floyd.

"She'll come out of it. She's had a going-over, all right, but she'll come out of it."

"There, son." Ed produced his first smile of the evening. "I guess you got here soon enough, after all. One of those last-minute rescues, like in the movies. Now look, Doc, I want to talk to Lil, just as soon as she's able. You'll let me know, won't you? Before she talks to anybody else. It's important."

"Sure. Alley-oop, Floyd. Grab her legs, will you?"

"Yes, sir."

Reverently, with a face of radiance, Floyd bent and grabbed her legs.

THIRTEEN

"Her cat?" repeated Gen. "Whose cat?"

"Why, Marcella's." Vonda sounded not so much impatient as surprised that this explanation should be necessary. "She wouldn't just go away and leave it. Somebody must be looking after it for her. I just wonder who?"

So did Gen, now that she thought of it. Whoever was taking care of Marcella's cat for her might very well be a little gold mine of information about Marcella herself—her friends, her habits, her troubles. Which was what Gen needed if she was going to prove to Mrs. Walter Flat-face Bowman that Alex was not in it up to his precious neck, for anybody's money.

"A neighbor, maybe?" she offered. "Somebody that lives in the same apartment house?"

Vonda beamed at her. "The very thing. Now, let me see, what was that address? It's the strangest thing, the way addresses elude me. Phone numbers, now—why, to this day I can remember Marcella's phone number, it was unlisted, and I'll never forget how impressed Mr. Stone was when he called me up and asked for it, and I reeled it right off—"

"Brad? Brad asked for Marcella's phone number?"

"Why, yes. So thoughtful of him, you know. It wasn't long after she finished the job for Alex, and he said in case she was still available there might be something for her at his office."

"And was there?" asked Gen. A likely story, she was thinking to herself; just another sample of Vonda's gift for scrambling facts. She made a mental note to ask Brad about it, when she got a chance.

"Apparently not, dear. I always meant to ask him, but somehow it slipped my mind, along with her address."

Gen remembered the address. She was probably going to remember it for the rest of her life. "I suppose the police have already been there. Let's walk over, anyway, and see if we can find out anything. Where's Dwight? Should we take him along?"

He was at his own apartment, Vonda reported, looking for draft number three of his Preface; it contained a section which he had dropped from succeeding drafts but which, he had decided after considerable deliberation, ought to be reinstated. "Such a scholarly man," said Vonda. "I have great admiration for scholars ... We can call him afterwards. People feel a little freer about talking—don't you think so?—when it's just a couple of women. Something just a tiny bit *official*, when it's a man."

True enough. Particularly when the man was Dwight, with his genius for casting an uneasy pall over any social gathering. Aware of a disconcerting pang of respect for Vonda, Gen repaired her face and hair, and they set off for Leroy Street.

It was a frowsy block, almost visibly steaming in the remnants of muggy daylight, shrill with the screeches of half a dozen kids playing hop scotch on the pavement. There was a resplendently gleaming motorcycle parked in front of Marcella's house, and a fat woman with her hair done up in curlers was cramming a bulging paper bag into the garbage can.

Vonda addressed her chattily. "Good evening. I wonder if you could be the one we're looking for? Though I suppose that would be more luck than we have any right to expect. Not that it's such a large house, but it's just that life isn't usually like that. Is it?"

Curiosity, suspicion, and plain bewilderment struggled for first place on the woman's sluggish face. "Who you looking for?" she asked after a minute.

"That's just it, you see. We don't know exactly, because we don't know who Marcella—"

"Marcella Ewing?" Suspicion had the upper hand, at least momentarily. "The police already been here. I told them, I don't know anything about it."

"Oh well, the police." Vonda made an airy gesture of dismissal. "We've got nothing to do with the police. It's business with them, of course. With us it's just a matter of friendship, in a way, because Marcella was so fond of her little cat, and we couldn't bear to think there was nobody to look after it, now that she's gone. Such an awful thing, isn't it?"

"Terrible," agreed the woman, cautiously. She fumbled at the hardware on her head, meanwhile measuring Vonda and Gen with her eyes. "You're friends of hers, you say? I didn't know she had any friends. Girlfriends, anyway. I didn't know anything about her. Like I told the police."

"Oh, dear. We were so hoping you could help us. But maybe there'll be somebody else in the house who knows about the cat."

"If that's what you're worried about, talk to the Harelip." The woman had started up the steps; she threw this suggestion back at them, over her shoulder, in a voice tinged with malice. "He's nuts about cats. That ain't all he's nuts about, if you ask me. He's the only one she had anything to do with. She was all palsy-walsy with the Harelip. I don't know what the police got out of him, but I'll tell you one thing, I bet it wasn't all he knows. Ahlberg. 2-A."

"Thank you so much, dear," Vonda called after her as she shuffled down the hall. "You've been so sweet and helpful."

She really means it, thought Gen, scanning the row of buttons for Ahlberg 2-A. She just doesn't see any of the spitefulness or suspicion or meanness in the world. And here she is, trying to track a murderer. "I have a feeling the bells are all out of order," she said. They looked it, somehow. But after a long, long pause Ahlberg 2-A buzzed back, and they started up the dark, narrow stairway. It smelled of disinfectant and dirt and fried fish. Gen looked up, and saw, peering over the banister at them, a man's face. The light was too murky for her to make out his features, beyond a shock of dark hair and a pair of gleaming eyes. But as soon as she heard his voice—which was long on breath, short on consonants—she knew that here was "the Harelip" they had been directed to.

What he said was, "Who wants Ahlberg?" There was a kind of desolate, panoramic sweep to the question. A voice—and a defective one—crying in the wilderness. Who, indeed, wanted Ahlberg?

Gen felt a surge of acute dubiousness. But nothing fazed Vonda. "We're friends of Marcella's," she called cheerily. "We're trying to find out about her cat."

He waited until they got to the top of the stairs. In a silence that seemed hostile to Gen, he watched them, all the while brushing one hand nervously across his mouth and chin. Then, with an air at once truculent and anguished, he thrust his disfigured face at them, as if it were a horrendous mask.

Staring contemptuously into Gen's eyes (for he had caught her slight, involuntary recoil, he had invited it, in a way he gloried in it) he spoke again. "I've got her cat. You want to make something out of it?"

He was not very old. Twenty-three, perhaps, wirily built, and dressed in a pair of blue jeans and a sweat shirt. There was a defensive swagger about the way he held his shoulders back and his elbows slightly out. Gen, self-consciously avoiding the two deformed flaps of his upper lip, saw that he needed a haircut, and that his eyes were large, dark, and wild with a lifetime of bitterly remembered wounds.

"Why, what would we want to make of it?" Vonda, who had been behind Gen on the stairs, stepped forward now, holding out her hand and smiling. "Mr. Ahlberg, you just take that chip off your shoulder and mind your manners."

Her easy, bantering tone obviously caught him off guard. Surprised into shaking hands with her, he scowled at her (only Vonda didn't seem to notice) and hurriedly adjusted his shield of mistrust. "You don't need to think you're going to take her cat away from me. She left her with me, and I'm not going to give her up. It was me that gave her to Marcella in the first place, and—" The words rushed out of him; his speech defect gave everything he said an exaggerated, breathy vehemence.

"Well, of course!" cried Vonda. "We only wanted to make sure she's in good hands. Marcella would want you to have her, I know. You're the logical one."

"What do you know about it?" said Mr. Ahlberg rudely and (it struck Gen) quite reasonably. "Maybe you're from the police. Maybe you're not a friend of hers at all."

"Well, but I told you—" Vonda stopped, brought up short by what was apparently a new phenomenon to her. Here was someone who didn't believe what she told him. The idea shook her. But only for a moment. "You have a cat of your own, Mr. Ahlberg?" she asked politely.

"So what if I have?"

"Very simple. I'll know Marcella's cat from yours, and that will prove that I knew Marcella." Her face broke into a reassuring smile.

There was a brief pause while Mr. Ahlberg considered the proposition. Then, with an abrupt, sly laugh, he turned and pushed open the door of Apartment 2-A. "Come on in," he said, over his shoulder. "You asked for it."

If it had been left up to Gen, she would have turned tail and fled the moment she followed Vonda into the apartment. Because her first impression was that the place was swarming with cats. All colors, all sizes. Cats everywhere. They prowled at every window, they slunk under every rickety piece of furniture, they peered out eerily through the half-gloom. She shrank to one side as Mr. Ahlberg shut the door behind them and clicked on a glaring overhead light. It fell bluntly on the mean disorder of the room and on their host's face, which—again with that savage, anguished gesture—he thrust at Gen. She was determined, this time, not to give him the satisfaction of recoiling, and, when his gaze wavered before hers did, she felt that she had won a secret victory.

They both turned to Vonda who—head tilted, preposterous earrings swinging—was facing undaunted the six pairs of yellow cat-eyes. At last she gave a cry of delighted recognition. "Ah, kitty, kitty. There she is. Ah, the nice little cat, the pretty little cat."

It was, in fact, one of the least prepossessing animals Gen had ever seen. Its five sleek companions were behaving with that mixture of dignity and curiosity natural to the mentally sound cat. But this one had been born a derelict. It cringed; Vonda's voice set it to vibrating as if all the strings of its miserable calico body had been plucked. It shied away from her outstretched hand, streaked for the safety of Mr. Ahlberg, crouched at his feet, still vibrating.

"Okay," he said grudgingly. "So you knew her. What of it?"

Gen would have pressed the point. But not Vonda. Her glance flitted around the room, taking in the flimsy furniture, the bare, dusty floor, the window shades that hung askew, the card table with its clutter of dirty dishes, ketchup bottle and peanut butter jar. "You men," she said, "and your bachelor's quarters ..." She paused, apparently electrified by the blown-up photograph which hung above the table. "Oh, so it's your motorcycle we saw parked down in front!" she cried. "Look, Gen! Did you ever see anything so dashing?"

Like a knight on a charger, Mr. Ahlberg sat astride his glittering vehicle, his hands resting lightly yet commandingly on the handle-bars, his head bent so as to hide the unsightly flapped lip. His helmet with the white chin strap fit like a glove, his belt was studded with gems, his boots were polished to a mellow sheen. He was flawless and magnificent.

"Beautiful," said Gen, and turning, caught his look of hungry pride.

"Otto Ahlberg, June 15, 1954." Vonda read off the inscription in the corner of the photograph. "Oh, Otto, what fun it must be, racing around on that wonderful machine!"

"It's all right," said Otto. He blushed. Then, as if suddenly angry, he switched off the overhead light. The room sank back into blurred dusk. "That was taken the day I bought it."

"You must have a wonderful job to afford it," said Vonda guilelessly. "It looks like it cost a fortune."

Otto snorted. "Yeah. I've got a wonderful job as a shipping clerk. You know how long it took me to save up? Three and a half years, that's how long. I even stopped eating lunches."

"And it was worth it!" cried Vonda. "Man does not live by bread alone! Why aren't you out with it, enjoying this nice long weekend?"

His face twisted into what Gen mistook at first for a kind of snarling laugh. Then he shook his head fiercely, and she saw the tears that were squeezing out of his eyes.

"There, dear." Ignoring his irritable gesture, Vonda reached up and smoothed the dark, over-long strands of his hair. "Stupid of me to ask. We're all upset about Marcella, too. It happened in Gen's house, you know, and—"

"My fault. My fault." The words wrenched their way out past the gulps that shook Otto from head to foot. He broke away from Vonda and, stumbling over to the couch, collapsed there with his face in his hands. "I shouldn't have let her go. I should've just sold it and given her the money ... I'd have done anything for her, anything ... She didn't need to borrow from those others, only she didn't tell me in time …"

The meaning of his strangled words did not register with Gen at first. Torn between pity and a cowardly urge to get out of there, somehow, anyhow, she could only stand still, an unwilling witness to Otto Ahlberg's disintegration. This was a far cry from what she had expected—the gossipy, kindly neighbor who would know, and tell, all about Marcella's private life. Yes, she had been naive enough to expect something cozy; she hadn't, until now, felt the impact of murder, which wasn't cozy at all.

"My fault. I shouldn't have let her go …"

Even Vonda was temporarily at a loss. She stood with her hands half lifted in distress, her eyes brimming with sympathetic tears. Vonda had done her share, anyway; it was time Gen rose to the occasion. She made herself go over and sit down beside Otto.

"You mean she wanted to borrow money from Alex?" she asked. "Is that why she went out there?"

Otto's head bobbed up and down. "To pay for the divorce. I could have gotten enough for the motorcycle, it's good as new, I'd have done anything for her. But no, she had to go out there, and they killed her. Dead. Dead …"

"A divorce? Why did she want a divorce, all at once?"

"Why? Why? So she could marry one of those others. Damn them, damn them … She didn't tell me because I wouldn't listen. I couldn't stand to hear about them, but I knew, and I would still have …"

"Haven't you any idea who it was she was going to marry? Because if you have, Otto, you must tell the police."

At once she sensed a change in him. He made a shuddering effort to swallow his sobs, and he rubbed his arm fiercely across his eyes. "Police!" He spat the word out. Even though his grief was under control now, Gen still had an impression of some strong, nameless emotion beating in him like a pulse. In the failing light she could see the film of sweat on his forehead under his tangled mop of hair. He looked like an anarchist, and he sounded like one too.

"Police! A bunch of filthy-minded— 'Who paid her rent? Who came to see her? Where did she go nights?' Making her out a tramp! What do they know about it?"

"But, Otto, she must have—"

"Yes, and you too!" He turned on her furiously. "You're not a friend of hers. I can tell. You didn't like her, you're against her, just like the police. I can tell."

The trouble was that it was true. Gen could only sit there in helpless silence, an impostor unmasked and ashamed of herself. This misguided, wild-eyed boy was, for the moment, impressive; a grotesque knight defending the honor of his lady's name.

"There, dear." Once more it was Vonda who saved the situation. "Gen only meant that you knew Marcella better than anyone else, and so you might know who killed her. She was such a quiet little thing, shy, so soft-spoken. Like a dove. I met her, you know, last summer when she did some work for Gen's husband, Mr. Blair. Mr. Theobald and I are one of Mr. Blair's employees, too, and—" Quaintly put, thought Gen. Yesterday she would have counted Mr. Theobald and Vonda, combined, as less than one average employee. Today, she found, her opinion had changed. It was true that Vonda hadn't any brains, in the ordinary sense of the word. Still ... That pleasant, prattling voice of hers was succeeding where Gen had failed; it was soothing Otto, making him relax in spite of himself. Marcella's cat leapt up and plastered itself across his knees, giving off its uneasy, garbled version of a purr as he stroked it. The other cats stared and prowled.

"But then maybe Marcella told you all this," Vonda was running on. "I remember her cat because once I brought some work over here to her. It's true we weren't close friends, the way you were. I expect you know Jimmy, don't you? Her husband?"

"That bastard," said Otto bitterly. "He never turned up except when he thought he could get some money out of her. They're looking for him, I saw it in the paper. They got that Walt Bowman. Well, I hope they get them all, all those others. Animals. Not fit for her to wipe her feet on. Damn them, damn them ..."

He was off again, and this time, Gen felt, he would never stop. For a moment all the street sounds faded away, with the last of the daylight. The screeching kids outside were silent, the rush of traffic hushed, there was nothing but Otto's voice, incoherent with hate and grief. He rocked back and forth on the sway-backed couch. After a while the sobs began again, choking off any attempt at words. But when Vonda tried to comfort him, he pulled away from her savagely.

"Get out ... Leave me alone ..."

Gen scuttled down the stairway ahead of Vonda. It seemed to her that the first words they had heard Otto say, that haunting question "Who wants Ahlberg?" still hung, unanswered, in the stale-smelling hall. Vonda was sniffling. "He loved her, poor boy—"

Yes, he loved her. Enough to kill her? wondered Gen. Could his mind have twisted murder into a kind of rescue—from those others, the animals, from life itself?

"I guess we're not such hot investigators," she said, trying to smile. "If he knows anything, he's not telling us or the police or anyone else ... What are you doing?"

"I'm going to leave him a note," said Vonda. "In his mailbox. Our names, and where we are. So if he changes his mind, or thinks of something, he'll know where to reach us. He might, when he's not so wrought up. He could come out on his motorcycle."

Right again, thought Gen. He might even have come out yesterday on his motorcycle— Oh, but someone would have seen him! Surely, surely.

"I think it's a lost cause, but go ahead." She paused. "Was he right about me? I mean—wouldn't I have liked Marcella?"

"Of course not, dear." They were out on the street now; Vonda was busy stowing pencil and scratch pad away in her canvas shopping bag, between the thermos and what appeared to be two hard-boiled (Gen hoped) eggs. "No more than you liked her cat. Natural enemies. You know, like rabbits and hawks."

FOURTEEN

Gen had to admit it. Exasperating as Vonda was, she could also be an oddly comfortable companion. On occasion, and this seemed to be one of the occasions. Her own explanations were elliptical; she expected no more from her fellow creatures. Gen didn't have to find a delicate way of signifying her intention, which was to get back to Alex tonight if she had to walk. Vonda took it for granted.

"Now let me see," she planned, as they turned off Leroy Street. "We can stop at your place to pick up your bag, and then go on to Dwight's. I told him I'd either call or be there by seven thirty ... Oh dear, I'm afraid we're not going to make it by then."

In view of the fact that it was now almost eight, Gen was inclined to agree. "Never mind," she said. "He's probably happy mulling over his Preface. Where is his apartment? I've never been there."

Way over west on Bethune, Vonda reported; one of those fabulously cheap cold-water flats, a whole floor, up above a shop where they made antiques. Dwight had had it for years, since before the war, and he had done wonders with it. Perfectly charming.

The exterior was far from charming, Gen thought when, a little while later, their cab driver put on the brakes and announced, a bit dubiously, that this ought to be it. It was a section of warehouses, deserted at this hour, with an occasional plumbers' supply or machine shop, each one closed up tight, each one discouraged-looking. Peering through the dust-dim window of the place where they made antiques, Gen saw a disemboweled chair, left there to die in public. A ferryboat tooted mournfully; there was a dank, old, river smell.

The contrast—after they had groped their way up two flights of creaking stairs and Dwight had opened the door to them—was startling. For once Vonda had been accurate: his place was perfectly charming. All mellow color and modern, airy furniture and subtle lights. Here, in this hideaway of his own, Dwight had at last shucked off the stale mementoes of his father's career that cluttered all the rest of his life. Gen was willing to bet that not so much as an ashtray had come from that paternal treasure-house out on the Island. Here were Dwight's books, the pictures he himself had chosen, he and he alone had painted the walls, polished the wide floor boards, and bought the striped curtains. It showed in his face, which flushed up proudly at Gen's admiring exclamations.

"You like it? I'd forgotten you hadn't seen my little snuggery before." (He would call it that, thought Gen.) "It's taken a lot of work, but to me it's been worth it. It's the only place I've ever fixed up, so for all I know I may have violated all the interior decorating rules ..."

He paused hopefully, and Gen obliged with the assurance that his taste was excellent. It happened to be true, but Gen suspected—much to her surprise—that she wouldn't have had the heart to say anything else. She had always checked Dwight off as too dull a dog to bother with, but tonight it struck her that there was something touching about his smile—so wistful, as if there were an eager-to-please little boy flitting around behind the pedantic façade. Maybe that was what Alex saw in him. Maybe that was Alex's special talent, a gift for seeing behind people's façades, a perceptiveness that gave life, for him, an extra dimension. While she herself went her impatient, shallow way, taking everybody at face value, all unaware of what she was missing.

Trust Dwight, though, to nip the first tender buds of her tolerance. He went all earnest and explicit. "I do hope, Gen, that you've decided to reconsider and come on back with us tonight. For Alex's sake. I don't know whether you realize how hard this has hit him or how much you mean to him."

She must have looked the way she felt, because he got flustered and stopped.

"I'd appreciate a ride out with you very much," she said in her haughtiest voice, "if it won't inconvenience you."

"Do show Gen the rest of your place!" cried Vonda. "The kitchen, such a dream with all those cupboards you built, and the bedroom, and all!"

"Yes, please do," echoed Gen, who was already a little ashamed of her own touchiness. All three of them exchanged anxious smiles and, thus encouraged, Dwight launched into a guided tour of the rest of his kingdom. In a moment or two he had forgotten his hurt feelings in a lovingly detailed recital of the problems the kitchen had presented, the inspiration that had come to him in the middle of the night about the color scheme for the study, the long-drawn-out search for the one right bedroom rug. Gen's mind wandered, but it didn't matter. All that was required of her was an occasional admiring murmur, which she could supply in all sincerity. Still, she thought as she stole a glance at her watch, they did have that long drive ahead of them. There must be some tactful way of cutting short this domestic saga. Her eye, scanning the bedroom for a likely change of subject, fell on the very thing (to borrow Vonda's phrase)—a woman's hat perched up on one corner of the dressing table mirror. It was one of those berets covered with iridescent "fish scale" sequins; against the delicate green wall it gleamed like mother-of-pearl.

Dwight was winding up for another involved episode, and Gen really didn't think she could face it. "Why, Dwight Abbott!" she exclaimed. "You old dog, you! What's a lady's hat doing in your bedroom?"

Cut off in mid-flight, Dwight looked for a moment completely blank. Then he blushed, so thoroughly that both Vonda and Gen laughed out loud. It was too funny to see that sober, scholarly face turning schoolboy pink and to hear the deliberate voice disintegrate into a stammer. And wasn't there, anyway, a tinge of pleasure in Dwight's confusion, a sort of secret pride in the idea of his own devilishness? Gen told herself there was, and then—as Dwight managed to get out a coherent sentence—felt her own face flaming with embarrassed remorse.

"It's— It's one of Clarice's," said Dwight. "My wife, you know. She sent all her trunks and things on from London by boat. They got here a couple of days after her plane crashed. I've always meant to sort them all out, but I don't know, I can't seem to bring myself to give her things away. They're all here." He turned to one of the closets and opened the door, revealing a row of dresses and tweedy suits, several years out of fashion now, and all stamped with that unmistakable British dowdiness.

There was a miserable silence. "I'm so sorry, Dwight," Gen said at last. "Me and my funny jokes."

"It's all right." The wistful smile flickered across his face; he stroked one of the dresses, a dejected brown crepe. "It's stupid of me, anyway. Nonsense to keep them. Maybe some time you'll help me sort them out, Gen. She was wearing this one the first time I ever met her."

"Of course I'll help. Any time you want me to."

"Eight years ago," said Dwight, staring off into space. "It doesn't seem possible ... I went through some of her letters while I was waiting for you. Stupid to keep those, too, I suppose, but I'm going to take them out to the Island tonight. There's more storage space out there. And that reminds me." He shut the closet door briskly. "We'd do well to get started. I assume you've had dinner?"

Gen hadn't, now that she thought of it, but the hot dog she had had at the beach was going to have to serve. Maybe she could wangle a hard-boiled egg from Vonda's shopping bag on the way out. The important thing was to get back to Alex fast: she had an illogical sense of urgency about it. Directly traceable, she decided, to that awful wife of Walt's. What if the woman had managed to talk her own husband out of jail and Alex in? It didn't seem possible. But Gen reminded herself that a week ago a murdered girl right in her own living room wouldn't have seemed possible, either.

At last Dwight got all the doors and windows locked to his satisfaction. At last he gathered up his briefcase (full of Preface, no doubt) and an ugly tin suitcase (full of Clarice's letters) and led the way down to the deserted street and the corner where he had parked his car. At last they were on their way.

Vonda curled up in the back seat and promptly went to sleep.

Gen sat in front with Dwight and jittered. He was, of course, what she called an over-precautious driver, but he vetoed, with polite firmness, her offer to take a turn at the wheel. He undoubtedly didn't trust her.

She realized, too, that he was doing his ponderous best to divert her with small talk. He discussed the weather exhaustively. As he had remarked to Brad this morning, they were fortunate indeed, and he only wished he could have spent the whole day at the beach, like Brad, instead of making this long drive for the papers he had overlooked yesterday. From these pleasantries he passed on to his Preface, outlining in minute detail what he hoped to accomplish with Mr. Lindsay's life during the next two weeks.

"What about your poems?" asked Gen. "Anything cooking in that department?" (She had noticed it before: she always lapsed into slang with Dwight.)

"Oh well," said Dwight. "I just dash those off, you know. They can't properly be classified as work." His tone was half-proud, half-deprecating. "I suppose they're amusing in their way, but after all, I'm a scholar. I want to produce something more solid, more authoritative, than a mere collection of frivolous verses."

"Personally I'd settle for the verses," said Gen. Particularly when the alternative was prose as leaden-footed as Dwight's, she added to herself. "It's no disgrace to be amusing. You've made yourself a name with them, so don't go sneering. Besides, they're not all that frivolous. There's a good deal of bite to them."

"You may be right. Clarice enjoyed them. Of course none of them had been published at that time. She had a remarkable sense of humor. I've always felt that both you and Alex would have found Clarice very congenial."

"I'm sure we would have," said Gen politely. She remembered that closet full of dowdy clothes, and felt a pang of pity for Clarice. How grim it would be, to have a remarkable sense of humor and a husband like Dwight. But then he might have been different, with Clarice. Love might have released in him the sprightly streak that never saw the light of day, except in the poems he called inconsequential.

"I still don't see why it had to happen," Dwight burst out, with sudden bitterness. "Why she had to die. She was all I ever had ... I've never made friends easily, you know, with either men or women. Clarice was the same way. Lonely. No family of her own anymore. She'd looked after her widowed mother ever since she grew up, but her mother had died several years before, so she had nobody left."

He paused, and then—before Gen's fumbling tongue could find any adequate words—went on, no longer bitterly, but in the hushed voice of one recalling vanished happiness.

"She had a job in a bookstore. I used to spend a good deal of time browsing around the bookshops in London, on the off-chance of picking up some Lindsay items, and one day, after I'd stopped in her particular shop several times, she and I struck up a conversation, and ..." For a moment, as he half-turned toward Gen, the street light—or something—lent a kind of radiance to his dull face. "It seemed so natural, the way we got to talking, I mean so natural and easy. We often remarked about it afterwards, because both of us had always had difficulty talking to strangers before, and yet there we were, chattering away as if we'd known each other for years. Why, believe it or not, I took the liberty of inviting her to dinner that very evening, and she accepted!"

"Good for you," said Gen, and she really meant it. She could see them in the murky light of a London bookshop—Clarice in her forlorn brown crepe; Dwight in his uniform (none of his clothes ever seemed to fit him right). Two lonesome creatures making the magical discovery that they could talk to each other.

"I don't suppose anything like that will ever happen to me again," said Dwight. "I'm not like Brad, with his— What are those flowers he always buys for his current favorite?"

"Lilies. That's what I call them, anyway. They have another name, something religious sounding, but it's simpler to say lilies. Whatever you call them, he must have spent a small fortune on them."

"That's what I mean. One romantic attachment after another. Though the present one, the redhead, seems to be of longer duration than usual. He was attempting a reconciliation with her this morning on the telephone. I couldn't help overhearing. Apparently she resents his interest in someone else." Dwight produced an abrupt chuckling sound. "She hung up on him."

Gen found herself remembering Vonda's odd little story about how Brad had called her, months ago, asking for Marcella's telephone number. He had said last night that the dead girl's name meant nothing to him. Could that have been a bit of glib pretense? Or a genuine slip of memory? There was also Vonda's airy inaccuracy to reckon with. Anyway, Gen decided, she wasn't going to mention it to Dwight. It would seem disloyal: that chuckle of his had been tinged with an unpleasant kind of relish.

"I sometimes wish I could be as casual as Brad," he was going on. "Or Walt. I suppose his affair with Marcella was just one of many."

"Probably," said Gen. "And I don't blame him, considering the kind of wife he has."

"You've met Walt's wife?"

"She paid me a call this afternoon. It's her opinion that Alex ought to be in jail instead of her precious Walt. Apparently she thinks Alex commissioned Vonda and Mr. Theobald to do the dirty work for him."

"What? She must be out of her mind!"

"I'm with you there. She doesn't need to think she's the only one that can investigate on her own, though. Vonda and I beat her to Leroy Street, anyway. We went over to see what we could find out from Marcella's neighbors."

"Now look here, Gen." Dwight's face lengthened with disapproval. "I know how unsolicited advice irritates you, but really I must protest. This is a police matter, and in my opinion it's very unwise of you to meddle in it. It might even be dangerous."

"Pooh. We didn't find out anything, anyway. All we did was talk to the boy she left her cat with. Tried to talk to him, rather. He didn't make much sense."

"Furthermore," Dwight went on, sternly refusing to be deterred from his course, "you might defeat your own purpose and do Alex's cause more harm than good. Assuming, that is, that there were any grounds for suspecting him, which I am glad to say there are not."

"Pooh," said Gen again, but with less assurance. "I don't see how."

"There's no predicting how such a thing might be interpreted. You might even be accused of having gone there to suppress or destroy evidence. I don't honestly think it will come to anything like that, but on the other hand it's not inconceivable. You just see if Alex doesn't agree with me."

"Maybe I won't tell him," said Gen. But of course she would; she was aching to tell Alex everything, to patch up, with the cement of impressions shared, the cracks in their private fortress. That was what marriage was, a fortress against the lonesome, prowling winds of life. It did not matter about the weak spots and makeshifts; every fortress had them. Hers—hers and Alex's—must not, must not be allowed to crumble.

Dwight, she discovered when she took a minute to listen, was now floundering in a bog of apology and self-reproach. He had said too much; it was none of his business; Gen had every right to be offended ...

"Oh, stop it!" she said impatiently. What a genius the man had for alienating your sympathies, just at the moment when he might have won them! "So I did something foolish and you told me so. Forget it, will you?" Dwight looked wounded, as usual when she snapped at him, and she decided to put them both out of their misery by pretending to take a nap.

Perhaps she really dozed off; when she opened her eyes again they were not more than a couple of miles from Rudy's and the dashboard clock showed midnight. Her heart set up a preliminary thumping.

"Do you think Alex might be at Rudy's?" she asked.

Dwight evidently welcomed this little overture as a sign that he was reinstated in her good graces. "We'll stop and see," he said. But there was no sign of the familiar, shabby car, and when Dwight returned from a quick look inside, it was with the report that according to Rudy, Alex had left an hour or more ago. "He's undoubtedly out at my house," explained Dwight. "There's apparently been some more excitement out here tonight. I didn't get all the details, but I gather that Marcella's husband is supposed to have emerged from hiding, stolen Rudy's Ford, and attacked some local girl."

"Another girl!" gasped Vonda, who had wakened and was now leaning forward in the back seat, rigid with alarm. "Was she strangled too? Where is he? Did they catch him?"

Dwight blinked apologetically. "I'm afraid I'm not clear on that. There seemed to be a number of conflicting reports, but—No, I think he's still at large."

"At large!" moaned Vonda. "That human beast, stalking the countryside—"

In spite of the crawling sensation along her own backbone, Gen had to laugh. "Oh now, Vonda, nobody's going to get you. Let's find Alex. He'll know what's been going on." The thumping of her heart had passed the preliminary stage; it was like a drum rattling out its urgent message:

Make haste. Hurry. Hurry back to Alex.

The message didn't get across to Dwight, though. He proceeded at the same, deliberate, excruciating pace, and there was nothing for Gen to do but clench her teeth and endure it.

And then, after all the build-up, all the prolonged ruffling of drums ... "I don't see the car anywhere," said Gen in a small voice as they turned up the driveway. "I guess he isn't here, either."

"Dearest!" cried Vonda, leaping out of the car almost before it stopped. "Are you all right? Oh, thank God you're safe!"

Mr. Theobald, who was sitting on the steps of the cottage, placidly eating a bowl of yoghurt, looked startled, in a dim way. He had not heard about tonight's developments. Why no, he didn't recall having seen Alex, either. He had spent a delightful day on the beach, enjoying the ozone, had just awakened from a long, refreshing nap.

"There are any number of other places to check," said Dwight encouragingly. "Alex may have been here while Mr. Theobald was asleep, and left a note up at the house."

A nice theory, but Gen didn't believe it. She felt suddenly exhausted, and as she followed Dwight up the broad steps it occurred to her that today had been, in a way, typical of her whole life with Alex—the crucial moments when they just missed each other (through nobody's fault); the precarious balance of her feelings lost by some trivial accident; the almost-understanding ...

In the shadows at the end of the verandah a movement—abruptly begun, abruptly ended—caught her eye. Her heart leaped up. "Alex?" she cried out.

The silence was extraordinary. Not a leaf rustled, not a breath was drawn anywhere in the spellbound world. How white the steps looked in the moonlight, white as bleached bones; and how starkly black the pool of shadow at the end of the verandah! Could she have imagined the movement, or whatever it was? No, Dwight had seen it too. He was standing with his hand on the door knob, as frozen as she.

"Marcella's husband," she whispered, and no doubt she would have gone into Vonda's human beast routine if Dwight had not hushed her with a gesture.

"Who's there? Come out of there, whoever you are!" His voice rang with a surprising amount of authority. One of his hands slid toward his jacket pocket; he took a step away from the door. There was the flicker of movement again, and a stealthy sound, feet shuffling over the porch floor.

Gen heard herself gabbling: "Dwight, you mustn't! He's desperate, he'll—"

"Shh!" He half-turned toward her. The moonlight lent to his face a luminous quality, like that of a small boy rapt in a game of cops and robbers. Dreams of glory, thought Gen ... He spoke in a clipped way, out of the side of his mouth. "I've got a gun, I can handle him. You run back to the cottage and call the police. I can hold him here till they come. Hurry!"

She turned obediently, plunged down the steps and across the grass to the cottage. "What are you doing here? What do you want?" she heard Our Hero rap out, before her racing feet carried her out of earshot.

FIFTEEN

"Hey there, Lil," said Ed Fuller, when at last her eyes stayed open. "Feeling better?" For the past ten minutes, ever since Doc had said it was all right for him to come in, he had been sitting here trying to decide what tack to take with her. It might be smart to get a little tough, just to teach her a lesson. Only she looked so distressed, with that puzzled frown on her face, and the way she kept trying to swallow, as if her throat was all parched inside, that he found he didn't have the heart.

"I won't die," she said in a scratchy whisper. "I don't *want* to die."

"Sure you don't." He patted her hand, rather shyly. She had put up a fight, all right; Ed liked spunk. "Don't you worry, you're not going to die. Like I told Floyd, he got there just in time."

"Floyd? He—did?"

"You bet he did. He figured there was something wrong, the way you sounded on the phone, so he hustled over. In the nick of time, just like in the movies."

She winced as if something were hurting her; her eyes got very big and dark, and tears welled up in them. For an uneasy moment Ed wondered if he ought to call for Doc, but then her mouth twisted over to one side, and he realized she was trying to smile. "Where is he?"

"He's gone with Mr. Blair to get your mother. Matter of fact, I expect they're back by now. Probably right outside in the waiting room. You can see them in a minute. But first, Lillian—" He made an official, throat-clearing sound—"Let's you and me have a little talk. I know your throat hurts, and I'll make it as easy for you as I can, but I expect you to tell me the truth, and the whole truth, Lillian. You've acted foolish somewhere along the line, and we both know it, so there's no use trying to cover it up now. I'm counting on you to help me. Okay?"

Her head bobbed up and down soberly. You wouldn't know she was the same kid, thought Ed, remembering the fresh way she had acted last night. And it wasn't just a matter of her hair being smoothed back from her forehead, or the lipstick being wiped off so you could see what her mouth was really like. She'd learned plenty since last night; he didn't need to worry about teaching her a lesson.

"Now," he said, "let's go back to yesterday. Did you know where Jimmy was last night, when I asked you about him? Were you lying to me about him? Holding anything back?"

Lillian shook her head no. Her eyes did not waver under his tough, searching scowl. Either she didn't scare easy, or she was telling the truth.

"All right. Now. When was the next time you saw him?"

"Last night, late. When I got home I found him hiding on the porch."

He had to lean forward to catch her hoarse whisper. That must make his scowl even more impressive. "Oh, you did. And in spite of the fact that you knew we were looking for him, you didn't notify us. Why not?"

"Because I—" She stared up at him, winking back her tears, defiantly pretending that they were not there. She even achieved a shaky, one-sided grin. "Figure it out for yourself," she croaked, with a flash of yesterday's pertness.

He felt his scowl slipping. No doubt about it, the kid had spunk. But spunk or not, it was his duty to see that she stopped impeding the law. He went on doggedly, prodding her, extracting from her, in nods and shakes of her head and rasping, broken phrases, the whole sorry story.

Ed sighed when it was finished. "Yep, Lil, you acted foolish," he pointed out dutifully—if rather absently. She wasn't the first to be taken in by Jimmy and his thick eyelashes. But she was likely to be the last, for some time to come. Jimmy was going to have a lot more to explain than just a handful of rubber checks, whether or not the pocket comb meant what it seemed to mean. It meant plenty to Jimmy, that was clear; enough to make him lose his head and try to choke Lil when it was mentioned. And it just so happened that the owner of that comb, whoever he was, had the same taste in hair tonic as Jimmy; Ed had found a bottle of the stuff among the few belongings left in Jimmy's room. The hair tonic, a couple of dirty shirts, and a stack of pulp magazines—that was all his landlady had to show for her trusting nature.

So there was no need to ask Lil to identify the comb. She'd had about enough questions. Looked like she'd been put through a wringer, thought Ed, and again he patted her hand shyly.

Her eyelids fluttered open. "Have you—caught him?" she asked, and he could see that she didn't know herself whether she wanted the answer to be yes or no.

It was no. "We've got Rudy's car, though. He didn't go very far in it—I guess he figured we'd be sure to nab him, if he didn't ditch it. So he drove it into some bushes a few miles down the highway and left it there. He could have hitched a ride, afterwards, or he could be hiding out again someplace close. Either way, we'll get him before the night's over. Now look, Lil, there's one other thing I want to get straight because I got a feeling it's going to come up, sooner or later. Yesterday afternoon at Rudy's, when Jimmy was buying you those drinks. Did he stay right there at the bar, from the time he came in with Walt to the time all the excitement busted loose? Or did he leave for a while—say half an hour or so—and then come back?"

She was all set to shake her head no. But then she changed her mind. Once more she went through the painful process of swallowing. "He—I don't know."

"What do you mean you don't know? You were right there, you'd notice if he was gone for any length of time—Or weren't you? Do you mean you went somewhere yourself?"

That was what she meant, it turned out. She had managed to tear herself away from Jimmy because she had promised to pick up her Mom's sinus prescription in town, and get her summer coat from the cleaner. A couple of the kids—she named them—had driven her in and back. How long had she been away from Rudy's? Thirty, maybe forty minutes.

She didn't ask why he wanted to know. She knew without asking—he could tell, from the miserable look in her eye—that Jimmy could have gone on a little expedition of his own, during her absence, and that she was like as not pulling his alibi out from under him. Walt's wife had dug up his drinking companion of yesterday, to swear he had never left Rudy's. But it looked as if Jimmy wasn't going to be able to do likewise. It also looked as if he was going to be sadly in need of the alibi he didn't have.

Off on the wrong foot, thought Ed moodily; I shouldn't have been so hasty about clapping Walt in jail. I should have paid more attention to what Alex said. Look at it one way, and I've been taken in by Jimmy too, just like Lil.

He wondered if it would make her feel better, to tell her that. He'd like to cheer her up somehow, before he left; there ought to be some way to tell her that what seemed like the end of the world hardly ever was, that the reason they put erasers on the end of pencils was because people were all the time making mistakes …

But before he had a chance to spout a word of these philosophical gems, there was a tap on the door and Floyd stuck his head in. "Excuse me, Mr. Fuller, but you're wanted on the telephone—" His eyes shifted to Lillian, and he was at once struck dumb.

"Okay." Ed hoisted himself up wearily. "Come on in, Floyd. Lil and I have had our little talk, so it's—" He let his voice trail away. No use talking when there was nobody listening. Which Floyd certainly wasn't.

Neither was Lillian. The way she was looking at Floyd you'd think she had never seen him before in her life. Maybe she never had. She didn't hear Ed when he said, "Thanks, Lil." As he padded out the door and down the hall, Ed smiled to himself, a little sheepishly. Well, anyway, he hadn't made a fool of himself trying to tell Lil about life.

The phone was at one end of the waiting room, where Lillian's mother sat on the edge of her chair, ready to jump out of her skin, poor woman. She had come just as she was, from her brother's diner, and she still had a grease-spattered towel tucked around her waist. Alex, who had driven Floyd out to fetch her, was sitting beside her, wearing the self-conscious expression of a man doing his best to supply moral support. At Ed's approach, she floundered to her feet; as far as he could figure out, she was trying to ask him about four questions at once. He patted her shoulder encouragingly.

"Everything okay, Mrs. Schroeder. Lil gave me the whole story, so I've got a good many things straightened out that I didn't have before. She's going to be all right. Go on in and see for yourself. Doc said you could, as soon as I was through talking to her."

He couldn't tell whether any of this registered with her or not. "It just *gets* me," she began tensely, "to think—" But she lost track of whatever it was, and stared at him in a beseeching way, as if she were begging him to finish the sentence for her. "Thanks," she stammered, before she scuttled off down the hall.

Alex smiled wanly. "She's got me climbing the walls too. Longest half hour I ever put in. I thought you never were going to get through ... There's the phone over there."

Ed stepped into the little stall and picked up the receiver. "Hello?" he said.

The voice that answered was at once brisk and breathless, as if its owner had made up her mind to keep cool, whether the sky happened to be falling or not. "Mr. Fuller, will you come at once, please. I think it's Marcella's husband. He's got him on the verandah."

"Good. Who's got him? Where do I come?"

"Oh." There was a blank moment. "Why, out here. I mean, Dwight Abbott's house. On the verandah."

"Be right out. Right away. Who's this calling?" But she had already hung up. Not that it mattered too much, Ed thought as he hustled out of the stall. He could almost place the voice; not quite. His eye fell on Alex, still dawdling in the waiting room as if he didn't know what to do with himself.

"By God," exclaimed Ed. "That was your wife, Alex!" And of course it was; the voice had had that funny little snap of impatience to it that was one of the first things you noticed about Alex's wife. "Claims they've got Jimmy out at—"

"Who? Where? *Gen?*" Alex made a kind of wild-eyed lunge toward the phone booth.

"She ain't in there," said Ed drily. "Out at Dwight Abbott's. Come on if you're coming."

SIXTEEN

Alex and the jalopy outdid themselves; they stayed right on Ed's tail all the way out to Dwight's, slewing around corners on two wheels, rattling in every bone and bolt. It was a triumph of mind over matter, an achievement that left very little energy for other mental activities.

Gen out here, Gen in danger, she couldn't have made the phone call to Ed if she was being strangled, yes but that was how many minutes ago, anything can happen in how many minutes, Dwight's got a gun ...

The shot split through the night just as they made the final turn, into the driveway. Alex's hands jerked on the wheel, and the jalopy all but scraped one of the stone pillars and reeled to a stop halfway up the driveway, a little past the cottage, which was ablaze with lights.

Ed Fuller was already out of his car. He looked like a startled bear, ponderously poised for flight. Somebody screamed. Somebody else— farther away, on the other side of the big house—yelled. Alex got out of the jalopy and hollered, too. "Gen! Are you all right? Gen!"

He caught only a glimpse of her at the cottage door before Vonda, gabbling that they would all be killed, pulled her back. Then there was a thud of running feet and Dwight charged into view—a disheveled, exhilarated figure, brandishing his gun. "This way!" he panted, gesturing toward the back of the big house. "He made a break for it and headed for the beach!"

Ed Fuller took off in a surprising burst of speed, and Alex, without really planning it, found himself drawn along in his wake. His feet seemed to fly over the ground. He caught up with Ed at the gate in the wall, and as they plunged down the path to the beach after Dwight's shadowy figure, he felt for all the world like a boy again, whisked back in time to one of those stirring childhood games. The mysterious rustlings of night and wind, the low, excited voices, the prickle of urgency along his spine, his pounding heart—it was Run Sheep Run, down to the last thrilling detail.

He had to remind himself that Dwight's gun was real, that his other comrade—the wheezing one—was a duly appointed officer of the law, and that they were chasing a bona fide criminal.

"He hasn't got a gun," Dwight was whispering. They had paused with one accord near the last scrubby clump of bayberry bushes, where the path stopped being a path and fell abruptly away to sand and sea. Moonlight spilled in a shimmering band across the water; it was calm tonight, swelling in lazy, powerful lunges at the shore. As far as Alex could see, there was no other movement, no human fugitive scurrying for cover in all this majesty. "I'll never forgive myself for permitting him to—"

"What did he do? Jump you?"

"I kept listening for your car—he was hiding on the verandah when Gen and I came up the steps, you know—and I knew it would be only a matter of minutes till you got there. So I kept listening. I couldn't have turned my head for more than the merest fraction of an instant, and he was past me in a flash. My glasses were knocked off when he shoved me against the pillar—fortunately they weren't broken—but by the time I had recovered them and collected myself—"

"Where was he when you fired at him?"

"Scrambling over tile wall. I didn't take the time to aim properly, all I wanted to do was scare him into—"

"Never mind." Ed hitched up his pants. "He got away. Let's try and find him. I'll stay up here and cover the bushes. You fellows take the beach. Not much chance we'll catch him, but if anybody does, holler. And sit on him till the rest of us get there."

Not much chance was right, thought Alex as he and Dwight set off in opposite directions along the beach. Theoretically, an empty stretch of sand didn't seem to offer much cover. But at night like this, with the moon casting weird, sharp shadows everywhere, all Jimmy needed to do was lie low. Any dune or hollow would serve as a hiding place, if he just had sense enough not to move. Time after time Alex was fooled by pieces of driftwood; even strands of seaweed took on grotesquely enlarged shapes in the tricky light. The upper reaches of the beach were still choppy with footprints. As far as Alex could see, the sand nearer the water's edge was trackless. But this meant nothing: Jimmy might have missed the path as well as the gate through the wall. He could have hit the beach at any point, and with his few minutes' start his footprints would have been washed away by now. He might even be scared enough to seek a hiding place in the water itself. In which case he was by this time a thoroughly chilled specimen. Alex himself was none too warm. He hunched his shoulders in his thin jacket and hurried on, trying to look everywhere at once.

The very improbability of the project added to his feeling that it was a game, that the danger lurking all around him was a delicious, Run Sheep Run kind of danger. And it heightened the flavor of adventure to imagine how astonished everyone (including Alex) would be if by some freakish chance he should actually stumble on to Jimmy. There was always that chance. After all, Dwight had fallen over him on his own front porch.

Yes, and had promptly let him get away. Typical of Dwight. Of Alex too? Certainly not; he was no acrobatic marvel, but he was better coordinated than Dwight. It would be a different story if Jimmy were armed. But he obviously was not: subject to panic as he had shown himself all along, he would undoubtedly have shot or knifed both Dwight and Gen on the porch if he had had the wherewithal. Alex suddenly shivered. For a minute, as he remembered Lillian huddled on the floor, the marks on her neck, and Floyd's bloody nose, it didn't seem like a game at all. Jimmy had done plenty of damage with no weapon other than his two bare hands. If you wanted to dwell on things, there was also Marcella and Horace Pankey ...

Supposing at this very moment Jimmy was creeping up behind him, raising above his head a stone or a chunk of driftwood like the one Alex carried in his own hand? Supposing that sound—that one—was the whisper of a foot pushing into the sand, poising itself for the crashing blow? Alex's scalp crawled. He whirled—and there was nothing there. Only the darkness, only the slick band of moonlight on the water, only the eternal plunge and slap of the waves.

But the first fine edge of his excitement was lost; what had been adventure began to turn into drudgery. He became aware of the sand in his shoes, and of the tiredness in the backs of his legs. His hands and face felt sticky with salt and the sea dampness. He wondered how long this performance was supposed to last. Dwight was probably stubborn enough to keep on prowling all night long. But Ed was a man of common sense; he would call them back when he figured it was no use. Alex decided that he personally wasn't proud; he would give it another ten minutes and then start back, whether Ed signaled or not.

It was a remarkably long ten minutes. He plodded on, conscientiously alert for any shadow that moved, but his heart was no longer in it. He felt chilly and tired and lonesome for Gen. Well, she would be waiting for him. Bless her capricious heart, she had come back, and tonight he would behave like himself instead of like Walt. It wasn't going to be easy, telling her about his little skirmish with Marcella, but he wouldn't botch things up the way he had last night. And Gen wanted to understand, in a way she must already understand, or she would never have come back. Ah, bless her.

He took another look at his watch (one more minute to go, but the hell with it), turned around, and started back at a considerably brisker pace. He zigzagged between the higher slope, where the going was tougher but where duty told him he ought to look because he had skimped on it before, and the edge of the water, where the sand was firmer under foot. He paused when he got close to the breakwater. He had paid no particular attention to it the first time around, but now it occurred to him that a man who didn't mind getting his feet wet might find those stout piles an excellent hiding place. They gleamed dark and wet in the moonlight, with the waves churning into suds around them. A very chilly scene.

Who was going to know the difference, if he skipped the breakwater and went on home to Gen? At once his conscience set up a great yammer about he would know the difference, and if a thing was worth doing at all it was worth doing well. Oh, all *right*, he thought, and he took off his shoes and rolled up his trousers.

It was just exactly as chilly as it looked. He advanced warily at first, trying to hold back against the cold, frothing suck of the water with its load of sharp shell fragments and slimy rags of seaweed. After a couple of minutes his feet got too numb to notice. It cheered him a little to think that, if Jimmy was here, he was damned uncomfortable. He made a methodical tour of the whole works; with his loud-mouthed conscience nagging him every step of the way, he peered behind each pile. It was all bewildering shadows down here, and the constant hiss of the water seemed to numb his ears, as the coldness of it did his feet. At the last pile he slipped and barely recovered his balance. His temper he did not recover. He did not even try. He just clung there and cursed Jimmy, his conscience, and the Atlantic Ocean.

Something splashed behind him. Too late, he turned and caught a glimpse of a large, looming shape. It came at him. He dodged clumsily, and as he went under, flat on his face, he heard an unearthly yell.

After a chaotic spell of floundering, he felt himself being dragged out of the water by his heels. People were yelling back and forth: "Hey, there! You got him?" The answer came from right above him: "Hurry up! I've got him!"

Alex recognized the two voices. After a couple of minutes they were both right above him. He let himself be turned over. In a deafening silence he sat up and spat out a quart or so of salt, sand, and seaweed.

"Alex?" wailed Dwight. He didn't even have the decency to hide his disappointment. "But I could have sworn it was Jimmy, the way you were sneaking around down there! I turned back, you see, and then it struck me that you might not have thought to search around the breakwater, so I ..." Before the force of Alex's glare, his voice dwindled away.

Ed Fuller was tactful enough not to say anything, except, "Come on, let's go back to Dwight's place and get you dried out." But Alex could tell, from the way he rubbed his hand over his mouth, that it was all he could do to keep from laughing his damn fool head off. Thought it was funny, did he? Alex brushed aside their helping hands and stood up, drenched to the bone, shuddering with cold and rage.

Once more Dwight broke out in blundering speech. "We must have double-tracked on each other. It never occurred to me that you were anywhere near. I wouldn't have had it happen for the world, Alex, I'll never forgive myself—"

"So don't," said Alex.

Except for the chattering of his teeth, there was no more conversation on the way back to Dwight's house.

Still, he would have recovered his sense of humor, he was already feeling a little ashamed of himself when they toiled up the steps in a weary, bedraggled procession ...

The door flew open, and there stood Gen and Brad. They looked like two happy people with a secret. He had his arm around her waist, in one of those famous, careless poses of his. Her eyes were dancing with excitement. So were Brad's. He took one look at the three of them—especially Alex—and guffawed.

"What in the hell happened to you?"

Ed Fuller had given in and was grinning openly too. "We've been combing the beach for Jimmy, and Alex—well, somehow or other, Alex got ducked."

"Why, you poor creature," said Gen absentmindedly. She did not move out of the circle of Brad's arm. "Hurry up, Brad, tell them. Because I'm busting to, and I shouldn't, it's your story. So hurry up and tell them."

"Tell them nothing. Let's show them. Step this way, gentlemen, and no jostling, please." With a dramatic flourish, Brad turned and led the way into the study. There, propped on the sofa, was a young man in a checked sports jacket and slacks, neatly trussed up with clothesline. He glowered at them out of shallow, light-colored eyes. He did not say anything on account of the handkerchief that was stuffed in his mouth.

"May I present Mr. Jimmy Ewing." Brad was practically licking the cream off his whiskers. "I'm sure you must feel you already know him, you've heard so much about him."

"Well, I'll be—" said Ed Fuller. He hitched up his pants. After a minute he closed his mouth.

As for Dwight, he started about six questions and abandoned them all. The result was a wordless spluttering. Very gratifying to Brad, no doubt. Alex set his teeth, shivered, and dripped.

"We gagged him because he kept talking dirty," said Gen. "He says he didn't kill anybody, and he never got a break in his life, and Lillian double-crossed him, that's why he choked her."

"But how did you catch him? I mean, where did you find him?" At last Dwight got a couple of his questions into words.

"They also serve who only stand and wait," said Brad, with what struck Alex as an insufferably pious air of modesty. "There was nothing to it, really. I didn't even know what had been going on until I got back half an hour or so ago, and Gen told me you boys were out ransacking the beach for Jimmy. So we decided to come up here to the big house and have a drink while we waited for you to get your man—"

(Oh you bet, thought Alex bitterly. It wouldn't ever occur to Brad to lend a hand in any such tedious, uncomfortable—and unsuccessful—project as searching a beach at night.)

"Well, he must have backtracked as soon as he saw you were heading for the beach. I don't know what his idea was, coming back to the house, I don't suppose he knows, either, but anyway, that's what he did. Dwight had left the keys in the door, and when Gen and I stepped into the hall …"

"Brad was wonderful," Gen broke in. "He really was. I hadn't even caught on that anything was wrong, and he whizzed past me, and bam, there was Jimmy laid out on the floor, and it was all over."

Brad treated everybody to a big smile, and Gen to a pat on her head. "Just luck. You were no slouch yourself, sweetie. You didn't lose your head and scream, and you not only thought of the clothesline, you found it."

"Great little team, aren't you?" croaked Alex. They all looked at him, and it seemed to him that even Jimmy's sullen stare was tinged with scorn and amusement. God knows Dwight—with his hair on end, his glasses crooked, his seersucker trousers wet to the knees, and his generally crestfallen air—cut a sorry enough figure. But Alex himself must be twice as ludicrous, and he was making it worse, and he could not stop. "If you'll excuse me now, while you relive your moments of glory, I'd like to wring myself out."

"Do, darling. You're actually making puddles," said Gen. She made a tentative gesture toward him, but he stalked past her, and as the door closed behind him he heard her chattering away again: "At first we were going to take him into town to jail, but then Brad said what was wrong with keeping him here till you got back, we could relax and have a drink while we waited—"

Trust Brad to find the slick, easy way. Success, as usual, handed to him on a silver platter, without his having to lift a finger; while Alex and Dwight were bumbling around, tripping over each other's feet like a pair of fifth-rate comedians ... Trust Brad, too, never to miss an opportunity for relaxing and having a drink. Especially with Gen. And that was another thing: Alex had seen the martini pitcher out there on the desk, and the two glasses. It was clear enough that Gen wasn't wasting time on superstitious nonsense like not drinking martinis with anybody except Alex. Of course Brad was wonderful, he really was. Brad said this. Brad said that.

SEVENTEEN

When he returned to the study, rubbed dry, wrapped in a bathrobe, but still sore in spirit, he found that Ed Fuller had departed with his prisoner. Gen and Brad were sipping their martinis, Dwight a brandy; it was a scene of cozy animation.

"They'll let Walt out of jail now, won't they?" Gen was saying. "Because Jimmy must have—Alex darling, sit down and have a drink. What can I fix you? A martini?"

"I'll have a brandy, thanks," he said stiffly, ignoring her invitation to sit beside her (and Brad) on the sofa, and choosing instead a chair near Dwight. He was aware of all their eyes on him—Dwight's anxious, Brad's bright and knowing, Gen's wavering between tenderness and exasperation. If Brad had not been there ...

But he was very much there. "I had a feeling all along that Walt wasn't guilty." (Oh, sure, Alex commented silently; you're the expert, you caught Jimmy.) "Even before Jimmy lost his head and started charging around the countryside. Somehow, Walt just didn't strike me as the type."

"What do you mean, the type?" Alex swallowed his brandy at a gulp; it sent a fierce glow through his middle. "What makes you think Jimmy's the type?"

"Well, why not?" asked Brad, with an irritatingly reasonable air. "He seems to be kind of a perennial juvenile delinquent, from what I saw of him. And from what Ed Fuller says about him, too. Bad checks. Petty blackmail. None too bright. I'd say he was pretty much tailor-made for the job. He admitted he saw Marcella night before last, and that he knew she was coming out here. She was broke, he said, and wanted to ask you for a loan. My hunch is that he put her up to it because *he* needed the money, and then he cadged a ride out here with Walt because he didn't quite trust her to carry through."

"But she *did* come out here to borrow money from Alex!" cried Gen. "For herself, not for Jimmy. Otto Ahlberg told us—"

Alex stared at her. "Who?"

"Otto Ahlberg. He's taking care of her cat, and she told him so. She wanted the money to get a divorce. So she could marry somebody else."

They were all staring at her now, in a silence that seemed to tingle through the room like a charge of electricity. Dwight leaned forward slightly, blinking in nervous concentration. Brad did not move at all; his glass was halfway to his mouth, and there was a queer, fixed smile on his face.

This is important, thought Alex. But for the moment he seemed unable to go on from there.

Gen had no such inhibitions. "Don't you see?" she rushed on impatiently. "That makes it point all the more to Jimmy. He didn't want the divorce, for some reason or other, and she did, and that's what they quarreled about."

"No," murmured Alex. "You've got it wrong ..."

But Brad interrupted. "I think Gen's hit it. Jimmy wouldn't want a divorce, because Marcella with a husband to protect her wouldn't be such an easy mark for his little tricks. It all figures, Alex. If you'd seen him, if you'd talked to him the way Gen and I did—"

"Okay." Alex gulped down his second brandy and felt the inner glow grow fiercer. "I didn't catch him, and you did. I don't know what type he is. But I do know—I mean I did know Marcella. A little better, I think, than you know Jimmy."

"I'm sure you did," said Gen crisply. "Though didn't you say you remembered her, Brad? And you too, Dwight? I think it's very interesting, the way everybody knew Marcella. Everybody but me."

"It's only a matter of circumstance," Dwight began. But whatever bungling dissertation he might have embarked on was cut short by Brad.

"We're all aware of the fact, Alex, that you knew the poor girl and knew her well, but I can't see what that's—"

"It's got plenty to do with it!" Alex had not intended to shout. Startled, he lowered his voice to a vehement whisper. "I don't know who murdered Marcella, but I know why they did it, and if you think it's a simple case of juvenile delinquency you're out of your mind."

Brad met Alex's glare with an imperturbable grin. "Flattery will get you nowhere, but thanks anyway. Why *did* they murder Marcella?"

"That's what I can't understand," said Dwight. "She seemed like the last person on earth anybody would want to harm."

"But that's just it! After you got to know her—" Alex caught the danger signal, the yellow gleam in Gen's eyes. But it was too late to stop now. Somehow he had been maneuvered (by Brad? by his own childishness?) into telling all of them what he had meant to tell only Gen. He swallowed desperately. "You started out feeling sorry for Marcella because somebody else was mistreating her, and you wound up doing the same thing yourself. There was something about her that—that turned you into a first-class heel. She did it to Walt. She did it to me. We got away from her in time. But somebody else didn't. She'd been trying all her life, and she finally made it. She turned somebody into a murderer."

There was a moment's silence. Dwight shifted in his chair, as if to get a better grip on this unfamiliar idea; Gen stared at her hands, which were clenched in her lap; Brad stubbed out his cigarette thoughtfully. He spoke first.

"Quite a fancy theory you've got there. I still don't see why it lets Jimmy out. Matter of fact, why doesn't it get him in even deeper? He never got away from her entirely. He walked out on her, sure, but he kept coming back. I don't see why it lets him out at all ..."

"Because he's a sub-Walt, that's why. I mean, he sounds like one ..."

"A *what?*" Dwight goggled at him. So did everybody else, including Alex himself. The word had sprung out, as if by spontaneous combustion. What's more, it was accurate.

"A sub-Walt." As he went on talking, he began to feel a clairvoyant kind of excitement. His mind seemed to work freely and precisely, crystallizing thoughts that until now had been no more than a muddy welter. "It's like this. The men that got mixed up with Marcella sort themselves out on different levels. The sub-Walts are the ones on the lowest step. Plenty of them, I suppose. To them Marcella would be an easy lay and nothing more, and so they'd be able to shuck her off without a qualm, as soon as they got bored with her—as even they would do. Without a qualm," he repeated. "Lucky kids, the sub-Walts."

He got up and began pacing the length of the rug, his hands dug deep in his bathrobe pockets. "We come next to the second level. The Walts. Lugs, but not pure lugs. Oh sure, she was an easy lay to them, too. But they also felt sorry for her. Lust plus pity. That's the mischievous element, that plus-pity." He paused, pleased with the phrase. And it was true, too. In his inarticulate, thickish way, Walt must have suffered much the same pangs as Alex when he broke loose from Marcella. Certainly he had had dim glimmers of what was really dangerous about her—that strange, corrupting power of hers to make sadists out of ordinarily decent men.

Brad leaned forward. He looked absorbed, for once in his life serious. "That brings us to the Alexes?"

"That's right." Alex tried not to look at Gen. And failed. Her head was pulled up high. There was nothing to do but go on. "There's not very much difference, really, between the—Alexes and the Walts. I caught on to what was happening to me quicker than Walt did. Let's say I've got a sharper sense of danger, a little more insight. And a bigger vocabulary. I'm more articulate than Walt."

"Yes indeed," said Gen. "A silver-tongued orator."

Neither Brad nor Dwight seemed to have heard her. "Let's see now," said Dwight. He settled his glasses on his nose; it was a scholar's fussy gesture, automatic with him. "We have the sub-Walt, as you put it; the Walt, the Alex. Who's on the next step?"

"I don't know, because I don't know who she wanted to marry. But whoever he is, he gets my vote. Why wasn't *he* paying for the divorce? I'll tell you why. Because he didn't want to marry her, he wanted to get away from her, like everybody else. Only he couldn't. He was stuck with her, he found out there was only one way left of escaping from her, and ..."

"This is ridiculous!" Gen jumped up. Her eyes were blazing. "Perfectly ridiculous! All this gobbledygook about different levels and who's on the next step! For Pete's sake, Jimmy's practically confessed! Why make a big production out of a perfectly plain, commonplace, obvious thing? So she and Jimmy had a fight, and he followed her out here and lost his head and killed her. But oh my no, we can't have anything that simple." Her scornful gaze fastened on Alex. "We've got to go into a psychoanalytical tailspin. We've got to dress the whole sordid business up so that we won't seem quite so miserable and cheap. Well, maybe Brad and Dwight will buy your highfalutin theory, but I won't. I'm sorry, but I ..."

She was close to tears, and Alex knew it. If they had been alone, he might have managed to make amends for all the damage to her pride. But there was the little matter of his pride, too; her words had stung like nettles (it was the truth, perhaps, that hurt?). And they were by no means alone. His eye fell on Brad, who was watching Gen with interest and admiration, and the humiliation of tonight's fiasco poured through him all over again.

"Nobody's asking you to buy anything." He bit off each separate word. "Have it your own way. Jimmy's a black-hearted murderer, and Brad's a great big conquering hero because he caught him when the rest of us couldn't. All I was trying to do was explain—"

"You might at least have had the decency to do your explaining in private—"

"There's just one thing I'd like to ask you." Through the haze of his fury, he was dimly aware that Dwight and Brad were jostling each other, both trying to get out the door at once. "If I'm such a cheap, miserable specimen, why the hell did you come back out here tonight?"

"I haven't the faintest idea," said Gen. "Will you excuse me now? I'm going to bed."

EIGHTEEN

It couldn't be said that Gen woke up. She had never really been asleep. Too miserable even for tears, she had lain listening—at first to the subdued voices, the footsteps on the stairs, as Dwight got Alex and Brad put away in second-floor bedrooms; later to the genteel, melancholy voice of the study clock chiming out the hours. She had watched the darkness change to the wan light of not-quite-night, not-quite-morning; had heard the first bird calls; had huddled for a few minutes on the window seat, peering out at another fine day.

Now, at the sound of someone tiptoeing downstairs and into the kitchen, she scuttled back into bed and drew the covers up to her chin. If it should happen to be Alex, and if he should happen to be planning to bring her a cup of coffee as a peace offering, he would find her sleeping the sleep of the just and the untroubled.

Whoever it was in the kitchen was making coffee, all right; and they were being very quiet. She couldn't be sure whether she heard whispers or not. It might be two of them—or even all three. There was a muffled clink of dishes, a thud as the icebox opened and shut. But no one tapped at her door. And after a while whoever it was went out the back door and drove off somewhere in one of the cars. The clock chimed nine times.

She decided that it must have been Dwight and Brad, tactfully clearing out. And that Alex must be waiting for some sign of life from her. And that it would be a nice gesture on her part to get up and make the coffee. Besides, she was hungry.

There were two dirty cups in the kitchen sink, in confirmation of her theory. But, though she clattered and thumped for all she was worth,

Alex did not appear.

All right, then. Let him sulk. It was nothing to her.

She carried her breakfast tray out to the terrace and settled down in one of the old-fashioned wicker chairs. It was pleasant here in the dappled shade, with only the birds and a couple of frisky squirrels for company. Very pleasant. Very restful, not to have to talk to anyone or be talked at. There was nothing like solitude to restore one's soul.

Hers needed restoring, and it was all Alex's fault. He had been a poor sport last night from start to finish—sore at poor old Dwight for ducking him by mistake; sore at Brad for doing what he would like to have done himself. With complete disregard for her feelings he had broadcast his affair with Marcella; and he had capped the whole performance by losing his temper, right along with Gen. I'm the one with a grievance, she thought, and if he wants to go on being silly and harboring imaginary grudges ...

Suppose he did just that? Supposing, this time, he didn't get over being mad at her?

She stared at the tray in her lap. A large, lean ant was marching purposefully across it. Well, as far as Gen was concerned, it was all his. Even the coffee seemed to stick in her throat. As she bent to put the tray down on the grass, she became aware of a sudden, jangling headache, and the sound of the motorcycle, coming at this moment, was like glass splintering inside her skull. She sprang up, as if to defend herself.

It looked, indeed, as if Otto Ahlberg might be planning to run her down with his glittering machine. He braked the thing to a dramatic stop just short of the terrace and remained astride it for a moment, surveying Gen, the house, and the grounds with a lordly air. Finally he pushed up his goggles and dismounted.

"Where's the other one?" he asked. "I wanted to see the other one."

Oh sure. Nobody in the world wanted to see Gen.

"I haven't seen Vonda this morning," she said. "She's staying at the cottage. We can go down and see if she's there."

He took a flat, newspaper-wrapped package from the sidecar, and together they walked down the driveway toward the cottage. So he had brought something for Vonda. At once Gen's mind swarmed with the bizarre possibilities of a gift from Otto Ahlberg. She did not dare look at him; surely her face would betray the curiosity that devoured her. And she did not trust her own tongue, even with an innocent question like "Did you have a nice trip out?" Once loosened, it might all by itself spill out the other questions trembling on its tip. Which would send Otto leaping for cover like a frightened deer. He was leery enough of Gen, as it was.

So nobody said anything on the way to the cottage. It was empty, just as Gen had expected; the uproar of Otto's arrival would certainly have brought Vonda running if she had been within earshot.

"She's probably gone to the beach," said Gen. "Would you like to wait for her? Or the beach isn't far, if you'd rather go look for her."

Otto shifted his package from one hand to the other. He shot a wary, speculative glance at Gen, and she mustered up a smile that was meant to indicate her complete lack of curiosity and at the same time her willingness to be helpful.

Apparently she pulled it off. "The thing is—" began Otto, and then broke off, as if alarmed by his own rashness. He glared at her. "I got to thinking, and I thought I'd bring her this. Seemed like she really liked Marcella, and—and, well, I've got the cat. She ought to have something too. Only fair."

"I see," said Gen. She allowed herself no more than a glance at the package. Might it be photographs? Pretty thick for that. Phonograph records? What possible mementoes might a girl like Marcella leave behind?

"It's her scrapbook." Otto blurted it out fiercely. "Her cat scrapbook. She started it a long time ago. Kept adding to it. She asked me to keep it for her, when she left the cat with me. Almost as if she knew—"

He left it at that. The unfinished sentence, broken still further by Otto's mutilated speech, brought to Gen's mind a poignant picture of Marcella entrusting her two treasures—a derelict cat and a scrapbook—to this wild-eyed boy before she set off on her last journey.

She had an impulse to put her hand over Otto's, make some comforting gesture, the way Vonda had done last night. But no, she wasn't like Vonda, she couldn't do it without self-consciousness. It would only heighten Otto's resentment of her, that illogical resentment that had sprung up—out of what? Had some special intuition conveyed to him Gen's true feeling about Marcella? Or was it more general, some plus or minus in Gen's personality? Whatever the reason, Gen knew that she was never going to be forgiven for having seen him go to pieces last night. Vonda had seen too, but Vonda was different ...

She said (and sure enough, it sounded self-conscious), "I think it's very generous of you, Otto. Vonda will be very pleased to have something to remember her by."

"I could leave it here for her, I guess," said Otto tentatively.

"Of course, if you like. The door's open, you can put it inside. I'll tell her about it when she gets back. Why don't you take a run down to the beach, as long as you're so close? She'll be sorry if she misses you, and you'll probably find her down there."

"Well, maybe—" He considered. He wavered. He seemed to search Gen's face for signs of trickery. Then he stepped inside the cottage and, with a deep, solemn sigh, set the package down on the table.

Gen, trotting along beside him on the way back to the terrace, decided that there would be something frivolous about inviting him to have a cup of coffee with her. Unless he volunteered a social pleasantry of his own first.

He didn't. He didn't speak at all until he had settled himself on his motorcycle and adjusted his goggles. His farewell statement was as withering as his greeting had been.

"It's not for you," he reminded Gen. "It's for the other one." He did something violent to the machine. It went into a shuddering, sputtering fit. Away he roared.

Gen watched until he was out of sight. It was absurd to feel hurt because he was suspicious of her. Especially since his doubts were fully justified: she had every intention of whipping right back to the cottage and going through Marcella's treasure with a fine-tooth comb. Sentiment or no sentiment. A cat scrapbook didn't seem a likely source of clues, but you never knew.

She whirled, at the sound of a window being flung up in the big house behind her.

"What the hell was all that racket?"

The top half of Alex was framed in one of the second-floor windows. He looked terrible. Puffy-eyed, shirtless, hair standing on end, and cross as two sticks.

"Otto Ahlberg," she called back.

"*What?*"

Yesterday gaped between them, an unbridged chasm, and to try to explain at long distance like this, practically at the top of her lungs, made it all impossibly complicated. Besides, if Alex was still mad at her—and he didn't look very friendly—what was the use? She just stood there tongue-tied, goggling up at him like Juliet in reverse.

And before she could get organized, Dwight and Brad drove up. Brad bounced out of the car, picked her up, and smacked her heartily. She could feel Alex's evil eye upon them. Perhaps Brad could too: he waved toward the second-floor window and called out an offensively cheery greeting. "Hey there, Slug-abed! Didn't expect you to come to till after noon. Come on, let's all go to the beach. How about it?"

"You and Gen go ahead." Dwight, who was already moseying up the steps, pawing through a handful of letters and papers as he went, smiled vaguely at everybody. "I'll join you later. I like to take care of the mail first thing. Get it out of the way. Morning, Alex. How are you?"

"Vile," croaked Alex. "Thank you."

"What's eating on *him?*" asked Brad, all mock innocence. "Come on, Gen. Get your stuff and let's go. No more days like this till next summer."

"Wait. I mean—" She sent one more despairing cry across the chasm, which seemed to be getting wider, more unbridgeable, by the minute. "Alex! Want some coffee?"

But it was too late. "Thanks, I'll make it myself. You and Brad run along to the beach." The window slammed shut. The rumpled, scowling face was gone.

NINETEEN

She hesitated, half disposed to wait for Alex in the hope of patching things up. But no: Brad had that amused, knowing glint in his eye; even Dwight took it for granted that she was going to the beach. It would be too humiliating to surrender to Alex's childishness so publicly. She stuck out her chin and went inside to change.

She forgot about Marcella's scrapbook until, dressed in her bathing suit and carrying her beach bag, she started down the steps with Brad. The sight of the cottage reminded her. "Wait a minute," she said, and, feeling like a sneak thief, she darted down to the cottage, inside, and out again with Otto's package.

"What you got?" asked Brad. "Lord, you look guilty! Guilty but good," he added, and his eyes made an appreciative tour of all of her.

It was the first kind word to come Gen's way this morning. "I think you're pretty, too," she said. "I have here a document that may prove to be of vital importance ..." She tucked the scrapbook into her beach bag, and as they set off, arm in arm, she gave a sprightly account of Otto's visit.

Brad was more amused than electrified by possible clues in the scrapbook. "But don't worry, I'm with you," he assured her. "I can't resist snooping, either."

The beach was dotted here and there with sun bathers, stretched out like human sacrifices on the sand. A group of weedy adolescents plunged in for the first swim of the day, shrieking at each other. And at the water's edge smaller children squatted in happy absorption with their pails and shovels while their mothers—equally contented with their chatting or knitting or reading—kept an easy-going eye on them. Under the pure, wide sky the water sparkled and swelled and whipped itself into exuberant foam.

There was no sign of Vonda and Mr. Theobald or of Otto; perhaps they were in the mood for solitude this morning too.

"Let's find a secluded spot," said Gen. "This way. There's hardly ever anybody down here."

They trudged on past the breakwater, past the last sun bather, to a stretch of beach populated only by themselves and a little troop of sandpipers. There they settled down, and Gen (it was ridiculous, the way her hands trembled) drew out Otto's package and unfolded the newspaper wrapping.

The scrapbook was of imitation leather cardboard, tied at one side with imitation gilt cord. It was dog-eared, and in one place the cover had been repaired with scotch tape.

"Getting cold feet?" Brad was grinning at her. "Go on. Open it."

Gen could not have said what she had expected to find in Marcella's scrapbook. Not astounding revelations, of course. But something— something more provocative than this vapid procession of magazine and rotogravure clippings. There were pictures of cats with bonnets tied on their heads, cats perched in the tops of boots (complete with the inevitable caption), cats peering at themselves in mirrors, baskets full of beribboned kittens. There were newspaper stories about heroic cats who had notified their owners that the house was on fire, thus saving everybody's life; about determined cats who, lost or stolen, had traveled incredible distances to get home again; about adventurous cats who got themselves stuck in pipes or other unlikely places and had to be rescued by the fire department. There were sentimental poems. Gen turned the pages with a growing sense of disappointment.

"Well, anyway, Vonda will love it," she said. "Not that I mean to belittle Vonda. She may not be a mental giant, but she's got a kind of intuition about people ... She said I wouldn't have liked Marcella at all."

"You would have despised her," said Brad. He was propped up on one elbow, lazily watching Gen's progress through the scrapbook. "I mean," he added quickly, "I only saw the girl once or twice, but I've got an intuition about people too. She was a poor stray cat of a person. You didn't really want her around, and yet you couldn't get her out of your mind. Something haunting about her."

"So I gather. Judging from the effect she had on Alex—"

"Oh, stop it, Gen! You're being tiresome. Any man—even a husband-type man like Alex—is apt to get involved in these affairs once in a while. They don't mean a thing."

"But that's just the point!" she cried. "That's the indignity of it! I could understand, if it hadn't been just a poor little stray cat of a girl, if it had been somebody—"

"In a pig's eye," said Brad affably. "You'd still call it an indignity, if Alex had taken up with the brainiest, most ravishing woman in the world. You're just plain possessive."

"Oh sure." Gen gave him a bitter look. "It's all my fault for being possessive. I should just smile and say, 'Well, well, boys will be boys.' I don't notice your redhead behaving like that. Silly girl, she's like me, she resents these little affairs that don't mean a thing. It would serve you right if she resented them enough to check you off for good and all." That shot had hit home; the look on Brad's face told her so. She discovered that she was feeling much better, and swept on energetically.

"Or if Alex had *told* me about it. But no. Not a peep out of him all this time, a whole year, and then last night he has to air the whole business in front of you and Dwight, instead of waiting till we were by ourselves—"

"Oh well, let's face it, last night Alex just wasn't at the top of his form."

"He certainly wasn't," agreed Gen. "You say I'm being tiresome and possessive. Ha! What about him?"

"This about him." Brad lay back again, smiling; his teeth flashed white in his tanned face. "Strange as it seems, the guy's devoted to you. Also, he's aware of the fact that I'm an extraordinarily attractive fellow. Most ladies of discernment find me irresistible. Why shouldn't you? Very sound reasoning. If I were Alex, I'd probably be jealous of you and me too."

"All right, then." Gen laid aside the scrapbook and hugged her knees. It was always such fun, arguing with Brad. "If you're so much in sympathy with Alex, it seems to me the decent thing to do would be to remove your irresistible self. Or at least to stop needling him. You do, you know. At every opportunity."

"Certainly I do. It's for his own good. It develops his character," said Brad smugly. "Like Latin. Besides, I never do the decent thing. And I like it here. I couldn't possibly tear myself away from all the excitement."

"I give up. You're just a brat," said Gen. In a way, it was his very brattishness that made Brad entertaining. But she was never quite sure, with him, where the slick veneer ended and where the real stuff began. He was genuinely fond of Alex, no doubt about it: without his support—both financial and moral—Alex's dream of a bookshop would never have come true. And yet he had no qualms about heckling Alex deliberately and cruelly, reducing him to a rubble of childishness. For the first time it occurred to Gen as a serious possibility that he might have no qualms, either, about seducing Alex's wife … It was an upsetting idea. The expression on Brad's face didn't help any: he looked as if he were observing—and enjoying—every thought that passed through her head. To cover up her embarrassment, she turned back to the scrapbook.

Even so, she could still feel Brad's eyes on her as she flipped the pages.

The snapshot seemed to jump out of the page at her, a bit of black-and-white reality dropped in between a kitten-on-the-keys color print and another poem (not a clipping, for once; Marcella had apparently copied this one by hand onto what looked like a sheet of ledger paper). The snapshot was an amateur job, and yet quite clear, a picture of a girl sitting on some steps (Leroy Street, perhaps?) holding a cat up against her cheek. Gen was sure she recognized that abjectly dangling animal. The girl was slim and limp-looking; her feet were drawn back under her in a self-effacing way. Across her lap lay a spray of chaste white flowers.

"It's Marcella, isn't it?" began Gen. "Marcella and her—" She paused, aware that Brad's eyes had shifted from her to the scrapbook page. He was not listening to her. His attitude, the angle of his head, made her think of a pointing dog. He was that motionless, that intent. When at last he realized that she was watching him he smiled, rather mechanically. "I knew it," he said. "I knew we'd get a kitten on the keys before we were through." And he reached over and shut the book, as if he could bear no more.

But Gen's eyes had been a fraction of a minute quicker. They flicked back to the scrapbook, imprinting—precise as the camera that had recorded the snapshot originally—the image in Gen's mind of girl and cat, and identifying for her the spray of white flowers in Marcella's lap.

Her tongue felt numb; it was a minute before she could even begin stammering out her question. "Brad, that picture, I mean the snapshot …"

"The snapshot?" Brad's voice seemed just a shade too artless. "Oh, the snapshot. Yes, sweetie, that was Marcella. She was rather pretty, you know, if you bothered to look at her twice. You were apt not to notice it at first—Hey!" He interrupted his own chatter to peer back across the beach. "Here comes Dwight." He waved and called to the figure plodding toward them. Gen waved too, rather abstractedly.

When she turned back to Brad, she found him busy with the scrapbook, rewrapping it in the newspaper and slipping it back into her beach bag. He winked at her. "Do me a favor, will you, and don't mention this little masterpiece to Dwight. You know how he is. He'd insist on examining each and every one of those damn cute cats, and I honestly don't think I can take a repeat performance."

"Well," said Gen. "All right."

But he didn't leave it at that. "Be a good girl and keep your mouth shut, darling, and I'll stop needling Alex. I promise. Is it a bargain?"

"All right," said Gen again. "It's a bargain."

TWENTY

"Where's Alex?" asked Brad. "Still sulking in his tent?"

"I wouldn't say that." Dwight dropped down beside them and smiled warily in Gen's direction. In spite of his deep tan, in spite of his bathing trunks, he still looked scholarly and sedentary. The drooping shoulders remained, the general effect of sagginess, the fussy mannerisms. "I believe he was taking a shower when I left."

If only Alex had come, thought Gen, she could have found a chance to tell him about the snapshot. Alex had a sense of proportion about such things; he didn't let himself get carried away. That was what she herself was doing. Her imagination was simply running away with her. She swallowed nervously. Even supposing that Vonda's story was true, that Brad had actually called, months ago, asking for Marcella's telephone number—that didn't mean he had ever used it. And even supposing that he had used it, that he had known Marcella better than he was saying, that he had bought lilies for her (there was no mistaking those distinctive white flowers in the snapshot)—even all that wasn't necessarily of any great significance. He had bought lilies for many another girl in the past. No doubt he would buy them for many another girl in the future—whether the redhead liked it or not. Naturally he would prefer her not to know; it was obvious that the redhead was more than just a passing fancy, like the others.

If only Alex were here to say all this! It wasn't the same, for Gen to say it to herself.

With an over-animated air, she turned to Dwight. "So what's the news from the village this morning? Brad hasn't told me anything. Has Jimmy confessed?"

Not yet, reported Dwight. "Though he's admitted—not only that he went to see Marcella the night before she came out here—but that her trip was his idea. He persuaded her to ask Alex for a loan, while he himself got what he could from Walt. The combined proceeds were to cover his bad checks."

"But she'd already tried to call Alex," said Gen. "I mean, before Jimmy went to see her. Don't you remember? That's how she knew we were coming out. Vonda told her."

"Probably doesn't mean much," said Brad. Gen noticed that his manner, like her own, was a little livelier than normal. "He may have been trying before to talk her into his little deal. Anyway, even after she'd agreed, he didn't quite trust her. Figured she might turn chicken at the last minute and not even ask Alex for a loan, let alone put the screws on him. That's why he got Walt to drive him out to your place."

"Incidentally, Walt has been released," put in Dwight. An unexpected twinkle appeared in his eyes. Dim, but still a twinkle. "After the pleasant visit you had with his wife yesterday afternoon, Gen, I know you'll be overjoyed to hear it. The consensus seems to be, now, that—just as Walt maintains—Marcella was not at your house when he and Jimmy first went out there, that only Horace Pankey was there, that Jimmy slipped out of the bar later on and, using Walt's car, returned to your house and killed Marcella after a quarrel, and then Horace because he was a witness."

"But wouldn't somebody at Rudy's see him leave? How about Lillian, that little girl he was plying with liquor? She would have noticed—"

"Ah, but there's a gap!" cried Brad. "There's a lovely convenient gap while Lillian went into town to do some errands, and while nobody else kept track of Jimmy. She was gone for at least half an hour—time enough for Jimmy's skullduggery."

"He'd have to hurry," said Gen.

"So he'd have to hurry. Do murderers usually dawdle? And furthermore—" Brad brought it out triumphantly—"he admits it's his comb that they found beside Horace. How are you going to sidestep that one?"

"How does Jimmy sidestep it? He must have some explanation—"

"Oh yes. Count on Jimmy for an explanation. He claims that while he was dodging the police Thursday night he stumbled over Horace's body down at the bay. Yes, he recognized Horace, and yes, he realized this might have something to do with Marcella's death. All the more reason, from Jimmy's point of view, for him to stay out of sight. That's when he sneaked back to Lillian's house and talked her into hiding him. He noticed he'd lost his pocket comb somewhere, but didn't think anything of it until he found out, from Lillian, where he'd lost it. Then he went berserk and tried to choke Lillian, but so help him he didn't kill anybody. Somebody's framing him. That's his story, but he won't stick to it. They'll break him down, they've got too much on him."

"I suppose so." Gen paused, thinking. "There's still the business about Marcella's wanting a divorce. Did Jimmy know about that? No? So as far as he knew she was out here to raise money for him. She didn't tell him that she was going to try to borrow from Alex for herself. Then I wonder what they quarreled about?"

There was a moment of silence. Then Brad laughed lightly. "What goes on here? A mental sea change since last night? If you don't watch out, Gen, you'll be selling yourself on Alex's theory."

"Don't be ridiculous," said Gen—but rather absentmindedly. "You were the one who was swallowing it whole. You and Dwight both."

"Oh, well." Brad lit a cigarette and flipped the match away. "Alex is a great analyzer. Always has been. And you can usually count on him to come up with some angle that's different, that you'd never have thought of yourself, that sounds good—especially after a drink or two. It's a hell of a lot of fun, but—you put your finger on it last night, Gen—what happens is that Alex gets carried away and overcomplicates. He can't stand anything to be simple. If it's not subtle to begin with, by God, it will be by the time he gets through with it."

It was exactly the way Gen had felt last night. And she had not hesitated to say so. But now she felt herself stiffening in perverse defense of what she herself had so recently attacked. It was as if Brad were trespassing on her own private hunting grounds. Alex was fair game to her, then, but to no one else? All right, if you wanted to put it that way ...

"Alex's theory has nothing to do with it," she said crisply. "I would simply like to know what—if anything—Jimmy and Marcella quarreled about. And who Marcella wanted to marry."

Dwight cleared his throat apologetically. "May I make one point here. We have only Otto's word that she wanted to marry someone else. Are you sure he's—ah—dependable?"

"I believe him," said Gen. "She must have been involved with somebody else because somebody's been paying her rent. Not Jimmy. Not Walt. Somebody who's managed to stay in the background all this time. I bet he's the one she wanted to marry, and I bet—"

She didn't finish it out loud, but it was there in her mind. She bet, like Alex, that this somebody else had murdered Marcella. A secretive man. And an eligible one ... Like Brad? He was eligible. Well, so was Dwight. But only technically; Clarice's hold on him was as strong as if she were still alive. That closetful of her clothes in Dwight's apartment proved it, and the letters from her that he could not bring himself to throw away. Something tugged obscurely, briefly, at Gen's memory—something she meant to do or say? It slipped away from her.

"What did I tell you?" Brad was saying. "You've talked yourself into it. You've decided Alex's theory is great. Ain't she the loyal little woman, Dwight?"

Dwight looked from one of them to the other, blinking, clearly wary—as always—of both Gen's temper and Brad's jokes. "Loyal? Oh, I see. Alex's theory. It had its intriguing aspects, but in view of all the evidence against Jimmy ... I suppose the truth of the matter is that murder is seldom as involved—one might almost say as interesting—as Alex made it sound last night. Usually it's just a sordid, simple affair."

"My point exactly," agreed Brad. "Like Jimmy killing Marcella. Very sordid. Very simple."

"Oversimple." Gen pulled on her bathing cap and stood up. It wasn't any use trying to convince them, but she couldn't resist one last stubborn shot. "It could also be that Jimmy's telling the plain, simple truth for once in his life. Anybody going swimming besides me?"

Dwight sprang up at once; swimming was the one pastime he allowed himself. But Brad made a great show of shuddering at the mere thought of physical exertion and stretched himself out once more. He looked lazy as a cat in the sun. Only Gen caught the flick of his eyes toward her beach bag, where he had put the scrapbook to keep it out of Dwight's sight.

A wave of uneasiness rose inside her, but she thrust aside the temptation to tell Dwight about the scrapbook. No. She still could not bring herself to take her own suspicions of Brad seriously enough for that. Telling Alex would be different. Or she might simply ask Brad himself. Why not? After all, she ought to give him a chance to explain before she went tattling to outsiders. The idea cheered and relieved her.

She and Dwight had a fine time in the water. He was a strong, though rather clumsy, swimmer; and the ocean seemed to wash away all his inhibitions and pedantry, turning him into an eager, even rather engaging, boy. It was a transformation Gen had observed before, but it never failed to surprise her.

Tingling and gasping, they splashed out of the waves and back up the beach to Brad. And when, after rubbing himself dry, Dwight settled his glasses back on his nose, he was all tiresome scholar again. The fun-loving boy had vanished, had never been. He folded his towel precisely over his arm and picked up his sandals.

"You're not rushing off mad, are you?" asked Brad.

Oh no, no indeed, Dwight assured him earnestly. But there was his schedule; it never paid, he had found, to disrupt his schedule. An hour at the beach, no more, no less. ("Portal to portal, I assume?" inquired Brad. "And what about rainy days?") An hour of recreational reading or music, in case of inclement weather, explained Dwight. An hour of writing before lunch. Unless—as was the case today—a session of library research was indicated. The nearest adequate library was twenty-five miles away; it was a stroke of luck to have one that close.

"I should be back at the house no later than three. See you then," he said as he set off.

"Dwight and his schedule." Half-smiling, Brad shook his head after the stoop-shouldered, diminishing figure. "What a shame he doesn't find a nice nubile librarian and live happily ever after."

"Not Dwight," said Gen. (She was aware of a preliminary inner tightening: in a minute now she would ask Brad about the snapshot. In just a minute.) Meanwhile, she heard herself chattering on. "He's too devoted to Clarice's memory to even notice another girl. Do you know, he still has all her things, even her clothes. He brought a tin suitcase full of her letters out here with him. Can't bear to throw them away."

Brad's only answer was a kind of drowsy hum. He was lying back with one arm thrown across his eyes, and his head cushioned on Gen's beach bag. He's going to sleep, she thought nervously; I must blurt it out before he goes to sleep.

And still she hesitated, fumbling her questions over in her mind, anxiously studying Brad's face—rather serious, even a little sad in repose—and his rangy, clever-looking hands. Could anyone with a guilty conscience be so trustingly relaxed, so unaware that he was being watched? Gen herself began to feel guilty, like a spy. It would be easier, anyway, not to be looking at him when she asked him about Marcella. It would be easier yet not to ask him at all, to wait and see what Alex thought ...

What a spineless creature she was, shilly-shallying like this, while time sifted away! The longer she waited the more ridiculous the whole thing seemed. She stretched out on her beach towel, stared up at the sky, and took a deep breath. "Brad," she said, "Brad, there's something I want to ask you."

No answer. She waited, repeated his name, waited again. Still no answer. Another glance at Brad, and she saw he was asleep. His chest rose and fell regularly; his mouth was a little open.

So there was her suspect. Unavailable for questioning owing to the fact that he had fallen into a deep and dreamless sleep.

The absurdity of it flooded her with relief. She closed her eyes, luxuriating in the sun's warmth and her own tiredness. Later, she thought; it would all wait—Brad and her questions, Alex, Marcella and the scrapbook, poor stray cat of a girl, Jimmy and the very simple, very sordid ... That was what Dwight had said, and Alex had said sub-Walt, and Brad had said poor stray cat ...

She woke by degrees, letting herself drift blissfully with the tide of drowsiness. A fleet of white, fat-sailed clouds floated across the sky; the shrill voices of children reached her, mellowed by distance; the ocean plunged and slapped. She turned her head: no sign of Brad. He might be in the water, or he might have gotten hungry and gone back to Dwight's for lunch. She could use a sandwich herself. After a while she sat up, hugging her knees and yawning. As far as she could see, there were no swimmers in this section of the beach. She fumbled in her beach robe pocket for her watch, and found that she had slept for at least an hour and a half. No wonder she felt so good, so full of well-being. And of course Brad had gone in search of lunch: here was his note, weighed down with pebbles.

Smiling to herself, she began collecting her belongings. She felt, for the moment, all sweetness and light: how amusing Brad was, what a quaint creature Dwight, and Alex, her darling Alex ... She foresaw a tender reconciliation (his early morning crossness would have worn off by now; it always did) over a good hearty lunch.

Towel, robe, sandals. Sun tan oil, bathing cap and cigarettes stowed away in her beach bag. All present and accounted for? She paused, with a dim feeling that something was missing.

And something certainly was.

Marcella's scrapbook was no longer in her beach bag, nor anywhere else in sight.

TWENTY-ONE

More exasperated than alarmed, she made another search—though of course a scrapbook that size wasn't going to blow away or get itself overlooked, particularly when she had sat here and watched Brad tuck it into her beach bag. Brad ...

At once—in defense against the inner chill that crept through her—her mind set up a bustle of simple, comfortable explanation. Brad must have decided to return the scrapbook to Vonda's cottage. So that, if by any chance Otto should turn up again, it would be where it was supposed to be. You see? Nothing sinister about it at all.

She set off, not quite at a trot, for Dwight's house. The terrace—where she had somehow expected to find Alex, waiting for her—was deserted, the wicker chairs empty, her breakfast tray where she had left it on the grass. No one was in sight anywhere. She hurried down the driveway; she was a little out of breath when she pushed open the cottage door and looked inside.

The scrapbook was not there.

All right. So the scrapbook was not where she had expected to find it. Alex was not on the terrace where she had expected to find him, either. No need to get into a sweat about the one or the other. Like as not Vonda had come back and found the scrapbook, and like as not Alex was inside the big house, peacefully sleeping off his hangover and bad humor. She went back up the driveway and climbed the steps to the verandah.

She might call out his name, she thought as she stepped inside the cool, shadowy hall. Ordinarily she would have. It was so still, though. The spell of silence seemed to engulf her. She felt it closing around her trackless and thick as fog. Her sandaled feet produced no more than a whisper of sound on the hall floor, and the study door opened under her hand noiselessly.

There was no one in the study but the ladylike clock, tirelessly clicking its tongue over the same old bit of gossip. Aware of a rising uneasiness, Gen put her beach bag down and crossed to the desk.

Well, there it was. The scrapbook. Right there between the photograph of Clarice and the majestic onyx inkstand. A gulp of relief escaped Gen; a paltry, unseemly sound that startled her and then was swallowed whole by the silence.

This was ridiculous, this feeling of uneasiness or whatever it was. Big old houses often had a hushed atmosphere, especially—where was Alex, where was Brad?—when they were empty. It was broad daylight outside, and here was the scrapbook (not that it had any particular significance, anyway) where Brad must have left it. She flipped the pages with quite a flourish, to prove to herself that she was not intimidated, everything was all right now.

Only one of the pages had been torn out. Most of it, that is: a ragged quarter-page remained to show where someone had ripped out whatever it was that interested him. It hadn't been the picture of the kitten on the keys; half of that was left. Gen's breath caught. The snapshot of Marcella had been here, between the kitten picture and the hand-written poem.

She sat down slowly. The leather chair felt clammy against her bare legs, and she shivered.

It had to be Brad. No one else knew about the scrapbook—thanks to Brad himself. How insistent he had been about not showing it to Dwight! He must have thought that Gen had not noticed the snapshot or that, if she had, he could talk her suspicions away with some glib story. But he couldn't count on Dwight to be so gullible. And he hadn't taken any further chances, even with a simpleton like Gen.

That was how important the snapshot was to Brad. He could not afford to have himself linked with Marcella, not by the slenderest of threads, because that thread might lead to others, not so slender, and because Marcella had been murdered. Gen closed her eyes, as if to shut out what her mind was seeing. No use. It was the only explanation. And it explained everything, right down to the way Brad had dismissed Alex's theory as so much high-flown nonsense, and brushed aside Gen's questions about the man Marcella had been planning to marry. He had a very good reason for wanting the murder to be checked off as a sordid, simple, Jimmy-level affair; a very good reason for wanting that mysterious prospective husband kept out of sight.

No, thought Gen, no. It was too dark, too sinister, too impossible. This was *Brad* she was thinking about—Alex's best friend, the one who had not been lost in the shuffle of college, or the war or the hectic advertising agency days. They might seem like an ill-assorted pair—Alex so easy-going, Brad so slick and ambitious—but their friendship had survived in spite of everything, even the occasional flashes of mutual jealousy. Almost like one of the family—Brad the carefree, amusing brat, who flirted with her and flattered her and once in a while, when she needed it, stuck a therapeutic pin in her ego.

And who also (Gen remembered that not quite comfortable moment at the beach) was prepared to make as much love to his best friend's wife as the traffic would bear. "I never do the decent thing ..."

It was so still in here. No sound but the gossiping clock and Gen's own quick breathing. If only Alex were here! If only there were some friendly, comforting soul she could turn to!

There was the photograph of poor dead Clarice, and that was all. The eyes in the picture met Gen's with the strained expression of a homely, desperately shy woman who has been told to smile into the camera. Frozen in self-consciousness, Clarice peered out from under the curls on her forehead, with the bold strokes of her message to Dwight—"From your devoted, your one and only wife Clarice"—slanting across her lace collar.

She probably meant well, but she was no help.

Gen put her head down on the desk. Nobody was any help against this swarm of suspicions, this alarm that threatened to engulf her. She tried to recall Brad's face as it had always seemed to her—alert, humorous, affectionately mocking—but it turned into a mask that had slipped awry, revealing not only the new, ugly face beneath, but its own falseness.

Her throat ached. The silence hung all about her, waiting to close in on her sobs and smother them.

"Why, Gen! Gen, what's the matter?"

The voice was right here in the study. She jerked her head up and saw Dwight coming toward her, concern written all over his dull face. "I'm sorry, I didn't mean to frighten you—Why, you've been crying! Is something wrong?"

"Nothing. I mean, I'm just upset—I didn't hear you, your car or anything."

"That's because I walked up from the gate. I left the car at the garage to have the horn fixed, and Rudy gave me a lift home." He came closer, eyeing her—Gen, of all people, crying!—anxiously but warily. "Where is everybody?"

"I don't know. Nobody seems to be here." She could not control her wobbling voice. She felt a tear crawling down her cheek.

"Now this won't do, my dear." Dwight came closer and administered a cautious, kindly pat. "We can't have you upset. Here. One thing we can do is get some light in here." He went over and adjusted the blinds, and bars of benign sunshine streamed in. "This room can be extremely gloomy at times. The effect of so much heavy furniture, I expect. Now. Why don't you tell me what's bothering you?"

"I just—" began Gen. She felt herself melting under the influence of the friendly soul she had longed for. Dwight was such a good-hearted sort, after all; he might not scintillate, but you knew where you stood with him, you didn't have to be on the lookout for tricks. "It's Brad," she blurted out. "I just don't understand the way he's acting about the scrapbook ..."

"Scrapbook?" echoed Dwight. He pulled up a chair, fussed with his glasses, and turned the pages of Marcella's scrapbook with scholarly care, while he listened.

In her relief at pouring it all out, Gen talked fast and breathlessly. She finished on a note of tentative hope. "Maybe I'm just overwrought. Like those hysterical women that imagine somebody's following them, or making passes at them in the subway."

But Dwight's face remained grave. "You've never struck me as the hysterical type. No. I agree with you. It's odd, very odd. And yet— Are you positive about those flowers in the snapshot, Gen? You couldn't have made a mistake?"

"I'm positive," said Gen. "They're distinctive, you know. Not shaped like any other flowers. You couldn't miss them, even in a snapshot."

"But even so—" Dwight rubbed his fingers thoughtfully over the torn page. "Even so, I don't understand how it could be just the flowers alone. It's true they point to him, but after all, Brad has no monopoly on them. Anybody who wanted to could buy them."

"That's right," said Gen. She felt a spurt of hope. "Anyway, supposing he did buy lilies for Marcella, what's so damning about that?"

"Exactly. And yet there must be something damning somewhere, to make Brad react like this. Something besides the flowers, I mean. Try to think, Gen. Try to recall the whole picture, the whole page. Maybe that will bring it back to you."

Obediently, Gen closed her eyes and thought. Her mind's eye reproduced for her the snapshot—girl, cat, flowers—against the black scrapbook page. "The kitten on the keys picture was up here," she said, "and down at the bottom, on the right-hand side, a poem ..."

"A poem?"

"Most of the other poems were clipped from newspapers or magazines, but Marcella had copied this one onto a sheet of ledger paper. I noticed the handwriting because it wasn't weak and straggly, the way you'd expect Marcella's writing to be. 'Cat-O- Nine-Lives,' that was the name of it. The snapshot was in the middle of the page. I'm trying to remember—" She screwed her eyes tighter shut, while Dwight waited in silence. Was she overlooking some incriminating detail in the snapshot—a house number, perhaps, that might place Marcella, not on her own steps but in front of Brad's apartment house? He lived downtown, too, in one of those little old houses with steps in front. It was no use: her memory produced only the girl, the cat, the flowers against a vague background of steps. Undistinguished, anonymous steps.

She opened her eyes and shook her head. "I'm sorry," she said, and once more the enormity of the whole thing swept over her. "I can't believe it," she whispered. "I simply can't believe that Brad—"

"You know Brad better than I do," said Dwight, a little stiffly, and she was reminded of how often and often he had been subjected to Brad's deft needling. "Oh, we've always been on excellent terms, but I've never felt that I understood him very well." He paused a moment. His fingers began an urgent drumming on the desk; he studied Gen's face sternly, as if he considered her responsible for Brad's whereabouts. "We've got to get to the bottom of this. Where *is* Brad? Is his car here? And how about Alex? Where's he?"

"I don't know where anybody is. I didn't notice whose car was here when I came back. If anybody's here they're keeping mighty quiet about it." Gen spoke tartly; as usual, Dwight was managing to annoy her. These prosecuting attorney tactics of his—just as ridiculous as the Our Hero act he had put on last night, when they had found Jimmy lurking on the verandah.

He was striding purposefully over to the window. "We can soon check on the cars. If they're both here, that means nobody can be very far—"

From somewhere above came a sound, a muffled, wrenching thud. It stopped Dwight in his tracks. It yanked Gen to her feet.

"Upstairs," she whispered. "Somebody's upstairs." They stared at each other a moment, waiting. Another thump. Gen opened her mouth to yell for Alex.

"SSh!" hissed Dwight, and all at once he had one hand over her mouth and the other on her wrist. "I mean—I'm sorry, Gen, but don't you see, we've got to figure this out first. We've got to proceed with caution till we find out what we're up against."

"Let go of me." But she kept her voice low; Dwight's earnestness was for once impressive. "How do we know it isn't just Alex thrashing around up there?"

"We don't. My point precisely. We don't know it isn't Brad, either. And in view of his peculiar behavior …" He stood still a moment, chewing his lower lip. Then he headed for the window again. "Both cars are here," he reported over his shoulder.

"Then Alex and Brad are probably both upstairs, and—"

The expression on Dwight's face stopped her. "I hope not," he said slowly. "I don't want to be an alarmist, Gen, but I don't like this. I don't like it at all. Does it strike you that, if there's any foundation for our worst suspicions, Brad may be—well, on the desperate side by now?"

Gen felt a numbness rising, like an unwholesome flush, in her cheeks. It was only logical, of course; Dwight had simply followed her own fears to the end of the trail. Here it was: Brad possibly guilty meant Brad possibly desperate meant anyone crossing his path (anyone being Alex) in danger. That wrenching thud, muffled by distance. And now the ominous silence. The croaking of her own voice broke it.

"We've got to—" She took several uncoordinated steps—toward the door, toward Dwight, back toward the desk. "The police. I can call the police."

She reached for the phone, and again Dwight's hand was all at once grasping her wrist. The violence of his movement upset Clarice's photograph. "No! Not yet. Not till we've found out for sure. I can handle this. I'm going up there and find out." His other hand slid toward his jacket pocket, the way it had done last night, when he had the gun.

Her wrist hurt. She wrenched it free and looked down at it, too muddled even to protest. Then her eye caught the photograph of Clarice, and she picked it up, intending to set it straight. It was an absentminded, meaningless gesture on her part; she would hardly have been aware she was doing it except for Dwight. His hand made an involuntary, instantly suppressed flick toward the picture. She could feel him holding his breath. She could feel him watching her intently.

And in that curious moment two things clicked in Gen's mind. She recognized the handwriting on the picture, and she remembered the fish scale beret. Her eyes stretched wide and blank with shock.

"Why, it's the writing, the poem—" She stopped, but it was too late. Her gasp, her face had already betrayed her. There were sweat-drops glistening on Dwight's forehead; a ray of sunlight struck his glasses, reducing his eyes to two patches of glare; he had whipped the gun out of his pocket and was raising it and she could not move, she was turned to stone ...

Her hands fluttered up in a feeble effort to ward off the blow—for he was holding it by the muzzle, he did not dare risk the noise of a shot. Oh Alex, she thought. In the second before the gun crashed against her head she opened her mouth and let loose a scream of wild, defiant warning.

TWENTY-TWO

An hour earlier, Alex's brooding (he had settled down on the terrace with a lot of black coffee and a lot of blacker thoughts) had been interrupted when Brad came trotting through the gate. He looked bright-eyed and busy, like a terrier bent on an important errand.

"Hi, Alex!" he called. "Just the man I want to see."

Alex's response had not been cordial. "Take a good look. It's free. Exhibition closes promptly at three."

"Listen. Dwight's not around, is he? He didn't change his mind about going to the library?"

"He's gone. I suppose he was just the man you wanted to see too." Alex did not try to keep the bitterness out of his voice; one of the most galling things about last night was the feeling of being classed with Dwight instead of with Brad and Gen.

"What's eating on you?" asked Brad. "Oh. That's right. Gen. Look, Othello, relax. Right now you and I have more pressing business at hand. Come on in the study. I want your opinion on something."

Alex eyed him suspiciously. From under his beach towel Brad had drawn a large, imitation-leather scrapbook. "Marcella's," he said. He looked both excited and mortally serious, and there was a note of genuine urgency in his voice that Alex could not resist. He surrendered to his own curiosity—or maybe to habit; Brad had always known how to draw him back into the charmed circle when he chose—and stood up.

At that moment the gate in the wall was pushed open, and Walt, in bathing trunks and a sports shirt of fabulous design and color, came puffing through. When he saw Alex his beefy face—ruddier than ever from the exertion of running—broke into a big smile.

"Hey there! Alex! Howsaboy, Alex, howsaboy?" He pumped Alex's hand enthusiastically. His china-blue eyes beamed with comradeship.

"Hi, Walt. They let you out, I see."

"You're damn right, they let me out. Yessir, like the fellow says, you can't keep a good man down." He gave a shout of laughter; his sports shirt, which was unbuttoned, heaved and billowed joyously, and all the little golden hairs on his solid chest twinkled in the sun. "Well, I was hoping I'd get a chance to see you before I left. Old times' sake, or something. So anyway, here we were, Shirley and myself, down at the beach, and I spotted your wife with this guy—" He jerked a thumb toward Brad. "—only I wasn't sure how it would set with Shirley, and anyway your wife went to sleep. So when this guy picks himself up and leaves, I saw my chance and followed him. I figured if he knew your wife he'd know you. Been trying to catch up with him all the way from the beach. But brother, he was in a hurry, he was sure making tracks."

Alex mumbled an introduction, and Brad, who had been fidgeting like a kid kept in after school, cut short Walt's Pleased-to-meetcha. "Look, Alex, we haven't got much time. Come on. Both of you. What's the difference?"

Nobody could miss the urgency in his voice. Not even Walt. Mystified, awed into temporary silence, he trotted along beside the others into the study.

"Here. We'll make the preliminary comparison first." Brad was already at the desk, with the scrapbook open in front of him. "Take a look at this, Alex. See if it means to you what I think it means to me."

"This snapshot, you mean? Well, it's Marcella, all right, Marcella and that damn cat, and—Good Lord, Brad, don't tell me you were buying lilies for Marcella!"

"What?" It brought Brad up short for a minute. "Why, that lowlife! Stealing my stuff. I didn't even notice—oh well, forget it. I mean the poem."

"The poem?" Alex peered at the sheet of ledger paper, faintly yellow against the black background. The handwriting was bold and striking; the poem itself had a certain pert distinction. "Not bad at all. What about it? Did you say this is Marcella's—"

"Yes." Brad reached out for the photograph of Clarice with its inscription across the bottom. He laid it down flat alongside the poem. "Yes, this is Marcella's scrapbook."

For a long, motionless moment they stared at the two bits of handwriting. Alex's mouth went unaccountably dry. "I don't think I understand," he faltered. "I mean, why would Marcella happen to have—" He finished inanely; "It's the same handwriting."

"Right. I was pretty sure of it, when Gen showed this to me at the beach. That's the kind of mind I've got, a grab bag."

"Gen? Gen knows about this?"

"No. She had her eye on the snapshot. Like you." Brad's grin was a trifle wan. "Now, our next move—"

"Wait a minute. What goes on here?" Walt's voice was plaintive with bewilderment. "I mean—well, for instance, where did the scrapbook come from in the first place?"

Brad disposed, with no great patience or clarity, of the question—which must have been one of dozens seething in Walt's mind. "The character on the motorcycle brought it out. Marcella left it with him, along with her cat. And she told him she was coming out here to borrow money from you, so she could get a divorce and marry somebody else. You were calling each and every turn, Alex, with that screwy-sounding theory of yours."

"Look, Brad, there's probably some perfectly simple explanation—" Alex began it firmly enough, but when Brad's eyes met his, he let it trail away. And after the one glance at each other, they carefully looked somewhere else.

"Maybe." Brad looked at his watch. "There's just about time. According to Gen, Dwight brought a tin suitcase full of Clarice's letters our here yesterday. More storage space here than in his apartment. So where would this storage space be? Upstairs, I guess?"

"We can't ransack his stuff behind his back!" But—Alex's eyes turned again to the scrapbook—they couldn't let this pass either, this fantastic link between Dwight and Marcella.

"It's us or the police," said Brad. "At least we're his friends—or as near to friends as the poor devil has ever had."

"What if he comes back and catches us?"

"He won't. We'll hear his car. And if Gen comes back, she'll holler for you." He ripped the poem out of the scrapbook and stood up. "We'll take this with us, just to check. Come on."

"It'll be locked," said Alex miserably. "We'd better take something along to bust it open with."

They found an out-sized screwdriver in the kitchen, and started up the stairs. Alex, aware of a plucking at his sleeve and a noisy swallowing sound behind him, turned to find Walt's eyes fixed pleadingly on his. "Just one thing, Alex. Who is this guy Dwight?"

"He's the guy that owns this house. That was a picture of his wife down there on the desk."

"Oh," said Walt hopelessly. "Thanks." He swallowed again, and plodded on.

Alex and Brad were still avoiding each other's eyes. Silence gripped them—the silence of their own embarrassment (an inadequate word, an inadequate reaction, and yet it seemed to be what Alex was feeling) and the silence of the big, empty house drenched in the drowsiness of summer afternoon. Their feet made no sound on the carpeted stairs; they moved with the quick stealth of practiced burglars.

"Here?" Brad paused in the second-floor hallway. Elegant green-and-gold paper was fading on the walls, and the cream-colored doors on either side faced them like a row of bland, impeccably mannered servants.

"Third floor's more likely," whispered Alex, and they moved on.

It was years since he had been up here. Dwight's room, he remembered, had been on the third floor, along with the maids' bedrooms, and a long, narrow attic room with sloping walls where they used to play on rainy days. A long time ago. The third floor lacked some of the luxurious air of the rest of the house. The carpeting continued, but the wallpaper was plainer, and the doors here were stained dark, with glass knobs instead of the fancy brass jobs on the floor below. There was an unaired, mothball smell, and it was very hot. Alex felt his grip on the screwdriver growing slippery with sweat.

The first two doors they opened turned out to be those of the maids' bedrooms. Small, stifling, the beds draped with faded spreads, the mirrors dim with dust. In one of them a wasp, furious at their intrusion, buzzed and bounced against the ceiling. The third door opened on Dwight's den. They paused a moment, peering in at the built-in bunks, the prep school pennants above the book shelves, a pair of boxing gloves gathering dust in a corner. Then Alex closed the door quietly on these few forlorn remnants of Dwight's boyhood, and they passed on to the attic room.

It was cluttered with cartons, packing boxes, trunks, odds and ends of discarded furniture. A discouraging prospect, thought Alex, particularly when all they had to go on was "a tin suitcase." But it took Brad no more than five minutes to spot what they were looking for.

Alex and Walt were poking rather aimlessly in a stack of cast-off luggage when they heard Brad's jubilant whisper. "Here! This must be it. Yep. It's got a British shipping tag. We're in business."

It was wedged up against the slanting ceiling near one of the alcoves, on top of a couple of trunks and a caved-in hamper. Brad clambered up, dislodged it, and set it down carefully in the middle of the floor, where there was a small, dusty clearing in the jungle of junk.

The job of getting it open (and it was indeed locked) proved more noisy than difficult. There was quite a wrenching thud when Alex's efforts with the screwdriver got results. But they had all been keeping an ear cocked for Dwight's car; one of them would have been sure to hear him if he had come back. They squatted down beside the tin suitcase that had been Clarice's, and its contents, which had also once belonged to her.

With no sense of shock, or even of surprise, Alex lifted out a handful of the papers and shuffled through them. There were a few letters. The rest was poetry—the tart, sprightly light verses that, in the last five years, had been appearing regularly everywhere under the name of Dwight Abbott. They were written on sheets of ledger paper, in the distinctive, vigorous hand that Alex was never going to forget. He had seen it twice before—once in the inscription on Clarice's photograph, and again in Marcella's scrapbook.

"Poetry? What—" began Walt. Then he shook his head in a dazed way and held up his hands, as if the answer—whatever it might be—was more than he cared to cope with. "Never mind. Skip it. I don't get it, but what the hell, skip it."

"This one's in a current magazine," murmured Alex. "'Vacation Vacuum.' I noticed it the other night."

"I know. A lot of them are familiar." Brad sighed. "He shouldn't have kept them, once they'd been published. He shouldn't have kept her letters, either."

There was pathos in Clarice's letters—the pathos of an intensely shy, lonely, intelligent woman timidly groping for appreciation. She had never even dared show her poems to anyone but Dwight. She hadn't had any idea how good they were. Perhaps Dwight hadn't realized their quality either, at first, thought Alex; he was no great shakes on perceptiveness. But somehow he had stumbled onto understanding. There was pathos here, too—the pathos of a man as lonely as Clarice, lonely but mediocre, and starved for recognition, snatching at the only chance that had ever come his way, or was ever likely to. More than pathos, Alex reminded himself, as his glance returned to the page torn from Marcella's scrapbook. Tragedy ...

"Marcella must have been in his apartment," Brad was saying slowly. "She must have been there a lot. Because Clarice's poetry wasn't anything he tossed around indiscriminately. It explains where Marcella spent the nights she was away from her own place, and who's been paying her rent."

"And who it was she wanted to marry," added Alex. "That was what got her murdered, really. Poor stray cat of a creature, even Dwight didn't want her for keeps. Especially Dwight. You know what a snob he is. He couldn't have stood it, being stuck with a socially unacceptable wife like Marcella, and yet he couldn't get away from her because she knew about all this." He gestured toward the open suitcase. "Not that she'd *mean* to blackmail him. But it amounted to the same thing. He had to keep her away from his friends—me, for instance—for fear she'd let it out."

Brad nodded sombrely. "And there wasn't any way for him to do it. If he shucked her off, she'd be sure to come running back to you for a job, or help of some kind. If he married her, she'd be all over the place. So he did neither—and she still turned up out here, there wasn't anything to do but kill her." He picked up the scrapbook page. "You think he knows about this?"

"He can't. If he knew, he'd have moved heaven and earth before now to get it back. No. He probably got drunk one night and let her in on the whole fraud—guilt compulsion or something—and then she snitched this one behind his back, because it's about cats, and then—"

Gen's scream (he knew at once that it was Gen) ripped through the house with a terrible, primitive directness. Alex felt it rather than heard it; with it leaping in his blood, he shot out of the attic and down the first flight of stairs like a horse unconcerned with anything beyond the rake of the spurs.

Behind him Brad yelled: "Look out! He's got a gun!"

In front of him on the stairs loomed a sort of grotesque mask of the face he remembered as Dwight's. It came at him head-on. He did not think; to think would have been to stop, and to stop was impossible. In a miracle of reflex action his hands gripped the banisters, swinging the upper part of his body backwards, while the projectile of his feet flew out ahead. He felt them connect with something made of muscle and bone. He heard a shot. He plunged on.

Then he was downstairs, in the hall, and he had started to shake. By the time he reached the library he was weaving like a drunk. It was a moment or two before he saw Gen, and the sight seemed to draw all the breath out of him. She was crawling (his imperious darling), crawling doggedly toward the door. Her movements had an endless, clumsy patience, like those of a bug on its back, struggling to right itself. There was a dark stain on one side of her face.

"Gen!" He tottered over to her and bent to take her in his arms. But, still intent on her painstaking journey toward the door, she did not lift her head; she frowned at his legs, as at another obstacle in her path. He took her face between his two hands and raised it gently.

At last her eyes focused on him. "Ax?" she croaked. She put her hand out incredulously. "Ax? You—all right?" And her face crumpled up; she began to cry.

It was not so much an embrace as a mutual collapse. Alex's unsteady legs buckled and he was down on the floor too, clinging and clung to, mumbling incoherently. Then he heard Brad's voice, calling his name, and when he turned he saw Walt in that ridiculous sports shirt of his, hovering in the doorway. He still looked dazed, but he seemed to be in working order.

"He's got him," he reported huskily. He stared at Gen. "Look, you want me to call the doctor? Looks to me like—"

"Dr. Nichols," said Alex. He picked Gen up and put her on the couch. "I'll be right back," he whispered, and kissed her before he went out into the hall.

He did not see Dwight at first; he saw only Brad, standing on the stairs with Dwight's gun in his hand. "Is Gen all right?" he asked over his shoulder.

"I think she's going to be. He meant to knock her out, but she must have ducked. Walt's calling the doctor, and we'll have to get the police—"

"Yes," said Brad, "we've got to call the police." He moved to one side, and Alex saw Dwight. He was sitting on the stairs. He looked sprawling and disjointed, and his face had gone to pieces. His glasses were missing; Alex saw that he was holding them in his hand.

"I had a right," he was saying monotonously. "Clarice was my wife. She wanted me to have them. Clarice *loved* me."

And again Alex could feel only an acute embarrassment at what should have been moving. Even in this extremity, Dwight had no stature; it was somehow typical of him that he should be absorbed in the footnote of plagiarism instead of the main theme of murder.

"It's Marcella," Brad reminded him. "Marcella's the reason we've got to call the police."

"Marcella," repeated Dwight. He made an effort to pull himself together. The result was a peevish sort of pomposity. "They can't prove anything. They haven't any evidence."

"They'll get it, though." It was as if Brad were a teacher, explaining to a confused pupil. "They'll find somebody who saw Marcella going to your place, or leaving it, somebody else who saw you out here the day she was killed, hours before you say you came out. You can't have covered your tracks that completely. It's just that there's been no reason, until now, to inquire about any of your comings or goings. There is a reason now, and they'll find—"

"And the fish scale beret." It was Gen's voice. She was coming out of the library door, lurching but dogged, the way she had been when Alex discovered her crawling across the library floor, bent on finding him. Behind her loomed Walt's anxious red face.

"What?" Dwight shambled to his feet and peered myopically over the banister.

"The fish scale beret in your bedroom. You told me it was Clarice's, but it couldn't have been, it's too new-fashioned. They didn't come out till a couple of years ago. I remembered it before, when you ..."

She wilted against Alex's shoulder.

Alex tried to stop looking at that dull, defenseless face—so familiar, so ruinously strange—still peering over the banister. The sight of it filled him with a vague, expectant dread, and yet he could not look anywhere else. He kept on watching. He kept on waiting—for whatever it was that he dreaded.

"All right," Dwight said at last. "I knew her. That's no crime. I'm not proud of it, but—I suppose if they investigate they'll discover it—I had an affair with her, I paid her rent."

"You kept it mighty damn quiet all this time," said Brad.

"I told you I'm not proud of it! Can't you understand—" Dwight swallowed convulsively. "No, you can't. You with all your girls, and those white flowers you always buy them. None of you can understand. You don't know what it's like to have nobody, nobody—Clarice was the only one, and I lost her. Not just when she died. That was only one of the ways I lost her. The other ways were worse, because they were my own doing. My own damnable doing." In a theatrical, almost biblical gesture, he lifted his two fists; from one of them dangled the end of his broken glasses. "Don't you think I lost Clarice all over again, every time one of those poems was published under my name? And how do you think it was, when I betrayed her with Marcella? That's what I did. I betrayed her, time after time after time. I kept it quiet, yes. Even at the beginning, when I called Vonda and asked for her phone number, I told her it was Brad because I was ashamed to give my own name. Do you think I wanted people like you sniggering behind their hands over what was going on? Marcella, a tramp like Marcella, after Clarice! Of course I kept it quiet. I was trying to hide it from everybody in the world, only I couldn't hide it from myself ..."

It was very quiet for a moment. And Alex still waited. Whatever it was he dreaded was still to come.

"I couldn't get away from her. She took it for granted I was going to marry her. Marry her! All I wanted to do was get away from her, only I couldn't—I couldn't let her come out here and talk to you, Alex. She thought she was keeping it a secret, but I knew what she was up to. I would have known, even if I hadn't been there when she tried to call you at the shop." His eyes strained toward Alex, and here it was, the beseeching cry of brother to brother. "You knew her, Alex! *You* must understand."

Alex thrust his hand out as if to ward off a blow. "Don't," he said, but nothing could stem the familiar surge of identification, the me-and-Walt feeling of last summer that had made him crawl with shame. Walt was right beside him, breathing heavily; their eyes met for a second, in a flicker of understanding. Me-and-Walt. How tame it seemed now, how innocuous, compared to me-and-Dwight. We got away in time, thought Alex, and Dwight didn't. There was a special set of circumstances, and

Dwight didn't get away. That's the hair's breadth of difference between us.

"I knew her. I understand."

That was why he had no choice but to call Ed Fuller. He turned toward the study door. With his arm around Gen's shoulders—and with Walt trailing along on the other side of him—he started walking toward the phone on the desk. He kept his eyes fixed rigidly ahead. Murder, he told himself. Not just Marcella. Horace Pankey too. Remember that. Murder.

His hand was closing on the phone when there was a commotion of rapid sound—from the driveway outside the racket of a motorcycle and at the same moment footsteps thudding up the stairs and Dwight's sudden scream: "They won't get me! They'll never get me!" Through the window Alex saw the incongruously jolly sight of three people on a motorcycle (the two in the sidecar were Vonda and Mr. Theobald) careening to a stop just beyond the cottage. They were laughing; they had a holiday look.

Rooted to the middle of the library floor, Alex waited for the shot. Beside him Gen and Walt waited too. But there was no shot. There was a crash that echoed through the whole house, and a final, sickening smack.

"Jesus," whispered Walt.

The three people had gotten off the motorcycle. They no longer had a holiday look. They were running toward the terrace.

So Alex and Gen and Walt knew, even before Brad came back downstairs and told them. "Out the attic window. Before I could stop him." He still had the gun in his hand; he looked down at it in a puzzled way. "I should have shot him, I guess. I tried to, and somehow I couldn't . . ."

There was nothing to say. But Walt tried. "Yeah. The poor devil. What I mean—" His hands moved helplessly. "Yeah. The poor murdering devil."

THE END

An Affair of the Heart
Jean Potts

ONE

"Don't just sit there thinking it." Kirk poured himself another brandy and gave her the hard-eyed smile. "Go ahead. Say it. Tell me how many brandies I've had. Three? Four? Anyway, more than the doctor ordered. Martinis before lunch, too. Not to mention what went on after lunch in that sturdy little bed of yours. You couldn't stop counting even then, could you?"

"No need to be coarse," she said. Sometimes the light touch worked. A display of hurt feelings only spurred him on; and last month's episode had scared her out of any more open quarrels with him. She stretched her bare legs, wriggling her feet in the feathered mules he had brought her today, making the wispy tendrils of marabou wave, flutter ... Fibrillate? Such a gay-sounding word for what had happened to Kirk's heart last month. Not unexpected considering the nature of the initial attack, according to the doctor; nervous tension, overexertion, any undue excitement—who knew what might have brought it on? Lorraine knew, that was who: by trying to break off with him she had made it happen, as surely as she was agitating the feathers on her slippers at this moment.

Kirk might have died, and if he had, she would have been responsible.

"I love my new team of mules. Very femme fatale." It was the sort of thing she had said often before—Kirk was as proud of his own presents as a child, and as greedy for praise—but today she was saying it with calculation, in a conscious attempt to divert and please him. How tired she was of her own machinations! What a relief it would be to speak first and think afterwards!

And this time it wasn't working, anyway. At the other end of the sofa Kirk hunched over his brandy like a lion over its kill. "It's cause for celebration, seeing you again," he announced in the belligerent tone she had come to dread, "and by God I'm going to celebrate it. I'm not an invalid and I won't be treated like one."

It compounded the treachery of his heart's antics, that there should be so little outward sign of them. He looked fitter than she had ever seen him: a vigorous, well-built man, not really young any more—forty-nine to Lorraine's twenty-six—and certainly never handsome, but still with plenty of the good old basic appeal. That, of course, but not just that; men were drawn to Kirk too, even men who disliked him could not deny the crackle of excitement he generated.

So little outward sign. The same lined, mobile face, vulnerable in spite of the ruthless touch to the mouth; the same gray-sprinkled hair and keen dark eyes behind horn-rimmed glasses, which Kirk used as a stage prop, something to slide up or down his nose, twirl in his hand, or aim at the opposition in the course of an argument. But several times during lunch Lorraine had noticed—and pretended not to—him rubbing his chest, as if to stroke a refractory creature into submission. And afterwards, the flights of stairs to her apartment had left him breathless.

It was the fourth brandy. Two martinis before lunch. Coffee. All forbidden by the doctor. So were fits of temper and quarrels like the one he seemed bent on picking with her at the moment.

"I said I'm not an invalid!"

"Somebody's been treating you like one?"

"Everybody! All the time. That quack doctor, with his big fat understanding face and his 'suggestions.' One long weak drink before dinner. Great. Just great. Hilda. She's bought a scale, for God's sake, she weighs my food! The kids. And now you. Even you. Watching and nagging and—"

"Kirk, that's not true. I haven't said one word."

"Oh, of course not. I mustn't be crossed. I must be humored. You think I don't know how your mind works?"

"All right. But it's only because I don't want— It's only because I love you." She did not look at him as she said this. She was not sure it was true. Half-true, maybe; not the whole-souled truth of a year ago. Even before Kirk's first attack she was beginning to get a little restive, a little less ecstatic about the other woman role she had leapt into so gladly and blindly. It was petty of her, no doubt, but she missed having dinner dates. Kirk could hardly ever get away except for lunch and, though he claimed he didn't mind her going out with other men—not in the least, not the slightest bit—there was always a caustic session with him when she did. It wasn't worth the bother. But more and more often on empty weekends she would become aware of a subterranean, smoldering resentment. Crumbs. She was relegated to living on crumbs, the leftovers of Kirk's time, and she was not geared for it, she was too much of an egotist herself to be satisfied with anything but first place.

Then she got to know Hilda, and her nuisance of a conscience began working overtime—perhaps to make up for Kirk's—pricking and prodding and yammering. And diminishing Kirk. Yes. The more she saw of Kirk's wife, the less enchanted she grew with him. It shocked her, that he could accept so much decency and trust and devotion as his due, with no thought of repaying it in kind. What Hilda didn't know wouldn't hurt her. Apparently it was as simple as that to him. Why worry about intrinsic wrong or right as long as he had what he wanted?

He was pointing the horn-rims at her accusingly. "Why didn't you finish what you started to say? You don't want me to die in your bed. That's what's really bugging you, isn't it?"

"I don't want you to die at all!"

"But especially not here. So embarrassing for you, having to explain—"

"Stop it!" The shrillness of her own voice alarmed her. But there were limits, after all; he had pushed her far enough. "Of course it's bugging me. Have you ever thought of what it would do to Hilda if—if anything should happen while you're here in my apartment? Don't you realize it would destroy her?"

He looked her straight in the eye and said, "Listen. I don't care what it would do to Hilda or you or anybody else. Because you'll be alive, and I'll be dead, damn it. Dead." He lurched to his feet and glared down at her in a fury of defiance, despair, something else that she did not recognize for a moment; she had never before seen fear in Kirk's face. It was there now, a flare of incredulous, outraged fear. "Dead. Finished. Through with everything. But I can tell you one thing, I'm going to get in all the living I can while I've got the chance. I've been doing some good hard thinking these last few weeks in the hospital. And I'm not settling for any more half measures. We've wasted too much time as it is, you and I. The minute I saw you I knew you were for me, and I haven't changed my mind since. If time's running out, then I'm going to spend what's left of it with you."

"Kirk," she said sharply, through the astonished ringing of her ears, "are you asking me to marry you?"

"Sure, if that's the way you want it." He gestured magnanimously, surged toward her, and pulled her up against him. "Whatever you say, darling. Just so we're together."

"But we can't— But Hilda— You can't be serious!"

He was, though. And there was something awesome about his egotism: the possibility that she might not be delighted with his proposal never so much as crossed his mind. He saw her sorry attempt, last month, to end the affair as a perfectly natural—and, to him, perfectly satisfactory—reaction. Of course she was frustrated, so was he, at having to dodge around as they had been doing for the past year, snatching a few secret hours together when they could. It was no good for either of them; he was glad now that she had blown up; otherwise he might never have seen the light. As for Hilda …

"At least we won't be lying to her anymore. I'm not proud of the way I've treated her. But on the other hand, it never was exactly a love match. I mean, there I was with two kids on my hands, and there was Hilda, ready, willing and able to help me raise them— It was her idea as much as mine. More, really. It's going to be a shock to her, I know, but—"

Lorraine closed her eyes against the image of Hilda's cheerful face stricken blank with the brute force of the blow. A double blow: she was not only completely unsuspecting of Lorraine, she obviously thought of her as a staunch friend, someone to confide her worries to, turn to for advice and of course—Hilda being Hilda—do favors for. There was no safe or graceful way of ducking the favors. Ever since Kirk started his independent agency, Hilda had been helping out at the office; in addition to relying on Lorraine as a free-lance artist herself, she had several times steered her on to desirable jobs for other advertising agencies.

Now, with her face pressed against Kirk's shirt front, Lorraine broke into uncontrollable sobbing. He picked her up—oh God, she thought, his heart, he mustn't—and sat down with her in his lap, cuddling her as if she were a child. "Shh, darling. Please, there's nothing to cry about …"

Nothing? There was everything to cry about. Not just Hilda and the waste of her life. Kirk, with death breathing down his neck, snatching recklessly and savagely at the love he still believed was his for the taking. That was what she wept for most of all: the thought of how rapturously happy his proposal would have made her a year ago. But he had waited till now, and it was too late, too late, they had lost their chance.

There was no way out. If she no longer loved him enough to marry him, she still loved him too much to tell him so. And the possible consequences were too terrifying. It might kill him—literally, physically—and the burden of guilt would be hers as surely as if she had picked up a knife and plunged it into his poor faltering heart.

Through a blur of tears she saw his face, gentle for once, full of unguarded tenderness. He waited until she had quieted down. Then he said soothingly, "I realize we can't just rush off and get married tomorrow. First we've got to figure out the details. We don't want to make it any harder for Hilda than we have to. I don't know whether it's better to try to break it to her gently or just let her have it and get it over with. Either way, it's not going to be much fun."

We. We. He was counting on Lorraine, then, to help with the dirty work. All right. At least it gave her a legitimate excuse for marking time; and that was what she had to have, time to figure out her own set of details.

"Give me a chance to think." She pushed back her hair, which fell—thick, shiny, almost black—to her shoulders, and stole another unobtrusive glance at her watch as she did so. Kirk was due to leave at five. Fifteen minutes to go. She had a sudden, piercing memory of how fast the precious hours with him used to fly, hours that today seemed to drag with the weight of unadmitted tension. "I'm still in a state of shock myself. Please, Kirk. Promise me you'll wait to tell her till we've really talked it over. Promise. Give me your word."

"Don't worry, darling, I won't jump the gun. Not bloody likely. How does Thursday sound to you? Hilda's got a meeting with a client in the afternoon and a dinner date afterwards, so I can get away any time. Meanwhile, bend your mind, so will I, and we can thrash it all out over a drink."

"Thursday?" Three days from now. Surely in three days something would occur to her. Or if not to her, then to Mary or Teddy. They were her tried and true standbys; without them to confide in, she did not know how she would have gotten through the last few months. Good old Mary—that was how Lorraine thought of her sister, though in fact Mary was the younger by a couple of years—had known about Kirk from the beginning, of course. Teddy, who occupied the apartment below Lorraine's, and to whom intrigue was the breath of life, had no doubt guessed it long before she broke down and told him. "I think Thursday's all right," she said. "I've got an appointment uptown at four, but it shouldn't take too long. Anyway, you have a key, so if I'm a little late it won't matter, you can let yourself in."

"Right. Thursday, then, as early as we can make it. Oh God, look at the time, how did it get so late?" He drew her to him for a prolonged goodbye kiss. "Won't it be great when we don't have to watch the clock anymore? Lorraine, Lorraine ..."

"Yes," she said, past the ache in her throat. "Oh yes. Great."

As usual, his departure was a flurry of nearly forgotten gloves, briefcase, glasses; of last-minute reminders and promises to call. As usual, she stood at the door, watching till he reached the landing of the narrow stairway, with its once elegant threadbare red carpeting. There he paused for the last look back. He seemed somehow defenseless, with his uplifted head, the collar of his topcoat rucked up in back, his face flickering into a smile that was half-rueful, half-exultant.

And death breathing down his neck, she thought again. For all his crackling vitality, the drive and sweep of his ego—death was still there, waiting for the moment to douse the light.

TWO

When the phone rang, Mary made a dive for it, got tangled up with the cord, and started off talking into the wrong end of the thing. "Lorraine?" she croaked. "Wait a minute … there. Are you all right? What is it?"

"Just calling to give you the all clear." Lorraine sounded quite blithe and bubbly. "What's the matter with *you*?"

"Nothing. Not a thing. Except I've been sitting here jittering for the past hour and a half, waiting for you to call. Five thirty at the latest, you said, and here it is—"

"Oh my, so it is. Mary, you poor dear, I'm sorry, truly I am. I went down to Teddy's after Kirk left, and we got to talking, and I simply lost track of the time."

"Okay. Skip it." It wasn't the first time. Nor, in all probability, the last. Even at the height of her jitters, Mary had known they were unwarranted. If anything dire had happened, she would be the first to hear about it. Good old troubleshooter Mary. "No disaster, I take it? Safely through another day?"

"Yes. No. I don't know." No more bubbles in Lorraine's voice now; instead, a throb of despair. "What am I going to do, Mary? Listen to what he's come up with now!"

Out it all came, and Mary, obediently listening, felt an ominous sinking in her midriff. Marriage! Trust Kirk for the surprise twist. Of all the possibilities she had worried about—and there were plenty—this particular one had cost her no sleepless nights. On the contrary, she remembered lashing out at Lorraine once, in exasperation and sisterly concern: "You don't imagine he's ever going to marry you, do you? You're not that silly, I hope!"

She didn't often blow up like that, opposed though she had been to the affair from the beginning. Who wouldn't be? Kirk was not only married to somebody else, he was too old for Lorraine, too much the "blue sky guy," the professional charmer who saw nothing wrong with taking everything and giving nothing. Or anyway, precious little. Yes, of course he was in love with Lorraine. She was quite a charmer herself, and—Mary could not deny it—more accustomed to taking than to giving. Novelty was part of Kirk's appeal to her. And then he had caught her on the rebound, when she had just broken off with Roger and was in a dangerously flighty and devil-may-care mood.

"You can't marry him," said Mary. "It's out of the question. Impossible."

"I know it is! I know it. But how can I tell him? Look at what happened last month when I tried to bow out. It could kill him. He might die, and it would be my fault; I'd be to blame. I can't tell him the truth. I don't dare! What am I going to do?"

The old familiar song. Lorraine had the problems; Mary was supposed to have the answers. "Now don't panic. Give me a little time to think." Quite often she did think of things. Like the "alert" and "all clear" system in effect since Kirk's first heart attack. That had been her idea, her answer to Lorraine's frantic question, "Supposing he should die up here in my apartment? You have to call the police, don't you, in a case like that? Everybody would know what he was doing here. Hilda, everybody. I couldn't possibly say it was business, Hilda knows I don't work here, I work in my studio."

Yes, you had to call the police. But if you first called two willing standbys like Mary and Teddy, to provide some semblance of a casual, impromptu social gathering—then Hilda would have at least a rag to cling to, she would not be stripped entirely naked, with all the world to see. Lorraine too, of course, though give her credit, she was less terrified for her own sake than for Hilda's.

"He won't tell Hilda, will he?" Mary asked. "He wouldn't be that mean?"

"I'm sure he won't. He promised. I told you, I managed to put him off till Thursday. But after that—"

"How about Teddy? Does he have any bright ideas?"

"He's all to pieces. Hysterical. He just had a frightful row with Ernest. And now this."

Mary sighed. It figured. In some ways Teddy was an ideal standby: certainly he was enthusiastic, and certainly he could be relied upon, if need be, to put on a convincing show for the benefit of the police and Kirk's family. He loved theatricals almost as much as he loved secrets and plots. But he was a broken reed when it came to the practical, logical working out of a problem. Teddy did not think; he emoted. So did Lorraine, on the subject of Kirk.

That left Mary. She sighed again. Then she caught the waiting quality of the silence, and realized Lorraine must have lost her, somewhere along the conversational line. "What?" she said.

"Not what. Who. You haven't even been listening. I asked you to guess who just called me, a few minutes after I got back from Teddy's." Lorraine's voice was bubbly again. Like champagne.

"All right. Who?"

"Roger! Can you imagine, after all this time? Of all the people in the world I never expected to hear from again …"

"I know. Well. Are you going to see him? I'm assuming that's what he had in mind."

"He asked me to meet him for a drink tomorrow, and I was too rattled to think of an excuse. But now I'm not sure I should. What do you think, Mary?"

"What do I think? I think what I always thought, that you were out of your mind to let him get away. If you'd listened to me in the first place, you'd never have gotten into this mess!" Hurt silence. She had a vivid mental image of Lorraine's face: the expression in her eyes—those limpid, dark-blue eyes with their sooty lashes—would be both humble and reproachful; the soft mouth was no doubt quivering a little. "There. I'm sorry. You can't help it, I suppose. I only wish Roger hadn't waited till now."

The perfect time would have been four or five months ago, when the bloom on the Kirk affair was beginning to wear a bit thin, and before his attack. But Roger had no way of knowing that; he wasn't the first man to do the right thing at the wrong moment.

"I only wish, too," said Lorraine sadly. "It scares me. I mean, if I did go out with Roger, and if Kirk found out about it—"

"No reason why he should. You don't have to tell him."

"No, but— Maybe Roger was right when he called me a tramp!"

"A tramp? Roger? When did he ever—"

"Well, as good as. When we had the big blow-up. He said I was fickle. Flighty. I am, too! With him, and now Kirk. I loved him so, and now— God help me, I almost wish he'd die before next Thursday—" She broke off, half-sobbing. "No, no, of course I don't mean that. It's just that I don't know what to *do!*"

Neither did Mary, for all the soothing noises she made, her promises to think, her assurances that of course Lorraine wasn't a tramp, of course there was always a solution, no matter how tough the problem. They rang a bit hollow in her own ears. Apparently not in Lorraine's: she had a child's complete, touching faith in Mary, and anyway it was her nature to bounce from one mood to another, with or without any good reason.

Mary was made of less volatile stuff. When they had hung up she stayed where she was, in the big easy chair, with her knees drawn up to her chin and her eyes fixed on the rug.

It did no good to tell herself that all Lorraine's romances were inclined to be stormy. This one was different. This time it was not just a private matter between two people falling in or out of love. Kirk had a wife, a son, a daughter. So far they had been mercifully spared, but they wouldn't be for long, if he persisted in his crazy new course. They too would be sucked into the middle of the whirlpool, to sink or swim. Mary didn't know about the son and daughter—maybe they were chips off the old block, as self-centered as Kirk—but she wouldn't want to bet on his wife's chances of survival. No, it seemed all too likely to her that Hilda, paralyzed by shock and grief, would go under without a struggle. And all for nothing; because the one certainty was that Lorraine must not, could not, would not marry him.

Only, if she were to hit him with the truth, what about his chances of survival? Tough he might be, but not indestructible, and in that very weakness lay his greatest strength. There he stood, brandishing his damned, damaged heart—consciously or unconsciously, it made no difference—daring anybody to keep him from getting what he wanted.

For a moment Mary tried to imagine calling him up, insisting on meeting him in some public spot, a restaurant or bar, explaining to him … Her bones went watery at the mere thought. She knew she would never in the world have the nerve to go through with any such performance.

Oh, this one was different, a far cry from Lorraine's other romantic crises. How simple they seemed by comparison, more exciting than disturbing, the natural product of Lorraine's impulsive temperament.

This time it could be a matter of life and death. Mary shivered. In the literal sense of the phrase. A matter of life and death.

THREE

There was no getting out of it, Wednesday morning when Hilda wound up her phone call with: "I've got a check for you. Why don't you stop in and pick it up? As long as you're going to be in the neighborhood anyway."

In sidestepping lunch, Lorraine had used errands uptown as an excuse, and she had made the mistake of being specific about the location of those errands. Now all she could think of to say was, "That's a good idea. Fine. I'll be seeing you." She said it and hung up. Then she added to herself, "Oh God."

Bad as it was, it still wasn't the worst. For a panicky moment, when she first picked up the phone and heard Hilda's voice, she had thought: This is it, I might have known Kirk wouldn't keep his promise to me, he's blown everything wide open, he's told her.

But that was just Lorraine's own bad conscience, conjuring up what she dreaded most. Hilda had sounded exactly the way she always did—hearty and brisk and unself-conscious. Had said the things she always said: "How's tricks?" and "Can't complain," and "Bye now." Lorraine's hypersensitive ear would have caught even the slightest shade of difference. There had been none to catch.

Today of all days, she thought, to have to face Hilda, today of all days. Somehow the fact that tomorrow, God willing, would mark the end of her affair with Kirk—or anyway, the beginning of the end—made her feel guiltier than ever. As if her rejection of Kirk added the crowning touch to her betrayal of Hilda.

Rejection was what it was going to be, though Kirk might not immediately recognize it as such. Then again, he might. In which case ...

She couldn't help feeling that Mary, usually so reliable as a problem-solver, had rather let her down this time. Not that she had any brighter ideas herself. And Mary's plan of delaying tactics just might work. After all, Lorraine really did have that one-shot job hanging fire out on the West Coast; it could quite legitimately be scheduled for sooner instead of later. Furthermore, it could be prolonged. The theory was that with time on her side and a whole continent separating her from Kirk, she would be able to ease out of the situation more or less unobtrusively.

That was the theory. How well it would work was something else again, something she would find out when she saw Kirk tomorrow. Meanwhile, today, there was Hilda. No getting out of it.

So here she was in Kirk's office—he wasn't in yet, at least she was spared that—perched on the edge of the chair, smiling uneasily across his desk at Hilda, who had no office of her own in the two-room suite, and worked at whatever desk happened to be unoccupied.

"Come on in," she had called out when she heard Lorraine at the outer door. "Sit down a minute. Tell me what you've been up to." That clear voice of Hilda's, ringing with open-hearted welcome. Her beaming face with its high color, the little space between her two front teeth, the laugh lines around her eyes, the curly graying hair that seemed forever on the point of springing out of the bun she pinned it into ... In spite of her matronly figure and the glasses strung on a cord around her neck, she had a kind of schoolgirl bounciness, an artlessness, a vulnerability— Or maybe that was just Lorraine's bad conscience again. After all, Hilda had survived twenty years of being married to Kirk; that took stamina.

"I haven't seen you in ages," she was going on. The frank affection in her eyes made Lorraine cringe. As usual. And, as usual, she felt a surge of resentment: it wasn't fair, that she and Hilda should like each other; why couldn't it have been a nice simple case of hate at first sight? "Haven't seen you to talk to, that is. Something told me that last night was no time for me to barge in on you. Two's company, you know, three's a crowd."

"Last night?" They had met at the Gotham, she and Roger. Their special place, their special corner, their own private Roger-and-Lorraine world rediscovered, more delightful than ever after the year and a half of exile.

"Oh yes, I was there too, having a drink with a client. You didn't see me, did you?" Hilda's smile broadened; she reached over to pat Lorraine's hand. "And no wonder. I wouldn't either, if I'd been in your shoes. My, he's a good-looking young fellow! Just the type for you. Is he new, or have you been keeping things from me? Not that it's any of my business …"

"Not new, really," mumbled Lorraine. Her face felt as if it were on fire. "We were a big deal for a while, only then we had this bang-up fight, over something or other, I don't know exactly what—" She did know, of course. She had pushed Roger just a little bit too far, that last party, playing up to the character with the sideburns. (What was his name? She had never seen him before or since.) One more pointless little episode, much like the others, memorable only because it was the one too many for Roger. "I *know* the guy doesn't mean anything to you!" he had raged. "That's what I can't take! If it was somebody you really cared about, okay, I wouldn't like it, but I could understand it …"

And maybe he would understand about Kirk, if and when she ever found the courage to put his claim to the test. Whatever else Kirk might be, he was no pointless little episode, no nameless character with sideburns. She did not love him as she used to. Had never loved him as Hilda did—was she capable of loving anyone with Hilda's single-minded devotion?— But he still mattered to her in a way that no one, not even Roger, ever had before or ever would again.

"Oh well," said Hilda comfortably. "Fights happen. Sometimes about the silliest things. I think the maddest I ever got at Kirk was over a set of living room drapes, can you imagine. Anyway, you had this fight. And then?"

This can't go on, thought Lorraine, I've got to get out of here. But she remained nailed to her chair, condemned to listen to her own voice nattering on with the next installment of maidenly confidences: "And then he called me the other night. After all this time, more than a year. I never thought he would, but he did, he called me, and—"

"Of course he did, bless his heart, if I ever saw a young couple in love it was you two last night. And more power to you." Hilda hitched forward, her plain, open face aglow. "I'll tell you the truth, Lorraine, it's bothered me that you didn't seem to have any special beau. A pretty girl like you, more than pretty, beautiful—yes you are, let's face it, beautiful—it just didn't seem right, the way you were always available for rush jobs, weekends, evenings, anytime. Not anymore, I bet. Not anymore!"

And now, at last, Lorraine found it possible to make the simple, liberating gestures: the glance at her watch, the startled exclamation, the jump to her feet. "Look at the time, I really must run ... What? Oh yes, that's what I came for, isn't it?" She waited, giddy at the prospect of release, while Hilda scrabbled for the check. "Fine. Thanks. Yes, so nice to see you—"

The outer door opened. She turned and saw Kirk come breezing in. "Well! Look who's here," he said genially; he took these occasions in his stride, maybe he even enjoyed them. "Hi, Hilda. Am I interrupting a top-level conference or something?"

"I just stopped in to pick up my check. I had an errand right next door so I stopped in and ..." A sudden, chilling premonition seized her. Like a paralysis; she could neither run for the door nor keep up the line of chatter which was her usual defense in a crisis.

"And we got to talking," Hilda chimed in cheerily. "Nothing to do with business. Woman stuff." Yes, here it came; and Lorraine stood tongue-tied and immobilized, powerless to stop it. "Lorraine was telling me about her new beau—well, not new really, but he hasn't been around for a while. He is now, very much so, if I'm any judge. I happened to see them last night, and my, he's a handsome young fellow. Just right for Lorraine, exactly her type."

"Well, bully for her," said Kirk. He stood as still as she, baring his teeth at her in a dangerous smile.

Another moment, and surely even Hilda would have sensed the tension. But somewhere in the city there was an angel of mercy who picked the right time to call Banning Associates. The phone buzzed; Hilda scooped it up. Lorraine recovered her powers of locomotion. So did Kirk. He followed her to the door, opened it for her with a courtly flourish, and held out his hand.

"Congratulations, my dear." He was still smiling his tigerish smile. "I'm so happy for you and your handsome young fellow. You must tell me all about him some time soon." Under his breath he added, "Tomorrow."

"Yes. Yes." Beyond his shoulder she could see Hilda, with the phone cradled against her neck, signaling goodbye. She pulled her hand free of Kirk's grip to wave back. Then she fled down the corridor.

Tomorrow. He would never buy the California trip gambit now. No amount of glibness—and she knew how glib she could be; knew and deplored—could explain away both Roger and a trip which had been in the offing for months and was now all at once urgent. Kirk would see through her delaying tactics the instant she tried to launch them.

Tomorrow. It loomed ahead of her as menacing and inescapable, as heavy with potential violence, as a volcano.

FOUR

Wednesday was family dinner night with the Bannings. It was Hilda's idea, and they were all stuck with it. Including—especially—Kirk's son Gene, who had triggered the idea by moving out of the "home" apartment on 66th Street four years ago. Finding a place of his own had been his first act when he landed his job at the museum: he was twenty-two years old at the time, and itching for freedom. Even so, he seldom failed to turn up for Hilda's Wednesday dinners. Partly because she took so much obvious pleasure in them. "Like old times," she was sure to say at some point, looking contentedly around at her little family circle. "Just us chickens." She had a fund of such timeworn quips, and the fact that they were invariably greeted by groans from her audience did not prevent her from using them. They lent a nostalgic touch, these simpleminded predictables, a harking back to the family solidarity of Gene's childhood. It was more myth than reality now, for him, if not for Hilda or Isobel.

And yet not all myth; otherwise he would have given up the weekly visits long ago. Because they weren't always the cozy, relaxed occasions of Hilda's dreams. More often than not, in spite of all her efforts and all Gene's advance resolutions, he and Dad would get into one of their yelling matches about nothing, anything, everything ...

He couldn't help it, even now when he knew perfectly well what the consequences might be. Another heart attack. Possibly a fatal one. He couldn't help it, damn it, even now.

Why did he have to be so excessive about Dad? First the kid's blind hero worship, then the shattering disillusionment of his adolescence— But he was past both those stages. If he no longer loved Dad the way he used to (the way Isobel still did), he no longer hated him either. Time and experience had given him some perspective about Dad's philanderings. After all, Hilda wasn't exactly scintillating; she had about as much sex appeal as a Girl Scout; her very devotion robbed her of the excitement and uncertainty that, to a man of Dad's temperament, were no doubt essential.

But somehow, face to face with Dad, Gene lost his perspective. It was too much for him, the friction, the rankling remnants of those two violently contradictory feelings, which he had not quite outgrown even now, and neither of which Dad fully understood. The too-much love he had taken for granted; the sudden switch to hostility shocked and baffled him. Apparently he knew what he had lost, but not why he had lost it. Too proud, of course, to ask for an explanation, and Gene had no intention of volunteering one. Let him figure it out for himself.

On this particular Wednesday Gene left the museum earlier than usual; it was hardly five thirty when he let himself into the apartment—quietly, because Dad might for once be following the doctor's instructions to lie down for a while when he came home from the office. It seemed so at first: either that or nobody was there at all. The long hall was hushed and dusky. No lights under the doors that opened off it. No sounds of activity anywhere. Gene paused with his hand still on the door knob, pleasantly aware of the warm silence, the faint smell of lemon oil and lilacs. There was a pitcher full of them on the table under the mirror. Isobel's touch. She was mad for flowers.

He took a step forward, noiseless on the wall-to-wall carpeting, and then he heard Dad's voice, low and urgent, from the living room. "Listen, Lorraine, I was a bastard this morning, okay, but you've got to admit ... No, I'm at home, waiting for the gathering of the clan. Family dinner night. Hilda must have gotten stuck at the office, and the kids haven't showed up yet, either. If I hang up sudden-like, you'll know why ... Lorraine darling, I'm not asking you to explain now, let's leave that till tomorrow, I just wanted to ..."

So. The thud in the pit of Gene's stomach was not shock, nor even surprise. After all, he remembered that intimate note in Dad's voice from years ago. Different circumstances, different locale, different playmate. If that was the proper term; Gene thought it was. Lorraine darling. Lorraine. Wasn't there a girl by that name who did some kind of freelance work for the agency? Yes, Gene remembered meeting her. A stunner. So.

The last thing he wanted was to go on listening. Yet he stood rigid, momentarily incapable of calling out, clearing his throat, opening the door and slamming it shut again—anything to announce his presence and cut off the voice from the living room. "Look, darling—"

A key snicked in the lock; liberated, Gene turned and sang out, "Isobel!" loud and clear.

"Shh. Maybe Dad's asleep. Hi. How are you?" She had bought more flowers, daffodils. Above their bright frills her face rose like another, paler blossom. Isobel was very fair, as their mother had been. She wore her fine, straight blonde hair parted in the middle, hooked behind her ears, and then hanging loose. In her mini-skirt and suede jacket she looked much younger than she was, rather like a lost child, grave and delicate and in need of protection. Never mind that she was twenty-four years old now, presumably adult; to Gene she was still the little sister he must look out for. It went deeper than just the happenstance of physical appearance. Isobel really was more vulnerable than other people; she had never grown a shell, and when she was hurt her only defense was to shrink inward, hugging her wounds in comfortless, silent misery. Gene was enough like her to know.

Thank God Isobel hadn't been the one to overhear Dad's end of that telephone conversation! Or Hilda! It could so easily have been either of them. At the thought of how easily, Gene felt his hands go clammy with sweat. Okay, it hadn't happened. Could have; but hadn't.

"Who goes there?" Dad called from the living room. Very cheerful and hearty. ("If I hang up sudden-like, you'll know why …")

He was stretched out on the couch, the picture of paternal innocence, his glasses pushed up on his forehead and the evening paper on the floor beside his slippers. "No, I wasn't asleep. Just resting."

Isobel switched on the table lamp and bent to kiss him. "Look what I brought you. Aren't they pretty?"

"Almost as pretty as you. Hug my neck, baby. That's the way, that's my girl."

Isobel had always been his pet. Naturally enough, looking as much like their mother as she did. It was a fact of life; Gene accepted it without resentment. Such demonstrations of affection were foreign to his nature, anyway.

Tonight, in fact, he would have preferred to skip the customary handshake with Dad. But Isobel would be sure to notice and wonder; no point in upsetting her. Dutifully he went through the motions. That "sincere" handclasp of Dad's. Part of the advertising man's basic equipment.

"You kids come in together?" In other words, who if anybody overheard what if anything?

"Practically," said Gene. "Isobel must have been right on my heels. I'd barely shut the door behind me when she opened it again."

Dad nodded, completely relaxed now—if he had ever been otherwise. His confidence in his own luck was superb. "How are you, my boy? What's new and startling with the mammals of North America?"

His little joke. His comic tag line for Gene's job—which, as he knew perfectly well, had nothing to do with mammals. Apparently stone artifacts were not intrinsically funny. And mammals of North America were. And of course it had to be reduced to a joke, because Gene had chosen it against his father's advice or consent. Preferred to spend his life mousing around in the musty bowels of a museum, for God's sake, when by now he could have been making real money as Dad's right-hand man!

"As far as I know," said Gene evenly, "nothing. What's new in the rat race?"

"Hilda can tell you when she gets here. I'm still pretty much on the sidelines, myself. It's a damn good thing there was somebody in the family to take over when I conked out." He swung his legs to the floor and twitched his glasses into place on his nose. "That's all I can say. A damn good thing."

"Yes, isn't it," said Gene.

Isobel, on her way to the kitchen with her flowers, looked back at them uneasily. "Come on, Gene. You can get the ice out. Hilda'll be here any minute, and we can all have a drink."

"Yes, yes," said Dad. "That's the high point of my day, my one ounce of booze in a gallon of water. I can hardly wait."

How the hell were you supposed to answer that sort of thing? Not sympathetically. Not lightly, either. The only safe course was to ignore it. But tonight Gene was in a fairly abrasive mood himself. He said what he felt like saying: "Oh, stop bitching."

It jolted Dad, all right, if only for a moment. Then, with a cold smile, he aimed the horn-rims at Gene and prepared to blast him. "Listen, you young—"

The door opened, and Hilda bounced in, flushed, breathless, and spilling over with oil for the troubled waters. "Hello, everybody, Gene honey, how are you? Sorry to be late, a minor crisis at the last minute—now, now, Kirk, don't agitate yourself, I said minor, tell you all about it later. Well, and then the bus, we simply crawled, I declare, the traffic in this town gets worse every day. Oh Isobel, daffodils! Lovely. I thought steak for dinner, okay with everybody? It won't take long, plenty of time for a good visit first. Unless you're all starving ..."

On she burbled, valiantly staving off dissension, rushing to patch up the chinks in the family fortress with whatever came to hand. And somehow managing to do it—not so much through skill or subtlety as sheer zeal. She cared so much about all three of them. Dad came first, of course. But could any natural mother have given her children more devotion, more steadfast, warm affection?

Or more fun? That was what Gene remembered most clearly about his childhood, the good times they used to have with Hilda. Dad's restlessness had kept them on the move, from New Jersey to Connecticut to Long Island, finally to the New York apartment; for some reason he had been contented to stay here longer than anywhere else. It couldn't have been easy for Hilda, all the uprootings and resettlings. But she had never been too busy or tired to pile a load of kids into the car and take them swimming or fishing or picnicking; on rainy days she could always be counted on to think up new games; no project was too messy for her, no pet was forbidden, even in the face of Dad's periodic explosions: "What are we running, for Pete's sake, a menagerie? Snakes in the bedroom, hamsters in the kitchen, turtles in the bathtub. What about a pig or two for the parlor?"

She cared so much. Gave so much. Surely, for her sake, he could refrain from quarreling with Dad. But that was the point of the quarrels! They boiled up on her account, because he resented so bitterly Dad's stupid little ego-building infidelities.

Was Hilda really unaware of them? She had never given the slightest indication ... But then of course she wouldn't. To do so would seem to her disloyal. Disloyal!

"Just let me get things organized in the kitchen," she was saying, "and I'll be right with you." She had tossed her tweed coat, briefcase and purse down on a chair, and her arms were lifted in the familiar gesture, re-anchoring the pins in her bun of curly graying hair. Not a bad-looking woman, in her solid, hearty, outdoorsy way; but on the other hand not the glamorous ultra-feminine type to appeal to a man like Dad. A marriage of convenience. For him; not for her. She had been his secretary originally, and except for Mother's death, probably still would be. Yes, thought Gene. One way or the other, Hilda would have devoted her life to the man of her choice. Without ever suspecting, in her single-minded innocence, how shamefully she was being cheated.

Once more her anxious eyes flickered from Gene to Dad. Then, apparently reassured, she followed Isobel out to the kitchen.

Dad was on his feet, pacing between window and couch, twirling the horn-rims, now and then casting a puzzled glance in Gene's direction. "So where did I go wrong tonight? Just because I like my little joke—Don't be so damn touchy. Forget it. Anyway, you evened the score. 'Stop bitching, stop bitching.' That was dirty pool, if you ask me. You don't seem to realize it, but I've got a lot on my mind these days."

"I'm sure you have," said Gene.

Dad swept on, impervious to sarcasm. "Let's face it, the agency could go under. It's a one-man operation, and I'm it. I don't mean Hilda's not doing a great job, because she is. Great. But if she and that quack don't let me get back on the ball full-time pretty soon, we're going to be in trouble. We've lost one account already, and we could lose Argus, it's always been too iffy for comfort. That could be what she means by a minor crisis. She's done it before, you know. Soft-pedalled things so as not to worry me. What's she up to? Do you know?" He flipped the horn-rims into place and glared at Gene through them. "I've got a hunch, whatever it is, Owen Adams is back of it."

He had a way of spitting the name of Owen Adams out, as if it were a bite of rotten apple. The rotten apple which, for reasons of his own, he now considered Owen Adams to be. Owen's agency was the biggest in the field, and for more than ten years Dad had been one of his star performers, and a close personal friend as well. His decision to strike off on his own (taking with him a choice account) had come as a double blow to Owen: he hinted at treachery, offered bribes, predicted disaster as the only possible end to such a reckless gamble. That prediction did it, of course; Dad would rather fry in hell than give Owen Adams the chance to say I told you so.

"Oh, come on, now, Dad. You don't seriously believe that Hilda would—"

"Not Hilda. Owen. The bastard's been aching to get his hands on my agency ever since I started it. That's what he's after, never mind what Hilda believes. Just trying to help. Out of the goodness of his heart yet. I set her straight on that point, don't worry. I know about Owen and his helping hand. There's always a price tag attached. And another thing —" The door opened: Isobel again. At once he forgot his tirade and switched to sweetness and light. "There you are, baby. Sit down, let's hear what you've been up to today."

Gene headed for the kitchen, to see about drinks. Hilda, who was washing salad greens at the sink, did not see him for a moment, and he could not help noticing the unaccustomed sag to her shoulders, the drawn cast to her face. Well, why shouldn't she look tired? She had been living in a state of total tension for the past few months, ever since Dad's attack—alert, even while she slept, for the emergency that was all too possible. Gene remembered what the doctor had said about Dad's heart: like a worn-out inner tube, no predicting where it might give out again, or when. A graphic description. One that Hilda, unlike Gene, wasn't likely to forget even for a split second. And added to the tension itself, the effort to hide it; the struggle against Dad's reckless contempt for all restrictions; the burden of responsibility at the office …

She looked up. Her shoulders straightened, and her face with its forthright features and high color rearranged itself into something like cheerful animation. "He's looking better, don't you think so? More rested. If only I could get him to stop fussing about the office— We'll make out, you know, even if we lose Argus, and we probably won't. Chances are they're just bluffing again, the way they have before. We'll still make out, Argus or no Argus."

Maybe. But Dad wasn't just being egotistical when he talked about "a one-man operation and I'm it." It was his flair, his imagination and flexibility and flashes of inspiration that had made his agency a success;

without them it would have no more drawing power than any of its competitors. There were plenty of them, all no doubt waiting to pounce like vultures, and no amount of Hilda's dogged energy could fend them off.

She said, with sudden intensity, "Sometimes I almost wish we would lose Argus, and the rest of them too. Then he'd have to retire, the way he should have done when he first got sick."

"Dad? Retire? It would kill him!"

"It's more apt to kill him if he doesn't. Nothing could be worse for him than all this pressure and rush and worry. He's got to slow down, take it easy ... I don't mean retire completely. But we could at least get out of the city, Florida or somewhere, anywhere, there are all kinds of little businesses to look into. And I could always get a job to tide us over." She stared past Gene, off into a dreamworld—impossible, surely she must realize it—of no stress and strain, no city clamor or crowds or polluted air. And no Lorraine, either; if by any chance she was on the same wave length as Gene.

She sighed and let go of the dream. "Wishful thinking. I know it's never going to happen. It's all I can do to keep him away from the office even part of the day, and then I'm afraid he just sits here and stews about what's going on behind his back."

"Something seems to be bugging him," said Gene cautiously. "Something about Owen Adams and—"

"Oh Lord, is he still off on that pitch? It's my own fault, of course, ever since I made the mistake of mentioning Owen Adams' name he's been smelling rats all over the place. Just because Owen wrote me when Kirk first got sick. Said he was sorry to hear about it, anything he could do, and so forth. Such a friendly little note, really. Or so it seemed to me. But—Oh well." She shook her head ruefully. "I guess there are some things about Kirk that I'll never understand."

There certainly are, thought Gene, and let's hope you never have to try.

He switched the subject to Isobel after that: her new job was turning out to be not much improvement over the others, and she was talking about going back to art school.

When they rejoined the others in the living room Hilda lifted her drink and said brightly, "Cheers, dears. Isn't it nice, just us chickens ..."

Everybody groaned.

FIVE

Yesterday it had sounded like a good idea to Mary, Teddy's suggestion that they "sit this alert out together." She had snapped him right up on his invitation to come over for a drink during what might (she could only hope) turn out to be Lorraine's final go-round with Kirk Banning.

But now that she was here, she rather wished she weren't. Maybe it was her imagination—she wasn't the most tranquil soul in town herself—but Teddy seemed even more fluttery and twittery than usual. He kept jumping up to adjust the blinds, empty the ashtrays, press upon her more of the little "eaties" he had prepared. And of course he chattered constantly.

In his waspish, gossipy way Teddy could be quite amusing. The department store where he worked as a window decorator provided him with a fund of stories and characters that he no doubt touched up here and there in the interests of entertainment; he had a knack for mimicry, and a keen sense of human absurdity, including his own. Some of his funniest sallies were aimed at himself. He had other engaging qualities, too: a lively, if superficial, interest in practically everything on earth; generosity to an almost embarrassing degree; the impulse toward neighborliness and friendship that had drawn him into this business with Lorraine. All the same ...

"Please, Teddy. You're driving me out of my mind. Could you please, just for a minute, light somewhere and shut up?"

"I know. Isn't it awful? I can't help it." He was perched on the hassock at the moment, diminutive and somehow monkey-like in his tight jeans, turtleneck sweater and thong sandals. Sometimes Teddy's costumes were splendidly high style. On his days off, like this one, he went ultra-casual. Apparently he had been experimenting with his hair again; it was decidedly more auburn. "I haven't been able to settle down to anything all day. After lunch I went shopping for a lamp shade, out of sheer desperation, and my dear, I wish you could have seen some of the monstrosities, absolutely fascinating, there was one at that little shop on Greenwich—you know, I told you about it, the place where I found my Cupid clock, after months, I'm not exaggerating, literally months of combing the metropolis— Oh dear, there I go again. I'm sorry, Mary. I can't seem to help it."

The Cupid clock chimed. Six thirty. What was going on in Lorraine's apartment, two floors above? "Now let's not panic," Mary had said last night, when Lorraine called with her latest tale of woe. "Maybe it's just as well that he knows about Roger. Maybe he'll be so mad at you he'll want to break it off himself." It was clutching at straws, and they both knew it. Just as they both knew (though Mary admitted it only to herself) that her program of delaying tactics had very little chance of succeeding now. All right, she could think of nothing else. Neither could Lorraine herself, of course; or Teddy. Let's not panic, let's not panic ...

"He got here early," Teddy was rattling on. "I told you, didn't I, he was going up the stairs when I came back from shopping. It couldn't have been much past four. He didn't see me, just as well he didn't, though he probably wouldn't even recognize me. The only time I ever actually met him was ages ago, long before Lorraine gave me the scoop on their little amour. Then, half an hour or so later, I heard her come in—"

"That early? She didn't expect to get through with her appointment uptown before six."

"Maybe she cancelled it. Anyway, it was about four thirty when I heard her on the stairs and then Kirk saying something, I know because I'd just turned on that campy TV quiz show, I adore it, today they had the most— Maybe if I turned on something now?" Without waiting for an answer, he hopped up and began twiddling knobs. Mary closed her eyes against the expected onslaught of commercials, folk music, newscasters.

But the racket, when it came, was not that kind, nor from that source. It brought her struggling up out of her sling chair and sent Teddy flying across the room: a pounding at the door, a series of frantic pings from the bell.

Lorraine stood there, whiter than the coat she was wearing, eyes stretched wide, an unhinged look to her chin. "Please," she whispered. "I think he's—"

And not another word was spoken, not even by Teddy, until they somehow or other got themselves up the stairs and into Lorraine's ruffly little bedroom. Kirk lay sprawled crosswise on the bed, face down, except that his head was turned so they could see one sunken, half-open eye and half of his slack mouth. On the side of the bed nearest the door the toes of his shoes scraped against the floor; his right arm was flung forward, seeming to reach for something beyond the other side. He looked so diminished. So shrunken and remote; all the taut energy cut off, all the crackling ego extinguished.

"I found him," Lorraine began calmly enough. Maybe too calmly. "I was late getting home, and when I first walked in I thought he wasn't here, either. Only then I came on into the bedroom and—and—" She shuddered and swayed; Mary put her arms around her. "It wasn't my fault, it wasn't anything I said or did. Honest and true, Mary. I just walked in and found him ..." She broke into a storm of sobs.

And Teddy, who had threatened to swoon at first and then thought better of it, was now off on one of his non-stop monologues: mouth to mouth respiration, the Fire Department, the doctor across the street—

"Go get him. And listen, Teddy." Mary grabbed his arm and fixed on him the stern eye of authority. "We were here, you and I, when it happened. Remember? I'll figure out the details while you're getting the doctor. You hear me, Teddy? You've got to watch what you say."

He gave a scared gulp. His little monkey face bobbed up and down. Temporarily at least, she had struck him dumb. He sprinted off without uttering so much as a syllable.

She turned to Lorraine and said crisply, "Pull yourself together and help me. No use trying to pull this off if we don't make it look right. There have to be four glasses. With liquor in them. And we have to decide how Kirk happened to be here."

"But he's on the bed," wailed Lorraine. "How can we—"

"We have to," said Mary.

And so they did. Mary wasn't sure how. But by the time the doorbell rang they were ready. Between them they had managed to piece together an innocent, plausible explanation for Kirk's being where he was. At least they hoped it was plausible. Now was the time to find out.

Disaster was narrowly averted at the last moment, when Lorraine had already pressed the buzzer. "My coat!" she gasped. "I've still got my coat on!" She tore it off as if it were red-hot and bundled it into the closet, where of course it would be if—so their story was to go—she had gotten home at five thirty instead of six thirty.

And Mary hadn't even noticed! What else might she have missed, what other little oversight might crop up to knock their story into a cocked hat? No time left, footsteps on the stairs, too late for anything but prayer. In a tremble of dire misgivings, she opened the door and faced—not Teddy and the doctor from across the street, as she expected—but two sturdy young cops. Behind her she heard Lorraine gulp and burst into another fit of tears.

"Guy says you got a problem?" said one of the cops.

She stepped aside to let them in, and here came Teddy panting up the stairs, his coiffure in wild disarray, his power of speech fully restored. "He'll be right over, the doctor, two minutes, he said, and then on my way back I saw this prowl car, and ..."

She felt miraculously calm as she led them into the bedroom. They bent over Kirk, peering at him soberly, respectfully. Not touching him. "Who is he?" asked the one who did the talking.

"Kirk Banning. A friend, a business acquaintance, of my sister's. This is her apartment." She gestured toward Lorraine, and they gave her the kind of look men did give Lorraine. Tears or no tears. "Lorraine Walsh. I'm Mary Walsh. And this is Teddy Houghton. He lives downstairs, on the first floor. We were having a drink together, the three of us—"

"Four," Teddy was right there with the correction. "Kirk, Mr. Banning, was here too."

"I meant at first," she went on smoothly, with a quelling glance at him. "Before he called about the rush job for Lorraine. He was— He's in advertising, and Lorraine does quite a bit of art work for him. When he couldn't get her at her studio he called here. Very rush-rush, he said, and too complicated to explain over the phone." She paused for breath, and Lorraine took up the thread, in a touchingly quavery voice.

"So I said if he wanted to bring it down I could get started on it tonight, and when he got here naturally I offered him a drink, and—"

The arrival of the doctor interrupted her. Teddy had left the downstairs door on the latch for him; he came breezing in, a florid, jolly-looking fellow in his white office jacket. "Now then," he said, and headed in a businesslike way for Kirk.

Everybody stepped back to give him room. Watching. Waiting. Presently he straightened up. "There's nothing I can do. Sorry. My guess would be death due to a massive coronary, but of course that's only on the basis of a superficial examination, and with no knowledge of his medical history."

"He had a heart attack several months ago." Lorraine. Muffled. Very subdued. "Quite a bad one, I think. And then last month, a setback of some kind. What do they call it? Fibrillation?"

The doctor nodded. "What happened tonight? Did he just collapse?"

It was Mary's turn again. Home stretch on their story. "We don't really know. I mean, he seemed fine, having a drink and chatting. Then he excused himself to go to the bathroom, and after a while we began to wonder, you know, because he didn't come back. I haven't any idea how long it was, actually, nobody was paying much attention. Ten minutes, maybe? I just don't know. Anyway, we began to wonder, and at last Lorraine came in here to see if he was all right, and—and here he was on the bed."

The cops blinked sympathetically. Lorraine sniffled. Teddy, who had listened spellbound, let out his breath in a sigh of sheer admiration. The doctor nodded again. "Yes. All the same, I'd be overstepping the bounds of my authority if I—"

"Better call headquarters, huh, Doc?" said the talking cop. "Okay if I use your phone, Miss?"

This had been only a trial run, then. They would have to go through their story again, for the benefit of other, possibly more skeptical officials. All right, thought Mary rather giddily, bring on your tigers.

"An awful shock," the doctor was saying. He gave Lorraine's hand a more or less professional pat. "But I don't think there'll be any difficulty. Fairly obvious, especially in view of the previous attack. They have to check these things, you know, just in case. What about his relatives? They ought to be notified."

"Yes," whispered Lorraine. She cast an imploring look at Mary.

There was no answer at the Banning apartment. Torn between hope and dread, Mary waited out ring after ring, long after she knew it was no use. Could Hilda still be at the office? (Incredibly, her watch showed only seven o'clock.) No answer there, either. Mustn't panic. But they had to get hold of her. Hilda had to be told. Mustn't panic.

"Maybe his son?" faltered Lorraine. "He lives—I don't think he lives at home anymore."

He was, thank God, listed in the phone book. Eugene Banning. East 21st Street. Mary's own neighborhood. Again she dialed, no longer dreading her unhappy task, only hoping to get it over with.

He answered on the third ring, and in her relief at having found an audience she forgot the tactful phrases she had prepared and simply blurted it out—the raw, undiluted message.

He seemed a very cool type, Kirk's son. After a brief silence he said matter-of-factly, "I see. Hilda's at a reunion dinner, I know where to reach her. Let me have the address, please. We'll be right there."

But when she saw him face to face—as she did fifteen or twenty minutes later—the impression she got was not so much of coolness as tension. Basically he looked a good deal like his father. The same dark hair and eyes; the same generously molded features. But without Kirk's mobility, the quicksilver shift from one expression to another that had accounted for so much of his charm. His son's face was still and guarded; it gave nothing away.

And Hilda, poor Hilda, dressed not too becomingly for the reunion dinner in basic black and pearls, was obviously and mercifully in a state of shock. Mary had met her a couple of times before, at Lorraine's studio, and remembered her air of cheerful, wholesome energy. Now her eyes were dazed and tearless, her movements clumsy; her voice, normally so hearty and ringing, could hardly be heard.

By this time the authorities had appeared to take charge. Mary and Lorraine went through their story again, with an occasional well-timed assist from Teddy, who came through like a trooper, now that he had been fed his lines. Mary suspected that he was enjoying himself. Well, there was something rather exhilarating about it. A tricky job well done, and on such short notice, too. More luck than shrewdness, probably, but she and Lorraine had hit upon an explanation that, as far as she could tell, was as satisfactory to the authorities as to Kirk's family. The biggest stroke of luck being that they had had to invent so little. The rush job, for instance, which they wouldn't have dared to fabricate, with Hilda knowing as much as she did about what went on at the agency—the rush job was an actuality, right there in Kirk's briefcase for all to see. It had come in that afternoon, shortly after Hilda left for her client's meeting; he had called Lorraine about it earlier than they claimed, that was all.

The authorities raised no awkward, unforeseen questions. Apparently neither Hilda nor Gene Banning (though with a poker face like his, how could you be sure?) saw anything out of the way about the circumstances as presented.

It was Kirk's daughter who roiled up the waters, for Mary at least. Now and then Isobel helped out at the agency—running errands, mostly—and Mary had met her once or twice before. So she knew what Isobel looked like, and Lorraine had provided a sketchy background: "A quiet little thing. Pretty, of course. In a way. Not a bit like Kirk. He dotes on her. Spoils her outrageously." That was all she had to go on, and it certainly did not prepare her for the atmosphere of violence that Isobel brought into the room now. A random sort of violence, directed at nothing in particular, everything in general. Almost as if the girl were a poltergeist.

She was out of breath from the stairs, and she had obviously been crying. Not now, though. In her pinched, mascara-streaked face her eyes were brilliant with what looked more like rage than grief.

Her brother sprang to her side. "We didn't know where to reach you, Isobel. The best I could do was call Pam and give her the message—"

"I don't believe it," she said, low and jerky. "No. He's not, he can't be. No. I don't believe it." She stood rigid, refusing the comfort of Gene's protective arm. Her eyes made a withering circuit of the room, accusing them all, blaming them all. No one escaped that impartial hostility. "You weren't home, either," she added to Hilda, who blinked as if she had been slapped.

"Isobel, honey, I—"

"Well, you weren't. Two flights of stairs. He's not supposed to climb stairs." That shot was for Lorraine. It hit home, too. "Why didn't you—" She caught her breath sharply.

They had moved Kirk's body to a stretcher and were maneuvering it through the narrow door between the living room and bedroom. Diminished to the limit now. Reduced to nothing but an inert mound under the blanket. Mary drew back, like the others, to make way.

Through the door, across the living room, out into the corridor. After that a series of muffled thumps as they started down the stairs, and a husky voice: "Watch yourself, will ya. Chrissake, watch it."

One of the officials closed the door and spoke in a low voice to Hilda. Something about Kirk's personal belongings, which had been removed from his pockets and now lay in a little pile on the coffee table. Hilda stared at them dully. Wallet, loose change, keys, pen, extra glasses, all the essentials that were no longer essential.

"His medicine isn't there," said Isobel, but muted now, almost hesitant. "His pills. The ones he was supposed to always have handy. They're not there."

Mary edged closer to the bedroom door and bumped against Lorraine, who was doing the same.

"That's right, they ought to be here." Hilda poked hopelessly at the pile. "Only he forgot them so often, you know. If I didn't think to remind him, he'd go off without them, half the time. He hated the whole business, pills, the doctor's instructions, having to be careful. He just couldn't seem to accept being ill. He just wasn't the type …"

Right. No one who knew Kirk would argue the point. And it was because he wasn't the type that Lorraine (at Mary's prompting) had pried out of him a supply of the pills to keep here, in case of an emergency. On the bedside table. They had been there for weeks. Must still be there. Surely, surely.

By now Mary had a clear view of the little table. In the uncompromising light from the wall lamp above it, its top was bare except for an ashtray.

Lorraine was right beside her, looking too. Then her eyes, scared and beseeching, shifted to Mary—a glance that, for all it revealed, was still somehow veiled. In Mary's memory something else stirred and rose to the surface: time, a discrepancy about what time Lorraine had come home. Six thirty, according to her. But Teddy had said four thirty, just after he turned on his quiz show …

He could be mistaken; he often was. The pills could have been knocked off the table, onto the floor.

All the same, Mary felt an ominous inner chill, an intimation that she and Teddy, with their kind hearts and good intentions, might have blundered into something quite different from what they had bargained for.

SIX

"I don't see what you're bitching about," said Teddy. "Pills, shmills. They wouldn't necessarily have saved him, even if they'd been there for him to take. Probably wouldn't have made any difference, according to what the doctor told Hilda. His own doctor, the one that prescribed them."

"Of course that's what he told Hilda," said Mary impatiently. "She already blames herself for not reminding Kirk to take them with him. Why make her feel any worse? It's not just the pills, anyway. I know you've changed your tune now about hearing somebody go up the stairs at four thirty, but—"

"I was mistaken!" Teddy shrilled. "You know how suggestible I am, especially when I get in a twitch. And I was that day, if you remember, you weren't at your best, either. There I was, all keyed up for the action to start, and—well, and so I heard things before there was anything to hear. I'm sorry, but that's how I am."

It was Sunday, and they were sitting in a tearoomish joint across the street from the memorial chapel where they had just attended Kirk's funeral services. Together, naturally. The three conspirators. Still together. Drinking coffee and snapping at each other. Two-thirds of them, anyway. Lorraine wasn't saying much of anything. Her profile, withdrawn and sad under her fetching little hat with its wisp of black veil, was outlined against the window. Since Thursday night she had been staying with Mary in her apartment. Her own place, once so dear to her, gave her the shudders now; she could not bear the thought of setting foot inside it. Later on, perhaps, but for the time being there was no need: Teddy was happy to pick up her mail for her and water her plants.

"Look, Mary." Teddy leaned toward her earnestly. "It's all settled. The autopsy showed what he died of. Natural causes. A perfectly simple, straightforward heart attack. Nobody else is making any waves. Luckily for us, I might add. My gawd, when I think of it, if they'd turned up evidence of foul play ... Sorry, sweetie," he added, as Lorraine winced. "Not that we did anything wrong, of course. A slight rearrangement of the facts, a few minor adjustments. And in such a good cause. A downright noble cause. Personally, I think we carried it off very well. All this quibbling about a few pills that happened to be missing. They'll turn up yet. Wait and see if they don't. Under the rug, or behind the radiator, or somewhere."

"We took the place apart, Lorraine and I. They're not there. They are just not there, Teddy. And they couldn't have walked off that table and out of the apartment under their own power. Somebody took them away. There's no getting around it. Somebody must have been up there before Lorraine came home and found him."

(At six thirty, she repeated to herself. That was what Lorraine said, and that was what Mary believed. She did, she did.)

Silence. Teddy applied himself to dunking a lump of sugar in his coffee, methodically dousing it up and down until it disintegrated. Lorraine spoke at last, tentatively, "I'm not positive they were there when I left to go uptown. I mean, I didn't check. Actually, I don't remember checking in the morning, either." She did not look at Mary. "It didn't occur to me until just now. But the maid was there the day before. If she knocked the bottle off and spilled the pills—and she's always doing things like that—she'd just vacuum them up and not bother to tell me. I don't know why I didn't think of it before, but—"

"There you are!" Teddy, restored to his normal sprightliness, spread his hands in a gesture of triumph. "What did I tell you? So simple, after all. It's why I don't have a maid anymore. When Mrs. Smyth—she was my last one, Mrs. Smyth with a y—when she smashed my Tiffany lamp and not only refused to admit it, but had the unmitigated gall to tell me I had done it myself, well, I mean, it was too much. I drew myself up to my full five feet one and three-quarters and I said in a voice of thunder, Mrs. Smyth, I said, this is it, I have had it, we have reached the parting of the ways."

He rattled on: from maids to taxes to air pollution to vacation spots to God knows what. By some circuitous route—Mary missed several stops along the way—he eventually got back to the funeral, which had been notable chiefly for its brevity and the fact that Isobel had not attended it. An attack of migraine. "I can't help thinking it was just as well," Teddy confided. "Not that I'd wish migraine on my worst enemy. But Isobel's a little—well, nervous-making, if you know what I mean. Or didn't she strike you that way? Of course it's probably not fair to judge her by the other night, naturally she was shook up, as who wasn't, I'm sure she's a lovely girl. She just seemed sort of spooky to me. They're not much like Kirk, are they, either Isobel or her brother? I mean—"

"Please," murmured Lorraine.

"I am sorry, sweetie. Stupid me, of course you don't want to be reminded. I won't do it again. I promise. Because there's no point, is there?" He smiled at them, brightly, anxiously. "It's all over. Past and done with. Nothing for any of us to do now but forget the whole thing."

"I'll never forget Kirk," said Lorraine, with a catch in her voice. "Never."

They finished their coffee and—minus Teddy, who was meeting somebody at the Guggenheim—went home, where Lorraine spent the next hour and a half getting ready to go out to dinner with Roger. Well, thought Mary, and why shouldn't she? After all, never forgetting Kirk was quite a different matter from devoting the rest of her life to remembering him. That would have been morbid.

Mary had a date herself. The new accountant at the office, after a good many false starts, had finally worked up the courage to ask her out "for a bite to eat and a movie." The bite to eat consisted of spaghetti at a fifth-rate Italian restaurant. The movie was arty and grim. The accountant had damp hands and a nervous habit of sniffing, heretofore unnoticed by Mary. It was raining and they couldn't get a cab. At the door of her apartment building Mary said good night decisively. Exit the accountant, sniffing.

She couldn't help it, she began to cry, once she had reached the sanctuary of her living room. Lorraine wasn't back yet, of course; she had the place to herself. She leaned against the door, gulping abjectly.

And the phone rang. Not even a good cry, she thought, even that was too much to ask for. She was constitutionally incapable of letting her own phone go unanswered. It might be something important, something ...

It was Teddy. In a swivet. "Mary! I've been trying to get you for hours. Are you free to talk? I mean, is Lorraine—"

"She's not here." She blew her nose. "What's the problem?"

"Are you sure you're all right, dear? You sound a little ... Well. The thing is, Lorraine's apartment, I went up to water the plants—the fuchsia, poor thing, not long for this world—anyway, somebody's been *in* there, Mary!"

"You mean a robbery? Somebody broke in?"

"No, no. The lock's okay. And nothing's missing, as far as I can tell. All the same, somebody's been in there since Friday night. I went up then, you know, to get Lorraine's other shoes for her, and I know just how I left things. Don't try to tell me it's my imagination. It can't be."

"All right, Teddy. Calm down and tell me—"

"I'm perfectly calm, thank you. And I'm not in the grip of liquor, either, if that's what you're thinking. Two martinis before dinner. Not a drop since. I don't mean to alarm you unduly. I just feel you ought to know the facts."

"So do I. Nothing's missing, you said."

"As far as I can tell, I said. Unless you want to count the stack of magazines and papers I brought down to my place Friday night.

Lorraine said it was all right, she always passes them on to me. No, it wasn't that anything was missing. And I didn't find any foreign objects, you know, like a handkerchief with somebody's initials or the stub of an Egyptian cigarette. None of that jazz. It's hard to explain in words. If you were here, of course, I could show you ..."

They both let it hang for a moment. Then Mary said, "You win. I'll get over there as soon as I can."

It was still raining, a dispirited drizzle that seemed more like November than April. But without the accountant and his blighting influence on everything including cabs, she had no difficulty in snagging one.

Teddy was already clutching Lorraine's keys when he opened the door to her. Bright-eyed, tensely determined to keep the lid on the excitement that simmered inside him, he led the way up the stairs to Lorraine's apartment, turned the key in the lock, and stepped aside to wave Mary in first.

She entered briskly, before the reluctance she felt—and refused to admit, too silly—could get a real hold on her. The living room was still and stuffy, no more disordered, and no less, than she remembered it from Thursday night. (Well, Teddy had made no spectacular claims.) She began to relax. Even the bedroom did not bother her too much. The bed was stripped down to the mattress, and the chest of drawers was pulled out from the wall, as she and Lorraine had left it after their search for the missing pills.

"All right," she said. "Show me what you mean."

Teddy, who had been pattering at her heels in heroic silence, instantly burst forth. First of all, the stack of papers and periodicals on the magazine stand beside the couch. Having picked up the top pile for himself, he remembered distinctly, unquestionably, beyond all doubt, that the *National Geographic* had been on top when he left Friday night. He pointed dramatically. *Harper's* was on top now. Not the *National Geographic*.

Next, the toss pillows on the couch. He knew good and well he had switched them so as to segregate the lemon yellow from the shocking pink. Because it set his teeth on edge, that combination, always had, he simply had a thing about it. Again he pointed, dramatically, accusingly. Lemon yellow and shocking pink were cheek by jowl.

Furthermore, the couch cushions themselves. Mary would remember that tomato juice had been spilled on the middle one? Yes, and the stain had never really come out; it still showed up in certain lights, he was willing to swear that it had been turned stained side down Friday night. Well. He switched on the floor lamp and stepped back, arms crossed over his gun-metal jacket and pale pink shirt. The stain was there, all right, faint but unmistakable.

Trivialities. But for that very reason forceful. They were just the sort of minute details practically no one but Teddy would notice; just the sort an intruder might easily overlook. On the other hand, Teddy was excitable, subject to flights of fancy, and far too fond of a good story to boggle at embroidering the facts if they weren't quite as sensational as they ought to be.

Mary eyed him sternly. "Teddy," she said. "If you're making this up—"

"So help me." He raised his hand. And his voice: it was suddenly quivering with outrage and frustration. "Making it up! I like that! Just because I lied for your sister— So did you! You're in this every bit as deep as I am. Yes, and so is she. Deeper, if you ask me. This is the thanks I get. Making it up! I must say, it's the last reaction I would have expected from you. I didn't have to call you at all, you know, and believe me, I wouldn't have if I'd had any idea you were going to accuse me of— Give me one good reason, that's all I ask, just one good reason why I should lie about a thing like this."

"Teddy, Teddy." She patted his fragile, heaving shoulder, in an absentminded way. One good reason, she was thinking. There wasn't one. Not with Teddy as anxious as he was to rule out any possibility of a dubious angle to Kirk's death. The missing pills she had agitated over—Teddy had pooh-poohed them all along. His original story of hearing Lorraine, or somebody, come in at four thirty—he had scrambled to withdraw it when he saw its implications. The fact that his intruder pointed in the same sinister direction proved that he was telling the truth. If he had decided a lie was necessary, it would have been an altogether different lie, in quite a different cause.

As usual, his fit of temper was soon over. A few more soothing noises from her, and they were friends again, clutching each other's hands. "All right, I believe you. As you say, you didn't have to tell me, you could have just kept quiet and— Why did you call me?"

"I was scared," he said; and that too was the simple truth. She could see it in his monkey-bright eyes, in every line of his sunlamp-tanned face. "I still am," he added.

"I know. Me too."

"Only I had to tell somebody. And you're so good in a crisis, Mary, you don't get rattled the way I do. Besides, we're in this together, whatever it is." He looked up at her wistfully. "It doesn't have to have anything to do with Kirk, does it? I mean, it could be just—"

"Just what? Go ahead, if you've got any other ideas. I haven't."

"Oh God," said Teddy. "Let's go downstairs. This place gives me the fantods."

Back in his apartment, he poured them each a stiff drink. Then he perched on the hassock and began. "Okay, so somebody has a key to Lorraine's place. Somebody besides Kirk. Because these are his, she gave me his set Thursday night. Remember?"

Mary nodded. Kirk had kept this particular set on a separate key ring and, after he let himself in Thursday afternoon, had left them on top of the bookcase, as often before. So they had been missing from the little pile of personal belongings Hilda had poked through, on the coffee table. And yes, Lorraine had handed them over to Teddy later on, just before she left.

"Her own set. And Kirk's. Those are the only ones I know of."

"Some other friend, maybe?" Teddy ventured. "After all, she's had other admirers besides Kirk. Roger, for instance. I understand he's back on the scene again. Why not Roger? He could still have a key, from back in the good old days before they broke up."

"If he ever had one in the first place. And if he didn't give it back or throw it away in the meantime. Anyway, why would Roger want to go mousing around up there behind her back?"

"Why would anybody? If we could figure out why we'd probably know who."

"It's got to have some connection with Kirk, Teddy. It's just too much of a coincidence otherwise. First the pills, and now this."

Teddy cast his eyes heavenward. "Sweetie, no, you're not still on the pill kick! Not after what Lorraine said—"

"I know all about what Lorraine said!" Cool it, she told herself, and took a sip of her drink. "She was only guessing. She's not positive, the way you are about the pillows and all."

"So?"

"So it might tie in. I mean, supposing the pills were where they should have been when Kirk got there. Only then somebody else came— just as you said at first, you said you heard somebody at four thirty— and went off with the pills—"

"*The Little Foxes!*" Teddy gave a shriek of laughter. "I didn't know you'd seen the revival! Forgive me, Mary, I can't help it." An even funnier idea struck him; he all but choked over it. "And then I suppose they came back two days later to see if he was really dead. Is that the tie-in?"

"Oh, what's the use! They could have come back to look for something, I don't know what, but—I still think it could be the same person. *Somebody's* been up there, according to you." She paused, and added bitterly, "Or have you changed your mind and decided you're not sure, after all?"

"No, I'm sure," he said, subdued now, and shamefaced.

"Well, then, we've got to do something about it. We can't just let them get away with it, whoever it was, and whatever they were up to."

"It's not as if they did any damage, or stole anything. The police wouldn't even— Good gawd, Mary, you're not suggesting we go the police!"

"Maybe we should, at that."

"You're out of your mind." Teddy stared at her in open horror. "Stark mad. Demented. In the first place, they'd arrest us. For perjury or suppression of evidence or whatever it was we did. You realize that, don't you? You realize we're some kind of felons?"

"I don't think felons exactly."

"Oh, don't you. Just a little matter of lying to the cops. All we have to do is explain why we did it, and they'll understand perfectly. Sure. And that's another thing. We're not the only people involved in this, you know. What about Lorraine? Kirk's family? That was the whole point, to save Hilda's feelings. It will hit her even harder, to find out now. And for what? Nothing's going to change the fact that Kirk died of natural causes. If it was a question of murder, okay, I wouldn't argue with you. But it's not. An out and out heart attack. Exactly what everybody expected."

"I know that." Then why couldn't she drop it? Why this compulsion to push Teddy on to the bitter end? "But I still say there's something fishy going on. You admitted it yourself. You admitted you were scared. I don't see how we can just—"

"Listen." He hopped up off the hassock and bounced in front of her. Like a jumping jack. "Just listen to me a minute, and then see if you're in such a sweat to go screaming to the cops. Just stop and think about who might be responsible for your something fishy. Who's the logical person? I'll tell you who. Lorraine!" She shrank back in her chair, and he leaned closer, jabbing his finger at her. "Don't pretend it hasn't occurred to you. She'd about had it with Kirk. Remember? She tried to break off with him, even before Roger decided to stage his return engagement. And when Kirk went all over honorable intentions, that really threw her into a snit. She wasn't going to marry him, come hell or high water. I'm not saying she wanted him to die, but—"

But Lorraine herself had come close to saying it. The tremulous rush of her words over the telephone was still fresh in Mary's memory: "God help me, I almost wish he'd die before next Thursday—"

"But he picked the right time to die, as far as she was concerned." Teddy pressed on relentlessly. "And if there was any funny business with the pills, she had the best chance. We've only got her word for what time she came home Thursday afternoon. It could have been earlier than she says, early enough for a lulu of a fight with him before she came pelting downstairs to tell us he was dead. Maybe with the pills in her coat pocket. She knew she could count on us to lie for her. We've been primed to do it for months now. No problem there. No problem getting back into her apartment, either, in case she needed to; she's got the only other set of keys extant."

"In case she needed to?"

"If she did pull *The Little Foxes* bit—your idea, sweetie, not mine—maybe the pills weren't in her pocket, after all. Maybe she'd hidden them somewhere up there, and then, when you started raising such a stink about them, decided she'd better destroy them just to be on the safe side."

"No," whispered Mary. "No."

"Yes." With one of his flashes of intuition, Teddy dropped to his knees beside her and pressed his nimble little hands over hers. "Mary darling, you pushed me into it. I'm only saying what you've been thinking yourself. That's all."

Yes, that was all. She tried to stifle her first sob. Then—what difference did it make anymore?—she let go of everything she had been holding back for the last three days. Just let go. Caved in. And dissolved.

SEVEN

One thing about the funeral, thought Gene, it had seemed to have little or nothing to do with Dad. Short, too. And small: neither Dad nor Hilda had any close relatives.

Okay, it was over. Now back to the 66th Street apartment; Hilda had invited a few friends for a buffet supper after the services. Trust her to go through the motions. Well, she was entitled to any available scraps of comfort. Haggard as she was—like a stranger, without her high color and her hearty, ringing voice—she was still managing not to let go. And would manage, Gene felt, never mind by how narrow a margin.

It was different with Isobel. She was the one who needed looking after. The trouble was that he did not know how. She gave him so little to work on. No tears for him to wipe away, no hysterical outbursts to quell, no response at all. Yet he had to keep trying. There must be some way of getting past the wall of her apathy ...

As soon as they reached the apartment, he headed down the hall toward her bedroom, where they had left her stretched out flat with her migraine. (Real or imaginary? He had his doubts.) And with Myrtle on hand, in case of need. Myrtle was dependable. Devoted. For a decade or so she had come in to do the weekly cleaning and, on special occasions like tonight's buffet, to help with the cooking and serving.

He tapped lightly on the sage-green door. No answer. Was she asleep? Too walled off even to hear? Or simply ignoring him, willing him to go away and leave her alone? He waited uneasily for a moment or two. Then he turned the knob and eased the door noiselessly open.

She was not there. The little bedside lamp cast a mellow light on the pale blue coverlet, which had been thrown back, and the rumpled, hollowed-out pillows. Otherwise the room was shadowy with twilight. "Isobel?" He stepped inside. The bathroom door stood open. Not there, either. He switched on the center light. (As if that would make any difference.) "Isobel?" The overwrought edge to his own voice embarrassed him. No need to panic. Myrtle would have the answer. He bolted down the hall to the kitchen.

"What? Not in her room?" Myrtle closed the oven door and straightened up to stare at him through her bifocals. "Well, but— But then where is she?"

Oh sure. Myrtle would have the answer.

And just to make it perfect, here came Hilda. She listened quietly, closed her eyes for a moment, and then said, "Did you look in the other bedrooms?"

So they looked in the other bedrooms. No Isobel. Myrtle did all the talking that was done. She flapped around like a distracted hen, her scrawny neck outstretched, her eyes beady with worry. "I fixed her a cup of tea along the middle of the afternoon, not that she drank it, but— She seemed kind of drowsy, so I just let her be, that's the only thing for a headache, I always say, sleep it off—I was out in the kitchen, making the canopies, but I had my ear cocked in case she wanted anything, not a peep out of her, if she was going off somewhere why didn't she tell me—"

Because you'd have given her an argument, thought Gene. You wouldn't have let her go. It wasn't much of a trick for her to sneak out without being heard or seen: the hall was carpeted, and she didn't have to go past the kitchen to get to the front door.

They wound up back in Isobel's bedroom. Hilda, on her way to the closet to see what clothes were gone, stopped short and made a moaning sound. "Oh! Her magic lamp! It's broken. Oh no! Poor child, she'll be heartbroken ..."

Isobel's magic lamp was not only broken, it was shattered, splintered into a handful of glassy fragments on the rug beneath the bedside table. She must have knocked it off herself, flung out an arm in restless half-sleep and sent her treasure crashing—against the headboard of the bed, perhaps, or the table leg.

"Oh Lord," said Gene. "I suppose that's why she took off the way she did."

It figured. The broken lamp would have, for Isobel in her present state of mind, a mystical, symbolic significance. Of all the gifts Dad had showered on her, this was the one she cherished most, this cheap miniature replica of a kerosene lamp. He had bought it fifteen years ago or more, to cheer her up when she had the measles. "It's a magic lamp," he told her. "If you rub it three times, like this, and make a wish before you go to sleep at night, your wish will come true." Did she still go through that nightly ritual? She might, thought Gene, out of habit if nothing else. For in all the years since—through all the uprootings and resettlings, through summer camp and boarding school, even weekend visits—Isobel had never been without her magic lamp.

Hilda opened the closet door and looked inside. "She must have worn her blue slacks. And her suede jacket. It's not here, either. I don't know what to do, Gene. I just don't know what to do."

"Now let's not panic. It's the sort of thing Isobel does when she's upset, you know. She's probably just walking it off. Or she might have gone to Pam's. I can call her and see. Look, Hilda. You need a drink. Go on back to the living room and leave the research to me. Go on, now."

He shooed both her and Myrtle out the door—for some reason, which he did not analyze, he needed privacy for the job ahead of him—and then headed for Isobel's pale blue extension phone. It was also on the bedside table; he had a good view of the shattered magic lamp while he talked to Pam.

They had been friends, he and Pam, since high school days, though nowadays Isobel saw more of her than he did. Pam was married to a composer, as yet unrecognized, of electronic symphonies, and they led what seemed on the surface a slapdash, arty kind of life. Actually, it was nothing of the sort. Pam's feet were as solidly on the ground as ever, her head as full of cheerful common sense. She was making money out of her record shop, and she was thriftily salting a certain amount of it away to pay for the four children she intended to have in due time. Isobel had worked for her for a while a year or so ago, and they had developed a great fondness for each other—rather bossy in a big-sisterly way on Pam's side, admiring and trustful on Isobel's.

"Oh, Gene! Hi! Wait a minute." There was a racket, presumably electronic, in the background; she dealt with it briskly and got back on the phone. "How are you? How's Isobel?"

His heart sank. "You haven't seen her, then? Or heard from her?"

"Not since Thursday, when you called me, you know, about your father. I've had her on my mind, only I didn't like to call her, not just yet … What's the matter?" He told her, and after a moment's silence she said, "Yeah, I see what you mean. She doesn't take things easy. And she was all churned up Thursday, even before the business about your father—"

"You mean you saw her Thursday, before that?"

"Sure. Didn't I tell you? That's how I managed to get hold of her so fast. She dropped in at the shop in the afternoon, all shook up about something or other, she wouldn't tell me what. I tried to get her to stick around with me till closing time, but she wouldn't do it. So then I said how about meeting us at The Purple Cow for dinner—we go there a lot, you know, it's where all our crowd hangs out—and she said maybe, she'd see. I wasn't at all sure she'd show up, but when you called naturally I zoomed right over, and there she was."

"I see," said Gene. He poked at the pile of broken glass with the toe of his shoe. Shattered. In spite of the thick rug it had landed on. Almost as if—

"I was all set to go with her, of course," Pam was going on. "If it was my father, I know I'd want somebody, for moral support. But not Isobel. I'll admit it kind of rocked me, the way she cut me off at the ankles. 'I don't *want* you, can't you get that through your head? You stay out of this …' To tell you the truth, Gene, that's why I haven't called her. I mean, she seemed to resent me so, as if I was trying to push in where I wasn't wanted. I guess it was just because I happened to be the one to bring her the bad news, but she sounded like she was *mad* at me. You know?"

They said what little there was left to say. Yes, of course Pam would let them know if she heard anything. No, of course there was nothing to worry about, Isobel would turn up any minute now. Et cetera. Et cetera.

Who else was there to call? Gene stayed where he was, on the edge of the bed, mentally checking through the possibilities, such as they were. No particular boyfriend at the moment. At least as far as Gene knew. And Isobel had never been much for the girly-girly bit. Pam was the best bet in that department. Still, there must be one or two … He poked again at the broken lamp. Fidgeted with the drawer of the little table, idly pulling it in and out. All the way out, eventually, damn, there it went, spilling odds and ends over the rug. He bent to gather them up— lipsticks, eye shadow, pencils, clippings, an emery board, postage stamps. And a little bottle of pills.

Dad's pills. He recognized the name of the doctor, the "fat-faced quack" whose rules and regulations Dad had treated with such reckless contempt. What were they doing here?

Still holding the bottle, he turned, at the sound of the door opening. Hilda was back again. "Did you get hold of Pam? Has she heard any ..." Her eyes switched from his face to his hand. "What are you doing? What's that?"

"It's a bottle of Dad's pills," he said. "I dumped the damn drawer and everything fell out."

"Pills?" She drew in her breath sharply. "It can't be. He only had the one bottle, and he left them in our room, on the chest of drawers. You remember, we found them there when we got home Thursday night."

Yes, Gene remembered. He followed her through the bathroom that separated Isobel's bedroom from Hilda's and Dad's. Sure enough, there on the chest of drawers was the bottle Dad had left behind on the last day of his life. It was three-quarters full; the one in Gene's hand was half-full.

"I don't understand. Unless ..." After a moment's pause, Hilda went on, in an eager little burst. "Of course! That has to be it. Isobel must have kept an extra supply, she's probably been carrying them around for months, ever since Kirk first got sick. Because she worried even more than I did about how careless he was. It terrified her to think he might be caught some day ..."

As he had been. And in typical Isobel fashion, she was now blaming herself for not having been there when the emergency she dreaded so much had struck. It explained everything: not just the pills themselves, but the depth of her despondency since Dad's death.

"That has to be it," Hilda repeated. "It's the only— There! Isn't that the phone?"

There was no extension in this bedroom; they had had it cut off when Dad came home from the hospital. Gene made it back to Isobel's bedroom first, and grabbed the phone in the middle of a ring. "Hello?" he croaked. And then: "Isobel! Are you all right? Where the hell are you?"

"I went for a walk," she said in a small, clear voice. "I thought I'd better call you. I didn't want you to worry."

"We've been out of our minds! Going off like that, without a word to Myrtle. You might at least have left us a note."

"I'm sorry. I didn't think of it. I didn't think you'd be back so soon."

"Well, we are. And if you know what's good for you you'll get yourself back here where you belong on the double, before I—"

"You don't have to be like that about it," she said coolly. "I don't want to come back now. All those people. I don't feel like seeing them."

"Listen." He swallowed hard and started over. "Okay. But you can't spend the whole evening roaming the streets by yourself. How's your head?"

"My what? Oh. Better. Thank you."

"You're welcome. How about meeting me at my place? Or don't you feel like seeing me either?"

Silence. He waited, nervously aware that if she hung up on him, as she was perfectly capable of doing, he would be right back where he started. At last she said, "I don't mind, I guess. If you want me to."

"Good. Fine. I'll be there in fifteen or twenty minutes. Have you got money for a cab?"

He could only hope so; she had already hung up.

"She's all right?" whispered Hilda. She had been listening, of course, standing beside him with her hands clenched. There was such anxiety in her face that he was moved to put his arm around her. Neither of them went in much for that sort of thing, and they wound up in a rather uncomfortable clinch.

"Cool as a cucumber," said Gene grimly. He was still prickling over Isobel's perfunctory little apology. I'm sorry. As if he were a stranger she had accidentally jostled in the subway. As if he and Hilda were a pair of tiresome alarmists, making a fuss about nothing.

"Don't be too hard on her, Gene. Her magic lamp. That must have seemed like the last straw."

Maybe so. And maybe it was not by accident, but on purpose, that the magic lamp had been so well and truly smashed. Gene could remember a time when he might have done such a thing himself, as a gesture of defiance and disenchantment with Dad. It was one more point he intended to straighten out with Isobel.

But then, as the cab turned into his block, he saw her waiting for him in front of the brownstone where he lived. She looked so little, hunched up against the iron railing of the stoop, so little and lonesome in the drizzly twilight. The sight of her melted him.

He put his arm around her and steered her up the steps, in out of the wet. His apartment—a fairly good-sized room with sleeping alcove—was on the first floor. The sound of the key in the lock, as always, sent Brown Sugar into a transport of joyful welcome; he was a demonstrative dog who loved not only Gene but the entire human race. While he rhapsodized over his great good fortune—two people instead of one—Gene turned on the lights, helped Isobel out of her jacket, and poured them each a brandy.

Without the impetus of anger, he did not know where to start. And it was clearly up to him. There she sat in the corner of the sofa, big-eyed and straggle-haired, offering neither resistance nor cooperation.

Okay. Start. "I called Pam," he said. "I thought she might know where you were."

"Oh?" She shot him a queer, guarded look. Then she hooked her hair behind her ears and went back to waiting.

"I didn't know you saw her Thursday afternoon before Dad—before it happened. How come you weren't at work?"

"I was, in the morning. I couldn't face going back after lunch. They were about to fire me, anyway, so I thought why not save them the trouble. I know what you're thinking, but honestly, Gene, it's too deadly, this receptionist bit. Sitting there smiling and pushing buttons and typing things in triplicate. I mean, it's not as if it was ever going to lead to anything."

Probably not. Certainly not if you didn't stick to it. College had been too deadly for Isobel too; naturally she wasn't going to find an interesting job when she had no particular training. And of course no motivation. No need for her to make her own living, with Dad happy to pay the bills.

"I'm not blaming you," said Gene. "I just wondered, that's all, when Pam said you'd been down to the record shop in the afternoon."

"I went home first. I thought Dad might still be there. But he'd already left for the office. I didn't have anything else to do, so I decided to drop in and say hello to Pam."

"What were you so upset about?"

"Upset?"

"That's what Pam said. All churned up about something or other. You wouldn't tell her what."

"Pam said that?" She uttered an extraordinarily hollow laugh. "She's imagining things. Pam and her imagination. Always seeing signs and portents. Always imagining things."

"Don't give me that. She's as level-headed as anybody I know."

"Well then, she's lying. Or else you are. Lying to me, trying to—" She caught her breath and sprang up, trembling like a scared bird. "Is this what you got me here for? Just to badger and nag and pick me to pieces?"

"You know better than that, Isobel. All I'm trying to do is help you. But how can I, if you won't tell me what's wrong?" He stood up too, and put his hand under her chin to keep her from ducking. For a moment they looked straight into each other's eyes. Hers were over-bright, almost wild with alarm. Imploring, too—but for what, for what? If he was right in suspecting that she knew about Dad and Lorraine Walsh, then saying so outright would be as much of a relief to her as to him. If, on the other hand, he was wrong ... It could never be taken back, once it was said outright. And no one knew better than Gene how much damage a fallen idol did to the idolizer.

He gave her as much of an opening as he dared. "It's something about Dad. Isn't it? Don't be afraid, Isobel. Whatever it is, believe me, you can tell me."

Her eyes fluttered shut. She said, in a rapid whisper, "He forgot his pills. He left them at home, I saw them, I could have taken them to him. Then when he needed them—I had them in my purse."

"I know you did, honey. You had an extra supply, didn't you? In case of emergency, because he was always forgetting his."

"How did you— Who told you that? Hilda?"

"We figured it out between us, when I accidentally dumped the drawer of your little table this afternoon and found the spare bottle." She stood still as a stone, and as silent. He pressed on anxiously. "But they might not have saved him, even if he'd had them to take. Probably wouldn't have. You heard what the doctor said, that it was a miracle Dad's heart held out as long as it did. Please, Isobel, you mustn't blame yourself."

"But I—"

"You mustn't, you mustn't. It wasn't your fault any more than anybody else's. Mine, for instance. Or Hilda's. We could feel guilty too, Hilda and I, if we let ourselves get started. It makes just as much sense."

"But Hilda didn't know he'd forgotten his pills. I did, I could have taken them to him. That's what I started to do, only—" She looked off into space, blank-faced, once more walled off from him. "Only I wound up down at Pam's shop instead of Dad's office. The story of my life. I never seem to get where I'm going."

"That still doesn't explain what happened to shake you up before you got to Pam's."

"Nothing happened! Nothing. I told you I wasn't—" After a moment's mental scrabbling she came up with an answer. Of sorts. "Well, of course it gave me kind of a turn when I opened my bag and saw the pills. I'd rather not talk about it anymore, if you don't mind …"

He had to leave it at that. Whatever else, if anything, was agonizing her—besides misguided guilt over the pills—she was not about to tell him. Later, while they were eating the sandwiches he brought back when he took Brown Sugar out for his walk, he remembered the magic lamp and mentioned it.

"Yes," she said, in the composed little voice that meant it was no use trying, she was inaccessible, "it got broken."

"It sure did. I don't quite see how it happened. I mean, with the rug—"

"I don't know, either. It just happened."

So they finished their sandwiches, and listened to some records, and as long as they didn't talk about anything that mattered, she really did seem better, like herself again: his wispy, dreamy little sister, his responsibility, whether or not he always understood her. About eight o'clock she decided she wanted to go home. No, no, he wasn't to come with her, she was all right now, really, he needn't worry, she wasn't going to pull another vanishing act.

He did insist on seeing her into a cab. When none turned into the block after a few minutes, they walked to Third, rounded the corner, and all but collided with Lorraine Walsh and escort. Who had just emerged from the corner apartment house; her sister lived there, Gene remembered.

The escort, a clean-cut, all-American type, was making quite a production of protecting her from the foggy foggy dew. With her full cooperation. She was snuggled in the curve of his stalwart, proprietary arm like a cat on its favorite cushion.

She was a stunner, all right. Creamy skin, sooty hair and lashes, deep blue eyes. Even the little veil and woebegone expression she had worn to Dad's funeral this afternoon had not dimmed her sparkle entirely. She wasn't wearing them now. Had probably shucked them both off, the one as easily as the other, the minute she got home. One thing was sure: she hadn't wasted any time finding a replacement. Easy come, easy go.

Here she was chattering along—after her first gasp of surprise—smiling and friendly and vivacious. Resentment surged up in Gene, fierce and hot. At that moment he hated Lorraine Walsh—not for having been Dad's mistress, but for being alive when he was dead, for taking so lightly the affair that mattered so much to Gene himself. And would to the other members of Dad's family, if they knew about it.

"Can we give you a lift?" she was asking. "Roger's got his car ..."

"No thanks," said Isobel. "Here comes a cab." The curtness of her tone startled Gene. As she stalked past him toward the curb he caught in her face the clear, sharp reflection of his own feelings. Hate. Resentment.

She knows, he thought. Never mind how. I found it out. So did she. That's why she's giving Lorraine the brush-off. Everything else she's done, too. That's why. Isobel knows.

EIGHT

Lorraine was still asleep on the living room couch when Mary left for work. As well she might be; it had been a late night for her and Roger. Just how late Mary did not know. She had been too exhausted after her session with Teddy to wait up for a sisterly heart-to-heart.

And of course now was not the time for it, either. Lorraine was a slow starter in the mornings. Even if she were to wake up at this moment, it would be another hour or so before she was really with it. No use trying to talk to a zombie, thought Mary. Or—more to the point—trying to get anything out of one.

Lunch would be a good time. Better than waiting till tonight, when like as not Roger would be back on the scene. Mary was in no mood for waiting, anyway. Having spent the last few days dithering over what Lorraine might or might not have done, she now burned to find out for sure and get it over with. Anything was preferable to this nerve-frazzling uncertainty.

She left a note: "How about lunch? Call me when you get to the studio. *Important*."

At the door she paused for a last glance at Lorraine: the rich curve of her hip under the blanket, the thundercloud mass of hair, the pink, childish mouth, so defenseless in sleep, so innocent.

Get it over with. Find out for sure, she thought; and closed the door, none too quietly, behind her.

Lorraine called about ten thirty, earlier than she expected. "Mary?" She knew right away something had happened. "Oh Mary, I've been robbed! The studio—I just got here, somebody broke the lock and got in, everything's upside down, I don't know yet what's missing, there wasn't much worth stealing ... Yes, I've already called the police, that's the first thing I did, of course. They said they'd send somebody over right away."

First Lorraine's apartment, now the studio. Coincidence? No connection between the two? "I'm coming right down," said Mary.

"Oh Mary, you don't have to—"

"Yes, I do," she said. She hung up, galloped into her boss's office with a breathless news bulletin—"a family emergency, I'll be back as soon as I can"—grabbed her coat and ran.

Lorraine's studio was on the East Side, below 14th Street, in a block of small, not very flourishing business establishments and rooming houses. The rent was fantastically low; she had lucked into it a couple of years ago through an artist friend who had used it for both living and working quarters. It was a large, loft-like room with primitive plumbing and splintery floors, up above a coffee shop. Robberies were a commonplace in the neighborhood, especially on weekends when the stores were closed.

By the time Mary got there the police had been and gone. Which was just as well; the apartment business was not something she cared to blurt out to them at this point. Lorraine had a right to hear it first. Time enough after that to decide about telling the police.

"They told me what kind of a lock to get," Lorraine reported. "Anyone could have broken the old one with a nail file. No trick at all. They said it was a wonder it hasn't happened before. They were awfully nice. Not much help, but then what can anybody do? I was luckier than most. My little transistor radio's gone, and a couple of dollars' worth of stamps. I never kept any cash up here, so they didn't get much. And they didn't pour paint all over the stuff I'm working on, or tear it up. They do things like that sometimes, the police said, out of spite ..." She stopped for breath. Flushed and bright-eyed with excitement, she looked around at the paper-strewn floor and the disorder of her long work table. "It looks a mess, but everything's all right, really. It's just the thought of somebody busting into my place, pawing through my belongings."

"I know," said Mary. "Nobody heard anything, I suppose? Tony? Or The Beard?" Tony was the proprietor of the coffee shop; The Beard was the tenant on the floor above Lorraine. If tenant was the right word: he showed up at irregular intervals, sometimes to work on his ceramic creations, sometimes, when he and his girlfriend had had another fight, to sleep.

"Tony wasn't here, of course. He doesn't open up until seven thirty or so. The Beard came wafting up the stairs while the police were here. He wasn't here last night, either. Hasn't been around for the past couple of weeks. Neither of their places was broken into. Just mine."

Yes. Just Lorraine's. It didn't necessarily signify: something might have scared the thief off before he had a chance to ransack the rest of the empty building. On the other hand, if it had been no ordinary sneak thief but someone with a particular interest in pawing through Lorraine's belongings, both here and in her apartment, someone who had a key to her apartment and who was shrewd enough to make the studio job look like the work of an ordinary sneak thief ...

"Listen, Lorraine," she began.

The phone rang, and Lorraine scooped it up. "Hello? Oh, Hilda! I know, the rush job. It's ready. I wasn't sure you'd be in the office today, didn't know whether to call you or not. Yes, of course, if Isobel can come down and pick it up, that would be fine." She hung up and said, "Now then, a locksmith. That's the first thing, I suppose ..."

"Isobel's coming down?" asked Mary. "I thought she was laid out with migraine."

"She wasn't last night. We ran into her and Gene when we were going out to dinner. I suppose they'd been at his place, he lives in your neighborhood. Anyway, there they were, and I must say, she was very snippy. Downright rude. Roger noticed it too. I said couldn't we give them a lift, because it was raining ..." Lorraine had found the yellow book and was thumbing through it. "Let me see, locksmiths."

"How about Gene? Was he snippy too?"

"Not like Isobel. But he's always pretty much of a cold fish. Too busy fuddling around with the Mammals of North America at the museum to bother with ... Here's one, 14th Street."

"Listen, Lorraine, I have to talk to you."

"Go ahead. Just a minute, I'll be right with you."

Mary waited while she made the call. Then she said bluntly, "Maybe you ought to have the lock changed on your apartment, too. Teddy claims somebody's been in there."

"What?" Her mouth dropped open; her eyes got big. "Oh my God, somebody broke in there too? Like the studio?"

"No, not like the studio." While Mary ran through the details, she watched her sister's face, on the alert for the slightest flicker of anything not quite candid or natural. If, for example, Lorraine's eyes should slide away from hers— They never wavered. Incredulity. Shock. Mary herself must have looked much the same, listening to Teddy last night.

"But I don't understand," she stammered. "Nobody else has a key."

"Nobody but you."

"Well, of course me. I mean nobody who'd do a thing like that. If I decided to go back there I wouldn't sneak around about it. Why on earth should I?"

A very good question. Surely it was an indication of Lorraine's innocence, that she could ask it so forthrightly, with such complete lack of self-consciousness. But the real proof of her innocence—Mary saw it with belated, dazzling clarity—the real proof was of course the studio job. It was hard enough to believe Lorraine had found it necessary to pay a surreptitious visit to her own apartment; that she should fake a robbery in her studio was simply preposterous. The realization turned Mary giddy with relief.

"Why indeed?" she echoed. "Obviously it wasn't you. But according to Teddy somebody was up there. Think, Lorraine. You're positive nobody else has a key? Roger, for instance?"

"Roger? Are you suggesting that Roger would—"

"Never mind the high horse. Did he ever have a key?"

"No he didn't. Kirk had the only other set, and I gave his to Teddy. Nobody else. I'm positive. Not even the maid. She prefers it that way. She comes early, so I'm always there to let her in, and when she leaves she just shuts the door behind her and it locks automatically." After a moment's silence she went on decisively, "It doesn't make any sense, Mary. Even if somebody got hold of a key, why would they go mousing around up there without stealing anything?"

"I don't know, unless they were looking for something. Something they expected to find there, but didn't, so then they tried the studio. Only they didn't have a key for the studio, so they had to make it look like a robbery ..."

"But it was a robbery!" cried Lorraine. "Of all the gobbledygook I ever heard! That's exactly what it was. A routine sneak thief job. The kind that goes on all the time, all over town."

"Uh huh. No connection with the apartment deal. Just one of life's little coincidences. Do you really expect me to swallow that?"

"Why not?" Lorraine's eyes began to sparkle. "After all, you swallowed Teddy's little fable. Didn't you, dear? Ate it right up. Without a single grain of salt. He knew you would, of course. I suppose he simply couldn't resist, after the fuss you made yesterday. Trust Teddy to pick the right audience."

"What do you mean, the right audience? The last thing Teddy wants is to get me stirred up again, he's scared stiff I might decide to tell the police we lied about Kirk. And I might, too. Because it's not just the pills now, it's—"

Lorraine groaned. "Not the pills again! Please, Mary, I can't bear it."

"I can't either," said Mary rather wildly. "Only we have to. We can't just sweep it under the rug, the way you and Teddy tried to do yesterday. And I think he really did hear somebody come in at four thirty. And all that business about maybe the maid threw the pills out, that was a lot of bushwa. Wasn't it? They were there earlier. Weren't they?"

"I—" She hesitated. It wasn't exactly the veiled look this time. It was more what Mary thought of as the mule look, and as soon as she saw it she knew she was licked. Lorraine had dug in her heels; nothing short of dynamite was going to blast her into admitting the truth. She said, with cool finality, "I can't swear to it one way or the other. I'm sorry, but that's how it is. Whatever you're trying to prove, you're on your own."

Mary opened her mouth and closed it again. What was the use? And anyway, here came the tramp of feet on the stairs, and a voice booming out "Locksmith!"

He was long on conversation, the locksmith. "It's these kids," he explained, above the noise of his electric drill. "These hippies, whatever they call themselves. Can't tell the boys from the girls. Got no commitment, they claim. You know what I told my middle boy when he tried that line on me? Commitment, is it, I told him, you get the hell out of here and get yourself a job, I said, I'll give you commitment. They take you for much, Miss? No? You're lucky. One call I had last week, 20th Street, way over west, this guy and his wife come back from a cruise, Bermuda, or maybe it was Nassau, one or the other, anyway, they come back and lo and behold ..."

The arrival of Isobel put an end to this particular episode in the locksmith's memoirs. She looked hollow-eyed, exhausted. No one who saw her face today—never mind the childishness of her figure—would mistake her for a teenager. Friendly enough, though. Ready with the appropriate responses when Lorraine, who was inclined to chatter in moments of nervous tension, rushed headlong into an account of the robbery.

"It could have been worse," said Isobel. "I mean, supposing you'd walked in on them, whoever it was, and—"

"You can say that again," the locksmith contributed, and obliged with a full, zestful report on what had happened to his second cousin's daughter. "Oh, the things I could tell you," he finished as, regretfully, he tightened the last screw in the new lock. "There you are, Miss. That'll be fifteen dollars. They'll have a little more trouble next time. Bye now, and good luck."

When he had collected his tools and left, Isobel picked up the folder of sketches. "Hilda said to thank you for being so prompt with this last rush job, she'll send you a check the end of the week. She's calling it quits, you know. No use trying to keep the agency going by herself."

"I suppose not," said Lorraine rather huskily. "I suppose it's the only sensible thing for her to do."

"It's what she wanted to do, even before Daddy—when he first got sick. She kept trying to talk him into selling out and retiring."

"Retiring! But he never in the world would have—"

The phone rang. To Mary's relief: she foresaw drastic indiscretions. Against the background of Lorraine's voice ("Teddy? What's the matter, I hardly recognized you …") she sought to divert Isobel with the first bit of small talk that came to mind.

"I understand your brother and I are more or less neighbors."

"Oh? Oh. Lorraine must have told you we ran into each other last night." Isobel seemed rather flustered, maybe by the memory of her own "snippiness." "My migraine got better in the afternoon, and I went for a walk. Because Hilda was having this buffet supper, and I didn't feel like … Anyway, I wound up at Gene's place."

"That was Teddy," Lorraine said as she hung up the phone. Still on her chattering jag, apparently. "You met him, Isobel, he was there the night—My neighbor. He's been picking up my mail for me, now that I'm staying with Mary, looking after things in my apartment. Poor creature, he's holed up with a cold, that's all he called up for, to complain. Freezing to death, he claims, so I told him to go up and get my electric heater. If I can find the time, I'll pop in and cheer him up this afternoon or evening. He hates being by himself."

"Ernest?" Mary suggested.

"They're still not speaking. He'll be changing his will again, I suppose, any day now ..." She rattled on until Isobel left, a minute or two later; then, warily silent, she got back to sorting out her paint shelves.

Finally Mary said, "An odd girl, isn't she? I wonder if she could be wise to you and Kirk. It would explain why she snooted you last night."

"But she was perfectly all right today. It was probably just my imagination last night."

Oh sure. Like Teddy's intruder, and whoever it was he had heard coming in at four thirty the afternoon Kirk died, and the missing pills. Good old imagination, the answer to everything. Once more Mary felt herself sinking into the familiar quicksand of doubt, suspicion, shameful surmise. For—in spite of what the studio "robbery" proved—the fact remained that Kirk's fatal attack had come at a very convenient time for Lorraine and that she had had the opportunity to help it along, by fiddling with his pills, by quarreling with him, who knew how. Supposing someone else believed, rightly or wrongly, that she had; and believed furthermore that somewhere in her apartment or her studio there was proof that she had ... Isobel, for instance. She could have found out about Kirk and Lorraine. It could have been her Teddy heard on the stairs. The walk she had taken yesterday afternoon—she could have broken into the studio then. And somebody had a key to Lorraine's apartment. Why not Isobel?

"Now what's spooking you? You've got that look in your eye again." Lorraine's own expression was one of candid, sisterly exasperation. "Honestly, Mary, how you can even consider running to the police with the truth ... Don't you realize what it would do to Hilda? That was the point, in the first place, to spare her feelings. And it's still the point. There's only one decent thing I can do for Hilda now, and that's keep on lying. You think the police would keep it to themselves? Of course they wouldn't. They'd clobber Hilda with it, first thing, whether or not they took you seriously—"

And Lorraine would see to it that they didn't. Without her backing on the pills, precious little was left of Mary's theory. They might not even bother Hilda with such a flimsy story. Ah, but they might. In which case Mary's theory would still remain unproved, unprovable; nothing would be accomplished, nothing but the damage to Hilda.

"Don't worry, I'm not going to the police," said Mary. "No point in it. You've made that crystal clear."

"Well, good for me. Hallelujah. No point in getting in such a flap over Teddy and his mysterious intruder, either. You know how he loves to fabricate. He didn't mention a word about it to me over the phone. If Isobel hadn't been here, I'd have brought it up myself."

"You didn't tell him about the studio, either."

"That can wait, too. We can hash it all over when I see him ... Mary dear, about lunch. No telling when I'll get around to it, I've got a whole stack of work to do. And Roger and I did make a tentative date. He's leaving for Chicago, and won't be back till Thursday. You don't mind, do you?"

"No, of course not." Lunch would only be more of the same, thought Mary hopelessly. She was right back where she had been, bogged down in the same unspeakable misgivings. Literally unspeakable: she could no more put them into words than she could wipe them out of her mind.

"Mary—" She turned, at the urgent note in Lorraine's voice; for a moment they gazed at each other wistfully across the gulf that yawned between them. There was no crossing it, after all. "You were awfully good to come down. I can't thank you enough. For everything."

Mary did not trust herself to answer. She shut the door behind her and plodded down the stairs.

NINE

Monday morning when Gene, who was taking the day off from the museum, walked into the Banning Associates office, he found—not Isobel, the one he was looking for, nor Hilda either—but only Mrs. Schmidt. She worked there on an irregular, part-time basis, and she greeted him with muted, death-in-the-family burblings. Mrs. Banning would be back later: an appointment with the Argus people, no, that couldn't be right, she had seen them on Thursday, anyway, an appointment. Isobel? Yes, Isobel had been in too, she was out on an errand, a pickup from Lorraine Walsh. Poor child, didn't look well at all, she was taking it hard, naturally, so devoted to her Daddy, little did anybody think, when she stopped in Thursday ...

"Isobel?" Gene, who had been only half-listening, pricked up his ears. "I didn't realize she was in the office on Thursday."

Oh yes, Mrs. Schmidt remembered distinctly, because that was the day poor Mr. Banning passed away. "Two thirty or so. He was in the inside office, making a phone call; some rush job that had come in. Mrs. Banning had already left, and I was on my way out, in kind of a hurry, so Isobel and I didn't exchange more than a word or two. You know. Hello, nice to see you, goodbye. Poor Mr. Banning, I never dreamed ..."

Well, even before last night's encounter with Lorraine Walsh, Gene hadn't really bought Isobel's story of getting sidetracked and never reaching the office. This explained why she was in such a flap when she got to Pam's. She too had overheard one of Dad's phone calls—yes, of course, the rush job—to Lorraine Walsh. In his mind's eye Gene could see her, standing trapped in the outer office, listening while her idol crashed and crumbled. Had she made a scene? Or simply crept away without Dad's ever knowing she was there? It was something Gene intended to find out from her. There was no reason now for either of them to hold back; maybe, if they got it all out in the open, Isobel would feel a little less guilty about the undelivered pills.

Meanwhile, Mrs. Schmidt, after a good deal more burbling, finished the letters she was typing and departed. It was nice and quiet without her.

The inside office gave him an unexpected pang. It wasn't the same room without Dad at the desk, pawing through a clutter of papers, or tilting back in his chair, hands clasped behind his head, feet propped on the open bottom drawer. The papers were still there, but neatly stacked at one end of the desk; in the background the silver-framed photograph of Isobel, the mug full of sharpened pencils, the carafe that nobody ever used; up front a pile of mail and pink telephone slips. "Mrs. B.: Owen Adams, please call back ..."

Owen Adams? Extending his condolences? Maybe.

He was about to settle down on the couch with his newspaper when Isobel came in. Not looking well at all—Mrs. Schmidt had been right—and a bit put off at seeing him. Or so he suspected. Never mind. Now was his chance, before Hilda showed up. He plunged right in: "So you did get to the office Thursday, after all. Mrs. Schmidt just told me."

"Mrs. Schmidt talks too much."

"Yeah. And you don't talk enough. That's when you found out about Lorraine Walsh, wasn't it?"

"I didn't—" She was eyeing him warily. "No. I didn't know who he was talking to. Then afterwards ..."

"Afterwards? What did you do, march in and ask him?"

"Of course not. Certainly not. I never even saw him, he never even knew I was there. It wasn't like that at all. And if you think I followed him to Lorraine's—"

No such idea had occurred to him. The fact that it had to her was for some obscure reason disturbing.

"It wasn't like that, either," she was insisting. "I just went away. I forgot about his pills and just went away. Then afterwards, when I heard where he—what had happened, then I realized it was Lorraine." She switched past him to the window, stood there with her back to him, fiddling with the Venetian blinds. "How long have you known?"

"About Lorraine, you mean? Not very long. But—"

"Oh, what's the use of talking about it? Why do you have to keep harping?"

His answer, whatever it might have been, was interrupted by the arrival of Hilda. "Isobel?" she called from the outer office. "Did you get the—Oh, Gene. You're here too," she added, as they came through the door. She didn't look well, either, and there was an edge to her voice that Gene had never heard before.

"Yes, I got the stuff from Lorraine Walsh," said Isobel. "Any more errands for me to run?"

"You don't have to be like that about it. I told you I'd call the messenger service if you didn't feel like going. How does it look? All right?"

"I wouldn't know," said Isobel. "I didn't inspect it, I just picked it up. Okay if I go out to lunch now? I've got a date."

"By all means. Don't let me keep you."

Gene shifted uneasily from one foot to the other. Hilda re-anchored her bun of hair and started fumbling with the folder of sketches. Isobel shrugged into her suede jacket. At the door she turned and said abruptly, "Lorraine's studio was broken into last night. Maybe she told you? The police had just been there."

"The police? Broken into?" After a moment Hilda got back to her fumbling. "Why, no, she didn't ... What did they steal?"

"Not much, apparently. I thought she might have mentioned it. Well. I must run. So long, Gene."

Looking very tight-lipped, Hilda sailed past him into the inside office. He could see her at the desk, flipping through the mail. Leave her alone, he decided. Let her simmer down.

She didn't. He realized that, as soon as he heard her voice: "Gene! Would you mind coming in here a minute?" There were mottled patches on her face and neck. Like prickly heat. "All right," she said, "what has she been telling you? Don't deny it. You were in here together, the two of you, having some kind of a confab—"

"Hilda! What the hell's the matter with you?"

"It's not me, it's other people. You saw how she acted to me. She's turned against me, she's up to something. I've got a right to know. What was she telling you?"

"She wasn't telling me anything. I can't even remember what we were talking about." A lie, of course; for a moment his head rattled with the notion that she had overheard the Dad-Lorraine Walsh bit. No. Impossible. He had been facing the door and couldn't have missed seeing Hilda come in. Besides, if it were that, why would she sound so much on the defensive, so suspicious and hostile?

Toward him, as well as Isobel. "What are you doing down here, anyway? You didn't tell me you weren't going in to the museum today."

"But I simply forgot! My God, I didn't keep it from you on purpose. Why should I?"

"I don't know! I don't know anything, except—" Her hands jerked up to cover her eyes. "Except I can't stand any more of this spying and following and watching, as if I were some kind of a—"

"Now, Hilda, you're imagining things." But that was what made it so dismaying: that Hilda, of all people, strong, stable, sensible Hilda should give way to sick delusions. This particular kind of delusions, too; why should she suddenly decide that Isobel and he were conspiring against her? He began again, "Nobody's spying on you, that's ridiculous ..." Then his eye fell on the pink telephone slip, crumpled into a ball on the desk between them; and he saw the light.

"Owen Adams," he said. Instantly she stiffened. "You've got some kind of a deal cooking with Owen Adams. That's it, isn't it?"

"What did she tell you?" Her head stayed down. Her voice came out muffled and hoarse.

"Isobel? Nothing." But he could understand now why she had "turned against" Hilda. Any deal with Owen Adams—that dirty word to Dad— would seem like treachery to Isobel. Disillusioned though she was with Dad, she was still too close to him to condone Hilda's trafficking with the devil. Hilda herself couldn't have too easy a conscience; between it and Isobel she had worked herself into a miniature persecution complex, and no wonder.

"Listen to me, Hilda." He put his hand on her tense shoulder. "There's no reason for you to feel guilty. No matter what Isobel thinks about it, and no matter what kind of hell Dad would have raised. They're not stuck with the agency, you are. It's up to you to decide whether to hang on by yourself—"

"I couldn't. It's no use without Kirk. He knew it, too."

"Right. So you have to make the best deal you can, and if that means selling out to Owen Adams, then that's what you do. I'm only guessing, you understand, I don't really know what goes on, but whatever it is it's your business and nobody else's."

Her head lifted at last. The look she gave him was long and searching, full of tremulous relief. "You don't know what I've been through," she said. "First Kirk, accusing me of God knows what, when all I was trying to do—I didn't want him to die, that was all, I knew what would happen if I didn't get him to slow down, only it was no use, he wouldn't listen. And now Isobel ..."

"She's overwrought, remember. She's not herself these days."

"Well, neither am I," said Hilda, with a burst of asperity. "I have feelings too, even if I don't always show them." She paused, and Gene had a hunch she was looking back, not at just the last few harrowing months, but at all the years of her marriage. Dad had let her do most of the giving. Whatever else she knew or didn't know about him, she must have been aware from the start that with him it was more convenience than love. And must have figured it was worth it, anyway. Maybe it had been.

The phone rang. With a little sigh, she squared her shoulders and picked it up.

Gene made tracks for the outer office, and closed the door behind him. Just in case she had any lingering notions about his spying on her. "Lunch?" he suggested when she came out a couple of minutes later.

"I'd love to, but I can't take the time. Thanks, anyway." She held out her hand and gave him a reasonable facsimile of the warm, thorough smile that was her chief attraction. "Thanks for everything, Gene. You're just what the doctor ordered."

TEN

Teddy blew his nose again and tried to think of somebody else he could call up. But who was left, after Lorraine? And that had been a fizzle, because she wasn't alone in the studio, he could hear voices in the background, and so he didn't dare try out any of the little needles he had looked forward to using on her. In a nice way, of course. She was a dear girl, really, whatever tricks she may have played with Kirk's pills. Teddy did feel she might have been a touch more candid with him and Mary, in view of their efforts on her behalf. However, he wasn't casting any stones. No, he only wanted a little harmless diversion, something to take his mind off his sufferings. It was little enough to ask for. But he hadn't even been able to find out from Lorraine how much, if anything, Mary had told her. Utter frustration.

As for the possibility of her dropping in on him later this afternoon or this evening, he knew good and well she wouldn't find the time. Too busy palpitating over Roger to bother with a poor lonely shut-in. No doubt figured she had done her duty by lending him her heater. Well, and it was a comfort. He had trotted right upstairs to get it—no further signs of trespass in her apartment—and there it sat, glowing away in front of the couch where he was ensconced. Comfort, but of an impersonal kind. Not like having someone to talk to. He flounced his pillows. Cast a disconsolate glance at the ailanthus tree outside his window, shivering in the April wind. Sneezed three shattering sneezes.

He could sit here by himself and choke to death, or starve, for all it mattered to Lorraine. Or anybody else, when it came to that. Ernest ... No. He would not Not NOT call Ernest. Too humiliating. And then he looked so loathsome: red swollen nose, watery eyes, every square inch of him simply crawling with germs.

So there it was: solitary confinement, hours and hours of it, stretching ahead of him as monotonous as a road through a desert. Lorraine's advice came back to him, in all its callous cheer. Improve your mind, curl up with a good book. He sniffed and reached listlessly for the stack of magazines he had brought down from her apartment the other night. There were all kinds. News, travel, fashion, artsy-craftsy, literary ...

Hello, what was this? One that Lorraine had not even opened? No, the manila envelope bore no address, return or otherwise; it was too thin for a magazine, anyway. Some of her sketches, maybe, shuffled in among the periodicals by accident, something she might be searching high and low for. Teddy brightened up a bit: it would give him an excuse to call her again, this time, God willing, without an audience to cramp his style. No harm in checking, particularly since the envelope was unsealed. He undid the little metal clasp and drew out the contents. His first reaction was disappointment at finding—not the sketches he hoped for—but just a routine business letter. Or so it seemed, such was the sodden state of his wits, until he had skimmed through the top typewritten page. Then the message began to permeate. He read on, bolt upright now, and tingling to his fingertips, positively crackling with elation.

Charming, oh charming. This would guarantee him a visit from Lorraine, all right. Wild horses couldn't keep her away, once he had given her the scoop. He paused, with his hand on the telephone. Part of the scoop, just enough to whet her appetite for more. Waste not, want not. Make the goodies last.

"I've stumbled on to something rather interesting," he told her, his tone a masterful blend—if he did say so as shouldn't—of the casual and the portentous. "Really quite interesting. I'll be curious to see what you make of it."

"Who—? Oh, it's you, Teddy. Stop making like a half-baked secret agent. What are you talking about?"

"Don't let me keep you if you're too busy. I just thought you'd like to know. After all, dear, it's your problem too, isn't it?"

"My problem?" He heard the little catch in her breath and smiled to himself. "What do you mean, my problem? What are you talking about?"

He decided on silence as the most effective maneuver.

"Teddy! Please! If it's something about— Oh, now I get it. Ernest. I suppose you've come across something else about him and want to change your will again. Okay, if that's it, I still have the old one you gave me to keep for you. It's safe and sound in my little strong box. That's it, isn't it? Ernest again."

"I'd rather not go into it over the telephone. In the first place, it's so complicated. And then ... No, I'd much rather show it to you and let you see for yourself. If I had my health I could bring it up to the studio, that is, if you could spare the time. But I honestly don't think I ought to go out, in my diseased condition."

"Well, of course not. Won't it keep till later? Things are sort of rushed right now, and I'm meeting Roger for a late lunch, but I ought to be able to make it by five thirty or so. I was planning to come down, anyway. I told you."

She hadn't been anywhere near as definite about it. But Teddy tactfully abstained from pointing this out. "Certainly it will keep. I just couldn't resist calling you in advance. Run along now, and have fun. I'll see you later."

He would indeed. Mission accomplished; and very neatly, too. He gave himself a congratulatory hug. Then, contented as a bee, his head buzzing with delicious possibilities, he snuggled down and presently drifted off into a long, refreshing sleep.

Did it come to him in a dream? No matter. When he woke in mid-afternoon there it was, sprung full-blown to the surface of his mind, the most delicious possibility of all. So naughty. Ah yes, and so irresistible.

An excited little bubble of laughter escaped him. He bounced up and, after a flurried search of the directory, reached once more for the telephone.

ELEVEN

"Here you are, Miss," said the cab driver and sure enough, here she was, back at the old homestead for the first time since her flight to Mary's place Thursday night.

Lorraine took a deep breath and got out of the cab. She wasn't absolutely sure she had the courage, not even with the pep talk Roger had given her at lunch still ringing in her ears. "Darling, you've got to go back some time. Don't you see? The longer you put it off the harder it's going to be. The only way to exorcise a ghost is to go ahead and do it. If you want me to come with you—"

"No, no." That much she was sure of. Understanding as Roger was—and he was marvelously understanding, what a difference from Kirk; not that she had told him quite everything, of course—still, the ghost of Kirk was her problem, hers alone. No one could help her. Roger least of all.

She paused in front of the stoop with its iron railing and at the top the familiar bright blue door. A rather pretty house. A pleasant, quiet block, residential except for the espresso coffee shop across the street, where the usual collection of youngsters dawdled. (One girl near the window made her think of Isobel. But then the woods these days were full of long blonde hair and suede jackets.)

Everything just the same, she thought with illogical surprise. After all, it was less than a week, not the years it felt like to her. She found her keys and went quickly up the steps, through the tiny foyer, and into the shadowy hall. She did not stop at Teddy's door. First things first: she knew that if she postponed going back to her own apartment much longer, it would be haunted forever, and herself along with it. A few minutes wouldn't make that much difference to Teddy.

Funny the way Kirk had popped into her mind for just a minute, when Teddy started his dark hints. Of course it was Ernest, another episode in the series of quarrels and reconciliations that had been going on for a year or more. And of course Teddy had to make a mystery of it; intrigue was the breath of life to him. How many times had she been through these dramatic will changes of his—each one irrevocable, absolutely final? From the production he made of it, anyone would think he was bestowing on Ernest—or cutting him off from—at least a million dollars. In his candid moments Teddy laughed at himself about it. But that didn't stop him from repeating the performance whenever he and Ernest got into another spat. This one must have been more serious than most; usually they made up again in a matter of days.

Yes, of course it was Ernest again. She might as well get out the strong box right now and ... It startled her a little, to find herself already back in her own apartment. No qualms, no hanging back or gritting her teeth. Thanks to her preoccupation with the absurdities of Teddy, she had unlocked the door and walked in automatically, without even noticing what she was doing.

So that was the trick: to fix her mind on something else, anything else, and keep on being automatic. Take off her coat. Hang it up. Open the windows. Check on her house plants. Make herself a cup of coffee. Get the strong box down from the top shelf of the bedroom closet.

The bedroom. Where Kirk had died.

All right. But such a long time ago; or so it seemed, mercifully, to her. Years instead of days. Kirk belonged to another lifetime—someone she had loved very much for a while, then not so much, someone no longer here to love or not love. He had known how it would be. His words came back to her, that proclamation of rebellious, desperate rage: "Listen. I don't care what it would do to Hilda or you or anybody else. Because you'll be alive, and I'll be dead, damn it. Finished. Through with everything …"

She squared her shoulders and marched into the bedroom.

And the worst was over. Back in the living room she sat down, a trifle shaky but undaunted, with her cup of coffee and a cigarette. She would never want to live here again. But then Roger was talking about a house in Connecticut, and in the meantime, there was his apartment, bigger than this, a more convenient location. Kirk, she thought, oh Kirk, don't hate me, it's not that I'm heartless, it's just that I'm alive, Roger and I, we're alive …

But this was what she must avoid. Quick. Think of something else, something safe and automatic. She picked up the phone and dialed Teddy's number. There was no answer.

Well, it wasn't quite six, she would try him again in ten minutes or so. He might be in the shower. Or asleep. (He was the type who could sleep through two alarm clocks, turned up high, blasting off in unison right in his ear.) Or—most probable of all—he had recovered enough of his health to nip out on some errand or other. He couldn't stand being alone; she suspected that part of his reason for calling her had been to insure himself against a solitary evening.

There was the doorbell. Teddy, of course; if her guess was right and he had been out on a neighborhood excursion, he would be quite likely to notice the light in her apartment. She crossed the room to the buzzer, and as she pressed it she glanced down at the bookcase below it. Teddy had left her "junk mail" there. A sizable stack of it, and beside it a brown manila envelope that didn't seem to have come through the mail.

Mildly curious, she turned it over: no address on the other side, either. She stuck it in her tote bag; it could wait till later.

Teddy must be inside the house by now, perhaps still feeling too feeble to climb the stairs. In which case be would be waiting for her on the first floor outside his own apartment. She opened her door and called down the stair well. "Teddy? Are you coming up, or do you want me to come down?"

But it was not Teddy who answered. A feminine voice, young and diffident, only half audible. Lorraine moved out into the hall and peered down. Who …? She was not sure until her caller reached the landing below and paused there, her pale flower-face in its frame of limp fair hair uplifted. Then there could be no doubt.

"Isobel! What are you—" But that sounded neither polite nor cordial. "How nice to see you. Come on up."

"If you're sure it's all right."

At last—after an embarrassing welter of apologies on the one hand, over-hearty assurances on the other—Lorraine ushered her into the living room, where she stood, nervously twisting a strand of hair and darting rather sly glances all around. Maybe she too expected ghosts.

"You're alone? I thought—I'm not interrupting anything?"

"No, of course not," said Lorraine. "I was just having a cup of coffee. Would you like some? Or a drink?"

"No, oh no. Thank you. I just happened to be down this way, and ... I thought Hilda might possibly be here. She said something about calling you about the Argus stuff, and I thought ... Or maybe I got it wrong. I often do get things wrong," she added. Proudly? Defiantly? Wistfully?

"No, I haven't heard from her. Won't you sit down?"

After a moment's hesitation Isobel perched, in a transient way, on the edge of the wingback chair. Lorraine went back to her place on the couch and tried to look friendly and relaxed. She couldn't help harking back to last night's little encounter. What had prompted that snub from Isobel? Resentment, because she had somehow learned the truth about Lorraine and her father?

If so, then the real purpose of tonight's call might be to make some kind of dreary scene. Confrontation, denunciation, maybe even threats. Anything was possible, with someone like Isobel. The waif look, the air of adolescent vulnerability—what were they but symptoms of how disturbed she was inside? Disturbed, and disturbing. For Isobel was not a child; she was only a couple of years younger than Lorraine. And there was something distinctly un-childlike about the expression in her eyes as they met Lorraine's for a moment and then veered off on another sly tour of the premises.

Whatever she had come to say or do, she didn't seem to know how to get the show on the road. All right, let her fidget; she needn't expect any help from Lorraine.

"I thought you were staying with your sister," Isobel said at last. "Or have you moved back?"

"Not yet. I just came down to take care of a few things."

"It's such a charming place, isn't it. You're lucky to have it. This is my favorite part of town, I'd love to find something for myself down here, but I know it's not going to be easy ..." She jumped up and began to prowl around, restlessly and erratically, like a cat in strange surroundings, chattering in a disjointed way all the while.

Lorraine couldn't puzzle it out. What did she mean, an apartment of her own, when she didn't have a job, and never had had a decent one? Who did she think was going to foot the bills? Had she really dropped in just to discuss such a harebrained scheme?

At last she paused long enough for Lorraine to ask, "What does Hilda think about the idea? I'm assuming you've talked it over with her."

Not recently, it seemed. But Hilda knew she was dying to get away from home, after all, Gene had moved out, ages ago, why shouldn't she, everybody had to sooner or later, no, Hilda could always be counted on to understand, it was Daddy—

She stood rigid, clenched up all over—as though the word, the name, had touched off in her an electrical shock—even her eyes screwed tight shut. Lorraine felt a pang of pity, but pity laced with impatience. Before she could think of any suitable comment or gesture, Isobel said in a rapid mumble, "Excuse me, do you mind, is it all right if I—" and fled. Through the bedroom, and into the bathroom.

Was she crying her heart out in there? Opening her veins? She had slammed the door between living room and bedroom behind her, so Lorraine could hear nothing. She stood up, wavered a moment, and then sat down again.

Better not to intrude. Better to do nothing, just stay where she was and wait it out. If only she hadn't answered the doorbell! If only Teddy would show up! He ought to be back by now. That was one thing she could do, call him.

But he still didn't answer. And Isobel still remained in seclusion, doing whatever she was doing in the bathroom.

She stayed there for another five minutes. Very trying ones for Lorraine, who had never been much good at waiting. And it was so simple, after all: the girl had been doing her eyes, no cause for concern, she had of course just been doing her eyes. They now looked out, blue-shadowed, expertly lined, inscrutable, from under lashes that were fringed and dark as the center of a poppy.

As for Isobel's manner, it was composed, if a little abstracted. She had to run along, she was meeting some friends for dinner, it had been nice talking to Lorraine, good night. Away she went, leaving Lorraine to make what she could of the peculiar little episode. Which was very nearly nothing.

In the end she gave up trying to figure out Kirk's problem daughter. Too frustrating. And the same went for Teddy. She gave him one more try on the phone; again there was no response.

He might at least have left her a note, after getting her down here with his tale of woe and his everlasting crises with Ernest. Well, she wasn't going to stick around any longer, waiting for another enactment of this ridiculous will-changing ritual. Enough was enough; Teddy and Isobel between them had already taken up almost an hour of her time. She washed up the coffee things, pulled down the windows, turned out the lights, and set off down the stairs.

When she reached the first floor, she paused outside Teddy's apartment and pushed the bell a couple of times, not expecting an answer and not getting one. There was a pale line of light under the door, but then he usually left a lamp burning when he went out in the evening. Should she leave him a note? On an impulse, she tried the door. Odd: it wasn't locked.

She pushed it open and walked in.

TWELVE

By the end of the day Gene was in a queer, restless mood. For no very good reason: he had settled a couple of points, more or less to his own satisfaction, with both Isobel and Hilda in the morning. There would have to be another session with Isobel, of course—a little brotherly lecture on keeping her nose out of Hilda's business—which he had hoped to polish off over dinner tonight. But Isobel was not available. Another date. Maybe that was the loose end that was bugging him.

There had been no loose ends about his conference in the afternoon with Dad's lawyer. It simply confirmed what they already knew—Banning Associates, which had always been half Hilda's, was now all hers. And aside from a modest insurance policy with Isobel named as beneficiary, the agency was just about the sum and substance of Dad's assets. He could make money—a lot of it, in his time—and he could spend it; saving it had never interested him. Or Hilda, either, though Gene remembered that she used to get rather wistful occasionally about "having a place of our own."

Well, maybe now she could have a place of her own. If she still wanted it, and if she worked out a good enough deal with Owen Adams. In any event, she would have no trouble finding a job. As for Isobel ...

Yes, Gene decided, that was why he had this uneasy, almost ominous feeling; he could neither get his mind off Isobel nor think of anything constructive to do about her.

Diversion was what he needed, and he got it from an unexpected source when he took Brown Sugar out for his pre-dinner walk. They had no sooner hit the sidewalk than he heard someone call his name, and turned to see Mary Walsh. She looked rather pink and flustered. Naturally enough, he supposed, considering the hand she must have had in cooking up that story of how Dad happened to be where he was when he died.

Not that Gene held it against her. On the contrary, he was grateful to her for lying. And to Lorraine. And to the little fellow, what's-his-name. Thank God they were good enough liars to pull it off.

At the time he had not cared to inquire into the true circumstances of Dad's last afternoon. Now—with Mary Walsh strolling along beside him, making small talk—he felt a surge of curiosity, a momentary impulse to blurt it out: "Thank you for lying your head off last Thursday, now would you mind telling me what really happened?"

Instead, he suggested a drink, and to his surprise she took him right up on it. "Let's go to my place," she said. She had a slight, engaging lisp. "You have to walk the dog, anyway, and I'm expecting a phone call. So if you don't mind?"

Very friendly. Pretty, too. She didn't have her sister's flashy good looks, no question about that. But then neither did Gene have his father's taste for dazzle and glamour.

He watched her with appreciation while she mixed them each a drink and then sat down in the other easy chair, with Brown Sugar panting happily on the floor between them. Just pretty enough. By no means flamboyant, by no means plain. Her hair was reddish-brown and curly, her ankles and waist were slender, she had a round, fresh face and a mouth that turned up at the corners, even when she wasn't actually smiling.

Which she wasn't, most of the time. He didn't realize it until she said "Cheers," and lifted her glass. She did smile then, not all the way, just enough to give him a glimpse of what the real thing would be like, and to make him notice afterwards—never mind the turned-up mouth—her look of strain and worry. As if something were preying on her mind, too.

Inevitably, his thoughts turned to Lorraine. She must be as much a problem sister, in her way, as Isobel. Again he felt the throb of curiosity—not only about Dad's death, but about Mary Walsh, who didn't look like a liar but was, who was being so unexpectedly friendly, and who wasn't doing much smiling.

"I saw your sister this morning," she said. "Down at Lorraine's studio. She stopped in to pick up some sketches. I'm glad her migraine didn't last long."

A harmless pleasantry. Nothing more. "Yes, she was pretty much all right last night. Maybe Lorraine told you? We ran into her and her—friend."

"Isobel mentioned it too." Her eyes flicked toward him, and away. "I think she said she went for a walk in the afternoon?"

"That's right." And what of it? Why shouldn't Isobel take a walk if she felt like it? "She's been very much upset about Dad, you know. She was always much closer to him than—well, than I was. There were a good many things we didn't see eye to eye on. Like the agency. He had this notion I ought to go in with him, don't ask me why, it's not my line at all."

"I know. Mammals of North America."

"I don't know where you got that idea," he said stiffly. Like hell he didn't: Dad to Lorraine to Mary. And it still put his back up, that witless witticism of Dad's. He watched her face go red. Suddenly he asked, "Why don't you tell me what's worrying you?"

"Nothing's worrying me. What makes you think I—"

"You're losing your grip. You did a much better job of lying last Thursday."

For a moment she sat bolt upright, rigid as a girl in a tintype, with her eyes fixed on him in a tintype stare. Then she said, "Oh."

"Yes. Oh. I know what Dad was doing in your sister's apartment. I didn't really buy your little bundle of lies."

"You pretended to. That's lying too, in a way, and for the same reason. Hilda. You did it for her sake. Well, so did we."

"Possibly. I'm sure that's the pitch your sister made when she got you to lie for her."

"She didn't make any pitch! It was my idea, not hers. Lorraine didn't care about herself, she's not like that, you don't know anything about her or you wouldn't—"

"I know she's got a very loyal sister," he said. "And a very worried one. Why, I wonder? Could it be that you're not so sure as you used to be about Lorraine's noble, unselfish nature?"

Bull's eye. She bounced out of her chair, her fists clenched, her face once more bright with telltale color. "And what about your sister? Isobel and her migraine and her therapeutic walks. Could it be that you're doing some worrying yourself?"

It seemed that he had gotten out of his chair, too, and of course that brought Brown Sugar lumbering to his feet, anxious not to be left out of the game, whatever it might be. He wagged between them, panting with anticipation.

After a moment Gene said quietly, "Of course I've been worried about Isobel. She knows it was a lie too. She overheard Dad talking to Lorraine on the phone, earlier that afternoon, before he died. He'd forgotten his pills again, and she stopped in at the office to give him the extra supply she always carried around with her in her purse."

"She had an extra supply? Just like—" Mary caught her breath. "But he didn't have them. They weren't there."

"That's what's eating on her. The phone call shook her up so much that she went away without giving them to him, without even seeing him. So now she's convinced herself that it's her fault he died."

"You mean just because she didn't give him the pills? She didn't follow him to Lorraine's and make a scene, or anything like that?"

"Who says she did? Lorraine?" He shoved Brown Sugar out of the way and grabbed her by the wrists. "What is all this anyway? You're acting as if there was something— He was my father. I've got a right to know how he died. I can guess, you know. It doesn't take a genius to figure out what actually happened. They had a fight, he and Lorraine. I can even guess what it was about. That all-American type she was cuddling up to last night, he didn't just spring full-blown out of the pavement. Like as not she started looking around for new talent as soon as Dad got sick. They had a fight and—"

"They did not." Mary flared into speech at last. "She never saw him alive that day. He got there early, about four, and let himself in with his own key because she'd already left for an appointment uptown. By the time she came home at six thirty he was dead. I was downstairs in Teddy's apartment, she rushed right down to tell us, and we ... She didn't quarrel with him. She didn't. She never saw him alive."

Or so she claimed. Only her word for it. But there was only Isobel's word for her story, too. Which wasn't quite the same story—Gene could not help remembering—as the one she had told to begin with. "Mrs. Schmidt talks too much." Isobel herself hadn't wanted him to know about her visit to the office, hadn't admitted it except under pressure. What else might she be holding back? How could he be sure of her word?

He was still clasping Mary Walsh's wrists; looking down at her, he felt a flash of rapport, a recognition of the fear he saw in her eyes. They were in the same boat, he and Mary. She was no more sure of her sister's word than he was of his; and no less determined to deny it. If that made them enemies, it also locked them together in an extraordinary intimacy.

"Lorraine's studio was broken into," she said, very low and hurried. "Just another sneak thief job, according to the police. And maybe they're right, maybe it was just a coincidence. Because before that—"

The phone rang. The call she was expecting? Her boyfriend, no doubt. She hesitated for a moment, as if tempted not to answer it. But on the third ring she picked it up.

Gene headed for the window, where he intended to stand with his back to her, pretending not to listen. He didn't get that far.

"Hello," she said; and then *"What?"* so sharply, like a whispered scream, that he spun around. Her face was chalk-white.

A wild, unnerving gabble reached him from the phone. Mary's voice cut into it, authoritatively now, and urgent. "Lorraine. You've called the police? ... All right. Yes. I'll be right there." She hung up and turned to Gene. "I have to go down there," she said. "Something's happened to Teddy."

They did not discuss the matter. He simply picked up his coat, helped her into hers, and went with her.

THIRTEEN

What had happened to Teddy was death, and it had happened with disproportionate violence. After the mindless horror, that was Lorraine's first conscious thought: so much violence expended when so little would have sufficed to crack that eggshell-fragile skull. Like using a sledge hammer to swat a fly.

He sprawled in the middle of the living room rug, a scrap of a body, pathetic in its finery. Chartreuse Nehru jacket and pants, Congress boots of fawn suede. One little hand, the right one, with the heavy forefinger ring, stretched toward Lorraine, beseeching, accusing.

Her only other impression—before she backed out and ran screaming to pound on the superintendent's door at the rear—was of extraordinary disorder. A whirlwind seemed to have struck the room, turning everything upside down, scattering books, magazines, cushions, tearing open drawers.

The superintendent took one look, turned green, and as always in moments of agitation completely lost his grasp of the English language. Spanish poured out of him in a staccato torrent. So it was Lorraine who called the police—on his phone, not Teddy's; nothing could have induced her to set foot beyond the doorway of that room.

Then she thought of Mary, her bulwark, her mighty fortress. The relief of hearing Mary's steadfast voice—"I'll be right there"—broke her up. Blubbering, she clung to Santos, whose babbling continued unabated against the background of steel band music blaring out of his radio. They waited in the hall outside his apartment; through the open door Lorraine could see into the little foyer where bouquets of garish plastic flowers flanked a picture of Jesus with his beard and bleeding heart. A crudely innocent scene that for some reason comforted her.

The police were not long in getting there. It was all a confusion to Lorraine: more and more of them came, swarming into the hall, asking questions, issuing cryptic orders, setting up a kind of heavy-footed, methodical bustle. Other officials appeared, technical experts carrying their cases of equipment, a white-coated interne, and of course the detectives who in the end took over the questioning.

They segregated Lorraine and Santos; he was led off to his quarters (where the steel band was abruptly silenced), and after some discussion it was decided that Lorraine's apartment would be an appropriate place for the quiet little talk her detectives had in mind. There were two of them. Mr. Cooper seemed to be the one in charge; she didn't catch the name of the other.

Mr. Cooper was a polite, youngish fellow with a receding hair line and sympathetic blue eyes. All the same, she felt a little forlorn as she started up the stairs. Santos, unintelligible though he was, had been a familiar face. Now there was no one. She was on her own, shaken and bewildered and about to be grilled ...

At that moment she heard Mary call her name, and spun around. There she was, bless her, oh bless her round face and staunch soul, she had talked her way past the police and was coming up the stairs with her hands outstretched and her neck ready to be fallen on. Swamped with relief, Lorraine rushed to meet her. It was only after she had gulped out an explanation to the detectives—"My sister, she knows Teddy too"—that she realized Mary was not alone.

The identification process took even more time: Gene Banning? Yes. Gene Banning. He had been having a drink with Mary, it seemed, so here he was hovering in the background—and with rather a proprietary air toward Mary, too, as if he had every intention of sticking with her.

The detectives obviously accepted him as Mary's boyfriend and left it at that; who was Lorraine to inject unnecessary complications? It wasn't as if she had any real misgivings about Gene Banning, anyway. A touch of uneasiness, less than shame, more than embarrassment. Perfectly natural under the circumstances.

He and Mary waited outside during the first part of the interview. "If you don't mind?" said Mr. Cooper. "After we've had Miss Walsh's report, I'd like to talk to you." Probably he saw it as a time- and labor-saving device: eventually he would have to work his way through the list of Teddy's friends and acquaintances; here was a chance to kill at least two birds with one stone. Three if you counted Gene, and nobody told Mr. Cooper not to.

Once more Lorraine went through her harrowing little story. No, she had not touched the body or anything else. Had not gone farther than the doorway. Did not even know, until Mr. Cooper told her, that the terrible damage to Teddy's head had been inflicted by one of his recent acquisitions —"such a fun piece"—an ornate gold-headed cane he had hung on the wall for decoration.

From there Mr. Cooper, who was as thorough as he was polite, took her back three years ago to the beginning of her friendship with Teddy. The neighborly greetings and sociable chats; the small favors; the occasional drink together; the confidences exchanged. At this point Mary and Gene were invited to join the party, which meant a repeat performance for their benefit. Mary corroborated; Gene had nothing to say and said it.

Gradually, inevitably, Mr. Cooper's interest focused on Ernest, whose chronic quarrels and reconciliations with Teddy were responsible for all those changes in his will.

"That's why he wanted to see me tonight," Lorraine explained. "At least that's what I gathered from the way he talked on the phone, as if he'd made up his mind to cut Ernest out of his will again. He didn't come right out and say so, but then that's how Teddy is, a great one for making mysteries. He dropped all these dark hints about something he'd found out, too complicated to go into over the phone, and so on. It sounded like Ernest again, another go-round with the will, they've been on the outs for a week or so now. So I got out my strong box—that's where he keeps his will, here it is, and I have the key in my purse, if you want me to open it ..."

"Please," said Mr. Cooper. He must be a slow reader, Lorraine thought, judging from the time he spent studying Teddy's will. Or maybe he was memorizing its terms.

"It was all a little bit ridiculous," she said. "Teddy didn't have much of anything to leave to anybody. He was too extravagant. Half the time he was overdrawn at the bank, and most of the stuff he owned isn't really valuable."

"People have been murdered," said Mr. Cooper, "for as little as a dollar and forty cents."

Then he made a brief phone call in which—though with his back turned to them and his voice so low it was hard to be sure—Ernest's name seemed to figure.

More questions about Ernest: did Lorraine know him? No. She had met him once or twice, very briefly. Might not even recognize him if she saw him again. Did he have a key to Teddy's apartment? He used to have; she didn't know about now. Did she have one? At the moment, no, though Teddy usually left one with her when he took out-of-town trips so she could look after his house plants. He did the same for her. The past few days, for instance, since she had been staying with her sister ...

She hadn't meant to go into that. Too late now. "I didn't realize," said Mr. Cooper. "May I ask how you happen to be staying with your sister?"

So of course the business about Kirk came out. Even Gene came to life and helped with the explanation. The expurgated version, needless to say—though Lorraine had a bad moment of remembering Mary's threat to go to the police with the truth. But she wouldn't carry it out now, not with Gene on the scene. Wouldn't carry it out anyway. It had been an empty threat, quickly retracted. Nothing to worry about. Nothing at all.

Mr. Cooper listened sympathetically, nodding now and then to indicate that he understood. "Yes, I see what you mean. Very upsetting for all of you. Now then, to get back to this business of Teddy ..."

His questions were wasted on Gene, who had met Teddy only the once and knew nothing about his private life. And Mary contributed little beyond confirmation of what Lorraine had already said.

She spoke in a subdued, unsteady voice, and with her head bent most of the time, possibly because she was on the verge of tears. It was an uncharacteristic pose for Mary; ordinarily when she talked to people she looked them straight in the eye. On the few occasions when she did take her eyes off her own clenched hands, it was to send tentative searching glances toward Lorraine and Gene. As if she were waiting for a signal of some kind. Preoccupied with waiting, in fact, almost to the point of losing track of Mr. Cooper and his investigation.

No signal was forthcoming from either Lorraine or Gene. Poker-faced (and yet with that haunting resemblance to Kirk), forever on guard, he stared off into space, thinking his cold-fish thoughts. It occurred to Lorraine that, under the strain of keeping her face expressionless, she might give much the same effect as Gene. The idea cheered her up. Relaxed her.

Most likely she had imagined it all, had read a lot of fancy significance into Mary's behavior instead of checking it off to sheer, simple nerves. Naturally Mary wasn't quite herself tonight. Who was?

"I believe that about covers it for now." Mr. Cooper and his assistant stood up; the grilling was over. "You've been very cooperative. Very helpful. Later on we may want to double-check a few points, depending on how the case develops. Meantime, you can reach me at this number, in case anything further occurs to you, anything that might have slipped your mind at the moment. Even if it doesn't seem to have any bearing. You never know what's going to turn out to be important."

He had reached the door when without warning Mary surged out of her chair. "Wait. Listen. I can't help it, this is murder, Teddy's been murdered, it isn't right not to tell you—"

And tell him she did. In spite of all Lorraine's self-assurances to the contrary—wishful thinking, she saw that now—and in spite of Gene's presence.

He took it without turning a hair. No news to him? With a face like

Gene's there was no way of knowing. Anyway, that part of it could wait. Right now the one, burning issue was Mary, standing there in the middle of the room, Truth on a Monument, reeling off the story of how and why they had lied about the circumstances of Kirk's death.

Mr. Cooper heard her out, with his habitual air of patient, polite understanding. Now and then he cocked his eyebrow at Lorraine, seeking her confirmation. And getting it, of course. What else could she do?

"I see," he said when Mary ran out of steam. "And you think this may have some connection with what happened tonight?"

"Maybe. No. I don't know. Only you said even if it doesn't seem to have any bearing. And—and Lorraine's studio was broken into over the weekend ..."

"Oh?" He moved back into the room, away from the door. Again he aimed the cocked eyebrow at Lorraine. It was time for positive action.

"Broken into and robbed," she said briskly. "You'll find a record of it at the police station. I called them—for all the good it did me. Well. They did tell me what kind of a lock to get. Oh, I'm not blaming them, they can't be expected to track down a beat-up transistor radio and a few dollars' worth of postage stamps. I'm lucky it hasn't happened before, considering the location and the setup." She gave him the address of the studio, then struck off again, boldly. "Really, Mary, I don't know why you— Oh, of course! Teddy's tale about somebody prowling around up here. I'd forgotten till just now. How did it go again? Something with the sofa cushions?"

"Here? You mean your apartment was robbed too?" Mr. Cooper pricked up his ears and advanced another step or two.

"No, not robbed. Not broken into, either. That was the mystery, you see, because there aren't any keys except mine and the set I gave Teddy. You tell him, Mary. I only heard it second-hand from you. Teddy never said a word to me about it."

Mary, very red and rattled, stammered out the details. They sounded gratifyingly thin. After all, a couple of cushions switched around; some magazines disarranged, according to Teddy's recollection. "I don't care," Mary finished stubbornly, "I don't see why he'd make up such a thing if it wasn't true. I know he sometimes embroidered the facts, touched them up a little here and there, but—"

"'A great one for making mysteries,'" quoted Mr. Cooper, with a twinkling glance at Lorraine. "I take it you agree with your sister in general, then. But not in this particular instance. Did Teddy have any theory as to who the prowler might be, or what they were after?"

"He thought it was something connected with Kirk. Mr. Banning."

"I see. It was a pretty dramatic experience for all of you. Very much on your minds, naturally." Mr. Cooper let the unspoken inference hang in the air: Teddy unable to resist the temptation to add a few splashes of color; Mary predisposed to accept them at face value. And Mr. Cooper predisposed to regard Teddy's death as a fag affair. That too. "I appreciate your telling me all this, Miss Walsh. We'll check it out, of course."

"You mean—" Mary was stammering worse than ever, poor dear. (But I had to cut her off, thought Lorraine, no telling how far she might have gone, she might even have gotten off on Kirk's pills.) "You won't have to—Hilda. Does Mrs. Banning have to be told how it really was?"

"I simply can't say, at this stage of the game. It may turn out not to be necessary. If so, believe me, she won't be told. I have no wish to—"

There was a rap at the door, and when he opened it Lorraine caught a glimpse of uniformed figures. After a moment's low-voiced conversation in which—again—Ernest's name figured, Mr. Cooper and his assistant said good night and took their departure.

Mary said jerkily, "All right. You hate me, both of you. I hate myself. Only I had to tell him. I couldn't go on lying, not after Teddy—" She burst into tears.

Lorraine said glibly, "Mary darling, of course I don't hate you. Why on earth should I? Don't worry about Hilda, they'll leave her out of it. They've got too much on Ernest." She started across the room, her arms outstretched.

But Gene beat her to it. Two unhurried steps, and he had Mary firmly, consolingly, in hand. Above her bent head and heaving shoulders he fixed on Lorraine a look that for some reason set her to shivering. Something flickered in that poker-face of his—but not a cold fish, no, she had been off on the wrong pitch there—something grave and uncompromising. It made her feel like a flighty child abruptly called to account.

He said, "Do you think it was Ernest?"

FOURTEEN

Next to her on the bus sat a young woman with a baby asleep on her lap and another child, a little boy of two or so, wedged in beside her. His legs stuck out straight in front of him; he wore corduroy overalls, dirty little sneakers, a shrunken sweater. The lower half of his face was smeared black from the licorice he had been eating. Above this unfinished minstrel make-up effect—comic, startling—his melting brown eyes looked out, sad as a clown's. Then, as the people across the aisle began to laugh at him, they filled with tears of bewilderment and alarm.

"You've got a dirty face, dearie," she said, and patted his hair, soft as feathers. His eyes switched to her, trusting and comforted; his grubby starfish hand reached for her; the mother smiled at her shyly.

They don't know, she thought. If they knew, they would cringe, freeze, everybody on the bus, the driver, everybody, would run screaming. It doesn't show. How can that be? How can they possibly not know what I am, what I have done? Unless I imagined it. Maybe I did. Not just tonight, the whole five days, maybe it's all been a prolonged, agonizing fantasy, and when I get home he'll be there and my mind will give some kind of a little click and work right again ...

But she mustn't go home yet. That was not the point of the bus trip. There was something else she had to do first. Very urgent. Crucial. Somewhere else she had to go. Something she had to find. Yes. The little semi-black face beside her went into a slow whirl and changed into another little face—but different, not innocent, bright with malice. The bus too spun out of its safe, commonplace griminess into a scene of dazzling menace. The pattern of the Danish rug, the sling chairs, Cupid clock, gold-headed cane. The violence, violently remembered.

And the moment of terrible, hopeless hope was past. She had not imagined it. He would not be there when she got home. He was gone forever. Dead. He had died of the quarrel with her, died reaching for the pills she had carried away with her in her purse. Never mind that nobody else in the world knew or that it didn't show. She knew: what she was, what she had done, what she still had to do.

She rang the bell and stumbled down the aisle of the bus without looking back.

There was a phone booth on the corner. She called Mary Walsh's apartment first, just in case. But the conclusions she had reached—after that spell of frantic wandering when her mind not only did not work right, it did not work at all—were apparently correct. Anyway, no one answered. Her second call, to the doorman of Mary's apartment house, also went according to plan.

"This is Mary Walsh," she said. How easy it was—just a matter of pitching her voice low, and inserting the slight, characteristic lisp. She had an ear for such things. "I wonder if you would do me a favor?"

"Sure, Miss Walsh. Glad to."

"Well, it's like this. I wonder if you'd let a friend of mine into my apartment so she can pick up an envelope, something that belongs to her. She needs it tonight—I just talked to her on the phone—and I won't be home till late, neither will my sister. We're way downtown, and she's way up town, otherwise I'd let her have my key. So I told her I'd call you so you'll know it's all right to let her in. She's on her way over now, ought to be there in a few minutes. If you'd just take her up and open the door for her so she can look for this envelope of hers. She can let herself out. It may take her a little while, because I'm not quite sure where I left it. Okay? Would you mind?"

"Not at all, Miss Walsh. Glad to help you out."

"Thanks a lot. Her name— Her name is Kane." Where had that sprung from? Kane? Cane? Cain?

"Got it, Miss Walsh. Kane. I'll be on the lookout for her."

Everything was going to be all right, after all. Good omens everywhere: the chilly spring air, the trees in the park beginning to leaf out, even a misty new moon to wish on. She was Mary Walsh's friend, walking along—not too fast, not too slow—to Mary Walsh's apartment, where the doorman was on the lookout for her, to pick up the envelope that belonged to her.

It would be there, of course. Had to be. The only place left where it could be. That was what Teddy meant when he said, "In a safe place." The search of his apartment had been wasted time and effort. If only he had told her, instead of smiling his bright, malicious smile, dropping his maddening hints ...

No. It would still have made no difference as far as Teddy was concerned. Foolish, meddlesome Teddy, he had sealed his own doom—not by calling her, not even by refusing to give her the envelope, but by telling her that unforgivable lie. She had never meant to hurt him; she never would have, except for the lie. And his taunting face as he told it, the triumph in his voice, goading her past endurance. She had lashed out in mindless rage, not knowing what she was doing until it was done. All she could recall now was the way his expression had changed, from triumph to utter astonishment to the first (and last) flash of terror. Guilt? She had none to spare for Teddy; she had spent it all—was still spending it, her endless, aching supply of guilt—on the other, original sin.

But she mustn't think about that. The envelope. It had to be at Mary's place. She had to find it, the envelope that had already cost her so much—too much.

"I'm a friend of Mary Walsh's," she began to the doorman, and from there on he took the words right out of her mouth. Sure thing, Miss Kane; he was ready with the key, all set to take her up. The only hitch came when the sound of his key in the lock started up a furor of barking and scratching from inside.

"A dog?" he said. "A dog in Miss Walsh's apartment? Miss Walsh got no dog."

But even that worked to her advantage, once the door was open. "Brown Sugar!" she cried, and of course Brown Sugar went into his customary fit of delighted greeting. "Mary told me he was here, he belongs to a mutual friend ..."

It was good enough for the doorman. "Okay, then. I'll get back downstairs. She said it might take you a while. All you have to do is shut the door when you leave, give it a good slam, see, make sure it's shut tight."

Her presence of mind—or nerve, or whatever it was—held out until he was gone. Then she sank into the nearest chair, her legs trembling, her hands clammy with sweat. Brown Sugar? Here, in Mary's apartment? Gene must have been here too, then. She had not figured on that. But all right. Gene must have been here when Lorraine called. As she had undoubtedly done; accurate figuring there, at least. And wherever Mary and Lorraine were now, whatever they were doing, Gene must be with them. Lucky for them. He was good in a crisis, Gene. Staunch.

Was it the thought of Gene's staunchness, not for her, never again for her? Or was it Brown Sugar? Not the unexpectedness of finding him here; just his warm, loving presence. His eyes made her think of the little licorice-smeared boy on the bus. So trusting, so vulnerable. Brown Sugar did not know, either. His thumping tail, his muzzle nudging up her arm in make-believe nibbles ... She gave way to a sudden, scalding gush of tears.

For a moment only. The envelope must be here. Must be found. With Brown Sugar pattering at her heels, she set to work, methodically, quickly. The other searches had taught her economy, different though each of them had been. Lorraine's apartment, where she had tried—but failed, according to Teddy—to leave no sign. The studio, where she had left sneak thief signs. Teddy's apartment, where panic had driven her into a rampage of pointless, brainless ransacking.

This time there was no panic. The death of hope put an end to that sort of madness. Nothing to hope for; nothing to panic about. Emptiness. The vacuum of total despair.

"It's not here," she told Brown Sugar. Her voice had a hollow echo, as if she were talking into a bottle. Not here. Not here. Was she herself here? She felt disjointed—eerily weightless in the head, light enough to float, while at the same time the rest of her was dragged down by leaden inertia.

Here, yet not here. Her one connection with reality was Brown Sugar, the pressure of his head in her lap, his soulful amber eyes fixed on her face. She seemed to be sitting on the couch. A comfortable couch; if only she could stretch out on it, just lie down and … Why not? As he had died, stretched across Lorraine's bed. (But there was nothing wrong with the machinery of her heart; it pumped on, strong, steady, undamaged.) Or even as Teddy had died, struck down before he knew what was happening. (But there was no one to strike her down.)

And besides. Besides. The other reasons why not escaped her. All the same, she was aware of them, bobbing around up there like her head, heavy and earthbound like her legs. Powerful reasons that in the end pulled her up off the couch.

"I don't know what to do," she said. "I don't know where to go."

Something else. Somewhere else.

From the door she looked back at the forbidden comfort of the couch, the warm reality of Brown Sugar, who stood in the middle of the room with his tail at half-mast, once more forsaken but forever loving. That was not for her, either.

She remembered to give the door a good slam behind her. Downstairs, the doorman was busy talking on the house phone. He smiled and nodded; so did she. A friend of Miss Walsh's, stepping along briskly, sure of where she was going.

Well, and maybe she was sure, at some subterranean level. The way a lemming is sure. Impelled by a force beyond her understanding or control.

She reached the corner and without a moment's hesitation turned down town, toward the house where he—and Teddy too—had died.

FIFTEEN

"I think it could have been Ernest," said Lorraine.

Of course. It was what she wanted to think. What Gene too would prefer to think—except that unfortunately he wasn't all that good at rationalizing. Neither was Mary; she had tried and failed, which explained why she now stood weeping, with her face plastered against his shirt front.

Meanwhile, Lorraine pressed on: "They were always having these violent quarrels. And he knew about the will. That was Teddy's favorite weapon. Only he wouldn't tell Ernest where he kept it. So that could be why the place was all torn up, because Ernest wanted to destroy the will before the police found it. They'd see right away that it gave him a motive. He's the most likely one. I mean, if it wasn't Ernest ..."

"I know what you mean," said Gene. "If it wasn't Ernest, Mr. Cooper will be getting back to us."

All right. So it shook her. An unpleasant fact that for once in her charmed life she could not sidestep or gloss over or manipulate out of sight. The possibility of a link between Teddy's death and Dad's was something Lorraine too was going to have to face, whether she liked it or not. She obviously didn't. But then neither did Gene or Mary or anybody else.

She said, with an attempt at bravado, "What of it? I have nothing to hide from Mr. Cooper." Her voice cracked, just a little.

He felt Mary stiffen in his arms. She unburied her face and twisted around to look at Lorraine. A searching, anxious look; after a moment Lorraine's eyes shifted.

Nothing to hide? They were not going to tell Gene, of course, any more than he was going to tell them certain misgivings of his own. He would have no choice, if and when Mr. Cooper got back to them. He was incapable of the kind of performance Lorraine had just put on, and he knew it.

A performance, yes; never mind how much of it had been innocent self-delusion and how much deliberate misrepresentation. It was not for him. Not for Mary. Maybe not even for Lorraine again: tonight Mr. Cooper had been too hot on Ernest's trail for more than a casual sniff at the side issues. They would not be side issues, if he came back. If. If ...

"Would anyone else like a drink?" asked Lorraine. "You look as if you could use one, Mary."

She did indeed. Rumpled hair, tear-swollen eyes, face drawn with fatigue. And the turned-up mouth that Gene found so touching. "That's how I feel," she said. "Is there any brandy?"

There was. They sipped it out of snifters. Comforting heat, like a burst of sunshine in the chest. The color returned to Mary's face; she leaned back on the sofa beside Gene and kicked off her shoes. Lorraine sat in the big blue chair with her feet curled under her, pretty and graceful as a cat. Gene thought, but without resentment, about how many times Dad must have seen her like that.

There was a tranquil atmosphere—possibly due to simple exhaustion—in the room, a suspension of hostilities and suspicion. And at the same time a sense of expectancy that made this brief respite all the more valuable, something they must make the most of before whatever it was they were waiting for happened.

Presently it occurred to them that they had had no dinner; and since

Lorraine's stock of groceries ran to artichoke hearts and frozen pea pods, they decided on the Italian place at the corner as their best bet.

A couple of policemen were still on guard outside Teddy's door, and out on the street curious passersby and block residents clustered in little groups. Staring faces. A subdued buzz of voices that broke off when Gene and the two girls emerged, started up again when they passed.

The restaurant, too, simmered with rumor and avid speculation. Their table—the only one available—was between the front window and the crowded bar, where late word had apparently just come in: Ernest was now in the hands of the police, but he had been on a binge for the past two weeks, ever since his last row with Teddy, and they were going to have to sober him up before they got a confession out of him. They'd get it, all right, no question about that. Guilty as hell. These queers ...

Lorraine kept starting up feverish little bursts of chatter and then leaving them to die of neglect. Mary crumbled a bread stick. Moment by moment Gene's nerves grew tighter, rawer, closer to the snapping point.

That tranquil spell just past had been a hallucination. Brandy- and shock-induced, and every bit as irresponsible as Lorraine's wishful thinking. His way of staving off the dreadful possibilities that now obsessed him.

Isobel, Isobel. Wherever he turned, there she was: her lost-child face glimmered up at him from the checked tablecloth; her slight figure—hunched and lonesome, the way she had looked yesterday, waiting for him in the rain—swirled among the passersby outside the window he was facing. And above the hum of bar gossip her voice, faint and despairing, called out to him for help. The conviction that she needed him, now, this instant, was suddenly overpowering.

"Excuse me, I have to make a phone call." He knocked over the salt cellar getting up; out of the corner of his eye he saw Mary's square little hand reaching automatically to right it.

Then he was in the phone booth, staring at the doodlings on the wall while the phone in the 66th Street apartment rang on and on, unanswered. It was the same when he tried Pam's number. He tried both places again, just in case he had made a mistake in dialing. No such luck.

He sent out a silent cry of his own to his little sister, wherever she might be: "I don't know how to find you, I don't know how to help you ..."

After that he pulled himself together and headed back toward the table by the window. The waiter had brought their food, but neither Mary nor Lorraine was doing anything about it. Some kind of a conversation (argument?) had sprung up during his absence; they leaned toward each other, tense and absorbed, oblivious of Gene's approach.

He caught only bits and pieces of what Mary was saying. "I don't care ... you know as well as I do ... bound to come out sooner or later ... those pills couldn't have just ..."

"What pills?" he said, somewhere between a whisper and a croak. Their heads jerked up, puppet-like; their two faces, startled into blankness, seemed for a weird moment identical.

Lorraine found her tongue first. "It's nothing, really. Just this notion of Mary's about the extra bottle of Kirk's pills I used to have—"

But Mary broke in hotly. "It's not a notion! No, and neither was Teddy's story about a prowler! You just twisted it around to make it sound that way to Mr. Cooper. I should have told him about the pills, anyway. They couldn't have walked off by themselves. Somebody was up there ..."

Not Isobel, not Isobel. He slid into his chair and focused his eyes, and mind, on Lorraine. "Nothing to hide, you claim," he said. "That's a little hard to believe, if you don't mind my saying so."

"Why should I care? Go ahead and say it. It's what you're thinking—that I walked off with Kirk's pills and left him to die. Well. Isn't it?" She added bitterly, to Mary, "Thanks to you. You and your 'somebody was up there.'"

"You can leave Mary out of it. She's not to blame. You've been using her all along, taking advantage of her because she's your sister and trusts you—"

"And what about your precious sister?" She leaned forward, pale and brilliant-eyed with rage. "Hasn't it occurred to you that Isobel might have a few things to hide, too? She had as much opportunity as I had to walk off with those pills. More. Kirk was already dead when I got there."

"So you say."

"So I say. What does Isobel say? Does anybody know where she was that afternoon?"

"Certainly I know," said Gene. "So does Mary. I already told her." Now he told Lorraine: the extra supply of pills Isobel too had kept on hand, her ill-timed stop at the office—Lorraine had the grace to blush a little over that phone conversation—her consuming, irrational sense of guilt.

When he was through Lorraine said, "All right. So she says. What about yesterday afternoon? Where did she go on that walk of hers? It wasn't necessarily the middle of the night when my studio was broken into. The building was empty in the afternoon, too." Her eyes flashed even brighter. "And what about tonight? How did she happen to drop in on me tonight?"

It seemed to Gene that the table was rocking; he flattened his hands on it to hold it down. "I didn't know that," he said very carefully.

"Well. You know it now." She stood up. Still furious. "Excuse me, please. I've changed my mind. I'm not hungry. Good night."

She sailed off, without a backward glance at either Gene, who was still holding down the table, or Mary, who was making sounds of agitation and protest.

In the end, though, she stayed with him. It was more than he expected, maybe more than she intended. Never mind; she stayed.

He reached out his hand, and she clung to it hungrily.

SIXTEEN

Outside the restaurant door Lorraine stopped and took several deep, therapeutic breaths. She was still churning inside.

But at least she had rocked Gene back on his heels, jolted him, for once, out of his everlasting poker-faced cool. The business about Isobel hurt him, it really hurt. And about time, after all his shots at her: "Do you think it was Ernest? ... Nothing to hide ... Taking advantage of Mary because she's your sister ..."

Well. They were even now. Her only regret was that she had not realized sooner what a lethal weapon Isobel was. Had not thought of her at all, in fact. But with Gene (and Mary too) making such a muchness of that unexpected little visit, and of the missing pills, and all the other odd pieces that Lorraine, left to herself, would have gone on brushing aside—

She took another deep breath and set off up the street. One thing was sure, wherever she went from here it would not be to Mary's apartment. A cup of coffee, maybe, to settle her nerves? She hesitated in front of the espresso shop.

And there, coming out of the door, was Isobel. Wild-eyed, and apparently in mid-flight; when Lorraine grabbed her by the arm she went into a skid and, after a moment of blank staring, gasped out, "Teddy. They said that Teddy ..."

"Yes. Teddy." The coffee shop too would be boiling with the news. And very shocking news it must have been to Isobel, to throw her into this much of a state. "Listen, Isobel, I want to know. Why did you stop in to see me earlier?"

"I was looking for—" She snapped her mouth shut. Wariness in her eyes now. And hostility. "Let go of me. Why should I tell you anything? I have to call my brother. I have to find Gene." Her arm jerked, trying to pull free.

"Go ahead. He's right down there at the corner restaurant, and he's going to ask you the same thing. He's just as much interested in what you were looking for as I am."

"Gene?" Again Isobel stared. Then she said, with a queer kind of urgency, "It isn't true, what he believes about the pills. I never had an extra supply, the ones I took that day were Daddy's, that's how I ..."

"So you were lying," began Lorraine, but that was as far as she got. Isobel gave a last, despairing jerk and took off like a rabbit, her fair hair streaming out behind, her shoulder bag banging against her ribs as she ran.

Lorraine watched until she had disappeared inside the restaurant. Shelter. Refuge. The welcoming arms of big brother. All right. Maybe he could pry the truth out of her. And maybe all he would get was just another set of lies.

She crossed the street to the cozy little house with its bright blue door. Past the knots of curious stragglers and neighbors still milling in front of it; past Teddy's door; up the stairs and into her living room, where the three brandy glasses sat, forlorn reminders of a truce that had not lasted. Not for her, anyway. For Mary and Gene it seemed to be standing up nicely.

Roger, she thought as she put the chain on the door and slumped down on the sofa, she needed Roger. But he wasn't here, he was off in some Chicago hotel, she couldn't remember which. There were several she could try, she supposed ...

Her glance, straying toward the telephone, fell on her tote bag at the other end of the couch, where she had tossed it when she came in. It was on its side, gaping half open to show the manila envelope she had thrust there, an age ago, when the doorbell rang and it turned out to be not Teddy but Isobel. She had forgotten all about the envelope. Now she plucked it out of her tote bag.

Mildly curious, as she had been when she first noticed it, she undid the clasp and drew out the contents. A couple of typed letters. It was the note clipped to them that set her bones to buzzing.

She recognized the handwriting instantly: Teddy's dainty curlicues. The language too was pure Teddy. Reading it, she seemed to hear, like a weird obbligato, his voice as it had come to her over the phone in that last conversation, another age ago.

"Lorraine, dear: It really is rather interesting, *n'est ce pas*? I happened on it while I was mousing through the magazines I brought down from your place. Three guesses how it got there. I yearn to discuss it with you. Meanwhile, I've decided, shrewd operator that I am, that your apartment is the safest place for it. Because—too wicked of me, I know, but I simply couldn't resist—I called the rightful owner and dropped a subtle hint or two. Our conference is scheduled for six this evening. If you get here before then, so much the better. If not, I do hope you'll join us. My parlor. Dress optional. Bye bye, sweetie. Teddy."

There was just one letter, really—the original two pages on impressively heavy stationery and a carbon on crinkly onion skin. She skimmed through it. Read it a second time, word for word. Re-read Teddy's note. Then she sat—bolt upright, eyes shut tight—listening to the drumbeat of her heart and piecing together in her mind the one inescapable design of Kirk's death. And Teddy's.

There was no place in it for Ernest. He was an irrelevancy, the product of her own wishful thinking and of Teddy's delight in the devious, his urge to make a mystery whenever and wherever possible. Poor Teddy, the secret machinations that had been the breath of life to him had also been the death of him. What fun it must have seemed to him, what delicious fun to call the rightful owner and drop his subtle hints! "I simply couldn't resist ..." Less malicious than mischievous, he had been an incurable meddler, a muddier of waters that, this time, were far beyond his depth.

Lorraine could have stopped him, if only she had realized what he was dabbling in. If only she had read the letter in time; if only she had rung his bell first, instead of coming straight up here, bent on exorcising Kirk's ghost; if only, at the beginning, she had faced up to the fact of the missing pills, instead of trying to play the ostrich ...

It was too late now. Too late to do anything but call Mr. Cooper. The letter, and Teddy's note, proved not only who had killed Teddy, but who had followed Kirk here the day he died, quarreled with him, and walked off with his pills—but without the letter, which might very well have figured in that first and last and fatal quarrel.

The letter let Isobel out. Whatever she might know or suspect, Isobel could not have gotten hold of the letter. There was no reason why she should quarrel with Kirk about it, anyway.

But there was a very good reason why Hilda should.

Hilda, and only Hilda, had a reason for bringing the letter here and for making those frantic efforts to retrieve it once she realized she had left it behind.

Had she really imagined Kirk would ever agree to sign it? Maybe. She was not exactly naive. But she had not shared Kirk's conviction that Owen Adams was a greedy, vindictive bastard bent on taking over the agency.

Yes, to Hilda, Owen Adams' offer of a loan might seem the friendly gesture it purported to be; and in his letter of contract confirming their verbal agreement she might not see what lay behind the fog bank of reassuring phrases. A matter of form. Purely a technicality because, as it happened, Owen's personal free cash was tied up at the moment and the loan would have to come out of his own agency's money, which naturally he had to protect ... In case of death, disability, etc., etc., the obligation to be retired by a transfer of assets ...

Kirk's agency. There were no other assets.

Whether Hilda saw the implications or not, she was faced with the necessity of getting Kirk's signature. A personal loan she could have negotiated on her own. But not this. The two pressures had converged on her—the proposed loan, which she could no longer keep secret from Kirk; and her knowledge of his affair with Lorraine. She might even have followed him here with some notion of using that knowledge as a lever ...

The phone rang, jolting Lorraine back to the present. Mary's voice came on, breathy with agitation: "You're there, thank God. You're all right? Listen, Lorraine, Isobel's here, all unstuck, but she's talking at last, and about time, she's known from the start, that is almost from the start, that it was Hilda—"

"Yes," said Lorraine. "I know."

Mary raced on, oblivious to who else knew what, or how. "On account of the pills. Because she didn't have an extra supply. The ones she took from home were Kirk's—"

"Yes," Lorraine repeated. "I know."

She knew enough, at least. There was no longer any mystery about her own extra supply of pills. Hilda had walked off with them, thinking they were Kirk's, thinking he'd remembered his for once, and when she got back to her own apartment had replaced them in whatever spot Kirk would be most likely to leave them. If Isobel, who knew good and well they shouldn't be there, had spoken out— Instead, she had bottled up her suspicions along with her guilty conscience, her grief and disillusionment and warring loyalties. There might even have been a feeling—deepest of all, and most corrosive—that whatever had happened to Kirk, he deserved it.

Meanwhile, Mary: "... says she's been following Hilda. She's after something, nobody knows what. Saturday night your place, and last night the studio, and tonight your place again. That's why Isobel rang your bell, she was looking for Hilda. Then when she heard about Teddy ... I don't see how she could be making all this up. Do you? Lorraine?"

"No, she's not making it all up. I'm sure. Have you called Mr. Cooper? There's something I have to tell him, too."

"There is? Oh. I'll tell Gene, then. He's waiting to get through to Cooper now. We'll be over as soon as he reaches him, unless you'd rather— No, you'd better stay there. And listen, Lorraine, put the chain on the door. Because Hilda's got a key, and God knows where she is or what she might decide to do next."

"It's on. Don't worry. I'll wait here."

She noticed, as she hung up, that her hands were trembling. They went on trembling while she clipped the note back to the letter and its carbon. Evidence, she thought; the missing bit that would fill out Isobel's story. She reached for the brown envelope. Froze in mid-reach, acutely aware of a prickle at the back of her neck. And turned.

Hilda was standing in the bedroom doorway behind her.

For a moment neither of them spoke or moved. Then, as Hilda took a step forward, Lorraine scrambled to her feet and gasped, "What are you— How did you—"

Pointless, unfinished questions. She knew the answers to both. The what was the letter she was still clutching. The how was the key Hilda held out on her open palm.

"I had it made a couple of weeks ago," she explained. "From Kirk's. I found his, you see, he left it in his desk one day, and it set me to wondering. Because it didn't fit any lock that I knew of. I didn't know what key it was until I followed him here, that last day." Her tone was conversational, not unfriendly.

And she looked much as usual, solid and wholesome in her tweed suit. But then she came closer, close enough for Lorraine to see her eyes and to feel a chill of mortal fear.

It immobilized her. She was not even trembling anymore. Her feet were rooted to the floor, she had no breath to make a sound, only her heart pounded on and on.

"Give it to me," said Hilda, and Lorraine's arm, suddenly remembering how to move, thrust itself and the letter backward out of reach. "It's mine. Give it to me, you lying, scheming tramp, it's your fault he died, you're to blame."

"My fault!" Lorraine's breath came back in a painful rush. Pain in her shoulder, too; exploding like a skyrocket as she tried to wrench loose from the bite of Hilda's fingers. "I didn't quarrel with him and go off and leave him to die. It was you. And Teddy …"

"It was a lie. It wasn't true, what he said."

"What do you—"

"You. Did you think I'd ever give him up so you could marry him? Did you really think I'd let you have him?"

"But I didn't want to marry him! I wasn't going to marry him! It was all his—" She knew, the instant the words were out of her mouth, that she had made a fatal mistake. Like Teddy. He too had told Hilda the "lie," the unendurable truth that made a mockery of Kirk's death and brought down on Teddy that rain of shattering blows. It was there in Hilda's eyes—the glare, the violence, the will to kill.

With the strength of terror, Lorraine tore free and made for the door. The chain, the chain. She ripped it out of its slot, wrestled with the knob, slammed down on her knees in the hall, seeing out of the tail of her eye Hilda's face, mottled and savage, and the crystal vase she had snatched from the bookcase upraised in her hand.

It flashed on the way down, and Lorraine heard, above the thud of approaching footsteps, her own voice loosing scream after banshee scream.

Then black silence, and after that, Mary's face floating in and out of focus up there, along with all the other faces. Some with names, some without. Gene, and Isobel, and Mr.—whatever it was, the detective fellow.

And Hilda.

There was nothing left in her face—not the violence of a moment ago, not the warmth and life that had glowed in it when Lorraine first knew her. Nothing. Vacancy. The Hilda who had hated was as dead as the Hilda who had loved. Gene was on her right, one of the nameless ones on her left. Between them she stood, docile now, beyond all human response, looking out stony-eyed at her empty world.

THE END

Jean Potts Bibliography
(1910-1999)

Mystery Novels:
Go, Lovely Rose (1954; winner Best First Novel Edgar Award)
Death of a Stray Cat (1955; reprinted in omnibus as *Dark Destination*, 1955)
The Diehard (1956)
The Man With the Cane (1957)
Lightning Strikes Twice (1958; reprinted in the UK as *Blood Will Tell*, 1959)
Home Is the Prisoner (1960)
The Evil Wish (1962; finalist Best Novel Edgar Award)
The Only Good Secretary (1965)
The Footsteps on the Stairs (1966)
The Trash Stealer (1968)
The Little Lie (1968)
An Affair of the Heart (1970)
The Troublemaker (1972)
My Brother's Killer (1975)

Mainstream Novel:
Someone to Remember (1943)

Short Stories:
The Lady Afraid (*Woman's Home Companion*, Feb 1942)
You're All I've Got (*Woman's Day*, March 1942)
The Other Woman (*Collier's*, Aug 24, 1946)
Restless Redhead (*Liberty*, Feb 1948)
The Box of Apples (*McCall's*, March 1949)
A Family Affair (*McCall's*, Nov 1949)
The Bracelet (*McCall's*, Dec 1951)
The Heart Must See (*McCall's*, Apr 1952)
The Engagement Ring (*Thrilling Love*, Oct 1952)
Let's Start All Over Again (*American Magazine*, Apr 1953)
The Girl He Didn't Marry (*Woman's Day*, Jan 1954)
A Long Day's Journey (*Cosmopolitan*, July 1954)
The Ideal Gift (*Family Circle*, Oct 1956)
The Withered Heart (*Ellery Queen's Mystery Magazine*, Feb 1957)
Murderer # 2 (*Alfred Hitchcock's Mystery Magazine*, Jan 1961)
Just Like Jessica (*Redbook*, Feb 1963)
The Only Good Secretary (*Cosmopolitan*, July 1965; condensed version of novel)
The Inner Voices (*Ellery Queen's Mystery Magazine*, Apr 1966)
In the Absence of Proof (*Ellery Queen's Mystery Magazine*, July 1985)
Two on the Isle (*Ellery Queen's Mystery Magazine*, Jan 1987)
The Lady Macbeth Case (*Ellery Queen's Mystery Magazine*, Nov 1990)
Family Circle "Family in Trouble" series (commentary by John L. Schimel, M.D.):
Families in Trouble (April 1969)
Families in Trouble - Alone Again! The Agonizing Problem of A Lonely Wife (June 1969)
Families in Trouble - "My Youngster Is Taking Drugs" (Oct 1969)
Families in Trouble - "My Job Made A New Woman Out Of Me!" (Feb 1970)
Families in Trouble - The Credit Card Nightmare (March 1970)

Also available from Stark House Press...

JEAN POTTS

Go, Lovely Rose / The Evil Wish
A 1954 Edgar Award winner and a 1963 Edgar runner-up paired together for the first time. "If Hitchcock had written a novel, it would have been similar to *The Evil Wish*...two masterpieces."—Don Crinklaw, *Booklist*. Introduction by J. F. Norris.

Home is the Prisoner / The Little Lie
"In Potts' fictional world there are no true good or bad characters, just many shades of gray, but she writes them in a way that makes you care about them, warts and all."—*In Reference to Murder*. Introduction by J. F. Norris.

The Only Good Secretary / The Man With the Cane
"...a tight account of personal interplay, observant, sympathetic, lively and adroit."—Anthony Boucher, *New York Times*. Introduction by Bill Kelly.

Footsteps on the Stairs / The Troublemaker
"...propulsive enough to keep the pages flipping fairly quickly... If you enjoy the classic, traditional murder mystery, then surely you will be pleased with Jean Potts."—*Paperback Warrior*. Introduction by Curtis Evans.

The Diehard / My Brother's Keeper
"In a Midwest small town Miss Potts has set another wonderfully human, vivid and believable story about our own kind of people."
—*San Francisco Chronicle*. Introduction by Curtis Evans.

Lightning Strikes Twice / The Trash Stealer
"[*Go, Lovely Rose*] was an event in the mystery field. *Lightning Strikes Twice* is even better."—*New Orleans Times-Picayune*. Introduction by Curtis Evans.

STARK HOUSE PRESS, 1315 H Street, Eureka, CA 95501
griffinskye3@sbcglobal.net / www.StarkHousePress.com
Available from your local bookstore, or order direct via our website.